I0666214

Double Conundrum

Double Conundrum

Scott A. Dondershine

Stonewall Stories

Copyright 2018, Scott A. Dondershine.

Names, characters, places and incidents in this book are from the author's imagination or are used fictitiously. Any resemblance to actual events, locales or persons, living or dead, is entirely coincidental.

Published by Stonewall Stories, LLC
Formatted by Anessa Books

Acknowledgements

I could not have written this book without the assistance of a few special people in my life. My wife Diane, children Alex and Zachary, brother Steven, and father-in-law Edward Miller provided me with a mixture of space, editing advice, encouragement, and love that helped me along the journey. I remain eternally grateful. I also want to acknowledge the help of a variety of people who provided me with technical and writing assistance: my Agent Nancy Rosenfeld, professional editors Nina Catanese (plot development) and Beth Skony (copy-editing), Tim Colwell and Michael Adelberg (early-stage plot development and editing), and Tim Bell and Gil Armendariz (technical assistance).

PART ONE
THE WHITE MAN COMETH

Chapter 1
London

Red's ringing cell phone woke her from her sleep. She looked across her bed. Some guy was snoring, his disheveled hair flopped on the soft pillow, nose streaked with sweat. She struggled to remember his name. Mike? Or, perhaps, Charlie? *Does it really matter?*

Red pawed after the phone, blindly searching the wooden nightstand, hoping to avoid knocking something over. It wasn't there. She next tried the sheets, praying it wasn't close to the sleeping stranger. At last she found it, nestled between the sheets and the fluffy white duvet.

Her head was pounding, even though she hadn't had that much to drink the night before. *At least I'm not an alkie*, she thought. She had actually stopped drinking altogether for a number of years, in part testing the idea and in part, well, for other reasons.

"Hello," she whispered into the phone.

Monty, her boss, laughed. "Whispering? Tough night? Thought you swore off alcohol. Meet me in thirty minutes." He hung up before Red could respond.

Red looked over at her companion and poked him in the ass. "You need to leave. Now."

He looked up at her. "But..."

"No buts. We shagged, that's all, now bugger off. I need to go to work. When I get out of the shower, you and your pecker better be gone."

Red marched off to the bathroom while the nameless man pulled on his clothes. A few minutes later she heard the front door slam, to her relief. Sometimes it was hard to get rid of a man. *They can act like gum stuck on one's favorite shoe.*

Red, now free, looked in the mirror. She admired her toned muscles and curves, but not the rest. Her red hair, usually shiny and groomed, looked dull and shaggy. Her eye shadow had leaked to slightly beneath her eyes, smudging her normally clear complexion.

She took a moment to reflect on her life, something she often did the morning after a long night. She had joined MI6 after reading an article about enrolling in the Security, Languages, Intelligence, and Photography College, SLIP for short. Her father wasn't pleased when she told him. He laughed and said, "Girls in spy school? Have you gone bonkers?" His reaction hardened her resolve.

Red grew up on a farm a few hours' drive from Gloucester. The farm had been in Pa's family for years, and he worked on it his entire life. It defined him, and he defined it.

Red's father was difficult – on his best days – always loaded, constantly berating the family. Life became unbearable after her brother, Jimmy, nearly lost his life, lapsing into a coma after the loft in the family barn collapsed on him.

Red was only seven at the time of Jimmy's accident, but her father began to rely on her to replace the farm work Jimmy had performed. Red hated it, and her father resented her subpar performance, making him even more irate. He began to drink heavily, beginning a vicious cycle of more verbal abuse, causing Red to do even worse, enraging her father even more. He missed his son, and Red missed out on her childhood.

SLIP offered Red the opportunity to escape. She enjoyed being off the farm away from her dad, and she began working as an agent after graduating. Life was good. She was liberated, felt challenged and important – for the first time in her life. At least until she made a catastrophic mistake that would haunt her for years to come.

***

The flat was sparsely furnished. The living room, with its shiny wooden floor and simple furniture, was spotless – more due to lack of use and a recent cleaning by the maid than Red's own cleanliness. Her bedroom had a blue shag carpet, a bed, and a dresser – and that was it. Red didn't spend a lot of time there watching television or relaxing. She didn't like to dawdle.

She hopped into the shower stall in the bathroom adjacent to her bedroom. The cold water hit her like a Bloody Mary, jolting but refreshing. She toweled off and was ready twenty minutes later.

As was often the case, she didn't have time for a formal breakfast, instead grabbing two energy bars on her way out of the flat heading for the subway. She entered the Central Line station that would take her from the company-supplied flat near Holland Park to her office, a nondescript building located a few stops away on Bond Street.

She saw Jasper playing his saxophone and swore under her breath. She had already swiped her fare card but knew she couldn't continue.

Red exited the tube, making sure Jasper didn't see her. Once outside, she purchased a bowl of chili chicken fry from Lak, the reliable local food cart vendor. She then re-entered, swiping her card again.

Jasper stopped in the middle of his song when he spotted Red hustling towards him. "Aw, Ms. Red, my favorite! Where you been? Been a while, like always," he chided her.

She hadn't even said the chili fry was for him, but he knew and could smell the marinade, eagerly reaching his hand for the bowl. She always brought him the fry or another treat when catching a train from the station.

He once told her he wished she would just get him a cup of churros but Red retorted that her fare contained the only portion of vegetables, as meager as it was, he would likely ingest until the next time. Besides, there was plenty of flavor, what's not to like?

At the age of twenty, Jasper had escaped to London from where he grew up outside of Manchester. His mother had died, and, having no siblings or other close relatives, he had nobody else left to care for him. Opportunities for a person with his condition were limited.

Red happened upon him during one of his episodes. While others quickly walked away, Red gently approached him and held him tight, calming him down. He had the same amber-colored eyes and casual yet hard-working attitude as Jimmy, and they had developed a bond.

"I can't stay, Jasper. Got to go make a living."

He smiled and said, "As best you can, girl. As best you can."

She kissed his dirty cheek and walked towards her train.

***

Red walked briskly to her building, ignoring the wandering eyes of a few men going in the other direction. The revolving doors beckoned her to enter the tall, modern structure. It looked normal on the outside and bore the name Emblomics, a faux name that backfired and incited curiosity—"Oh, what an unusual name. What do you do in there?"—rather than anonymity.

Simone greeted her coolly at the security checkpoint. "You know the drill, Red," he said in a monotone voice.

She took out her metal, checked her Walther P99 pistol, and walked through the screener. She had completed this routine a thousand times.

Liberated at last, she took the elevator to the third floor, opened the glass doors, and walked toward Miss Moneypenny, real name Harmony. Harmony started to greet Red, who, still sore after being forced out of bed early in the morning on a Saturday, responded by winking as she passed. Red didn't even bother knocking on Monty's door before barging straight into his office. Harmony knew better than to attempt to slow her down.

Monty immediately put his feet up on his desk when he saw Red, and he gestured to a chair in front of his cluttered workspace. He leaned back. She half hoped his chair would fall backward and gave it right back to him, sitting down as he commanded but then pushing her chest out, enjoying the thrill of watching him squirm. Everybody in the office knew Monty was a closet homosexual. His getting married and acting like a pig was all part of an elaborate act. She sensed he tolerated insubordination, fearing the office would out him if he disciplined the agents and staff.

"Now, why do you have to do that?" he said in his high-pitched voice.

Monty had well-defined cheekbones and a large, rounded face. While some men gain weight in their buttocks or stomach, Monty gained his in his face and neck. By the time he turned fifty, his black hair had become littered with specks of white. Now fifty-five, his hair was an even mixture of salt and pepper. By sixty, Red imagined it would be pure salt.

"Why do you have to wake me up early on a Saturday? Are you mad?"

"Sweetie," Monty began in a condescending tone, "the Queen has called!"

Red stood and saluted him as he watched in horror. She sat back down and waited for him to talk.

He stammered, "We have a situation brewing in sub-Saharan Africa."

"Seriously? Can you narrow that down a bit?"

Monty stiffened in his chair and wagged his crooked finger. "Don't interrupt me, Red. I'll get to the point. One week ago, we received a report of a nomadic shepherd stumbling onto a ghost village located in Kenya near the South Sudanese border."

"Ghost?"

"Yes, literally. The poor shepherd described it as a ghost town. But then he wandered further into the village and discovered a grisly scene. About fifty dead bodies lay oozing with blood, vultures picking at the guts. This guy, he didn't stick around. He calls the Kenyan authorities, they check it out and seal the area in their usual half-assed manner. They don't know what to do. The coppers still haven't returned. Imagine, the police even being afraid. You know who they called?"

"You?" Red answered sarcastically.

"No, silly. Well, sort of. You know that Kenya used to be one of ours, until 1963. We like to check in on them every now and then, like...uh...an old uncle. And they gladly accept our help. They called somebody over at Downing Street, who then called me."

"And you called me, right?"

"Now you get it. Shit flows downhill. You need to hop on a plane and check it out. I'm told there is one survivor who is being held by the authorities."

Red straightened up in her chair. "But doesn't this sort of stuff happen all the time? Kenya is replete with tribal issues, especially outside the main urban centers. The so-called Western world usually doesn't care that much about a remote village being wiped out. It happens all the time. Fifty fewer Africans—what's all the fuss about?"

Monty replied, "All true, but this situation seems different. The survivor sat in stone silence in the police station. They had to slap him a few times. I'm told he stared at the wall for hours until finally uttering, 'The white man cometh. The white man cometh.' How many tribes of white folk are there in that part of the world? Venture to guess?"

"Not many."

"Actually, we don't think there are *any*. So, you see the point?"

"One white guy and everybody is suddenly scared? People going to start running from you next?"

"Funny. The Kenyans have the situation under wraps for now. But you better get there quick. Your flight leaves in an hour. Harmony will provide you with details."

That was Red's cue. He finished each assignment that way—directing her to Harmony, his lackey. Red stood up, ready to bolt.

As she approached the door with her back facing him, Monty asked, "Red, one more thing. Have you met with Dr. Hopkins yet?"

Red spun around, glared at Monty, turned back toward the door, and left without responding.

***

Kenya

Harmony booked Red on a direct flight from Heathrow to NBO in Nairobi. It was code for Jomo Kenyatta International Airport—the biggest airport in central Africa.

Red slipped into a grungy pair of faded jeans, an old loose white shirt, and a yellow sweater for the nine-hour flight. She removed her contact lenses and took ten milligrams of a sleeping pill immediately before the pre-boarding announcement. They would be flying through the night, and she needed as much sleep as possible for the arduous days to follow. It wasn't going to be a picnic.

Red stood in line with the other coach passengers. She could have squeezed Monty for a first-class ticket with a little pouting, but coach worked better for her cover—a journalist working for the *Daily Express*.

She took the window seat and immediately donned her blue eye mask, stretched out her legs, and put her head against the window. Red felt the presence of another human sit down beside her, his or her weight shifting in the tight seat. She felt like poking the annoying passenger but mustered up a scintilla of control. If she continued to fake being asleep, the interloper would settle eventually.

But the person kept moving around, ultimately laughing and declaring, "Red, I'm not buying it."

Bloody hell! She sat up and removed her eye mask. "Robert, what are you doing here? They sent you, of all people? They must think I'm still crazy."

Robert grinned at her with a twinkle in his eyes. He hadn't changed much on the outside since they had attended SLIP together about fifteen years ago. He had the same yellowish hair which still covered his round, bumpy face that possessed the same reddish hue. Red wasn't entirely pleased to see him, remembering about a pool at SLIP betting on how long it would take for him to drop out. He was awkward, barely able to pass the fitness tests, and he didn't show any initiative—a timid follower, not a leader. The candidates wondered how he had been admitted in the first place. Was he part royalty? The son of a knight?

Everybody made fun of him until one day Mr. Peters, their doddering forensics instructor, made a mistake in computing the angle a marksman would have to fire in order to shoot an object on a higher plane. Peters was flustered, forgetting the formula, then remembering it, but being unable to properly apply it to the problem.

Robert weakly raised his hand in the middle of the misadventure. Peters quickly called on him, eager to shift the ridicule to Robert. But then Robert went to work, explaining not only the formula but the calculation necessary to solve the hypothetical set of facts being discussed—all without use of a calculator or textbook.

After the incident, Robert gained a little more acceptance. Back then, the thinking was that he might not be great in the field, but he had the makings of a solid analyst.

Years later, Robert looked different. He must have gained more confidence, being assigned to the field, no doubt a byproduct of working for MI6. He looked at Red and announced, "I am the best photographer at the *Daily Express*—who else they gonna call?"

***

They landed a half hour late, on time for flights to Africa. The terminal looked more modern than most Red had traveled through in the so-called First World. Its high ceilings, large glass windows, and spacious areas provided a stark contrast to what Red knew she would see in the bush areas of Kenya. They were going to a part of the country without running water and limited support. But first they were to stay at their base camp, one to two days in the capital city.

The luggage was delivered on time, and they were ready for the next leg of their adventure. Robert gestured to a fit man who wore a plain white shirt and black pair of pants. The man, Mustafa, held a sign that read: *Welcome, Mr. and Mrs. Potwiler.*

Robert whispered in Red's ear, "That's us, honey. Didn't Monty tell you we're married?"

Robert reached for Red's hand, and she promptly shook him off. The practical side of her reasoned she was playing the part of the moody traveler. The truth, however, was she simply didn't trust him to lead the parade and wanted to reestablish the dominance she and others had over him at SLIP. She also vaguely recalled him taking a liking to her.

"I'll take these, ma'am," Mustafa said, refusing to let them carry their two large suitcases and Robert's camera gear. He began carrying one bag in each hand, reserving his shoulder for the gear. Red was impressed at how he moved all of the baggage with such little effort.

They maneuvered through the airport to Mustafa's car, stowed in short-term parking. Mustafa drove onto Mombasa Road on their way to the Kilimani neighborhood, where the company house was located. His car had tinted windows, making them less of a target for carjackers—a common problem in Nairobi.

Their car immediately became engulfed by a mass of European and Japanese cars and trucks. Mustafa explained that Nairobi, once known as East Africa's "City in the Sun," now had more traffic than its dated roads could handle. Smog polluted the air—not as bad as some of the Asian cities Red had visited—but not comfortable, either. Mustafa told them they would need to blow their noses before going to sleep.

The city contained an eclectic mixture of older structures, some having aged concrete columns and institutional windows and others of the charming modern variety. Like other major metropolitan cities, hustlers, tourists, businessmen, families, and shoppers trolled the streets.

Close to an hour later, they arrived at the three-story cement apartment building Harmony had arranged for them. They shunned the tourist hotels to maintain a low profile. It wasn't worth a chance encounter of running into anybody from the *Daily Express* or meeting any reporters on the off chance somebody else was investigating their "story."

Mustafa delivered the luggage to their flat and offered them their weapons for use in country. Red happily chose the same gun as her normal weapon of choice, a Walther P99. Robert grabbed the second firearm, a 9mm Beretta handgun. They looked over the weapons, making sure they were properly balanced and maintained. They would check the gun sights later if they had the opportunity for target practice, a luxury they weren't likely to have.

Mustafa felt relieved when the agents smiled at him after the inspection.

The three-room apartment provided ample space. Red took the bedroom and looked at Robert with a wide grin, pointing to the couch in the living room. He got the message without even a whimper.

They spent the rest of the day finalizing arrangements. Mustafa ran errands, buying supplies and food.

***

Exhausted, they turned in early, and they woke to the sound of honking. It felt as if they had never left London.

"Ma'am, we haft to go, haft to go," Mustafa said excitedly as he entered their flat.

Red mused they were probably the first spies requiring his service in a long time.

Mustafa drove them to a runway located about ten kilometers outside of the city, explaining with a faint smile they were taking a shortcut. The runway couldn't be found on any official map. The sky was cloudier than yesterday, and it wasn't just the smog. Outside the city, Mustafa turned off onto a dirt road of packed red African clay. A trail of dust followed the car and the truck in front of them, some of the dust landing on their windshield.

Red abruptly felt the car jerk to a stop about ten minutes later as Mustafa slammed on his brakes in the heavily populated slums about five kilometers outside of Nairobi's city center. She lurched forward as a soccer ball whizzed by the car and a pack of kids chasing the ball stopped. They were suddenly surrounded by dozens of kids of all ages. All of them were barefoot, and most had no shirts, even some of the girls.

Men and women approached more cautiously. While the kids smiled and laughed, the adults looked tired and frail. The women carried large beige jerry cans on their heads filled with what Red assumed was water from a UN-funded well. She knew that UNESCO had a large field office nearby.

Robert turned to Red from the passenger seat and pointed in the distance.

"Red, that is Kibera, the poorest area of Nairobi and probably all of Kenya. You will never see something like that again. You know how many people live there? Estimates range up to one million," he answered before she could say anything.

Red perked up and stared. It was incredible. "Mustafa, how big is this place?"

"'Bout two kyes, ma'am."

"Two kilometers? Wow. How do people live like that?"

Robert added, "And with an average wage of about one euro per day."

Mustafa got out of the car, shooing the kids away from the vehicle so they could continue. Red had the sudden overwhelming urge to join him.

As she reached for the handle, Robert screamed, "Red, no!"

But it was too late. She couldn't control herself, a maternal urge rushing through her body. *How can these poor kids live like this?* Her eyelids felt heavy.

More kids ran toward them, screaming, "White woman, white woman!" Mustafa laughed; Robert looked terrified. Red dug into her pockets, but nothing came out. She felt embarrassed. The kids, however, weren't threatening; they were used to being disappointed.

Red returned to the car, as Robert breathed a sigh of relief. As they drove away, she watched the children through the rear window until they disappeared, at which time she turned her attention to the surroundings. Both sides of the road contained rusted aluminum shacks that stretched as far as she could see. Garbage was strewn everywhere. Pigs, dogs, and cats roamed freely.

Mustafa maneuvered the car through a few more streets. The scenery didn't change until they pulled through the gates of a wire fence. Guards standing at the entrance let them in. A runway beckoned to them in the distance. No placard or sign, just a strip of barren earth, an adjacent dirt road, and two guards. Strange, but not for this place.

***

A Cessna was already on the tarmac ready for them to board. *Harmony on the ball! You go, girl!* Red thought. They were heading towards a dirt runway about five kilometers outside of Todonyang, a town in northern Kenya near the border of South Sudan.

The long flight allowed Red to doze. Mustafa tapped her shoulder and pointed out the window as they flew low over Lake Turkana.

"You'll never see something so lovely!" he shouted over the roar of the engine.

He was right. A swarm of flamingos skipped across the water looking for prey in the greenish-blue water. The surrounding land resembled the moon more than any territory she had ever seen, except for maybe Iceland.

"Fancy that," Red shouted, waking up Robert. "What are they looking to chow on?"

"You know where they get their pink from, right? The algae they eat turns their feathers from gray to pink!" Mustafa chimed, proud of his knowledge.

Red pointed to a gigantic circular crater on the edge of the water.

Mustafa answered her un-articulated question, "That's Teleki Volcano, which last erupted in 1921. See the black streaks on the end there? Lava."

She continued to follow the volcano from her vantage point, straining and twisting her neck as the view changed. It was in the shape of a perfect circle, and she noticed the lava fields to which Mustafa had pointed.

About an hour later, they started their descent.

***

A tall, lanky man with a pockmarked face dressed in a light-blue police uniform met them as they disembarked from the plane. He had rich dark skin.

"Welcome to the real Kenya!" he said to them, obviously excited, barely able to contain his nervous laughter. "My name is Amani."

Red got the impression she and Robert were the most important guests he had ever greeted.

Robert took out his camera, and Red started jotting notes in her reporter's notebook.

Amani chuckled softly. "You can put those away. I know you no reporters but secret agents, bang-bang." He cocked his right hand with his thumb up and index finger pointed at Red for emphasis.

The agents looked at each other, thinking the same thing.

Red asked, "Will you take us to the village now?"

He motioned to his topless Jeep. Amani, whose name Red later learned means "trust" in this part of the world, had a box of fried chicken, which he said he purchased from "Kentarken Wired Chicken."

Red looked at him and then the box, her eyes betraying her disgust.

He ignored her look of disdain and said, "Ha! you eat. You not be in the mood after you get there and mayb' *never* after dat!"

Mustafa and Robert dug in, wolfing down the grub. *Men...all the same.*

Red's feeble protest ended after ten long minutes. Finally caving, Amani handed her the scraps they rejected. They finished and began the final leg of their long journey. Robert and Red drank from their supply of bottled water they had brought with them from Nairobi.

The dirt road contained numerous ditches, some deep and wide, causing Red to bounce high enough she feared falling out of the roofless Jeep. Enormous mountains with peaks of varying shapes and sizes were visible in the distance. Trees were few and far between. The immediate area would have looked barren if it weren't for the locals around Todonyang, whose bright clothing of different colors provided some flavor. *Like cherry tomatoes in a salad*, she thought to herself.

People seemed content. They looked at the Jeep and its occupants, more curious than threatened.

As they traveled away from town, sightings became sparser, except for the mountains still looming on the remote terra firma. They eventually pulled off the road into an area where they could see huts in the distance. A shirtless man with an AK-47 slung over his shoulder stopped the vehicle. Amani said something to him that Mustafa seemed to understand but Red didn't. Not that it mattered—the guard waved them through and even smiled at Red as if to say, *Thank God you are here. Thank you!* His greeting made her a bit nervous.

They turned off the main street onto a smaller dirt road, continuing further into the brush and wilderness. Two soldiers dressed in Kenyan military uniforms initially blocked the path but then waved them through after spotting Amani.

A plump white man on the wrong side of fifty, his pale shirt dripping with sweat, approached them.

"Good day, lads! Took you long enough. I'm Harry from the embassy. You see, our hosts contacted the embassy. They have never experienced anything quite like this before." As he spoke, Harry wiped the sweat off his brow using a handkerchief he took from his front pocket.

Red surveyed the empty village, thinking about Monty's story about a nomadic shepherd describing a ghost village. She introduced herself and Robert without saying more, not wanting to engage Harry in conversation at this point. She would see it for herself and then would ask questions if needed.

She simply blurted to Harry, "Let's have a look, shall we?"

Robert cocked his head at Red but didn't add anything.

"I'll show you around," Harry said. "We think the attackers came up the road you traveled, ten to fifteen, maybe even more than that. They must have covered the perimeter pretty well so nobody could escape. And then they used a pincer movement to systematically wipe 'em all out."

"How do you figure that?" Robert asked.

Harry paused for effect, inhaled, and said, "Well...you see over there? There are impressions showing three pairs of boots deeper than anyplace else. That is where we think the victims were funneled to their deaths."

"How many dead?" Robert wanted to know.

Harry replied, "About fifty."

"And they didn't fight back?" Red asked.

"You have to understand, this is tribal country. Villages belong to different tribes. These guys were members of the Mogobishi tribe, relatively peaceful lads. You remember what happened in the seventies?"

"Explain," Red quickly chirped.

"In 1970, December, I think, Kenya reelected President Mwai Kibaki. The only problem was that many people didn't believe he had legitimately won. Kibaki hails from the Kikuyus clan, and his rival, a chap named Odinga, was supported by a large tribe—the Kalenjin tribe. To make a long story short, the two tribes also coveted the same land in Rift Valley—the portion of Kenya where you are now standing."

"So what happened?" Red asked, looking around at the huts, each one made out of wood, animal skin, and plant leaves.

"What do you think happened? It took a while for the kettle to boil over, but eventually, in 2008, Kenya, including Rift Valley, went up in flames!" Harry stammered, raising his voice as if she had insulted his intelligence. He continued, "About twelve hundred people died, and more than three hundred thousand people became refugees. Most of the violence was the Kikuyus against the Kalenjins."

OMG, Red thought. *Fatty is killing me! Get to the bloody point*. "And?" she asked impatiently.

"Well, the tribe that lived here consisted of a small group of broad-minded chaps, some from each of the Kikuyus and Kalenjins. You know, to show they could get along. They joined forces and called themselves the Mogobishi tribe."

"Appears somebody didn't believe in their Utopian idea," Red said, stating the obvious.

"Yes, indeed. But that is where this story gets interesting. You see, we don't believe the Kikuyus or the Kalenjins had a hand in this. We've been monitoring their movements, and we don't think they wcrc involved."

Red sighed, slumping her shoulders. "We kinda figured that, Harry. If it were that simple, we wouldn't have traveled all the way from London. So who are the leading contenders?"

"At first we thought another tribe, perhaps the Turkanas or Dassanechs, were involved. They've been involved in other incidents of intertribal violence and massacres. Now we think the Mustavi tribe slipped across the border from South Sudan. We found these in the bodies." Harry picked up an arrow. "Don't worry, this one went astray. But you see these yellow, red, and blue markings? These are the markings of the Mustavi tribe."

"Why would they be involved?" Robert asked.

"Not sure, but they are bad seed. See these pictures from the Internet?" Harry handed Red photos of tall and lanky boys and girls cutting razor blades into their skin, bright-red blood oozing everywhere. "They are marking themselves with their warrior colors."

"What did you mean when you said 'at first'?" Red asked.

"Remember I said there were fifty bodies? Well, fifty-one people lived here. And there was a lone survivor who died shortly after we pulled up. Wanna know what he told us?"

"Get on with it, Harry."

"His last words were, 'The white man cometh.'"

Chapter 2
Kenya

Amani drove Red and Robert to the morgue in Todonyang. Harry met his fellow Brits at the facility, located in the dingy basement of a police station. He showed them pictures of each body before it was moved to the facility. Each had at least one puncture from an arrow in addition to other scrapes and signs of physical abuse. Some had wounds made worse by vultures and vermin.

Something bothered them.

"Interesting. Fifty bodies and no survivors except for the one person who lasted a few days? Shot by arrows? And who is the white guy? The tribal chief?" Robert asked.

Harry dove right in, sounding a bit defensive, stating, "A white guy hanging out with the Mustavi? One of the fiercest tribes, people who mark their skin with razor blades? That didn't happen—believe me. This lone survivor, he probably *thinks* he saw God as he was ascending to heaven. Trust me. You realize one of the nastiest Sudanese tribes took them on. Probably a ridiculous tribal dispute. I bet some underling stole a goat or a lion. You never know with *these* people."

Harry didn't say it, but there was no reason for the Kenyans to have involved MI6 in the first place. It was a tribal dispute as far as he was concerned, and the "white guy" didn't exist.

Red put her hands on her hips. "Goat or lion? Really? This isn't some Hollywood movie, Harry," she said.

Harry stared at Red and stammered, "Whatever! What's the difference? Maybe it was an affair or something like that then. OK?"

Red replied sharply, "You mean like a tribal sex triangle?" She then looked at Robert. He tilted his head to the side and looked at Red. They ignored Harry, and Red thought, *This guy is an idiot. No wonder Downing Street banished him to some outpost in East Africa.*

"Did you run any toxicology screens?" Red asked the coroner, an elderly man with an obvious limp, listening to the discussion with a terrified look on his face.

"No, ma'am, we no have budget for that," he replied.

"Fifty-one guys die, and it isn't in the budget?"

"Yes, ma'am. That's right."

Red began to poke around after putting on gloves. "What's that coming from this guy's mouth? And that guy too. And the guy over there. Does that usually happen with arrows?"

Robert shouted, "Over here! This guy has a dark lesion on his skin. It looks new."

"Same with this guy," Red said, pointing to another body. "You guys need to lock this place down," she said to the coroner. "I'm going to take some samples with me. Can we get a cooler with some ice, Harry?"

Harry clearly didn't like taking orders from a female agent encroaching on his territory. He looked Red up and down, paused for effect, and replied,

"Sure, why don't I go to the nearest Tesco? They got those in these parts, you know."

Red, though, was not in the mood to argue. "Harry, figure it out. Go to a restaurant, supply shop, food store. The locals must purchase from somewhere, don't they?"

He grunted and left.

While Red was playing turf wars with Harry, Robert procured a few needles and syringes from the coroner. About a half hour later, Harry entered the dungeon with a Styrofoam cooler filled with ice. Red and Robert took a few samples while Harry and Amani arranged for the plane back to Nairobi. They didn't have a lot of time before all of the ice melted.

***

London

The next day, after better securing their samples in Nairobi, Red and Robert headed back to London. They relaxed on the plane until Robert's curiosity broke through. Red knew what he wanted to ask. He kept staring at her with the look of a child in a sweet shop. Red toyed with the idea of stringing him along for a bit, to make him sweat. But ultimately she wanted to get it over with.

Red finally had enough and turned her head to face Robert. "Robert, you look like a fish. Opening and closing your mouth without saying anything. What would you like to know?"

He looked up at her like a puppy. "I, uh, are you still shacking up with Jake Kessler?"

"Seriously? What, are you still in secondary school?"

"Uh, I'm sorry it came out that way. I didn't mean it to be so awkward...It's just that, well...you know, people talk."

"And you want to know because other people are talking? Come on, Robert, at least be honest with me."

Red shrunk down in her seat and looked at the floor. "It's really no big deal. We had a thing while working on the MKUltra case. The case ended, and we ended as well—several years ago, as a matter of fact. Nothing to it. It's in the past." She stopped herself from going on and on. "Anything else you want to pry about?" she asked sharply.

***

Red, in a dark mood, dressed to go knees up tonight, needing to shed some steam. But she couldn't go as herself. Her blonde wig made her younger and cuter. Men couldn't resist blondes. It's part of their DNA.

She looked over the dresses in her walk-in closet. Some were falling off their hangers, others fit snug. A few had fallen to the floor. Red had always been somewhat of a slob. A few minutes later she made her choice: a blue V-neck bare-back.

She bought the evening dress to use when she wanted to display her tattoo on the small of her back, a birdcage hanging from a tree branch with an open door and a red bird about to escape and fly away. The tattoo was acquired after graduating from SLIP as Red's own personal "fuck you" to her dad. She refused to be a bird caged in a man's world.

A pair of silver stilettos rounded out her attire.

The bar was located a few blocks away from Piccadilly Circus. People were dancing to a band playing a blend of Latin and jazz music.

The door she opened to enter the club had not even closed when she spotted a brown-haired man-hunk sitting at the bar. He ordered a drink and looked around. Red hoped he was looking for somebody to spend the night with.

She began to approach when her cell rang. She wanted to ignore the call, but her job was 24/7, her only constant at this point in her life. To screw up would prove her dad right: "Spy? Girls don't make spies!"

She reluctantly answered, going outside to take the call.

"Red, get down here now!" Monty screamed so loud into her cell phone she had to hold it ten centimeters from her ear.

Red sighed, realizing she could never completely leave her cage, and left. She returned to her flat, where she quickly dressed down. Ten minutes later, she headed for the tube.

Monty greeted her warmly at his office. He pointed to a seat, where she dutifully sat. Robert was already there, sitting like a schoolboy at the principal's office. He started laughing and then leaned over to whisper in her ear.

"You don't smell like you did in Nairobi."

Red remembered the perfume she put on, more difficult to get rid of than clothing and makeup.

"Are you two done yet?" Monty asked. "Because you made an interesting discovery. Did you know you brought anthrax back in that cooler? You're lucky you didn't contaminate anybody, including yourselves, or worse, yours truly."

"Anthrax!" Robert said, thankful that they had taken precautions to not touch or ingest the material. "That explains the lesions and foam."

"Yes, but the arrows and Mustavi tribe?" Monty deadpanned. "I mean, why would those buggers kill folks already dead? There are two possibilities: either they poisoned them with anthrax and then shot them with arrows to make sure they were dead, or some other dolts poisoned them first and *then* shot them. Neither makes a whole lot of sense, if I understand this right."

"Wait a minute," Red said, practically jumping up from her seat. "The white man—there was one survivor, you know. And remember what the poor guy said right before he died? 'The white man cometh.'"

"Oh, come on, Red. You guys put that in the report as an afterthought, now you think it's real and the key? I agree with your first instinct. Why would a white guy come to work with a fierce African tribe? Even if you manage to answer that one, how would that even happen? These guys don't jibe too well with the Western world, if you get my drift."

"Money?" she asked.

"Have you gone bonkers? What would a bunch of bushmen do with money?" Monty asked.

"Hmm," Red pondered.

"Hmm," Robert added helpfully.

"Well, while you two geniuses stew, let me add to your puzzle," Monty said after putting his feet on his desk.

Pig! Red thought.

He barked into his phone for Dr. Sanjeev Parchman to join the meeting from his office in the basement, where MI6 stowed its scientists.

Sanjeev arrived fifteen minutes later, eager for fresh air outside the dungeon. He pulled up a chair to join them. Red looked at him closely.

Sanjeev laughed. "You are wondering how an Indian has blond hair, no?" he asked.

She nodded, instantly regretting the impulse.

Monty rolled his eyes while Sanjeev explained, "My mum met my pa while he was visiting as a doctor in Mumbai. I was born here. I got my mum's complexion and my father's blond hair, blue eyes, and last name."

Monty interrupted, "Can you two stop playing United Nations?"

Sanjeev said, "I took the liberty of bringing some of the blood you took to the British National Lab Porton Down. I wanted to find out more about the anthrax."

"What more do you need to know?" Robert asked.

Sanjeev looked at Robert and then at Red. "The lab has equipment that lets us know the particular strain of anthrax. We can measure, if you will, the DNA. And studying the DNA can teach us its origin. And the origin can lead us to the source."

Sanjeev was no longer interesting to Red, who couldn't take his long-winded answers anymore. "Look, Doctor, can you get to the point?" Red asked.

"Ah, the point. The lab traced the particular sample to a place nicknamed Anthrax Island. Funny name, I know. The real name is Vozrozhdeniya Island, which is an island in the Aral Sea. It used to be part of the Soviet Union and is now controlled by Kazakhstan and Uzbekistan.

"The United States had its Project MKUltra program where it experimented with drugs. Our cousins also used the Marshall Islands in the Pacific for nuclear tests. Well, Russia didn't idly stand by while the West advanced, if you want to call it that. In the forties, Russia began using islands in the Aral Sea for biological warfare testing. They explored using anthrax, various plagues, and smallpox—as a weapon."

"When did the program shut down?" she asked.

"Good question, Red, and one that shows several parallels to America's Project MKUltra. Project MKUltra shut down after word leaked about the CIA's use of LSD and other drugs. A CIA operative, Frank Olson, actually died jumping from his hotel room in New York City after drinking LSD-laced brandy. The American Congress conducted investigations in the

1970s forcing the program to stop, or at least morph into something else.

"The Soviets had their own issues around the same period of time. They accidently released weaponized smallpox on the island, infecting ten people in 1971. A few of them died. A defector, Ken Alibek, spread word in the 1990s, forcing Russia to shut it down. He was the former head of the Soviet bioweapons program."

The good doctor obviously didn't know Red knew all about Project MKUltra, having worked with Jake Kessler several years ago to prevent the assassination of US president Ross Tucker. She simply nodded. Robert looked at Red and then directed his focus to Sanjeev, asking him, "What became of the island?"

"Well, it was abandoned after the smallpox incident, except for a pack of brave scavengers, who periodically return to the island in search of abandoned building materials. In 2002, the Americans and Uzbeks decontaminated some of the burial sites. Today, the island remains abandoned."

"How sure are you the strain of anthrax we found in Africa is from Anthrax Island? Could it be from somewhere else?" Red asked.

"The only way to know for sure is for you to go to the island to get a live sample of the substance. The lab determined it likely came from there, but we have to know for sure by getting an actual sample."

Robert said, "Wait a minute. Let's slow down. How is this even possible if the Americans cleaned it up and it hasn't been used in decades? I mean, how could our 'white man' have gotten enough from an abandoned island in central Asia to kill a whole village in Africa?"

"Good question, the answer to which could have devastating ramifications. If you confirm the strain matches anthrax from the island, then we have a real problem. A really big problem."

"Which means?" Red asked.

Sanjeev responded, "If it is the Anthrax Island's strain, then the bad guys probably know how to reproduce it. In other words, they can manufacture as much as they want."

"What would the connection be to the African village?" Robert asked.

"You expect me to know? I'm just a scientist."

Red sat up straight. "So somebody gets a hold of the same strain, adds to it, and brings the product to Africa to poison the Mustavi tribe? I agree with Robert, that makes no sense."

"Bingo," Monty said.

"Why would somebody do that?" Robert repeated the fundamental question.

Monty stewed for a moment and then eagerly said, "Well, that's what the two of you lads are going to find out! Starting at the source, of course."

And with a flick of his wrist, he banished Sanjeev back to his dungeon.

Chapter 3
Washington

A few years ago, Jake Kessler was a senior advisor to President Ross Tucker on security and intelligence matters. Jake and Tucker grew close, playing basketball together and sharing downtime.

Like Tucker, Jake kept himself in superb shape, working out as often as he could. He had an average-sized nose but one with a distinctive bend, as if he broke it and never had it reset. His lean face, square chin, and toned body made him appear younger than his middle age. His thick hair hid his bald spot, but it seemed to grow larger each year, and it wouldn't be long before it became pronounced.

Jake quit his presidential post after helping to prevent the assassination of President Tucker, an African American. A racist sicko named Paul King teamed with a remnant program doctor to perfect Alterando, a drug first invented through the shuttered Project MKUltra program. King intended to use the drug to brainwash an unsuspecting person into pulling the trigger.

Jake went rouge, choosing to work with Red as opposed to the Secret Service to save Tucker's life, not even telling the Secret Service or others in law enforcement until the aftermath. Jake had his reasons and in the end proved to have made the correct choice, but his methods had caused a great deal of resentment.

Now Jake was on the outside, forced to leave his job and banished from the White House. He would have to jump the White House fence and risk getting shot in order to see his friend again. Hard to imagine, but it was true.

Tucker referred Jake to Sherman right after leaving his employ. But the sessions with Sherman had not worked, frustrating Jake.

How much longer will I have to put up with the man? If anything, Jake felt worse and was more depressed than before he started.

***

Sherman's office was located near George Washington University, right off of Pennsylvania Avenue. Sherman, in his younger years, was built like a truck with trunk-like legs and a thick neck. His walls featured pictures of wrestling matches, including one where he hoisted a large trophy in the air. In another, he sported a gold medal, and Jake could see a banner announcing, "NCAA Finals."

He greeted Jake with his usual fake smile and lisp. "Welcome, Jake. Good to see you."

"Nice to see you too, *Sherrman*." Jake liked saying his name this way, although part of him hesitated, not wanting to provoke the shrink.

"Please sit down, Jake," Sherman said, motioning to his ancient green stained couch to the right of his desk. Jake complied. A glass of water was waiting for him on the glass coffee table located in front of the couch. The table sat on top of an oriental rug, which made Sherman's office seem too cliché even for a shrink.

Sherman sat upright on his chair in front of the coffee table. "Did you have a good week?"

Jake wanted to tell him to cut the fake Mr. Rogers act but held his tongue. Jake lay down, putting his feet up on the opposite end. "Sure, the Jets beat the Patriots."

"Ah, yes, an upset! Take your shoes off, will you?" Sherman complained. Jake complied, forgoing the opportunity to poke fun at his wrestler-turned-shrink. Sherman continued, "Adjusting to your job?"

Jake snickered. "They don't know what to do with me. Half the people think someone called in some favors to get me there. And sometimes I think the same thing."

"Do you miss your old job?"

He sat up and looked at Sherman. "Sometimes, yes."

"Why don't you go back then?"

Jake lay down again and stretched out his legs on the couch. "Can't, just can't."

"Why not?"

"I don't know. People still don't understand the choices I made."

"Wish you'd played it differently?"

"Looking back, no. If I had involved the Secret Service or others earlier, nobody would've believed me, and I would've lost my—excuse me, our—leads."

"*Our?*" Sherman interrupted, obviously pleased Jake used the word.

Jake stared at him, ignoring the moment and instead said in a raised voice, "It worked out right, didn't it?"

Sherman accepted his logic, at least for the moment. "Yes, it did. Let's talk about Renée. You told me last week she died after leaving a bar in Jersey City. Did the autopsy indicate how much she had to drink?"

"Well, um, she had a blood alcohol content of twice the legal limit when she died."

"Why was she at the bar on a weekday? Where did you guys live at the time?"

"New York."

"New York, OK. So why would she go to a bar alone in Jersey City?"

Jake looked at his feet and said slowly, "I...should have paid more attention. She, um, was having a difficult time."

"How so?"

"Well, she hated the press following us around like paparazzi and writing stories about us after 9/11. I mean, sure, I was the chief of police of NYC, but why hound me with dumb questions? Why snap pictures of us eating dinner? I didn't realize the toll it had taken on her while I was working twenty-four hours a day during that time. How could I understand?"

"Jake, you're a hero. Everybody knows that. You helped Giuliani put the city back together."

"I played my part," he said in a soft tone.

"Played your part? You led the NYPD through one of its darkest times. Take some credit. Figure out how to move on."

Jake sat up straight and tensed his shoulders, practically screaming in a snarky tone, "Don't you think I have tried?!"

"Jake, please lower your voice. Let's talk about that. What happened to Renée that day?"

"Sherman, we have already gone through this...many times. I told you that the bitch killed her."

"Intentionally?"

"Yes, she was driving like a lunatic. It was freezing out, but she wouldn't slow down."

"But wasn't she chasing someone?"

"Sure, she says she was after Saajid Badat, who had a connection to Richard Reid—the Shoe Bomber. Why didn't she stop, though?" Jake shouted.

Sherman looked at Jake, cocking his head. He must have thought he was brilliant. "What would you have done if the situation were in reverse?" he asked after a pause.

"You mean if I killed Red's wife?" Jake said, surprised he could actually make light of it.

"Funny. Good. Humor is a sign of healing. Please just answer the question."

"OK, Doc, I'll play along. Depends."

"Depends? Jake, humor me for a second. Let's say you were chasing somebody as important as an accomplice to the Shoe Bomber. And you hit somebody who slipped on ice in front of your car. Would you continue, knowing that if you stopped he'd get away? Or would you stop?"

"Of course I would stop!" he stammered, falling right into Sherman's trap. "If I had hit a pedestrian it means I was probably off course anyway. I would've also hit the curb or something else, slowing me down. And you think the terrorist would've stuck around to watch? No, he'd be long gone, but maybe the person I hit could be saved by first aid."

"First aid? After being walloped by a car? I mean, what would you have been able to accomplish other than losing any hope of catching up to the guy you are chasing? A person as dangerous as the Shoe Bomber, trying to blow up planes."

"I...I don't know," Jake said in a quiet, wavering voice.

"And don't forget there would be other people around who could've called an ambulance. I mean, it isn't like it took place on a country road. Let's get back to that. Let's shift gears and discuss how you discovered Red's car had hit Renée."

"Well, we discussed before that I fell in love with Red while we worked on the Project MKUltra case.

The bitch could've told me. But she didn't—even when we were falling for each other."

"So...how did you find out?"

"That's the really weird part. We saw each other a lot after we stopped Paul King's plot. Things were going great. Then one day she left. She couldn't even face me. She left a note for me to find."

"And..."

"And? Not much else to say. The note said nothing really. Some crap about her wanting to return to England. Not even giving me the chance to join her." Jake looked at his watch. "I think this is enough for today."

Sherman implored, "Let's continue, please. We're making a lot of progress here."

Jake hesitated. He was right to continue. They had made more progress today than on any other day. "Well, after she left, I started to think about what happened. Looking back, it seemed as if she was holding back on something. She didn't drink, not even a glass of wine. When I probed, she clammed up. It didn't seem like she was an alcoholic. No, her issue was different. I sensed she had a drinking problem as a reaction to some incident or issue in her past.

"So, I did some research. I pulled up a database— remember I had access to all sorts of NSA-like information—and I discovered she was involved in the Shoe Bomber case. I also learned Saajid Badat was staying in an apartment house in Jersey City the same evening Renée died. Witnesses remember a car chase near Renée's bar, and I read Badat had disappeared that same night.

"I was stunned. I didn't have the courage to confront her until a few weeks later, and even then I didn't want to speak to her. I sent her an email. She didn't respond to the first email or any of my follow-ups."

Sherman relaxed his shoulders and said in a soothing voice, "Look, Jake, that sounds horrible. I can't imagine what you're going through. But we need to figure out a way for you to let it go and live your life."

"Let it go? How do you expect me to let it go? I hope you don't say that to all of your patients. Like, 'Charlie, I'm sorry your wife cheats on you. You just need to let it go.'"

Sherman looked at Jake, trying to suppress a chuckle.

Jake sighed and then said softly, "You may be right. But look at it from my perspective. My wife dies, and then I fall in love with her killer?"

Sherman sighed and then shifted topics. "Let's talk about what else may be going on here. Your parents, Jake. You said last time your mom was one of the first female generals to serve in the Army. And your dad was a dentist, also Army. Interesting combination."

"That's right. They met when Dad was giving Mom a checkup at the base. What's that got to do with this?"

"Maybe nothing, maybe everything," Sherman replied. "It's just that it might help explain what you are feeling."

"Explain?"

"Just hear me out, Jake. Both your parents are disciplined people. I mean, military and all. Right?"

"Sure," Jake huffed.

"And you're disciplined too, at least until you left NYPD. You can't get to lead *that* force unless you're hard-wired. Agree?"

Jake nodded. "Where you going with this, Doc?"

"You felt the need to go out on a limb during the Project MKUltra case, and that left you vulnerable. Indeed, you were the person who King tried to drug with the Alterando. You would've been the perfect triggerman, using your access to Tucker as a senior advisor and friend." Sherman raised his voice as he spoke.

Jake sat stunned. He wanted to walk out but felt paralyzed.

Sherman continued, "You were embarrassed that King tried to use you in such a devious manner. Fortunately, you figured it out and faked using the drug to uncover the plot. You crossed paths with Red, who stumbled onto the plan while working on another case. The two of you joined forces and fell in love. You didn't tell anybody in the government about King and his plan, even though you understood the backlash you'd ultimately receive. You ignored the risk, flying blind, not being your usual disciplined self, because of your involvement as King's initial pawn *and* your affair with Red. Then you learned what Red had done years before – to Renée. A devastating development, a double whammy. It explains a lot."

Jake was speechless. Sherman was on to something.

Chapter 4
Iraq

Jake landed at 10:00 p.m. at Baghdad International Airport. The flight provided him with an opportunity to think about his session with Sherman the day before. Sherman was adept at his job and had helped Jake work through his feelings. The passage of time, and inspiration he hoped to find as a reporter, would further brighten his outlook, and someday he might even be fully refreshed to his usual self.

The weather in Baghdad was balmy. A small dust storm had cleared the area a few hours before his plane landed, leaving a humid stench in its wake.

Years of fighting had left pockets of debris, disheveled buildings, and bombed-out cars. People acted as if they didn't know who to trust, a difficult reality.

Jake's editor assigned him to a human-interest story in Iraq. Not the usual tale about terrorism, fractional fighting, dysfunctional government, but a story which, on its face, seemed strange. Almost like being assigned to interview Hitler's SS officers after WWII.

He was insulted at first. How far he'd fallen since his days working as a senior advisor to POTUS or leading the New York City Police Department. But he was the one who requested that he not be assigned to investigate or report domestically. First, he had run to Washington, quitting his plum job as NYPD chief. Then he became entangled in the Project MKUltra case, saving the life of President Tucker but in a way that alienated the intelligence community. He needed another change.

Fortunately for Jake, the *New York Times International Edition* hired him, evidently with reservations. He began to wonder about the assignment as soon as he boarded the plane. And now, part of him wanted to catch the next flight back to America.

***

A short, plump man dressed in black pants and a loose-fitting, white, Oxford-style shirt approached Jake as he stood by the baggage carousel. He had a black beard that had been carefully groomed, and his skin had the same color as a light-brown olive.

He said softly, "Welcome to Iraq. The sun is shining bright today. Did you find your bags?"

Jake mumbled his learned response, "Yes, it is even stronger than the last time I was here. They lost my bags but will bring them to my hotel. You can never be too careful in Baghdad." Uttering the secret password made Jake feel cool, as if he was part of a select cult.

Jake watched the apparent contact process his words. He didn't respond immediately, making Jake nervous, but then he replied, "That's too bad, Mr. Kessler. This way, please."

The two walked to the contact's car in silence. The local introduced himself to Jake once they were inside while handing Jake a cell phone keyed into the local cellular network for his use while in country.

"My name is Ali Kohinoor. I'm at your service, officially as your gopher and interpreter. I work for Protectorate Enterprises. Here's my identification."

Jake was familiar with Protectorate, a body shop with an array of cleared and non-cleared staff. He didn't need the more expensive cleared variety, just somebody he could trust. And Protectorate hired the best, enjoying a stellar reputation.

Jake looked at Ali closely. There were two types of interpreters working in Iraq: locals who wanted to make Iraq a better place, and nonnatives who were fluent in the language and needed a job. Ali seemed to fall within the latter category.

Jake asked him, "Iranian fluent in Arabic in addition to Farsi?"

"That's me!"

"Interesting. This phone clean?" Jake asked.

"Of course. Protectorate gave me seven for you to use on your trip."

"You familiar with why I'm here?"

Ali hesitated but then answered, "Yes, they briefed me, and I've made the requested arrangements. Tomorrow we visit the hole where they found him and two of them. The next day, the other three. Will that work?"

"Great, great. This place is still pretty dangerous, right?"

Ali laughed. "Yes, but it also depends upon which way the wind is blowing. We have an old Persian saying: 'If a man would live in peace, he should be blind, deaf, and dumb.'"

Jake laughed nervously and said, "A Persian working for the Americans as an interpreter in Iraq? Oh my, somebody doesn't like me too much."

***

They drove up to the iron gates of their hotel, where two massive German shepherds escorted by two young men wearing fatigues searched the car. One of the men shined a small but powerful flashlight in Jake's face and then traced the beam down to his feet, looking for anything out of place. A bulky black man slid his mirror underneath the car. Ali rolled down his window, greeting a fourth person sitting in a kiosk.

They must have passed all tests, as the gate soon opened. The hotel, originally built as one of Saddam's smaller monuments to his ego, had a grand foyer with a white stone staircase leading to the second level. There, a mixture of operatives working for a variety of intelligence agencies, NGOs, and journalists relaxed, enjoying a rare opportunity to savor different flavors of American and European beers.

A few of the occupants glanced up at Jake as he walked by. Only one nodded at Jake, the others looking at him skeptically. A stranger in a land where that could be dangerous. Fortunately, many of them recognized Ali, respectfully nodding at him.

Ali led Jake to a room on the third floor.

When they were alone Jake asked Ali, "I take it I'm not too popular, right?"

Ali answered, "Don't take it personally. You know what FUBAR stands for, right?"

"Of course."

"Well, what you're doing here is FUBAR."

***

Jake, with Ali translating, interviewed the first four doubles over the next two days. That left only one, Jabal Shamoon, which means "which glides away" in Arabic. Jabal lived in Tikrit. Jake planned on compiling his notes from the interviews he had already conducted on the two-hour drive from Baghdad.

Instead, he gazed through the window of Ali's Toyota, amazed at how Iraq still hadn't made any tangible progress since the Gulf Wars and the tragic events that followed. Kids played soccer in dirt fields along the highway, dogs scavenged for food, abandoned rusted and bombed-out vehicles and trash stood waiting for a pickup that would never arrive. The torrid heat baked the earth. A gusty breeze created miniature dust storms that must have made the locals indifferent about cleaning the landscape.

They pulled up to the four-story brown brick building where Jabal lived on the third floor. The inside walls had a few holes, evidence of one or more squabbles, errant throws, or collisions with furniture. There was no supervisor at the ready making the necessary repairs. The elevators didn't work and probably hadn't in a long time, forcing Jake and Ali to walk up the three flights.

Ali knocked on the door three times. A woman dressed in jeans and a blue shirt answered. Deep wrinkles covered her face. She seemed sad and tired.

Ali spoke to her in Arabic. She perked up once she realized they weren't with the government or a security force, beckoning them to enter and quickly shutting the door immediately after they walked through the frame. She looked out her peephole, presumably to determine if any nosy neighbors had witnessed the exchange.

After satisfying herself, she turned to Ali, who introduced her to Jake as Aisha, Jabal's mom. Although she was cautious with Ali, she greeted Jake like she had known him for years, kissing him on both cheeks. Her eyes sparkled, and her posture straightened.

Aisha gestured for her guests to sit on a couch in the living room. A plain wooden coffee table separated the couch from a simple chair. One lamp dimly illuminated the room, and a large section of a wall was covered with three shelves filled with books.

Jake spoke first. Aisha heard Ali's translated words five seconds later. "We are here to talk to Jabal."

She ignored the question, asking if they would like tea instead. They both accepted, knowing it would be rude to decline. Aisha disappeared into the kitchen, a small room separated from Jake and Ali by a doorway filled with about ten strings of red, green, black, and blue beads. The objects made a soothing noise as they collided. A pleasing thyme and rosemary odor emanated from the kitchen, invading the living room on invisible waves.

She emerged about twenty minutes later with a steel tray filled with a mixture of pistachios, thyme bread, a stone teapot, and three cups. Jake offered to help, but she declined his assistance, serving him tea while he held back the urge to ask if Jabal would be joining.

They sipped the tea and waited a few minutes. Jake broke the ice by talking through Ali's translation about the many books on her shelves. Jake couldn't read the titles but noted that, like himself, she liked to read. Ali continued to relay the mundane conversation encroaching onto sensitive topics such as the weather and the trip from Baghdad.

Fifteen minutes later, she asked Jake through Ali about his story.

Jake replied, "I work for the *New York Times International Edition*, and I am doing a human-interest story about the Saddam doubles. A story about what they are doing now. Have they been able to find work? How much do they really look like Saddam? Any plastic surgery?"

At first, Jake thought something must have been lost in the translation since she just sort of grunted. He explained further, "People are interested in knowing…"

She interrupted, "You mean *your* readers in *your* papers? To read in fancy houses over...coffee? To justify your war?"

Jake replied, pleading, "Aisha, my story *is* a human-interest story. Jabal's experience is important for people in your country and, yes, also in the West, to understand. Iraq has changed everybody, some for the better and some for the worse. People are evolving and are still asking questions. They want to understand."

"Understand? What do you mean? The transformation? Plastic surgery?"

Jake looked at her while she sipped her tea. This was not going as planned. And where was Jabal? Aisha had let them into her apartment and seemed to want to engage Jake. But at the same time, she was reluctant, challenging him instead.

Jake had learned a long time ago that people responded well to honesty. People could see through half-truths.

"I do have some questions about the process, how they came to look like Saddam. But that part is somewhat obvious. A story about that wouldn't be interesting. I'm more interested in learning about what they were *feeling*. Did they like doing what they did, taking the risks? Where did they come from? What about their families?"

She explained she was afraid and wanted Jake to promise he wouldn't publish Jabal's or her first or given name. He agreed, wondering what she was about to tell him. And she still hadn't mentioned Jabal's location. It became increasingly obvious she hadn't seen him in a while, an unexpected and disappointing development.

The trio sipped tea in relative silence for a few more minutes. Jake began to fidget. Ali touched his shoulder when Aisha was not looking as if to say, *Hang in there. Don't rush her.*

Jake waited, but when she finally spoke, she confirmed his worst fears.

"I haven't seen Jabal in five years."

He was taken aback. *Five years? Why did she accept the interview?*

Jake looked at her, his expression blank. He stood and began pacing. She rose too. Jake thought she was going to show them the door. Instead, she walked slowly to a table on the other side of the room. Jake began to walk toward her to see what she wanted to show him, but she held out her open palm, fingers tight as if directing traffic to stop. He obliged.

She handed Jake two pictures, and this time in broken English, she said directly to him, "Which one Saddam? Which one Jabal?"

He looked closely, squinting in the dim light. Jake turned his cell phone on in order to shine its flashlight onto the photos. He couldn't tell the difference. Both men had the same jet-black hair cut short, fully exposing their large ears and elongated foreheads. Jabal also sported Saddam's wide nose, two cheek moles, and thick black mustache covering the top part of his lip.

She gestured for him to sit back down and returned to her seat. Tears swelled in her eyes while she rested for a few moments. Jake felt sorry for her.

A few minutes later, she began to rant to Ali in Arabic. Ali tried to keep up.

"Jabal, he is a good boy. You need to understand, to believe me. He's had a difficult time. His father died fighting the Iranians." She looked up at Ali but continued, "I raised him myself. He didn't have time for school, you see. With no father, he had to work in a factory instead. He'd watch children his age going to school, experiencing life.

"I was bitter back then, heartbroken, wanting to crawl inside myself. But I held it inside, choosing instead to show Jabal his father died for a reason, that his death wasn't a waste. There are a lot of people like Jabal and me. We were proud to be Baathists on the outside. But on the inside, we were being eaten alive, with no purpose in life.

"Jabal grew into a young man but was sad. Then one day Uday Hussein saw Jabal at a rally. The bastard and two henchmen led him into a car. I thought he'd done something wrong. I tried to intervene, but they waved me off. I didn't know what to do until he called later that night. 'Mother, something wonderful has happened,' he told me. 'I'm going to work closely with President Hussein himself.' That was difficult for me to understand or accept. I didn't want to lose Jabal as I had lost my husband. But I...felt powerless...What could I do? Saying no could land us both in jail or...worse."

Ali continued to translate the remaining conversation.

"Did you ever try to talk Jabal out of it?"

"Yes, but I was weak and afraid. And Jabal seemed so proud of his work. He began to dress like Saddam even when he wasn't working with him. He practiced speaking like him in front of a mirror. He even walked like him. He never cared about anything important before. Now he felt important." She paused and then asked, "Do you have any children?"

Jake shook his head but then surprised himself by adding, "I was married once. But she died, and we never had kids."

She took his hand across the table and said, "I'm sorry. We are alike in that way. I can tell that you are still in mourning. It never stops, right?"

"Each day gets a little better than the last, but the pain still lingers." Jake shifted the focus. "How often did you see Jabal after they took him away?"

"Oh...he'd come back a few times a month at first. Then his visits became less frequent, and he seemed more distracted when he was here. His work was more important to him, I guess."

"What do you mean?" Jake said, noticing Aisha's calm but depressed demeanor.

"Well, Jabal, he had a hard time. Didn't have a lot to do other than work, you know, and he resented that. Saddam offered him an opportunity. He became important, advancing the country. He didn't appreciate the true danger and instead accepted his role with a childlike fantasy about power and importance. He also began to shut me out, not listening to me. And the truth is, I began to fear him."

"You thought he might report you?"

She began to sniffle, her voice becoming quieter. "I knew many cases where a child turned in a parent to the authorities. Some children begin to believe in the state more than family. Like children of Nazi families."

Jake was impressed at her level of knowledge and then glanced again at her books. He decided to shift gears. "Was he ever threatened by Saddam or anybody else?"

"Not sure."

"Did he ever have to step in to protect Saddam— you know, like in the line of action?"

"Not sure."

"Tell me what happened when America began threatening to invade. How did that affect Jabal?"

"Jabal, he was confident. I believe he started to love Saddam on some level...almost like...a father, you could say. Remember, his father died so young. He never really had a one, and that always tormented him. Now he had a father figure. And he trusted and believed in him."

"What about when America invaded and made progress?"

"Progress?"

"Sorry about that...let's just say America caused Saddam to go into hiding and on the run. Did Jabal begin to worry then?"

"At some point he became moody and upset. His temper became short. He seemed concerned. He wouldn't talk to me about it, but I could sense it, you know?"

"How did Jabal handle Saddam's capture and hanging?"

"Jabal, he stayed in his room a lot after that. And when he came out of his room, he tried to act like Saddam, as if somehow he could still help the cause. He didn't know what to do. He wasn't a thinker to begin with. His purpose in life went away."

"Then he left, you said about five years ago?"

Aisha leaned back in her chair and took a moment to compose herself. "Yes, he left during the night, and I haven't seen him since."

"Did he leave a note?"

She looked at Jake and didn't respond.

Jake repeated his question.

She looked into his eyes and redirected. "You said before that you will not use Jabal's first or given name. You still agree?"

"You should understand I'm professionally obligated to not break that promise. You can trust me."

She looked at Jake, unsure of what to do. He clasped her hand like she had done to him earlier in the interview.

She stood up and said, "Please give me a moment." She returned with a note which Ali translated. It said:

Dearest Mama,

I know this must be difficult for you to understand. But I was lost before President Hussein rescued me. I had no purpose in life. It is as if I was destined to work with him. For him and our great country.

The Party is important, and we were prospering before the infidels invaded our country. Now we are suffering. Criminals have taken over the streets. People are turning to alcohol and crime. We have no rules, and there is nobody left to keep us safe. Our country is no more, and all hope is lost.

Who will save us? The infidels? No. They are hunting us down like animals. They torture us with dogs and break their promises.

God willing, praise Allah, I promise to restore our society. I have friends who are helping me rid our country of all foreigners. And if I can't succeed, I will become a martyr, avenging the death of Saddam, teaching the infidels that they will not succeed. They can't take our country and our oil. God left it for us, not them.

We will resurrect, rise above the chaos. I have gone to the land of our cousins in order to prepare and to begin our struggle. We will succeed, even if I have to see you next in paradise.

Love, your son now and for eternity,
Jabal

***

That night, Ali and Jake talked alone at the pub in their Western-style hotel.

They sat at a booth. Jake ordered a beer, and Ali followed suit.

Jake asked him, "Why didn't you tell me Jabal was missing? You know my story is about the doubles and what they are doing now. Did you know what was going to happen?"

"I had hoped she would slam the door on us and that would be it. I had no idea she would say what she did. You think this is easy for me? A double running around thinking he has the powers of Saddam? To continue the fight? Saddam was a bad guy a very bad guy. He killed my aunt, uncle, and two cousins. And this just brings back the nightmares."

"I'm sorry to hear that."

"Remember, I'm Persian. Iraq invaded my country when I was in America studying at college in 1980. My family wasn't even involved in the war, at least as combatants."

Jake began to say something, but Ali cut him off, talking faster and in an animated tone.

"Uncle Mehrdad had an olive farm fifty miles outside of the border. He worked long hours, carefully pruning the trees and harvesting his bounty. When the war first began, the mechanized division led the assault into Iran and tore up the land right through the farm. My aunt was helping my uncle pick olives when she saw about two hundred Iraqis with tanks and artillery within half a kilometer of the farm. She was scared and didn't know what to think. She screamed. I mean, she had never seen troops before. She was a simple farmer.

"The troops, they saw her and chased her into the house. My uncle...he tried to protect her as best he could," he said, fighting back his tears.

"Ali, I'm so sorry. You don't have to continue."

He ignored Jake, as if he thought he needed to know. "The troops, they took my uncle and my three cousins outside. They could hear her screams as the men inside violated her...over and over. My uncle fought back as best he could...but all he had were rocks. He threw a stone at one of the men, and it hit him in the forehead. Right here," Ali said, pointing to his forehead, "according to my one cousin who somehow survived."

"I understand how difficult this is," Jake said as the waiter served them their drinks.

"No you don't, not yet, at least. The rock conncctcd, drawing a spcck of blood. Thc troops went crazy, gunning down all of them. Everybody died, except for my one cousin who survived long enough to tell the Iranian authorities what had happened."

"Look, Ali, we're on the same side here right now. We got rid of Saddam, remember?"

Ali scoffed. "Really? The country that helped Iraq destroy my country? Saddam became your little puppet helping America avenge its hostages and control the oil. That bastard wouldn't have become the leader he was, invading my country, without America's help."

"Ali, I'm sorry this happened to your family. America has made mistakes in the past, but it is usually on the right side of history. Look at both world wars, for instance."

"Hah! Wars you were dragged into. Too many other examples of invading to extend or protect your colonies or oil."

Jake wanted to defuse the discussion, but he felt compelled to address his comments. "And your country? There is a reason why America supported Iraq against Iran. You kidnapped our people as part of a revolution that ultimately has turned your society into nothing more than...a model for repression. What freedoms do your people have? Can you criticize your government the same way you have criticized America?"

Ali nodded. "I understand our shortcomings. Look, don't get me wrong. I have spent time studying in America and have worked for many Americans. I believe in American values and want to reform my country. I don't blame America for what happened to my family—it was a catalyst in some ways, true—but the real enemy was Saddam."

"On that we can agree. To Saddam's demise," Jake said, raising his glass. "Cheers."

Ali smiled. "Cheers. You will continue to need an interpreter. Yes?"

"Of course," Jake said. Inside, though, Jake didn't feel so confident. A few days ago he had wanted to quit, return to New York, and beg for a more meaningful assignment. The note changed everything. He had stumbled onto something important. Still, he couldn't shake the feeling that he was in way over his head.

"Well, now that your doubles story has brought back the nightmare of Saddam for me, can you at least let me see it through?" Ali said, raising his glass towards Jake.

"Yes, of course," he responded, clicking glasses with Ali.

Chapter 5
Aral Sea

Red and Robert boarded a plane at Heathrow. They were traveling to Aralsk, Kazakhstan, a town close to the Aral Sea. The Aral Sea, which technically is classified as a lake, used to be the world's fourth largest saline lake, ideal conditions for pike, perch, carp, and other species of fish. Communities used to pluck 160 tons of fish from the sea every day.

But the Soviet Union had other plans, and in the 1960s, it began diverting water from two rivers that fed the sea in an attempt to irrigate desert terrain for agricultural purposes. Growing cotton was deemed a higher priority than supporting fisheries. In a classic case of over-engineering, the attempt failed miserably as the diverted water dissipated into the ground.

In its heyday, Aralsk was a major Kazakhstanian hub for fishing and economics, of great importance to the region. Now as a result of the economic travesty, it's a hub for unemployment, rotting boats, and sedimentary chemicals from the diminished sea.

For the MI6 agents, however, it was a place from which to launch their next phase of the investigation. Indeed, many scavengers use the town as a launching point to Anthrax Island (located in the Aral Sea) in search of abandoned iron, copper, and other valuable metals and artifacts. The economically-deprived foragers are generally aware of stories about use of the island by the Soviets before the 1970s as a biological warfare proving ground.

The local authorities discouraged visits. Despite repeated assurances from the central government and the American cleanup effort in 2002, spores may still live in the soil and on unsterilized equipment, walls, and floors, unlike other agents which probably weren't active anymore.

Still, people continued to trek to the island in search of material to sell. Fate had already conspired against them.

***

After landing at the Aralsk Airport, the agents spent the night at a motel close to a dock on the Aral Sea. The motel's façade separated from the structure in several places, allowing for a disconcerting view into the wooden support beams. The roof looked splotchy, missing tiles in several places. Their rooms were full of mold and smelled like manure, reminding Red of her days growing up on the farm. Robert spent part of the night awake, wondering if he should check on the conditions in Red's room.

They survived the night, feeling fortunate the building had not collapsed on them while they slept. In the morning, they walked across the street with their gear to a wooden dock where they would catch a boat to the island.

The boat captain spoke to the boarding agents in choppy English with a thick accent. "And what do we have here, Dasha?" he said to his first mate. "Two English scavengers or a couple on cheap honeymoon?" They both laughed. "And look at their cute little jumpsuits with matching rubber boots." They roared even louder.

Red stared at the captain, boring into his eyes the way only a woman can, until he turned away. His name tag said Nuro. Fitting. Red could see pieces of his morning gingerbread in his scraggly beard and mustache. He was washing it down with coffee that dribbled onto his chest, resulting in a tan pattern down the middle of his blue shirt.

Red responded, "Captain Nuro, we're looking for artifacts, and we're also doing a story about the history of the island, if that's OK with you."

He responded, "Sure, whatever. Ship pick up at four. Remember, it's the only means of transportation. Miss it, you sleep over or walk the land bridge in the south. We no track your whereabouts and no wait. Understand?"

"Yes, Captain," Robert said weakly.

The agents took their seats, stowing next to them their backpacks carrying food, a respirator, anthrax detection kit, test tubes, vials, and other equipment. If the captain had made fun of what they were wearing, he would have had a cow laughing at the sight of their other gear. They had also rented from the transport company scooters they would use to move around the island. They parked them across from where they sat.

A few locals grunted as they watched them care for their new and expensive equipment. Nobody else seemed to have any provisions other than some food, water, overused gloves, and nylon or mesh bags. Some of the locals had old bikes that had traces of rust, but many would traverse the island on foot. Nobody else had scooters.

Red and Robert reached the island about three hours later, their boat anchoring in the shallow water. Getting the gear and bikes onto the island turned out to be a collective effort. The locals took small pieces that could be carried over the water and put them on the gravelly beach. They motioned for Red and Robert to follow suit.

Then they formed a line from the beach to the boat. There, Captain Nuro and Dasha began handing the heavier equipment, including the scavengers' bikes and the two scooters, one at a time to the first passenger in the water by the boat. Everybody pitched in to move all provisions to the beach without anything touching the water. Although Red was moved by the collective effort, it was difficult to keep an eye on the gear they had already placed on the beach.

They finished about thirty minutes later. The other five passengers, all of whom appeared to be scavengers, left immediately. The agents took inventory of their equipment. Red looked up, pleased, but she noticed Dasha scowling at her.

The agents organized their boots and clothing that MI6 had provided before leaving to search the island. They looked a bit funny but not completely out of place given the well-known, albeit ignored, rumors about biological agents on the island. They kept to themselves, not wanting to attract any more attention than they already had. Once they were alone they put on the rubber gloves and respirators as additional protection. About a minute later they removed and repacked both of the items, realizing they still had a long way to go before reaching the labs.

They hopped on their scooters and rode for a while until seeing the residential village. Then they slowed down.

Robert pulled up next to Red and said, "Wow, this place is a shithole." She laughed. He was right.

Red replied, "Yes, kind of scary. It looks as if somebody dropped an atomic bomb and everybody died. Spooky. See that building over there covered with overgrown weeds and the rusted shell of a car next to it?"

They dismounted and walked with the scooters toward the area.

Red said, "This must be Kantubek, the town where all of the workers lived." They could see several yellow brick and concrete buildings, all with broken windows. Birds flew in and out of the structures.

A dog spied them from the entrance. He lifted his leg to pee on the door frame. They moved on.

The next building was missing half of its roof. It must have caved in a long time ago. They entered. The ground floor was covered with small chunks and shards of concrete, glass, bricks, and other debris. A toy doll rested on a stained mattress.

A scavenger from their boat appeared from down the hall. He waved at them and they returned the favor.

Red had enough fun and said, "We're not going to learn anything in this place. We need to go to the labs, about two and a half kilometers south from here."

"True. I read there is a gravesite there. We should look for more on our way."

They drank some water and shared a few energy bars, walking the scooters out of the town, seeking a path clear enough to mount and ride.

***

A couple of scavengers passed, eyes boring into the agents. They were heading the opposite way toward the town. Red looked at them, and she and Robert walked faster.

One of them said something loud in Russian as they were passing. The other responded even louder, causing the first guy to howl.

A sufficient buffer formed between the two groups.

Red said to Robert, "I didn't catch that. What did those guys say?"

"Don't worry about it," he said.

"Tell me, anyway. I'm a big girl."

"Well, the first guy called you an English whore dressed like a rubber duck. The second guy suggested they act like Drekavacs."

"Drekavacs?"

Robert laughed. "Yes. You're obviously not up on your Slavic mythology. A Drekavac is a type of monster formed from the souls of dead unbaptized children. The monster goes around scaring the dickens out of people so they won't be naughty."

"Oh, cute." Red didn't like the development but wasn't too concerned. "Let's take the safety switches off the guns and stay close."

They found a path sufficient for their scooters, mounted, and proceeded, eventually passing an old rusted sign somebody had staked into the ground. It was in Russian and said *Биопрепарат*. Red knew what this stood for: *Biopreparat*, the name of the program Russia denied having in the first place.

They reached the labs and began walking again. The agents searched more buildings and found nothing other than empty cages that used to hold animals, individual rooms, and larger areas where they assumed the scientists worked.

Robert reminded Red they needed to return to the drop-off point by 4:00 p.m. They had about an hour left to search for a graveyard. They fanned out and searched as much as they could. Robert spotted something and called for Red's attention.

She looked at the small gravesite he found.

Robert said, "Damn! This can't be it. These graves date back to the 1920s. This is not going to help."

"Let's head back. We're running out of time, and I don't want to be stuck here."

They walked back, frustrated and tired.

***

They boarded just as Captain Nuro was about to leave.

Red smiled at him, winked, and said, "Sorry to disappoint you, Captain." She didn't wait for his response, shuffling past him.

He shouted after both of them, "Ah, you two. Should have left earlier. Fun to see you next day."

Red smiled at him, accepting that this was his way of greeting them. A truce of sorts.

They entered the seating area and stowed their gear, including the scooters. Their Drekavac friends smirked and gestured for the agents to sit next to them. They didn't take the bait.

***

Later that night they headed to the local saloon, which, according to Robert's translation, was named the BioTox. The inn's tagline apparently was "Get toxed at the BioTox." It looked out of place in Asia, resembling a country-western pub in the US circa the 1850s, with its swinging wood doors and dark-panel wooden walls and bar. All twenty patrons of the establishment turned their heads towards the agents when they entered.

They sat down quietly on the rusted bar stools, carefully surveying the room.

The bartender, an older guy with a foreboding frown and deep wrinkles more akin to those found on prunes, caught their gaze and said in English, "You're lookin' at stools made from iron and metal salvaged from the island. Sit down—they don't bite, you know."

Robert smiled and told Pruney to fetch two bourbons. Unofficially, they were there to relax after a hard day in which they accomplished nothing. Officially, they were hoping to find somebody to question. The Queen wouldn't be happy with them wasting her precious pounds if they returned empty-handed.

At SLIP the agents had learned to search a room using only their peripheral vision. Four of the six tables featured Kazakhs who wouldn't have been alive when the island was being used. They weren't likely to have any useful information about where the anthrax victims were buried or anything else relevant to MI6.

Robert walked to the fifth table and started talking with its occupants. He sat down and stayed for about thirty minutes. Everybody was laughing and having a good time. Then he abruptly stood and left.

He sat back down with Red at the bar and quietly said, "Nice folks, but they don't know shit." Since the sixth table was now empty, they were out of luck.

Pruney served them another round of bourbon. About thirty minutes after Robert returned, Captain Nuro's first mate, Dasha, walked in. He sat at the bar a few stools away from their table. He didn't even have to order. Pruney knew his drink: a straight shot of Stolichnaya.

Dasha looked content sipping his vodka. Robert greeted him in Russian; he simply nodded.

After a brief exchange of pleasantries, Red said, "Dasha, can we talk to you for our story?"

He responded in surprisingly good English, more understandable than the dribble spoken by Captain Nuro. "Depends. You buy?"

Robert nodded. "Let's take the table over there in the corner."

The three of them relocated to a table, the top of which was made out of plain wood punctuated by indentations. They moved the cheesy fake flowers out of the way and engaged in small talk for a few minutes.

Then Dasha asked, "You working on a story?"

Red replied, "Yes, it's about the history of the island." She didn't take any notes, relying on her memory.

"Well, I've been with the island for a long time."

"When did you first start?"

"I first worked as a teen doing odd jobs on the ferry. The ferry was the only means of going to and from the island in those days."

Robert straightened his posture and asked, "What do you mean?"

"Back then it was island. Now, not so. We've had water problems, you know? The level is so low there is a land bridge now."

Red chided him, "Yes, we already knew that. Your captain reminded us." Robert glared at her. She softened and asked in a pleasant tone, "Can we talk about the weapons program?"

Dasha nodded. "What do you want to know about it?"

Red replied, "Well, let's start with how much you know about what they did."

"Not much, really. I just did odd jobs, as I said before."

"But did you ever hear of anything?"

"Of course. I knew what they were doing. Heck, we all knew. But we learned not to ask too many questions. We were in the middle of the Cold War back then. Khrushchev and Brezhnev, not as bad as Stalin, but they still ran a tight ship. Ask too many questions and you wind up in Siberia," Dasha said quietly while emitting a nervous laugh.

Red shifted her weight in her chair. "Any accidents?"

He looked around the room, lowering his voice, prompting them to lean their heads in close. "You know, in this country, if you want information..." He didn't complete his sentence, but they knew what he meant.

Red dug into her pocket, but he interrupted her, saying, "Not here." Pointing to Robert, he said, "Meet me in the john in five."

When Dasha left, Red said to Robert, "I don't know how much this is going to cost. He better give us more than we can read in our file."

Robert left to complete the exchange. He returned to the table five minutes later.

Red looked at him. "Where is Dasha?"

"Don't worry. I gave him a hundred pounds and told him he'd get another hundred after."

Dasha returned shortly after that, sat down, and announced in a low, measured tone, "There were a couple of, how do you say, incidents? In the early seventies, the scientists released weaponized smallpox. Nobody on the island got infected. But a young man who used to fish in and around the island got very sick and infected three people. All four of them died."

"Where did he get infected?" Robert asked.

"Nobody would say for sure. But he used to dock his boat on the beach at the island, not too far away from where we dropped you guys off this morning. He would fish off a recessed area near there. And that is where people think he contracted the virus."

Red replied, "Interesting, but...what about anthrax? Any incidents with anybody contracting anthrax?"

"No," Dasha replied, "not that I know of. Well, on second thought..."

"You want me to meet you in the bathroom again?"

Dasha laughed. "I'll take credit for now." Red slouched in her chair, trying to act nonchalant. He continued, "I did hear about a scientist who dropped a petri dish."

"And?" Robert prompted.

"That's it. What else do you want?"

This was going nowhere. The information was available on the Internet. Red shifted gears.

"What happened when they closed down the island?"

Dasha leaned in again, and the agents followed his lead. He said softly, "They weren't too careful. We're talking about Russia, remember? Land of Chernobyl. And this program was secret. Sure, they scrubbed the place, but not enough. Did you know that America actually finished the job in the early 2000s. Embarrassing, huh?"

Red asked, "Do you think there are still anthrax spores on the island?"

He leaned in again and spoke softly. "I can't prove it. And there are a lot of people around here who don't want to know. But the truth is, that once in a while some scavengers get sick." He leaned in even closer. "The government pressures doctors to say it's cancer or some other disease. We don't believe what we're told, but we don't have a choice, either. There are no jobs, and we have families to feed."

Red said, "Didn't you say the Americans cleaned the labs and debris?"

Dasha laughed. "Sure, they got as much as they can. But I tell you, people still get sick. Less now than before the cleanup for sure, but it still happens."

"Is there any particular place on the island you think is still contaminated?" she asked.

Dasha looked at her and then at Robert. "Not that I can think of. I really don't know. At least not where any humans could have gotten sick."

"Meaning?"

"Well, there was an issue with big rats."

"Rats?" Red repeated, looking at Robert.

"Yes, before America came to clean up the place, a whole bunch of huge rats died. I mean, these suckers were huge. Biggest you've ever seen." Dasha held his hands apart, demonstrating the girth and size.

Red said, "Huh, that sounds interesting. What happened to them?"

"The Americans, they didn't do all the work. They hired some locals for part of it. I know some of the people hired, worked with them before. Anyway, they were put in individual protective boxes and buried on the island."

Robert glanced at Red, who then looked at Dasha. "What, you mean like a rodent burial ground?" Robert asked.

"Ha!" Dasha said. "That is funny. No. Well...sort of. A burial ground, but not one that is marked. And I know the place."

"Can you show us?" Red asked.

"Yes, but first let's go to the bathroom," Dasha said, looking at Robert.

Red slipped Robert five hundred pounds under the table before he left.

Chapter 6
Aral Sea

Captain Nuro greeted the Brits for the second morning in a row. "You again?"

They responded, in harmony, like old pals. "Good morning, Captain."

He put his hands on his hips, Red sensing his stare as they looked for a seat. He didn't want them becoming regulars.

Dasha was slightly more congenial, choosing to ignore the pair. The Drekavacs actually smiled at them as if they were now part of their club.

On the way to the island, Red let her head fall onto Robert's chest. Before dozing off, she felt his heart beat faster and through a slit in her eyes noticed a smile form on his lips. She awoke suddenly, head jerking forward and then up. Robert chuckled, and Red clubbed his arm, shooting him a dirty look.

The boat arrived. The Drekavacs got off first, followed by a few other scavengers. The Brits lingered, waiting to follow Dasha's lead. He bid the captain farewell and walked through the water onto the beach. The passengers and crew then repeated the process of the previous day, unloading everybody's gear, including the scooters.

After finishing, the Drekavacs scampered away like rats smelling food, only it was old copper and iron.

Red and Robert drove their scooters toward the labs, this time not bothering to don the protective gear. They would put it on before digging. They slowed their pace, knowing Dasha was on foot.

They arrived at the spot Dasha told them to meet him. It took longer than expected, but he finally arrived. "You have the money?" he asked.

Robert handed him a few bills. "You'll get the rest after."

Dasha nodded and then beckoned the agents to follow. He stopped about a half hour later at the base of a tree and walked twenty paces to the south. They watched him while putting on their respirators and gloves. Dasha pointed to the ground and handed them each a shovel. They dug while Dasha watched. A stray dog approached and then quickly left.

The dirt was loose and easy to move. Then came the smell. Red gagged. Bits of disturbed bone, wood, and other debris collected in the pile being formed. Robert began taking samples Red tested with her portable anthrax detector. A few positive hits. They found what they had come for. Monty might even congratulate them before finding something ancillary to complain about.

***

But, the Drekavacs had other plans. The agents didn't see it coming. Red's head suddenly exploded in excruciating pain. Warm blood dripped onto her ear as she stumbled and fell, disoriented from the initial and subsequent hits from one of them. The second Drekavac slammed Robert to the ground and stood over his limp body. Dasha stood and watched as if supervising a road construction project.

Red looked up from the ground at the first Drekavac. He stood over her and was preparing to kick when her training kicked in.

These guys are nothing, she told herself. *I've faced better, actual trained assassins.* Red rolled toward the Drekavac, quickly eliminating the space within which he could bring power to his kick.

Her strategy worked. His would-be jarring kick was no more powerful than a baby kicking in his mum's womb. And while he extended his kick leg, Red took out his plant leg, tripping him to the ground. She jumped up and kicked him in the nuts as he staggered back up. The man grimaced in pain while Red grabbed a rock and smashed it against his head. She was out of control. Blood splattered while she continued her assault.

Images of Jake Kessler and his dead wife, Renée, flooded her head. Tears welled. She could hear her dad. *"You a spy! Girls can't be spies. What a joke!"*

Red was hurt and furious. *How dare this guy jump us? And for what—a few hundred pounds?* She kept hitting her target using the rock as her fist.

Robert had also gained the upper hand against the second Drekavac. He was now pummeling him with punches until the Drekavac fell to the ground.

Dasha continued to look on. Red imagined he initially hedged his bets or may have even set them up. If they lost, he could share in the loot—money and expensive gear. If they won, his silence would allow him to join them as surprised victims, although without any bruises.

At some point, Red faintly heard, "Red, stop! Stop! You're bashing his skull in." It didn't register. As her assault continued, another image of Jake Kessler flooded her head. She started to cry while she finished him off.

***

Red jumped off the man, avoiding the pool of blood rushing from his head. Dasha froze, too scared to run away or intervene.

Robert screamed, "Why'd you do that!" He put the second attacker, who was already limp, in a chokehold and squeezed until he passed out.

At the same time, Red attacked Dasha, sending him to the ground. She wanted information.

"Who is the person you took to the island several months ago?" she screamed while leaning down on him and choking his neck.

No response from the startled man. He finally managed to say, "What person? I...uh...talk to lots of people."

"Don't be an imbecile!" Red shouted. "I obviously mean someone like us. Someone...who doesn't fit in." She could see the despair in his eyes.

"I...eh...don't know. Don't remember anybody like that. I swear! You can ask the captain."

He seemed to be telling the truth. And the operative working in Kenya or somebody working with him could have taken the land bridge or a different boat. Maybe one of the Drekavacs helped. There was only one way to find out if he knew anything. She squeezed harder.

He coughed up blood and started to gag. It seemed as if he wanted to talk. She loosened her grip. Instead of talking, though, he bubbled up nervous laughter. He was obviously scared and was not going to talk. They would have to take him with them and extract his secrets later.

Red pinned his arms and gestured for Robert to find something useful to bind his hands, material they might have passed. With the attention of the agents diverted, Dasha used the opportunity to lash out at Red, knocking her to the ground.

Now free, he began to run away. The Brits gave chase. He looked back at them over his shoulder, eyes diverted from the rock in front of him. He tripped, smashing his head against a larger boulder. A pool of blood began to form.

***

Robert's heart pounded as he looked at the carnage of two dead and one unconscious man splayed out in front of them like fish on dried ice.

"Why, Red? They were stupid to attack us, but now your personal row is going to send the whole world after us!"

She spat back at him, "They jumped us…and…the captain would've never believed our side of the story. Dasha was obviously in on it. He died trying to escape. We couldn't have gone back anyway. We just have to survive and buy enough time to get out of this place alive."

Robert stared, not even registering her presence.

She slapped him and screamed, "You need to grow up! This is the big time." She lowered her voice. "Now, let's calm down and take a deep breath. Don't stroke out on me and leave more dead bodies for me to tend to. We're going to have to move the bodies to that brush over there. I want you to start moving them while I call our local support. Can you manage that?"

Robert nodded as she began dialing. Stephen, their lone emergency contact, picked up on the third ring, his signal to Red the line was not secure.

"Stephen, this is Sunshine. We had a long hike and are now about two hours"—meaning kilometers—"away from our base. It just started to thunder and lightning, and we are stranded. We need a lift for us and our three tired friends. Can you arrange for a ride? Use the coordinates from my phone."

Stephen replied, "Sunshine, I can make it, but not for about three hours. I have to repair a flat tire. Can you wait that long?"

"I'm not sure I can. The lightning is very strong and is getting closer. I think the storm will be strong once it is upon us."

He responded, "I'll do my best. Take cover and wait." The line went dead.

They finally heard the whirl of the blades a few hours later. Red motioned for Robert to stow the bodies of the dead and injured attackers while she crept out of her hiding spot. She wasn't sure if they would be met by a search-and-rescue team called in by Captain Nuro or Stephen. Either way, the ordeal would end soon, although they might not live past the night under the former scenario.

Red spotted a dim light from a helicopter off in the distance. It was flying low with minimal lighting, not searching with big spotlights. A good sign. She went further, preparing to wave her arms.

The rescue helicopter came closer, sporting a brighter light. Red started to wave but then heard Robert shouting, "Look, Red, over there!" She wheeled around and saw what he was looking at. Another helicopter in the other direction, this one conducting what appeared to be a broader search with its spotlight illuminating large swaths of land. The rescue would have to be delayed. She signaled for the copter to leave. They were on their own, at least until the second helicopter, now bearing down near them, began searching elsewhere.

***

They huddled on the ground, making sure to use the brush as camouflage. It would be dark soon. They could run if needed, but they had to stay hidden.

"Make sure you are ready to fire," she whispered. Robert said, "You think?"

They chuckled softly, a good release of the mounting tension.

The second helicopter zigged in and out. It was getting closer and closer to them. They had to act quickly. Stephen's helicopter was watching from an extended distance, out of sight from the second helicopter.

Robert pointed towards a rusted shed in the direction of where they had walked. She remembered a thick patch of brush beyond it.

Red signaled to Robert and then the shed and counted down three, two, one. At one, Robert moved to his hideaway while Red moved to the brush. She could see Robert from her new location. They had a fighting chance.

When the low-flying second helicopter was close to Red, she took the first shot, aiming through the brush. The pilot turned away from the direction from which the shot originated and maneuvered the craft closer to Robert.

Robert now had a clear shot at the pilot. He would have to be near perfect. Simply grazing the pilot would make matters worse, leaving her exposed. Nothing happened. Red started to panic.

But then she saw the smoke. Robert must have hit the engine, causing a serious problem. The craft began a rapid plunge to the west of their location. She took cover and shouted, "Protect yourself!"

A fireball erupted, engulfing the area. They got into the shallow portion of the sea and waded back toward where they had come from. The rescue helicopter had already landed. They climbed onto the rescue helicopter and then immediately collapsed on the cold metal floor.

Stephen shook them a few hours later. "We need to move fast. We're now in Uzbekistan. You're going to transfer to that helicopter over there." He pointed in the direction of a larger and longer-range craft, one managed by the CIA.

They were airborne again about twenty minutes later.

Chapter 7
New York City

Eighth Avenue between 40th and 41st Streets used to be home to dilapidated one-story structures hosting sex shops, smoke shops, vendors selling fake IDs to teenagers, and loiterers. Wealthy, bored men from stale marriages in the suburbs paid $1 for a cheap peep or $10 for thirty minutes in a private room for a dirty, immediately-regretted pleasure. After the deed, they returned to their miserable lives, repeating the perverted pilgrimage the following week, telling their onetime trophy wives they "have work to do."

Rudy Giuliani vowed to rid Times Square of its blight and, through eminent domain, handed over a portion of the land to the New York Times Company and Forest City Ratner Companies. The companies built a building to house the *New York Times* and its affiliates, forever changing the landscape, relegating the shabby enterprises to tomorrow's problem.

Jake Kessler looked up at the building before entering. Its exterior featured a double-skin curtain wall designed by architect Renzo Piano to filter the sun, allowing in enough natural light without overheating the interior space. He entered the lobby and walked past the enclosed moss and tree garden before boarding the elevator to the 25th floor, home to the *New York Times International Edition* brain trust.

Jake strutted through the glass doors, entering the suite and the modern reception area, where he could see the group that had already congregated in the snug conference room across the hall. The off-white tiled floor and white ceiling tiles made the room bright. The brown leather chairs and long conference table offered contrast without sapping the room's energy. Water bottles and a tray of fruit were perched on the table.

Heads turned toward Jake Kessler when he walked into the space. People nodded and issued polite hellos.

His career had meaning again. The nervousness he experienced in Iraq had dissipated.

He had spent a lot of time in New York in the past, but that seemed eons ago. Although he had moved away after Renée's death, he missed navigating the busy boulevards and the feeling you get when walking toward hundreds of people of different shapes, smells, and colors, parting like the Red Sea allowing you to pass. Hundreds more walking in the same direction as you, but you can't even look at them without risking a collision. At first, it can be imposing. But then you realize everybody is in the same position. An odd but familiar comfort takes hold.

The newspaper's editor, Joseph Brommer, gestured for Jake to sit in the chair next to him at the table's end. The Swedish transplant had platinum hair parted in the center, exposing his thin nose, white eyebrows, and chubby cheeks. He straightened himself, smoothing the wrinkles off his crisp blue dress shirt and immediately jumped into the discussion.

"Jake, your report is interesting. But what makes you think you can pull this off?"

"Isn't his note pretty clear?" Jake said defensively.

"I read your report. But you need to *convince* me."

The atmosphere in the room changed, heads turning towards Jake, waiting for his response.

Jake calmly replied, "Two points Jabal made in his note. He wants to 'prepare for our people's resurrection.' You're up on the history of the Ba'ath Party, right? The party was founded to resurrect Arab nationalism, not like some of the radical groups which focus on forced religious conversion, but instead through socialism. Even the name Ba'ath Party translates into *restoration* or *resurrection*. And so, there is no doubt in my mind he is referring to the Ba'ath Party. He wants to work with other Baathists."

"But why Syria?" Joseph pointed out. Heads turned back towards Joseph.

"Well, that is the other clue. He says, 'I have gone to the land of our cousins.' This refers to Syria and in particular, I believe, Damascus."

"Damascus?"

Jake took the bait and ran. "As I said in my report, that's where the Ba'ath Party was formed in the forties." He felt like adding, *Did you even read the damn thing?*

Joseph thought about that for a few seconds and said, "Even if you're right, you can't just rush into Damascus and expect to find Jabal. His note refers to us as the infidels. What if he captures you?"

"I've taken precautions. Jabal's mother gave me the actual note, the original." Jake handed Joseph the note in Arabic, with an English translation attached.

"You say she gave it to you? She just handed it over—to a complete stranger?" Joseph looked surprised.

"Again, it's in the report." His annoyance started to show. "I visited with Aisha looking for Jabal. She and I, well, sort of connected, if you will, and she felt comfortable enough to share Jabal's note. She's scared for him and doesn't have a lot of options. Who else is going to help her, the current Iraqi government? Anyway, she seems to have not liked Jabal's work as one of Saddam's doubles. Saddam took advantage of him, changed him. She lost her husband in the war with Iran and doesn't want to lose her only child."

"So you're going to waltz up to him and give him the note? Won't he be upset you know what he's up to?"

"Waltz? No, I'm not waltzing. I'm continuing my story. Aisha gave me the note out of her concern for him. I'll only use it if I think it will help. If I think it'll make him want to at least talk to me. Besides, the note isn't even that difficult to interpret. He might have even wanted somebody to find him, maybe before he does something he regrets."

"Still, you're going into a hostile territory. You really want to risk your life on this?" Joseph asked. Jake started to interrupt, but Joseph held up his hand and continued, "Who knows who you're going to run into? What if you run into al-Qaeda, ISIS, or some other group of the day? Your press pass might make matters worse. You're Jewish, American, *and* a former government official – three strikes against you." Jake sat stone-faced as Joseph continued to raise his voice, culminating in, "Bottom line, you're just playing hunches. I ask again, is it worth the risk?"

Jake had predicted the tirade, and Joseph had a point. Still, Jake remained insistent. "I understand your concerns, but isn't this part of the job? I mean, reporters take risks all the time. People have died reporting from war zones. This is a good story. When was the last time your paper backed down from one? Maybe I should approach the *Washington Post* instead! Is that what you want?"

Joseph sighed while Jake continued, "I've looked into this and thought about it a lot. Syria can be a bit like a checkerboard. With good intelligence, we can avoid the red areas and stick to the black ones. Don't forget that I still know people in the intelligence community. It's *my* story, and *I* want to follow the strands."

Joscph startcd to reply but then stopped himself. After a pause, he nodded to his corporate security consultant, Hans Wolfgardener, a rigid and tall gentleman with a snarky frown, sitting opposite from Joseph, flanking Jake's position.

Hans left the room after receiving the signal from Joseph. Joseph watched him leave and added, "OK, but just remember that this was your decision. I have my reservations. Agreed?"

Jake shook his head yes, and Joseph continued, "Hans is getting a guy whose last name is, and I'm not joking, Leatherneck. His first name is Michael, and he's going to help you."

The savior arrived a few minutes later. If Jake had expected Batman, he got Robin instead. Leatherneck was about 5'11" with bushy black hair and an unshaven face. He had a dimple in the middle of his chin and wore thick glasses that looked old and bent.

Jake stared at him in disbelief, watching him plop down, making a loud thud across the table next to Hans.

He must have noticed Jake's reaction since he laughed and said, "Don't worry, I'm actually a former marine. I have an eye infection."

"Eye infection?" Jake repeated.

"Yeah, pinkeye."

This was getting better and better.

Hans interrupted the exchange, no doubt fearing it could get worse. "Michael, tell Jake about yourself."

"Well, my name is Michael, as you know. I was born and raised in Syria. I changed my name to Michael from Moussa when I came to America about thirty years ago. I used to go to Syria every so often to visit my grandparents until they died several years ago."

"No more family there?"

"Just a few remote cousins."

"Why'd you leave?"

"My father was a professor in Arabic studies. He got an opportunity to teach at an American college, and he took us."

"So you grew up here?"

"Yes, sir. I was raised in Texas and eventually joined the marines. I stayed for about ten years, seeing action in the second Gulf War. I *earned* the right to change my citizenship and stay here for the rest of my life."

"And now?" Jake asked.

Hans interjected, getting tired of Jake's skepticism, "He is a contractor, but he has done a lot of work for us. He's now at your disposal, and that's the important part."

The group talked for about thirty minutes longer. Then Jake dropped a surprise, asking, "What about Ali?"

Joseph looked like he was going to fall off his chair. "Ali? What do you care? Some interpreter you met in Iraq? He could be a liability, don't you think?"

"Look, guys, if we do this, I'm in charge. It's my lead. You didn't even want me to pursue this in the first place. Leatherneck—can I call you that?" Jake didn't wait for a response to his rhetorical question. "Good. Leatherneck's going to have to watch our backs. He's not going to assist me in reporting, but in other ways. Right?"

"Sure, Jake," Hans answered.

"The point is, I need an assistant. Ali has already proven himself to me, and I promised to include him. I see no reason to break that promise. He's got his own reasons to help, and we're going to need all the assistance we can get."

"But he's Persian. Won't that be a liability?" Hans asked.

Leatherneck jumped in. "Not necessarily. We're not talking Iraq. We're talking Syria, and Syrians are less sensitive to that. Many Syrians have worked closely with the Iranians for years. I think we can manage the risk. After all, he's an assistant on a story about the Saddam doubles. Not very threatening."

"Except if you guys start asking about revenge and resurrection," Joseph said.

Leatherneck and Jake looked at each other. Jake shrugged and smiled.

Chapter 8
Beirut to Syria

Beirut is a more reliable point of entry for Westerners than Damascus, given the fighting, poor security, and instability in Syria. And with the right visas or bribes, people can cross into Syria from Beirut through the busy Masnaa border crossing.

Masnaa has seen it all. Dead bodies of wayward Syrian men being returned to their country of origin, courtesy of the Lebanese Red Cross. Medical personnel working for Doctors without Borders crossing into Syria in search of sick and wounded. Desperate immigrants with fake papers attempting to flee grief stricken areas of Syria.

***

Leatherneck and Jake landed in Beirut a few weeks after meeting in the newspaper offices. Ali met them a day after they arrived, and the following day, the trio traveled in a car rented by Leatherneck from Lebanon to the Masnaa border crossing.

They each wore international press arm insignias, unsure of what kind of trouble they would encounter on the journey. The press was only slightly safer than other travelers, but every little bit helped.

Hans provided them with daily updates about which route to take, wanting to avoid the paper becoming an international spectacle. "Three *New York Times* Workers Beheaded" was not a headline anybody wanted to see.

They approached Masnaa ninety minutes after beginning the journey. Leatherneck eased the car into the accumulating traffic. Men and women walked in different directions, as if lost in a sea of confusion. Others prayed on rugs positioned on the sidewalk. Vendors sold falafel. Beads of sweat formed on the foreheads of all.

Lebanese soldiers manned the main road, leading vehicles into the white brick building that served as the checkpoint. Jake's heart began to pound faster as they approached a skinny soldier wearing glasses and an AK-47 draped from his arm. Leatherneck and Ali remained calm. It was obvious to Jake they had experienced this before.

Leatherneck, who was driving, rolled down his window as the solider approached. He said something in Arabic that Jake didn't understand. Leatherneck returned the favor. The soldier grunted and waved them through the building.

A second soldier stopped them as soon as they were about to exit. He looked at Jake and said loudly, "You, you American. You know Shaq?"

Jake couldn't believe it. "Shaq?"

"Yes, basketball?"

He replied calmly, controlling his anger at the stupidity, "No, I don't know him."

The tall, muscular, soldier grunted as if mocking Jake. His mustache and thin circular-styled beard made him look a little bit like Shaq but with a tanner complexion, possibly accounting for his fascination with the long-retired basketball player.

Scott A. Dondershine

Shaq and Leatherneck got into a heated exchange. Voices rose and fell, then the discussion ended. The third soldier pointed his pistol at Leatherneck while Shaq barked orders for the group to leave the car.

Leatherneck turned around and said in a soothing voice, "Guys, I'm sorry, but we have to leave the car." Ali understood, remained calm, and immediately hopped out.

Jake started to protest from the passenger seat. Leatherneck cut him off and said quietly, "Look, the worst thing we can do is create a scene. They don't know who we are, except we're part of the press, and they have no interest in winding up on the front page. These are not terrorists, after all. This is probably just a routine check. Make a fuss and it'll turn into a real problem."

Leatherneck and Jake joined Ali outside the vehicle. Shaq walked up to Jake and said in broken English, "You, go there." He pointed to a room. The third soldier pointed his gun at Jake, and Leatherneck nodded at Jake, telling him he had no choice.

Jake walked in, and Shaq locked the door from the outside. He was alone, trapped in a dimly lit room which had a smooth concrete floor, metal table, and two chairs. Jake sat down on one of the chairs, knowing a soldier would join him soon. Jake hoped that whoever walked in wouldn't come with pliers.

About fifteen minutes later, the door opened. Shaq emerged and sat down. "What you doing?"

Jake replied, "I'm working on a story."

"Liar!" Shaq jumped up and screamed at Jake. "I ask again! Why you going to Syria?" He sat back down again.

Jake stiffened and replied again, "I'm a reporter for the *New York Times International Edition*. See, my press credentials."

Shaq, who apparently needed his exercise, jumped up again. But this time he didn't immediately say anything. Instead, he whipped out a bag with what looked like gravelly tar and thrust it in front of Jake's nose. "What this, then! Your story?" He chuckled.

Jake said, "That's not mine. I've never seen it."

"Got it from car!"

Jake asked to see his colleagues. Shaq shook his head and walked out. The door lock clicked a couple of seconds later.

Shaq returned about one hour later with Lebanon's pirated version of Coke in his hand. Jake eagerly sipped it, ignoring his training as a cop.

Shaq said, "I know you, Jake. You former police chief. What you got for me?"

The development concerned Jake. A shakedown was one thing, but Shaq apparently used his time out of the room to investigate his credentials. Jake decided to try and defuse the situation. "Can I pay a fine?"

Shaq looked at Jake, not saying a word, leaving Jake to think about whether he read the situation right. Shaq paced the room, making Jake even more nervous. A few minutes later he said, "Depends."

Jake whipped out his wallet and handed the soldier a twenty-dollar bill.

He laughed and threw the money back at Jake. "This not Africa."

Jake handed him two more twenties. He continued to stare. Three twenties and two hundred-dollar bills later and they had reached a deal which Shaq sealed with a gesture for Jake to leave.

The third soldier pointed to the car. Leatherneck and Ali were both sleeping, apparently not concerned about the affair. Leatherneck was in the driver's seat, Ali in the back.

***

Jake opened the car, got into the passenger seat, and slammed the door. The others jarred awake, and their heads snapped up. Leatherneck looked at Jake and shook his head, a broad smile forming at his lips. Jake stared back, trying not to laugh but ultimately failing. Enough said.

The Syrian soldiers waved them on as they entered the country. Jake imagined they had a system with the Lebanese to not shake down the same car on both sides of the border. He feared the Syria extrusion would come later and be much more intense.

Forty-five minutes later, about twenty kilometers outside of Damascus, they slowed down in a line of cars. Leatherneck said to Ali, "Let me do the talking." Ali pouted but didn't voice any objection. Jake straightened up and looked alert. The three of them smoothed out their press armbands. Jake took out the temporary license the newspaper had secured from the Syrian government, making them even more legit.

Their car approached a series of small stacks of worn tires. Each stack was part of two lines angled toward the other, forcing all vehicles into a narrow funnel. Two soldiers in army fatigues stood on either side of the funnel, inspecting cars. More soldiers were perched at various points on the other side of the tires, ready to fire if needed.

Leatherneck pulled up. He started to roll down his window, but the soldier hit the glass and held out his palm towards the car. No further communication was needed. They apparently didn't care what the newsmen had to say. After a cursory look, the soldiers waved them through.

"Those guys army regulars or militia?" Jake asked Leatherneck.

"One never knows in this country. Sometimes there is little difference anyway."

A second checkpoint awaited them about fifteen minutes later. After emerging, Jake noticed in the distance a ring of buildings, some with walls sheared off. As they drove closer, Jake could see concrete rubble and rebar. Other buildings were intact, the same way a tornado destroys a group of structures in its path while leaving others standing.

They entered the city. Jake noticed the same mixture of preserved and dilapidated structures, in addition to signs of normality – people walking and shopping in local bazars and shops. A left turn onto Fayez Mansour Street took the group to Tishreen Park, where they could see children running. Roller skaters maneuvered on the park's pathways, carcful to not run over walkers. Palm trees and an apartment complex towered over the street.

A few turns later and they had reached their destination, the Farzat Hotel. The building, owned by Ahmed Farzat, offered a relatively safe place for Westerners to stay without attracting a lot of attention. Syria was already a dangerous country, with Damascus having a disproportionately high number of incidents. Ahmed was also a cousin of Leatherneck, making it less likely that their room would be bugged.

Ahmed received Leatherneck with a kiss on both cheeks. He shook hands with Ali and Jake and led them to their separate rooms. The inside of the hotel looked more like a small college dormitory than a hotel with its dimly lit hallways and plain reception area, but it was functional.

Jake's room was the size of its single bed plus barely enough room to walk around the mattress and metal frame. The bed had a green wool bedspread, which Jake feared had never been washed. The best room's best feature, a relatively new phone, wouldn't be used. Ahmed had picked up several different disposable phones for the group to use instead.

The bathroom, off to the side of a small hallway leading into the bedroom, looked even less inviting. White tiles covered the floor and three-quarters of the way up each wall except for the aluminum shower stall. Streaks of brown stains covered the grout and some of the tiles. A white sink stood opposite the shower, and a toilet that required squatting filled the corner on the same side as the shower. Jake thought he was looking into a white rubber room as he peered in from the hallway. But at least he would be able to strengthen his glutes.

Leatherneck banged on Jake's door about thirty minutes after they had arrived. "Ahmed is going to bring you and Ali a plate of falafel, pita, and hummus. It's getting late. I'm going to visit some family."

"I take it you don't think it's a good idea for Ali and me to check out the town? Too dangerous?"

Leatherneck responded, "I'm not sure. There are frequent power outages, and things happen too fast in this country. It's been quiet for the past several months, but every now and then it seems a new group of roughnecks or insurgents makes a push for their own personal agenda. Remember the beheading a few months ago?"

"Al-Nusra?"

"Yes, and they usually don't directly target Westerners, but this time they did."

"Don't worry about us. We'll stay put. We're not wandering off, especially when it gets dark out."

"I'll see you in the morning. And I hope to talk to a distant cousin who may have a lead on where our friend is and the best way to approach him."

Jake looked at Leatherneck. He had more resources in this country than he first led him to believe. That might be a good development. But it also meant that more people would know about their presence.

***

Leatherneck and Ali were already eating when Jake walked down to the first-floor restaurant the next morning. Ali had trimmed and shaped his black beard. His brown shirt and white pants snugly fit his smallish frame.

The restaurant featured the Syrian version of a continental breakfast. Jake walked up to the buffet, surveyed the interesting selection, and was happy he recognized much of the food including the small boxes of cold cereal and assortment of cheeses, nuts, and dates.

Leatherneck walked up to Jake, a broad smile forming on his face. He pointed to a bowl on the right side of the table. "That over there, my friend, is two kinds of yogurt. Not the fancy Greek kind you get in the States but better, to me at least. In that bowl is laban arabi, yogurt made from sheep's milk. Next to it is yogurt made out of cow's milk, laban baqari. The laban arabi is creamier. And you can't just pick off the pistachios on top." He hit Jake on the shoulder and chuckled as he said this, as if what he said was actually funny.

He pointed to a bowl next to the yogurt. "That is mamouniyeh. It is like hot porridge with cinnamon, and you use that bread over there to dip in it. Try it."

Jake passed on the laban baqari and the dates but tried the mamouniyeh in addition to cereal and nuts. He took his seat at the table with its stained white linen. Pictures of animals grazing and Syrians posing adorned the walls in cheap crooked frames. Ahmed obviously didn't put a lot of money into his establishment. Ali and Leatherneck had already cleared their plates of food and were drinking Syria's strong coffee.

Two other tables were occupied. A surly man looked at Jake, who said hello. The man ignored Jake and returned to his meal.

Leatherneck took the opportunity to update Jake and Ali on his activities the night before. "I met with my cousin. Good news, bad news."

"Give me the good news first," Jake said.

"An optimist, I see. The good news is that he's heard rumors that a Saddam look-alike is in town."

"And the bad news?"

"He might be hard to find, and he doesn't have a location. He did give me an idea, though."

Leatherneck explained what he had in mind.

***

The trio looked at the government building they were about to enter. They considered entering as their point of no return.

The red, white (with green stars), and black stripes of Syria's national flag stretched across the entire top of the structure – a ribbon without a bow tying up the building as a present to its fortunate citizens, crying out for their platitudes. Tiny windows, some visibly cocked open to let in "fresh" air, dotted across the exterior of each floor.

They entered, waited patiently for the elevator, and exited on the sixth floor. Leatherneck had arranged for a meeting with Elyas Qureshi, a low-level manager at the Syrian Arab News Agency (SANA). SANA was a quasi-governmental organization controlled by the Syrian Ministry of Information. They waited for Qureshi in the reception area.

After waiting fifteen minutes, an assistant emerged to show them to Qureshi's office. They sat in three black leather chairs arranged in front of his desk.

"Is this guy another cousin?" Jake asked Leatherneck.

He laughed. "No, not everybody here is my cousin. He's more like…a friend of a friend of a friend. I don't know him, though."

The assistant knocked on Qureshi's door. They heard him slam a desk drawer shut. Leatherneck whispered, "Probably his morning beverage. A lot of these guys act holier than God, but the truth is they're just like the rest of us."

The assistant told them to enter. Leatherneck and Jake sat at the two seats in front of Qureshi's desk.

The office was tiny, much smaller than those back home in America, and they had to cram into the space. The assistant dragged in a third chair for Ali, making it even smaller. A picture of the leader of Syria hung over Qureshi's desk, his eyes looking down on them, scowling, forehead frowning, as if to say, "This better meet with my approval."

Leatherneck acted as the interpreter after they had exchanged pleasantries.

"Mr. Qureshi…" Jake began.

"Stop!" Mr. Qureshi said, pointing at Ali. "He needs to put that phone away. No pictures or recordings. Got it?"

Jake turned to Ali and said sharply, "Ali, put that thing away and just take notes, please." He then turned to Qureshi and apologized, "I'm sorry, he didn't know."

Ali looked at Jake with a frown but didn't voice any objection. He slid the phone into his pocket and retrieved a pen and notepad.

Mr. Qureshi replied, "Thank you."

Jake sat close to the edge of his chair. "You're welcome. Let me tell you about our project, if I may."

Leatherneck was doing a good job translating, and Jake didn't need to pause for that long. Mr. Qureshi seemed to understand and nodded his approval.

Jake continued, "My newspaper, the *New York Times International Edition*, has readers throughout the world. They follow current events closely and especially the events leading up to, during, and following the second Gulf War."

"Mr. Kessler...Jake...I'm aware of your paper. We here in Syria, we have rights and can read, you know."

"Thank you. Well, there is one human-interest story that has grown stronger in recent years. It started out as another conspiracy theory but now has turned into a human-interest story."

"Conspiracy theory?"

"Yes, our readers were interested in the Saddam Hussein doubles. How some would appear in public putting their own lives in danger. Questions like: How many were there? How do they look so much alike? Any plastic surgery? Were they forced to do what they did or did they enjoy their chosen occupation? And so on and so on. Some people even believe one of Saddam's doubles got hanged and that Saddam is still alive, somewhere in Belarus or even Canada."

"Well, I can assure you that is not the case, Mr. Kessler."

"Yes, it seems that way. But still, the question has lingered." Jake looked at Leatherneck, waiting for his translation, wondering if there was a comparable word.

Leatherneck translated and then looked at Mr. Qureshi. He added, "Do you understand?"

"Yes, I think so, but how can I help with a human-interest story about the Saddam doubles?"

"Well, we were hoping to meet and interview a double we believe is in Damascus."

Mr. Qureshi looked at Jake, leaned forward, and said loudly, this time in English, "Mr. Kessler, you believe this to be so because we are Baathists? Everything in your world is clear, no? Saddam was a

Baathist, I'm a Baathist, and therefore we all know each other. One big happy family, eh? You need to study your history." He looked at Ali and Leatherneck and said in Arabic, which Leatherneck promptly translated, "And you two should know this to be the case."

Jake replied to this, "Mr. Qureshi, we have specific information that one of the doubles, a guy named Jabal Shamoon, is here."

"In Damascus? That's ridiculous. Why would any double be here?" He sounded defensive.

Jake tried to put him at ease. "Look, Mr. Qureshi, all we want to do is a human-interest story. Nobody is getting in trouble. As I said, my readers are interested in his life and the life of other doubles. We are hoping you can put us in touch with somebody who may know where he is. Jabal himself may be interested in talking, and if he isn't, then he can just say no and we'll leave. Can you make some calls?"

"Well, it depends..."

Jake knew what that meant, immediately taking out his wallet.

***

They went back to their hotel and waited. A day passed, then another. Nothing. Leatherneck received a message on the third day. They were to meet a man at 10:00 a.m. outside of the shrine of Sayyidah Zaynab. The instructions were clear: sit on the third bench to the right side of the main entrance to the shrine. The gold-leafed dome would be at eleven o'clock if one were staring at it while sitting on the bench.

Leatherneck left to scout the area at 9:00 a.m. He called Jake on his cell phone to give him the green light.

Leatherneck picked them up, and they drove to the southern reaches of the city, parked on the street, and walked toward the entrance. A gigantic shrine stood waiting in its immaculate condition. Leatherneck told them that Iranian and Syrian Shia militia had protected the shrine from various attacks over the years.

Shia Muslims built it to honor Sayyidah Zaynab, granddaughter of Prophet Muhammad. It featured ten blue-tiled archways with three larger green-tiled arches in the middle. The thirteen gave entrance to an open courtyard leading to the inside. The glistening gold dome was in the middle, and a multi-colored tile minaret protruded from one side of the structure, as if watching over, protecting the dome. Jake felt overwhelmed and anxious at the sight and history.

They located the bench and sat down, with the dome correctly positioned at eleven o'clock. It was 9:55 a.m.

They rigorously scanned the area, watching for any strange movement. Jake noticed Ali fidgeting with his leg while sitting on the edge of the bench. Leatherneck stood up and walked around, peering behind hedges and the main water fountain. Jake continued to sit, choosing to examine the residents and visitors of Damascus bustling through the area.

Leatherneck sat back down. A few minutes later a man walked to the back of Leatherneck's side of the bench and whispered something in his ear. The man then left abruptly.

Leatherneck leaned into Jake and Ali, and said, "We need to go to an intersection four blocks over from here and wait for further instruction. That's all he said. He walked away as I asked questions. We have fifteen minutes."

Ali said, "I don't like it. There is an old saying, 'He who turns avoids danger,' and I think we should turn."

Leatherneck cut him off. "We don't have time for that right now. I agree with you, though—I don't like it, either. It's in a secluded area."

Jake said, "We don't have to get into anybody's car. We can just go and see. Maybe someone will have us walk to a park where we'll meet with him in a neutral location, an area where we can feel safe."

Leatherneck responded, "Look, Jake. You are a former senior advisor to the U.S. president and a former chief of police from New York City, of all places. You're also Jewish. Remember Daniel Pearl? You even look like him. I can't guarantee your safety if we go."

"Daniel Pearl was killed by al-Qaeda in Pakistan. The Baathists hate al-Qaeda. The guy we're trying to interview seems like a harmless double."

Ali raised his voice until Leatherneck moved the palm of his hand in a downward steady motion. "Harmless double? These people killed my uncle and millions of people in Iran and Iraq. Did you forget the note? He is looking for revenge and resurrection. What better way to shed some light on his cause?"

Jake responded, "I doubt his revenge is killing somebody like me. What would that accomplish? He'd know that would quickly be forgotten—like Daniel Pearl. Anybody remember him? He's either planning something bigger or bluffing. Either way, I'm guessing he'll talk to us."

Leatherneck sided with Ali. "Jake, let's go back to the hotel and wait for another message. When it comes, we can explain we want to meet and have the interview in a public place. If they don't reach out to us, then c'est la vie. We'll find another way."

Jake was outvoted, and although he was in charge, he had to admit they had a point. He didn't want to be responsible for putting their lives at risk.

They began walking back to their car, in the opposite direction from where they were told to meet.

A van pulled up, slowed down, and then drove off. They walked faster, with more intensity.

Their car became visible, and they relaxed. They began to cross the street to where the car was parked. The same van approached them again, this time with its doors open. Three men were inside wearing black ski masks and carrying AK-47s. They ordered the newsmen to get inside.

They hesitated for a few seconds. One of the men inside the van said something in a measured tone, but Jake couldn't understand what he meant.

Ali responded in Arabic, and his face tensed upon hearing the response. He gestured for Jake to enter. Jake froze. Ali said in a calm voice, "They said they will take us to Jabal."

"And if we refuse?" Jake asked.

Leatherneck said, "You don't want to know. I don't think we have a choice."

Jake's feet refused to move, until Jabal's henchmen aimed their guns at him. He relented, and the newsmen began walking toward the van. The henchmen grabbed Leatherneck and Jake. Ali climbed aboard without assistance.

Chapter 9
London

Red's box arrived in the morning mail. All provisions were included for that night's leather theme. She was heading to Dynamo, a posh club in the Leicester Square area of London, for its monthly costume dance. And she had a special outfit in mind.

The nagging part of her brain didn't want to go; she should visit the gym or see a show instead. She didn't have a lot of friends, but she could reach out to the few single people in her office, like Robert, or at the gym. But her stronger emotions reminded her that she wasn't good at doing "normal." Her last attempt at civility, falling in love with Jake, didn't end very well. Besides, she felt frisky tonight and had already purchased an outfit.

She took the Tube to the club, wanting to first check in on Jasper. This time she made sure to purchase the stir fry before entering the station, and she was relieved when she spotted him at his usual spot.

He was on a "break" and greeted her enthusiastically with his amber-colored eyes, "Ms. Red, you look lovely tonight. Going out on the town, huh?"

They talked for a few minutes, until Jasper began trying to peek into the bag that Red handed him. It was time to leave. She hugged him. He flashed a small smile, and she left.

Red and green strobe lights illuminated the dance floor, providing enough light for her to decipher the single from the hitched (wedding rings were too creepy) and the groomed from the sloppy. Red whooshed through the crowd, dancing with half a dozen different men. Each complimented her on her seductive attire: black leather boots, dress, and cat-woman-styled ears. A black wig topped off her gothic style.

Red left four men after one or two dances each. They were either too boring, brutish, or bombastic. A fifth one had an arrogant air about him. Red was sure that if chosen, he would ruin her night with fantastic claims of his importance as barrister, aristocrat, or bourgeoisie government official who had managed to hide himself from the masses by partying at the club.

The sixth one was perfect, and he had an empty flat, his roommate being out of town. Red didn't ask if his mate was male or female—it didn't matter as long as he wasn't wearing a ring.

Red began to leave with her companion. The clincher was her clasping his waist just above his bollocks and yanking him toward the door. She looked back at the club when they were outside.

A few minutes later, they entered his flat. He lunged at Red, who dodged, letting him know that she was in charge. He'd have to wait. Eventually, she let him take her to his room. Red made sure her purse was nearby and then straddled and blindfolded him with one of his socks, using the opportunity to reach into her purse for two toys that she had received in the mail earlier in the day: handcuffs and a leather whip. Fortunately, the mailman didn't know what he had delivered. If he had, he would have switched the package for a stack of bibles.

Red left her prey's flat about two hours later, making sure he was fast asleep at the time. She wiped the sweat off her chest and face and returned to her flat. After grabbing a few more hours' sleep, she packed and then headed to RAF Northolt, outside of London.

***

The Horn of Africa to Kenya

The Horn of Africa is the most eastern portion of Africa, literally protruding out of the continent. The Horn looks like the byproduct of an accident – a puzzle piece that does not quite fit.

The land is, however, much more than an ill-fitting puzzle piece. Strategically located bordering three major bodies of water (Arabian Sea, Gulf of Aiden, and the Red Sea), the Horn allowed ancient traders to transport spices and other products between Asia, the Middle East, and Northern Africa. More recently, one particular country located on the Horn, Djibouti, became an important hub for NATO military powers.

Robert was already seated on the plane to Djibouti by the time Red boarded.

"Good day, mate," she said, mocking him and in a cheery mood. "It's going to be a long flight. Don't make the mistake of waking me if I fall asleep. Got it?"

"Well, looks like somebody had a long night last night? And she's still cheery. My, my," he said with a forced chuckle to hide the growing knot in his stomach. Now that they had confirmed the origin of the anthrax, they needed to find out more about the mythical white man and whether he directed the slaughter—and for what reason.

Their plane landed at a French air force base. After a brief rest, they boarded an Osprey that would take them to a British helicopter carrier conveniently sailing in the Indian Ocean.

On the carrier, they met the six members of the Special Air Service regiment who would join them on the mission. Rigorous briefings were held, every detail checked and verified. The weather had been clear for the past two days. No dark clouds obscured the view of the military satellite stationed high above. The mission would be riskier without the footage.

The last briefing ended, and they walked into the mess hall for what would be the final sit-down meal for a while. Sure, they packed MREs, but no matter how much effort scientists and chefs devoted toward making freeze-dried food, it could never come close to the real deal. Besides, how many times can a person eat the same freeze-dried French toast, barbecue beef, or chicken parmesan? The crew, not involved in the mission, looked at them with interest but knew not to ask questions.

Five hours later, at 11:00 p.m., the group of eight checked their weapons and equipment. They were equipped with night-vision goggles and fully automatic 9mm pistols, with spare magazines for each gun. They also had regular and smoke grenades, headsets, and throat mics. A few of the commandos carried an array of communication equipment, medical provisions, and heavier weapons.

Once set, they boarded two Osprey helicopters. One helicopter could have transported the group, but they also needed air support. The takeoff from the carrier deck was uneventful. They didn't need to be catapulted from the flight deck like a helicopter's flying cousin—an airplane—but Red still hated this part. Too much could still go wrong, very wrong.

She looked at Robert. Like Red, he didn't appear to be having fun. The commandos relaxed, taking in the scenery and using their headsets to talk to one another over the whirl of the engines. One began banging out lyrics to the tunes playing on his smartphone. Another yelled for the singer to stop. A third played with his cross. Robert looked like he was going to be sick. Red offered him a bag, but he shook her off. The gesture caused him to toughen up.

Although they had received the tacit approval from the Kenyan government, they knew they couldn't control the ungoverned fighters on the ground. In this part of the world, you couldn't know for sure who controlled the village antiaircraft gun. Satellite footage aided their attempt to choose a safe path. Higher altitude was even safer.

A refueling tanker joined the group about four hours into the flight. The tanker steadied itself in front of the first Osprey. Each pilot tried to stay on course at the same speed. Any sudden shift might cause all three crafts to burst into flames.

The pilots, however, had performed this midair daredevil maneuver many times, and Red marveled as the tanker's long fuel nozzle with attached basket slowly made itself to the Osprey. The female basket hooked into the male connection parts of the plane. A connection was made and fifteen minutes later the first Osprey was fully refueled. The process was repeated for the benefit of the craft carrying the two MI6 agents.

The pilots descended toward the landing zone in northern Kenya about an hour later. Fresh images from the reconnaissance planes flying above them confirmed there were no warm human globs moving around below. The Osprey descended while their escort scouted the area.

***

Lake Turkana

The group received the signal to begin rappelling down the ropes into the barren land near the Kenyan side of Lake Turkana. Fine brown clay littered with rocks dominated the landscape. A few acacia trees with their large arching tops would provide temporary shelter from the powerful sun scheduled to rise several hours later. Bits of moss and grass sprinkled the landscape in selective areas. The group could see the lake in the far distance using their night-vision goggles.

The commandos landed first and spread out, establishing a perimeter. Robert rappelled after them, leaving Red as last. He hit a rock when landing and twisted his ankle. Red saw him grimace in pain. She hoped it wasn't severe, as the mission couldn't withstand the loss of even one person, especially one of the MI6 agents. He began to move again, limping a little but still advancing at a reasonable clip.

The aircraft turned away. They were on their own without any further air support—at least for now. The GPS devices confirmed they were on schedule and at the right place.

The plan required them to hike fifteen kilometers around the edges of the lake, eventually crossing over into South Sudan. Many hostile tribes and villagers lived in the area. It would be nearly impossible to tell friend from foe. Allegiances changed on a seemingly daily basis.

The lake also offered its share of danger. The landscape looked pleasant, sporting a combination of golden reefs and barren landscape littered with interesting reddish-brown rocks. But the tranquil landscape masked the latent dangers of 900-pound adult Nile crocodiles lurking behind corners and venomous snakes filling crevices. They carried a few potions and an assortment of weapons in an attempt to address these dangers.

Portions of the trip took them into and through waters leading to and from the lake. They needed to enter the lake itself a few times in order to bypass jagged ravines.

Captain Kevin McNutten, the head commando, led the way. McNutten's square jaw, lean face, and jagged nose bent to the right told his story as a seasoned warrior. His neck looked like a thick log. Red was glad he was on their side.

On the group's second excursion into the lake they came across an earthy formation protruding out of the water. McNutten walked toward the area. The earth had little significance except it obscured their view of the other side. He instructed the others to take the safeties off the pistols and semiautomatics they were carrying.

McNutten crawled on his belly onto the earthen object to see what lay ahead. The rest waited in the water for the all-clear signal. Five minutes later, they began to wonder if something happened to their leader. Ten minutes after that, they knew something was wrong.

Red took control. She signaled for the commandos to stop and then pointed to Robert and herself and then the earth. They began to crawl. At first, they didn't believe what they saw.

Poor McNutten was surrounded on the land by three giant crocodiles he must have disturbed from their sleep. Fortunately, the group had received some training on the carrier on how to kill the animals in case they couldn't avoid a fight, the second-to-last-minute training, the "less important" information the instructors squeezed into the briefing. They approached cautiously, looking for a way to eliminate the threat without announcing their presence to the entire region, including any nearby tribal militia.

McNutten signaled for them to keep down and quiet. Other crocs could be nearby, and crocs move much faster in water than on land. While they could see the ones on the land near McNutten, the rest of the crew was still in the water. McNutten signaled with his hands, assigning one croc to each of the three of them.

They knew to attack the back of the neck, punching their sharp knives through the head and into the brain. The goal was clear. Using proper tactics to accomplish the goal, however, was another story. One wrong move and the crocodile could turn the tables and bite one of their heads off.

McNutten pointed to sticks on the ground. Red knew what he meant for them to do. She looked at Robert, who nodded affirmatively.

A few minutes later, they were in position. McNutten counted down using his fingers. On one, each person approached his or her designated animal, holding a stick picked up from the ground in one hand and knife in the other. The trick would be making sure the crocodile didn't move too quickly toward the group.

They moved gingerly. Once in range, each of them baited their animals into biting down on the sticks. Then they tried to keep the jaw closed tight on the stick using their hands first and then one arm and armpit the same way a boy might hold down his little brother in a makeshift wrestling match, allowing for a nuggie or other playful trick. Only this wasn't for play. They learned on the carrier that it was easier than expected to lock the jaw of a croc. The jaw was powerful biting down but much weaker when opening back up.

With lockjaw accomplished, they used their other arms and hands to quickly slice the crocs through the back of the head into the brain using their knives. Blood spurted up from Red's dying croc. She looked over to McNutten. His croc didn't die immediately. McNutten had to apply an extra twist of the knife to accomplish the deed. Robert was also successful in neutralizing his beast. The three of them relaxed and exhaled.

Red went back to get the others while McNutten scouted the next section. They continued wading through and out of the lake, using land where possible. Once ashore, they were consumed in thick, tall reeds. The danger now was crocs and snakes they couldn't see.

They advanced, this time working in pairs. McNutten held up his hand a couple of hundred meters later, and the group immediately froze in place, unaware of what scared him. Word filtered throughout the group that he had found a quiver of king cobras, unfortunately the most aggressive cobra breed. They could kill a few of these snakes but not a pack.

Fortunately, unlike with the crocs, they were able to detour around the quiver, careful not to arouse their interest. A short time later, their Garmin devices told them they had reached the planned rest area.

**

The group sat in a barren area, a place where they could see advancing wildlife or enemy tribes. The sun began to rise, offering a more complete view of the astonishing landscape. Red saw the top section of the Teleki volcano that Mustafa pointed out during her first venture to the area, protruding out of the lake.

The volcano looked more majestic this time around since the rising sun gently illuminated the red clay and nearby lava field. A pack of flamingos flew in the distance. She surprised herself by secretly wishing she and Jake were here alone on a romantic date.

McNutten approached Red, interrupting her thoughts. They shared a large rock. "Let's go over a couple of details, shall we? I just received an update on my satellite phone. At last check, our satellites showed the heat signatures for fifteen persons at the site. Eight looked to be smaller. Remember, we're here to complete our objective, nothing else. All eyes on me when we move."

"Are the birds ready to pick us up after?" Robert asked.

McNutten replied, "I hope so, but remember that nothing goes according to plan."

"Well," Red said, looking at her watch, "we should probably get going. Something tells me we're going to need more time."

The team mobilized and moved onward.

***

They crossed into South Sudan, an achievement they would not have even known, if not for their devices. The landscape didn't change from Kenya, still the same rocky brown clay with a few acacia trees mixed in the landscape for "variety" in the areas away from the lake. Golden reed dominated the marshy areas around the lake. They walked in and around the marshy areas using the clay areas where possible.

Suddenly, they heard shots. They immediately nestled into a thick patch of reed while taking stock of the situation.

Red couldn't see where the shots came from, but they weren't accurate. Some went over the heads of the group members while others flew around in no apparent pattern. McNutten told a group of commandos to flank the shooters while they returned fire from their position. He whispered they should try to take shooters alive to use as bargaining chips if they were from the same tribe the commandos and MI6 agents were seeking. The group was within a kilometer of the ultimate target objective.

Then the gunfire stopped. It was as if somebody called for a ceasefire. Strange. Were they being baited? Their flanking commandos returned with no news.

The group proceeded, carefully observing the surroundings.

One of the commandos spotted him first—a member of the Mustavi tribe, bleeding from his chest. An AK-47 in seemingly good condition rested on the ground next to him. Red recognized the markings on his body. They were the same as on the arrows she and Robert had picked up on their previous venture in the Rift Valley. The other tribesman must have fled, probably for help. They had to act fast.

They gave the tribesman first aid and carried him with them toward the camp. Ten minutes later and it was in sight.

McNutten began to talk to the fallen warrior in a language spoken by the Mustavi tribe. In addition to being a warrior, McNutten was also a central African tribal linguist. He calmed the prisoner down and convinced him his survival depended upon his approaching the camp as a peace offering.

The prisoner walked toward the camp. They followed at a safe distance, unsure if the offering would work. Minutes later, they had their answer. Five warriors walked out to meet them, each holding AK-47s. The warriors had the same markings as the injured tribesman. After a brief exchange with McNutten, the tribal leader beckoned for the commandos, Red, and Robert, to follow him into the village.

**

The village surpassed Red's modest expectations. The tribe was doing well, at least by third-world standards.

An outer ring, which Red later learned was called Enkang, was made of a mixture of sharp thorn bushes, dried earth, and cow dung. It protected the tribe from rivals and also served as a fence, preventing pigs and other animals from escaping.

Red counted seven huts arranged in one area of the village. Each was made out of branches pasted with cow dung, which dried into a kind of concrete. Some of the huts were raised off the ground resting on logs, protecting the occupants and any property from water. Although the shape of the huts differed—some were circular and some square—the roof of each hut rose in the center, allowing water to drain off the sides.

The bare-chested tribal patriarch had welts in a circular pattern covering his stomach and chest. He gestured for the group to sit down inside his hut. A woman with a lip piercing served hibiscus tea. McNutten, Robert, and Red sat on an earthen floor near the elder while two of the other commandos sat in the back. The remaining three stood outside the hut, weapons ready. McNutten translated a conversation between Red and the elder.

Red began by looking into the tribal leader's eyes. McNutten translated, "Thank you for your hospitality. Let me start by saying we have come a long way to meet you, and we are honored to be in your presence. We are here looking for information and do not plan on staying. We will leave and never bother you again."

The elder grunted and took a sip of tea.

She continued, watching him closely. "We understand you recently had a visitor?"

He sat still and didn't move.

Red added, "I'm only interested in what the visitor looked like and what he wanted."

He didn't budge.

"McNutten, does he understand your translation? Can you talk to him?"

McNutten asked him a few questions, and although the elder responded to him, McNutten didn't seem satisfied. McNutten turned to Robert and Red and said, "He understands just fine. He just doesn't feel like talking."

As soon as McNutten answered their question, a warrior entered along with one of McNutten's men. The warrior was sporting what looked like an AK-47 in pristine condition and whispered in the elder's ear. The elder didn't seem to respond to him either, instead shooing him away.

But it gave Red an idea. She said through McNutten, "Your tribe has some nice guns. Are they new?"

The elder looked at Red, traces of a smile forming. But he didn't answer.

She took a chance. "Are you interested in more guns? Your AK-47s are big. You should combine them with smaller, more modern weapons."

The elder nodded slow at first and then more rapidly.

"You answer some questions, and I'll arrange for you to have eight handguns." Red showed him the 9mm she was carrying.

He began pointing right at Red. She and Robert exchanged worried glances. And then Red realized what the elder meant.

"You answer questions, and you can have all of our pistols, but not our automatics. Deal?"

The elder stuck out his hand, which Red promptly shook. A server brought in a plate of breads, nuts, and food Red didn't recognize. Tea was served, and a tribal deal was born somewhere in South Sudan.

The elder talked about the white man who led them into slaughtering the Mogobishi tribe. He had also provided guns, not for information but for the privilege of killing off their enemies. It was an easy battle. They didn't even fight back. Most were already dead.

Red asked Robert for a piece of paper and pencil from the kit he was carrying. Growing up, Red would draw when she wanted an escape from life on her farm, a talent she developed over several years. She spent the next hour working with the elder to draw a sketch of the white man. The image looked vaguely familiar.

Red used their satellite phone to access the Internet and browse a database of pictures. The elder, clearly not understanding the technology, looked at Red as if she was an angel.

Red and the elder were able to parse through the pictures, settling on one that looked like the drawing. The elder began nodding.

Red said, "This guy? You sure?"

The elder looked at Red, smiled, and said, "Yes, just like that guy."

Chapter 10
Damascus

Jabal's henchmen frisked Jake and his crew, presumably for weapons or recorders. Finding nothing, the ringleader spoke in broken English, "We apologize for, eh, any drama. Need to be careful. You understand, eh?"

They all nodded, and the ringleader continued, "We take you to Jabal, yes? If you no cause problem, we go. Eh?"

They nodded again. "Sit and relax."

The group sat on the middle of the floor of a blue van with walls flaking of rust. It smelled like rotten food, probably emanating from the trash dispersed around the edges of the van. The henchmen surrounded and trained their guns on them.

The leader put a bowl of nuts and dates on the floor in the middle of where they were sitting. "You eat, eh?"

He probably thought it would relax the group, but it didn't. They ignored the offering and stared at the captors until Leatherneck spoke. "Thank you. We don't want any problems. We just want to interview Jabal, and then we are free to go. Right?"

"Of course, we understand. Location secret though. Bags on, now, please. Eh?" the head henchman said, pointing to the three large brown paper bags with holes for breathing, Arabic writing, and a smiling man on the front.

Ali and Jake looked at Leatherneck, who nodded his approval. After all, what choice did they have?

The bags were fitted on their heads. The jerky movements of the van, and inability to see, provided Jake with an eerie flashback to Disney World's in-the-dark rollercoaster, Space Mountain.

The longest fifteen minutes of Jake's life passed, until the van screeched to a stop. Jake could hear the front passenger door open and close.

Rap music began playing from the direction of the driver's seat. A rat-tat-tat noise became audible as the driver's hand began hitting the steering wheel to the beat of the song. *Rat-tat-tat, rat-tat-tat.*

Voices from outside the van talked in Arabic. Leatherneck strained to hear what they were talking about, but he could barely make out the words being spoken. *Rat-tat-tat, rat-tat-tat.*

Dark thoughts began to run through Jake's mind. *Why are we still in the van? What is taking so long? What will happen next?* Maybe it would turn out that Jake was better off in the van, as uncomfortable as that experience was. *Rat-tat-tat, rat-tat-tat.*

***

The passenger door opened and closed again, and the music quickly silenced. One of the henchmen climbed over to the back and pulled the bags off of Jake and his group, revealing their sweaty foreheads. They were directed into a dingy, mostly-empty warehouse where they could see stacks of food and two idle forklifts.

A man who looked like Jabal—with the same jet-black hair, large ears, and pudgy nose—sat on a chair in the middle of the empty portion of the warehouse floor. Three chairs were arranged around him in a semicircle. He gestured for the newsmen to sit down, greeting them in passable English. Then he said, "You travel a long way."

Jake replied, "Yes. We would like to ask you some questions. I take it you are Jabal Shamoon. Yes?"

"Yes. What is it you want?" Jabal replied confidently, sizing up Jake as he spoke. Jabal was in his element, in control of the situation. He did indeed bear an uncanny resemblance to Saddam, but at the same time he looked different. He was no longer pretending to be somebody else. His father and Saddam both died defending his homeland. Jabal wouldn't make the same mistake.

Jake ignored the question, trying to gain the upper hand. Control over the order and content of the questions was important. Jake also didn't want to act too subservient. Instead, he asked, "Did you speak to Elyas Qureshi?"

Jabal answered, "No. Qureshi spoke to someone who talked to me."

Jake, remembering Qureshi's bitter reaction when Ali began to take notes, pointed to his notepad and pen and said, "May I?" He also gestured to Ali, who also took out his pad.

"Yes. What is your story?" Jabal grumbled.

"I work for a newspaper interested in learning more about the doubles. Not just you, but others. How did you become a double? How did it make you feel? What was it like? How much of the look is real?"

"Real?" he interrupted.

This guy acts tough but really isn't too smart, Jake thought to himself. "Yes. You know, versus plastic surgery."

Jabal laughed. "I can assure you I'm real. No surgery."

He proceeded to tell them how he became a double, corroborating that he was indeed Jabal and also much of what Aisha had told him. Jake had other questions and moved up toward the front of his seat.

"What was Saddam like?"

Jabal looked at Jake for a few seconds before responding. "He was a leader—smart, quick, decisive."

"Did you like working for him?"

"Yes, of course. He was a lion in a land full of dogs. Somebody we all looked up to."

"Were there actions he took that you didn't like?"

"No...I mean, sure he was tough. But there were aggressors, people looking to kill him or terrorize the country. And we couldn't be intimidated. Only one way to deal with those types." Jabal moved the front of his shoe back and forth on the ground for emphasis, as if putting out a cigarette.

Jake continued, attempting to shift the discussion. "Did you talk to Saddam while he was in hiding from the Americans?"

"No, of course not. I didn't know where he was, and I was being watched."

"Do you remember the day he was captured?"

"Yes," Jabal said dryly, not offering any details.

Jake shifted gears again. "You said before that Saddam was somebody 'we' looked up to. By we, you mean the other doubles?"

He sat back. "Yes."

"How many others?"

"About four," Jabal said as he exhaled, looking a bit more relaxed.

"And you guys looked up to him in what way?"

"He was protecting our country from the same forces that pillaged the Palestinians and others—the Zionists and their American friends," he said, raising his voice while leaning in towards Jake.

Jake deflected. "Jabal, I only have a few more questions. How long have you been in Syria?"

"About five years," Jabal said in a gruff voice while staring at Jake.

Jake took out a pack of cigarettes. "Do you mind if I smoke? Would you like one?" He nodded, and Jake handed one to everybody but the three henchmen. They were on their own.

Jabal's shoulders relaxed.

Jake continued asking what he thought was an innocent question. "Are you planning on going back to Iraq?"

"I...uh...am not sure. Yes...at some point. If..." He waved his hand, holding the cigarette in the air, as if painting an invisible canvas when he spoke.

Jake wasn't sure how much he should press, but he ventured further. "Because..."

Jabal interrupted Jake, exploding with rage, causing Leatherneck to stir. "Because? How about *because* we're not safe? We've been driven underground. People are out for revenge."

"But there's been some reconciliation. Not all Baathists are jailed. Not the ones without blood on their hands, at least."

"True, but I look like him. Remember?"

Jake shrugged his shoulders and said, "Looks can be changed. Different hair, different dress. And I don't have to mention your name in my article. Or, better yet, I can discuss the future in my article. Integration of the doubles..."

"Integration?" Jabal squawked. "It's like fitting a square peg into a round hole. It don't work. Don't you get it?"

Jake contemplated what he said, seeing Jabal's point from his perspective. "Jabal, I understand where you are coming from." Jake then ventured into new territory, saying, "You know, I visited with your mom while looking for you."

Jabal fidgeted on his chair. "What...um...why?"

Leatherneck glared at Jake. Ali put his head down into his hands, slouching like a child.

"I was looking for you for this interview."

"What...um...she say?"

Leatherneck swirled in his seat and glanced back at the henchmen, calculating his next move.

"Well, she's worried about you. She talked about your dad and how you came to like working for Saddam. Kind of what you were saying before."

"What else did she say?"

"Not a lot more, just that she misses you." Jake then added, "She doesn't seem to know where you are."

Leatherneck stared at Jake, who was sure that Leatherneck would've screamed at him had he not been constrained.

Jabal considered what Jake said, drawing a couple of deep breaths of smoke. He exhaled a ring of smoke in the direction of Jake and said, "Did she show you anything?"

Jake didn't know what to say. *Should I lie about the note? He seems unstable. I can't provoke him, certainly not in this warehouse under these conditions with the three henchmen present.*

"Show me anything? No. We talked for a while. She misses you."

"Liar!" he screamed at Jake, sensing that Jake had more to tell.

"Why would I lie? I met with her in your apartment in Tikrit. On the third floor. She served us tea."

Jabal jumped to his feet and screamed, "You, an American spy, saw my mother in my apartment!" He pointed to Ali and shouted even louder. "And with him, that Persian rat?"

Jabal approached Jake threateningly, as if he had lost all sense of control.

Leatherneck stood, blocking his path while Jake pleaded, "Jabal, let's talk about this. Please calm down. I didn't mean to offend you."

Jake wasn't sure if he calmed Jabal down, but Jabal went to sidebar with his friends. They were pointing and gesturing at Jake, as if weighing evidence in their spontaneously created kangaroo court.

Leatherneck whispered to Jake and Ali that they needed to leave, immediately. Walking out while they were conferencing, however, could make Jabal even more enraged.

Jabal broke away from his henchmen and said to Jake, "Change in plans." He added wagging his finger, "This interview is over."

Jake, Ali, and Leatherneck stood to leave when two loud gunshots rang out from behind them where the henchmen were standing. Jake looked at Ali and Leatherneck, who slumped to the ground and fell off their chairs, blood pooling onto the hard warehouse floor.

Jake screamed, "Oh my God! What are you doing? What is going..." But he was cut short when the butt of a gun crashed into his skull. Blood trickled down his face as he lost consciousness.

***

Jake woke up with his hands chained over his head against an iron fence. His brain hurt, and his arms and wrists ached. Dried blood covered his hands and streaked his shirt.

A captor walked by outside the fence and shoved a tray of bread and water through a six-inch cutout in the bottom of the entrance to his cell. Jake looked at him, eyes pleading. He pointed to the tray and then spat through the bars onto the floor and said, "You. Zionist, American, infidel. Eat." Jake turned away, ignoring him.

Jake said weakly, "My hands." The guard unchained his hands, freeing Jake to eat.

About an hour later, Jabal let himself into Jake's cell, taking a seat on an overturned bucket.

Jake asked him, "Why are you doing this? I've come here with good intentions, with news from your mother."

"You! Liar. Good intentions? The same people who killed our leader? Forced him into a hole for weeks, living like a stray dog? Story? You doing a story about how *you* did that and how *we* feel about what *you* did?"

"But Saddam was a murderer. He started wars and killed hundreds of thousands of people. People like your dad."

"Liar! My dad was killed in a war with the same Persian dogs as you brought to me yesterday. He was defending his country."

Jake needed to calm the situation. "Look, Jabal, I'm not trying to take sides. I didn't participate in or start any of these wars. And we actually helped your country in the war with Iran. I'm a reporter now, and I'm just working on a story. You can call my editor."

"Jake Kessler, we know who you are. You worked as the Jewish police commissioner in New York City, the city of Jews. Then you worked as an advisor to President Tucker. You have blood on your hands, the blood of my people. And you're going to pay." At that, Jabal stood and whacked Jake twice in the face.

Blood spattered out of Jake's mouth; a front tooth felt loose. Jake felt the blows a few more times until he lost consciousness.

***

Jake regained his senses to find himself on the floor, his hands once again raised overhead and chained to the iron fence. Jabal was holding an empty bucket. Jake was suddenly cold as he was drenched in water from head to toe. Jabal overturned and then sat down on his bucket while Jake sat against the cold iron.

"What do you want with me?" Jake asked.

Jabal looked at him for a minute and then decided to answer. "We've decided to trade you."

"Trade me?"

"Yes, for cash. We need cash."

"But you know the American government doesn't trade for hostages. Don't you?"

Jabal laughed in a crude, bitter tone. "The American government? No. But your paper, yes." Jabal stood and walked out of the cell.

Jake looked around the room. There wasn't even a window, the only light emanating from a single fixture hanging from the roof. They must have been belowground; ironic, given that was where the Americans found Saddam. The room smelled like mold, although Jake knew that was the least of his problems.

The floor was cold, musty concrete. Spider cracks and pock marks were evident. The bars were flaked with rust. *They weren't built for me*, Jake thought. Kidnapping was always part of their plan. He was just an "opportunity."

Thoughts of Daniel Pearl flooded his mind. The good news was that Jabal seemed more pragmatic, less ideological than Pearl's murderers. Jabal, like Saddam, didn't seem to be a religious fanatic. The note Jabal left for his mother in Tikrit talked about revenge for Saddam, not the creation of a caliphate.

Jabal's agenda appeared rooted in gaining back power lost. And he would need money in order to carry out his plan, not having bin Laden's money or the oil money used to finance other groups. He needed his own unless he had a hidden benefactor, which Jake doubted.

The amount of money Jabal demanded would reveal whether he was bluffing and intending to kill Jake all along in order to bring attention to his cause, or serious in asking for money in exchange for Jake's life. If he asked for a few million, he was probably serious. If he asked for a few hundred million, he probably was not.

But even if Jabal would trade for Jake, would the *New York Times* or the US government pay? For starters, paying a ransom could be against the law, although there have been changes in this policy over the years. And while there sometimes were workarounds, Jake couldn't remember any instances where the American government (unlike the governments of France, Italy, and Germany) paid cash to recover a hostage. The closest the Americans came to trading dollars for blood was with Oliver North, but he derived a convoluted scheme trading arms to Iran to gain favor for hostages being held by proxies in Lebanon, and he was caught and prosecuted in the resulting scandal.

Jake also couldn't recall an instance when the *New York Times* paid a ransom. The only silver lining was that Jabal's merry band may not be considered a terrorist organization, at least not yet. The only people who knew about them other than Jake were Ali and Leatherneck, now both dead (thanks to his stupidity), and a few folks at the newspaper.

***

Jabal walked back in. "You haven't eaten. You need to eat. Need you alive."

Jake didn't want to give in, but he was starving. He had difficulty fasting even for Yom Kippur, a one-day fast which he knew would end with a big feast.

Jake looked at the bread and water, now about ten hours old. He reached for the tray and began eating.

Jabal said, "Good. Smile." He took a picture of Jake with his cell phone and walked out.

Two days later, he walked back into Jake's cell. "No friends."

Jabal started to walk out when Jake called to him, asking, "What does that mean?"

His response was chilling. "Do you really want to know?"

***

Jake knew he didn't have a lot of time left. The worst part would be the pain. He was prepared to die, and sadly part of him had already given up. The burden of the deaths of Ali and Leatherneck pushed his depression to new lows.

What was I thinking—a Jew, bringing a Persian and former US Marine to an abandoned warehouse in Syria to talk to a sadistic Baathist seeking revenge? Jake felt he deserved his fate.

Nobody will miss me anyway. Mom and dad are dead, and I have no children.

Visions of Renée stumbling into the path of a racing car driven by Jake's onetime lover, Red, filled his brain. Sure, Red blamed the accident on Renée and her drinking. But it was really Jake's fault. He was the one whose job produced incessant news stories and tabloid pictures about both of them. He was the workaholic ignoring her needs.

***

A man returned to Jake's cell the next day. He was wearing a mask, but his body size appeared to match Jabal. He seemed a little hesitant until four others, each with a mask, walked in behind him.

Two of the men walked up to Jake. The first immediately hit him with a punch that landed on his right cheekbone. Jake fell to the cell floor, hands still hanging above from the chain binding him to the iron. The second kicked him hard in the ribs, saying, "Why they no pay? Why they no pay? Nobody wants you, you Zionist spy!"

Jake sat up, only to be slammed in his head by another targeted fist. Jake's nose felt broken, and blood accumulated in his throat.

Jake whispered, "Just get it over with."

Two of them uncuffed him and dragged him by his arms which tingled from being bound to the iron fence above his head, his inert legs lifelessly following his body. Jake's face, dripping with blood, hung toward the floor. The inverted tips of his shoes came last, creating a line of blood, sweat, water, and dirt as they met the floor at the end of his body.

He would open his eyes with every other step. Images of Renée, and even Red reflected off the floor, offering a mirage of past failures. Nobody was going to save Jake, certainly not them. He knew that. They arrived at what would probably be the last room he would ever see—a brightly lit area with no windows surrounded by four whitewashed walls. A tall green plant, probably fake, was in one corner. A camera supported by a tripod sat in the middle of the room, facing the back center wall, which had a flag with a red triangle on the left and black, white, and green stripes running from top to bottom. A banner with Arabic writing was posted on the wall to the right of the flag. A white sheet lay on the floor between the camera and back wall. Jake dreaded what was about to happen, but on the other hand, the silver lining would be an end to his misery.

Jake's escorts bound his hands and then threw him onto the sheet, where he collapsed. Jake waited, sweat dripping from his forehead, stomach wildly churning, heart racing, hoping for a massive heart attack.

***

Two of the men walked out of the room. Jake knew they would return shortly, probably with one holding a razor-sharp machete.

They returned about fifteen minutes later, one carrying the anticipated machete and the other carrying a large knife. Jake heard Jabal read something in Arabic as he closed his eyes, waiting for the end.

Two henchmen walked up to Jake and stood by his side. He peeked, seeing the stainless-steel knife and machete, light reflecting off the blades. A third man placed an old burlap sack over Jake's head.

The sack had eyeholes. They wanted him to watch his execution.

Jake glanced again and saw the man reaching for his head with the bag. As he was placing it over his head, the machete-wielding man next to him raised the weapon. Jake closed his eyes as tight as possible. He thought mostly of Renée, but flashes of Red also entered his mind.

Then Jake heard a whoosh and a scream. Warm liquid splattered through the eye holes onto his face and eyes, obscuring his view. He heard a scuffle. His hands were still bound, forcing him to stand still as if waiting for a predetermined outcome. If his rescuers prevailed, he would be freed. If not, he'd be killed. Jake eventually freed his hands and removed the sack.

Two men holding a knife and machete were attacking the two other men. Everybody in the room but Jake wore a black mask. He couldn't decipher friend from foe in his dazed state. He felt helpless, overcome by a mixture of weakness, exhaustion, pain, and emotions.

Somebody ran out of the room, and the battle was over. One of the men took off his mask. He stood and looked into the face of a stranger.

***

The hero slapped Jake and said, "Ve need to get out of here. Now!"

Jake felt paralyzed, though, physically and mentally. So many questions ran through his brain. "How did...Where...When..." Jake couldn't complete a sentence.

"I'm Moshe. Right now you need to get a grip on yourself. Let's go!"

The other man took the masks off the two dead henchmen. He took a picture of them and confiscated the video camera that either Jabal or his men had used. Jake looked at their placid faces, anger bubbling up from his bowels.

One person's face bore similarities to Jabal but seemed different. Jake took off the man's shirt, looking at his right shoulder. Aisha had said that Jabal had a birthmark on his right shoulder, just below his neck.

"Jabal must have been the one who escaped," Jake said to Moshe.

The other stranger approached Jake. "Ve'll talk about this later. Ve need to get out of here, or all of us are going to die," he explained emphatically.

They left the room. Jake noticed two dead bodies to the right, each wearing a black ski mask.

Moshe said, "This vay. Hurry."

Jake struggled to catch up, limping along. Moshe dropped back to help him. They entered the warehouse. Two bodies lay on the floor. A third person stood in obvious pain but alive. The stranger approached and began comforting the wounded person while Moshe took pictures of the two dead bodies. Jake caught up to the stranger and the person he was assisting. The person laughed weakly and said, "Jake, we have to stop meeting like this."

Red then introduced Jake to Robert.

Chapter 11
Syria and Beyond

Moshe got the attention of Robert, Red, and Jake. "Ve need to get out of here now." He pointed to one of the men Red killed and said, "This guy looks like Saddam, another double. Like a cult or something. By the looks of you two, you're not in a position to fight, and ve can't hold 'em off on our own. Small talk vill have to wait. Quick!"

The four of them headed toward an old Camry. Moshe put his right arm under Red's left armpit and around her neck to her right shoulder. Robert did the inverse, completing the human splint. A bullet had grazed her thigh, giving her a deep contusion, a painful but temporary injury. They escorted her while Jake limped along last, climbed in the car, and closed the door.

"What about the bodies of my men?" Jake asked.

Red answered with labored breath, "I didn't see them. How about you guys?"

Moshe and Robert shook their heads. Moshe added, "I think they vould have gotten rid of them. It has been several days since the GPS signal vas last sent." Moshe turned on the engine and began driving away.

"GPS?" Jake repeated.

Red answered, "That's how we tracked you. Your guy, Leatherneck, he wore a GPS activator. It was in his shoe, sending his coordinates the entire time to Protectorate Enterprises. The activator sent out an alarm when the pulse in his foot stopped. Protectorate called its customer, your paper, and the paper eventually reached us."

"Why didn't they call the CIA or the FBI?" Jake asked Moshe.

Red interjected, "Good question. I asked the same thing, and don't take it personally, but they weren't interested. There wasn't enough to go on in the short timespan, and their reach here is limited anyway. Same with the FBI. They then tried their luck with MI6 because they knew we worked together before."

Jake grunted and asked, "Moshe, you don't sound like a Brit. Who do you work for? Mossad?"

Moshe responded, "Good guess. My accent?"

"Yes. You look Middle Eastern but speak like a Jew. Another Jew can always tell. How did you guys get involved?"

"From MI6, of course. This is our backyard, and vhen shit happens in our yard, ve get the call!"

Jake laughed to the extent he could without reigniting the pains in his face, neck, shoulders, and ribs. "Of course. Where are we heading?"

"Ve don't have too many options. Ve don't know how far Jabal's network goes into the Syrian government. And he escaped. He's probably telling them right now that ve just killed a bunch of their men. Jews coming to Damascus and people dying, not a pretty story. They vill assume you are returning from vhere you came from, Lebanon. So that eliminates that. The Turkish border is too unstable. So that eliminates that. Which leaves us one alternative. Guess?"

"Oh my God. You can't be serious. How are we going to do that?"

"Ve have our vays!"

***

Jake fell fast asleep, resting his head against his window, while Robert and Moshe navigated through Damascus. Robert looked over at Red. She was squirming in her seat, blood seeping through the fabric of her pants.

Robert said to Moshe, "We need to get her to a doctor."

Moshe replied, "No vorries. Ve have one."

"But how long till we get there?"

"Twenty minutes, maybe?"

"That's too long. She's looking pale. She's lost a lot of blood."

Robert shouted at Jake, "Jake, wake up. You need to help Red. I know you guys have your issues, but she's losing blood. Wake up!"

Jake raised his head and looked over at Red, immediately understanding the predicament.

Red looked at Jake with disgust. "Hey, I just saved your life. Could you throw me a bone please? Rip me a shred of clothing."

Jake snapped into action, quickly removing his shirt, exposing his bruised body. He ignored the smirk from Red, ripped two lines of cotton, and tied both together.

"You have a first-aid kit around here?" Jake asked Robert and Moshe.

Moshe told him to look in the back of the Camry.

Jake turned towards the back, fished around, and located the kit. He grabbed a cotton ball and antiseptic.

"Take off your pants," he commanded.

"Easy, sailor. I just met you again. Not on the first date," Red said, laughing weakly.

Jake, not in a joking mood, said, "OK. Have it your way. You put the ointment on."

Red finished applying the substance. Jake marveled at her toughness, not even wincing at the bitter pain he knew she was feeling.

Jake said, "Lift your leg, and I'll slip this under."

She complied, and Jake moved closer. He slipped the combined line of clothing under her leg and tied it as tight as possible. He moved away quickly. Red moaned, "Uh-huh."

Jake tried to fall back asleep. He noticed Red watching him from the corner of her eye, but he didn't care. He would never forgive her. He couldn't.

He had just fallen asleep when he was again jarred awake, this time by the ringing of Moshe's cell phone. Jake considered Moshe while he was talking. His six-foot two-inch frame packed with muscle filled the driver's seat. The spy looked overweight from a distance but had a linebacker's body. His dark kinky hair and olive skin gave him an exotic look. He even smelled like tropical suntan lotion.

Moshe talked in Hebrew for a few minutes. Jake hated studying Hebrew as a kid, not understanding why it was necessary. He learned the bare minimum, enough to fulfill his bar mitzvah requirements, and had forgotten it all after completing the deed.

Jake heard Moshe slam the phone down and issue a loud grunt. Nobody talked. Moshe made an immediate U-turn and began taking a series of turns.

Robert turned to him and asked, "What's going on?"

Jake noticed Moshe give Robert a look of distress. Moshe refused to answer. He didn't need to.

A few minutes later, the Camry turned into an underground parking garage. Moshe drove to the second level down, rapidly snaking around the curves of the downward turnstile. The wheels squeaked. Nobody spoke.

***

Moshe pulled in between two nondescript parked cars. Jake noticed one head lifting up in each of the stationary cars. Doors opened and out popped a man and a woman. Moshe greeted the man with a bear hug and the woman with a kiss on the cheek and then a friendly hug.

Moshe turned to face his passengers. "Jake, Red, gather all of your stuff. Don't leave anything behind, and go vith that skinny guy over there—Efraim. No fighting, OK?" He laughed at that. "Robert, get all of the other crap out and put it in Sarah's car," Moshe said, pointing at him. "Quickly, people!"

Jake looked back as his car drove away. Moshe was wiping down the inside of the Camry. He didn't bother to remove the license plates. Efraim told his passengers to get down on the car floor with their heads below the bottom window line. The car's tinted windows would further obscure the passengers.

They drove for about five minutes. A gate opened and closed. Efraim gave them the all clear, and Jake and Red climbed back onto their seats.

The car pulled into one of three garage bays within the confines and on the left side of the walled-in mini compound. Jake looked around as Efraim approached. The structure was in the shape of a horseshoe. There seemed to be several rooms above the three garages. The entrance was located to the right of the garages, part of the central structure. Jake could see a man with binoculars scanning the surroundings from the center upper-level room. The right leg of the horseshoe featured what appeared to be the kitchen on the ground level with an additional room on the second level.

From the outside, Jake imagined the enclave looked like an estate owned by another wealthy beneficiary of the rich/poor dichotomy prevalent in Damascus, somebody with government ties or otherwise off-limits, above-the-line people.

Moshe told Jake later that the property was rented, nominally by Radwan Sayed—a common Syrian name—from a management company. The owner, as is the case with many privileged Syrians, lived abroad and used a company to rent the property. Radwan, fluent and trained in Syrian culture and language, had applied and was interviewed by the rental company. He met all expectations.

Except all of it was a lie. The management company had no way of knowing that all of Radwan's papers were forged. He was not who he said he was. Mossad knew him as Efraim, but the neighbors knew him as Radwan, a kind and thoughtful neighbor who showered them with dates, olives, and other cherished items.

Jake and Red walked into the entrance where they introduced themselves to the two agents they had not met. A third agent, whom Jake recognized as the watchman, emerged to say hello from the top of the staircase. They were joined twenty minutes later by Sarah, who had arrived with Robert and Moshe.

Everybody took seats on two couches and a few chairs for the impromptu meeting.

Moshe began in English for the benefit of their guests. "I've received a message. They have blocks on the outer ring of the city. Ve can't leave. Not yet. Aaron, Lot, you guys vork on cleansing and turning the three cars. Can you do it by tomorrow afternoon?" He looked at his watch. "That gives you twenty-four hours."

They nodded.

"Good."

Red asked, feeling intrigued, "What do you mean by turn?"

Moshe chuckled. "Ve know how to change the look of a vehicle in case the cars ve use are spotted. Our cars look normal but are not...they're...how do you say...adaptable."

Jake shot him a puzzled look. Mossad was known for its ingenuity, but turning cars?

Moshe explained further. "Ve got the idea from your toys—erector sets. Pieces can be added and subtracted by unbolting sections and bolting others onto the basic frame, vich has been adapted for this purpose. You'll see."

Moshe looked at Efraim and said, "Get the kit and start vith Robert."

Jake asked, "Moshe, what is the plan, though?"

"Ve can turn more than cars, and that's vhat ve're going to do!"

"What does that mean, Moshe?"

Moshe looked at him sternly. "In due time, my friend."

***

Everybody left the room except for Jake and Red, who separated themselves as far as possible by sitting on different couches, a Syrian apartheid. An awkward silence followed. Red looked at Jake. Jake looked away. Red sighed, then Jake sighed.

Red needed to talk about the real reason she and Robert risked their lives to save Jake. It was true that Jake's newspaper, the *New York Times International Edition*, contacted MI6 concerning its missing newsmen, knowing about Jake's and Red's roles preventing Paul King from using Alterando to assassinate President Tucker. King had perfected Alterando, a brainwashing drug first developed through the CIA's illicit and scandalous Project MKUltra program.

Red's heart ached when she heard Jake could be in mortal danger. She lobbied Monty, but he was reluctant to let two of his agents become entangled in a rookie journalist's pursuit of a human interest story about the former Saddam Hussein body doubles.

Until, that is, Red reminded Monty there could be a connection to their investigation into the use of anthrax to wipe out the Mogobishi tribe from a village in the Rift Valley of Northern Kenya, creating a ghost town in the process. The only surviving witness revealed, "the white man cometh," referring to a white man directing the carnage.

The agents then located, near Lake Turkana, the Sudanese tribe that had massacred the Mogobishi. Red traded guns for information about the "white man." The tribal chief provided a detailed description resulting in a sketch bearing an uncanny resemblance to Saddam Hussein. Saddam, of course, had died years before.

Even the sometimes dimwitted Monty realized there could be a connection, providing the impetus for both agents to investigate further with support from Israel's Mossad service. Red pleaded for the opportunity to go, jumping at the chance to save Jake and pursue the lead at the same time. Robert agreed to support the mission and, of course, Red.

Red wanted to talk to Jake about the connection, but she first needed to repair their relationship and, if possible, regain his trust. She began the difficult conversation.

"Jake, we need to talk. Let's be adults, OK? We got close working together to save Tucker on the Project MKUltra case. We shagged. No big deal. No obligations." Red regretted couching the affair in the benign terms she used, but she was scared to say more. A passive-aggressive approach would have to do for now.

Jake stood in outrage, jumping right to the point, his pent-up anger boiling over. "No big deal? When were you going to tell me that *you* killed my wife?"

Red chose her words carefully. "I've been thinking about that for a long time." Her eyelids became heavy, her voice wavered. "At first, I blamed myself. I replayed what happened in my mind, over and over. And I got the same answer each time. It wouldn't have mattered if I was a twenty-year veteran or a rookie. She stumbled out of a bar and slipped on the ice, falling right in front of my car. She wound up on the street! And I was chasing Saajid Badat—the British terrorist accomplice to the Shoe Bomber. I couldn't have done anything. Please believe me."

"But you could've stopped! She may have been saved," Jake pleaded.

"I did stop. Trust me. But I knew by looking at her..." Tears streamed down her face.

"You could have taken her to the hospital."

"Seriously? Wouldn't it have been better to wait for an ambulance anyway? She could get treated right away by the paramedics. Besides, I'm with MI6 in a foreign country, and at best, I had just seriously injured a pedestrian, not to mention a woman who, it turns out, was the wife of the chief of the New York City Police Department. My training and rules require me to continue to chase important suspects. The guy I was chasing was in the business of blowing up planes, for God's sake! What good would it have been to get arrested, lose the mark, and cause an international incident? We had been tracking that bastard for months! Lose him? What if a plane blew up because I lost him? Really? CIA plays by the same rules when it operates in Britain. You know what would've happened if I'd stopped, so please don't lay that on me!"

Jake stared at her.

Red continued in monotone. "Jake, I've been twisted up about this whole affair ever since it happened. You know I developed a drinking problem, right? But I keep coming back to the same conclusion. Every bloody time."

"But why didn't you say anything when we were working together? And then when..." He stopped himself.

"I don't know. I started to on several occasions. But how could I? We were on a mission, remember? And we were both out on the thinnest of limbs. You, a senior advisor to the president caught up in an assassination plot, navigated by the infamous Paul King. And me, an agent working under deep cover for King and then joining forces with you against him. It was way too complicated to say, 'Hey, Jake, guess what I did ten years ago?'"

Red wiped her eyes with her sleeve and limped away. She needed to cool off.

***

The next morning, Efraim called Jake into his makeshift office. "I'm going to turn you into a Syrian Muslim."

"What kind?"

Efraim laughed. "Good question. Syrians come in all sizes and shapes. But the majority are Sunnis. And we're going to add to their lead. Sit down, please."

Jake complied. Efraim stood and walked around Jake. He approached his project the way an artist plans a painting. Except in this case, Efraim was not starting with a blank canvas.

Efraim said, "This is going to be fun. Don't say anything until I'm done, and please relax."

Jake loosened his stiff shoulders and stretched his neck muscles. He was still in a lot of pain from his captivity and the beatings he took. His nose hurt the most, and he feared it was broken. He took a few deep breaths.

Jake watched as Efraim used a piece of moldable plastic to cover his teeth. He pressed a slim portion against the upper teeth and a bigger piece against the lower jaw. The effect created an underbite and facial imbalance that had not existed before. He then carved out several pieces on both the lower and upper molds, mimicking the lack of fine Syrian dentistry and orthodontic services, at least among the lower class.

Efraim next turned his attention to Jake's nose. He told Jake, "Good news, bad news. It's not broken, but it's dislocated."

"You sure?"

"Yes. I'm going to have to fix it before I go any further but it'll eventually feel a lot better. Ready?"

Jake bit down on a towel and nodded.

Efraim stood facing Jake with his legs spread to lower his balance. He took both hands and yanked the dislocated left side of the nose back in place.

Jake screamed.

"That's it. You need a few minutes?"

Jake swallowed some water. "No. Let's get this over with."

Efraim applied putty around the nose but more on the right side than the left. Jake winced at Efraim's touch. Although Efraim tried to avoid the bruised spots, he couldn't prevent pain.

Jake's hair was clipped. Efraim applied a white cotton headdress, covering any remaining hair.

Last came the makeup. Efraim removed as much dried blood as he could without opening any wounds. He then applied a dark brown color topped off with a large mole that he glued in place. The mole, along with glasses, would hopefully divert the attention of any onlookers away from the wounded portions of his face.

Jake, after changing into a loose-fitting black shirt and pants, walked downstairs. He barely recognized Robert and Moshe, who had already been processed in similar attire.

"Oh, my. When you look mahvelous, yooooou feeeeel mahvelous, dahling!" Red said, drawing a sharp glare from Jake. She then headed upstairs for her turn.

An hour later, she emerged wearing a dark navy hijab and glasses. Her black cotton dress had the effect of rounding her body.

Next, Moshe taught them a few simple phrases to say if they were stopped. He also provided final instructions before they boarded their cars. Moshe, Jake, and Robert loaded into one car, while Efraim and Red boarded the second car.

The cars had been turned into Jeeps, one larger than the other, through the addition of metal onto the chassis. The agents had painted one of the Jeeps navy and the second one black. Both were intentionally roughed up, making them look old.

***

The Jeeps drove toward Hadar, a town strategically located in southern Syria. Flying out of the country would be too risky, even with the forged passports and documentation they were carrying. The Baathists would look toward the border with Lebanon first, given that Jake had entered Syria after flying into Beirut. The borders with Turkey and Iraq were too chaotic and dangerous—armed gangs, extremists, smugglers, and refugees from different wars roamed the area. That left Jordan and the Golan Heights as possibilities.

Hadar offered an element of surprise that Jordan didn't. The downside was that crossing the so-called purple line, separating Syria from the Israeli-occupied

Golan Heights, could be more dangerous than any other border.

The drive began uneventfully. But as they neared Hadar, Moshe spotted a checkpoint ahead of their position on the highway. He slowed down as Syrian guards directed him off the road to a checkpoint. A trail of thick dust followed the Jeeps as they were forced to stop.

Two regular Syrian Army soldiers approached each Jeep. The soldiers who had approached Jake's car began to ask questions, which Moshe answered in passable Arabic.

Jake, sitting in the backseat, began to panic, sensing an oncoming allergic reaction to the dust invading the car through the open windows. He didn't want to suddenly close his window and attract unwanted attention. He tried to hold it in, but he couldn't and began sneezing. Robert looked back at him from the front seat, eyes imploring him to stop.

But Jake couldn't help himself and began sneezing harder. He could feel globs of snot accumulating around his nose and face. He didn't want to wipe, fearing it would ruin the makeup. Then he sensed his mole becoming loose. Would it fall? Would the wounds on his face begin to show?

Robert shot him a second desperate look. Another soldier began to look more closely at the inside of the car and its passengers.

With Jake fighting the impulse to touch the mole and his face, Efraim's car was waved through. The soldiers interrogating Moshe turned away. Moshe followed, and the Jeeps continued on the highway. Jake and Robert breathed a sigh of relief.

A half hour later, Moshe and Efraim turned off the highway. They drove for several additional kilometers through a maze of other off-road paths until finally parking side by side. They were alone, somewhere in southern Syria.

Moshe rolled down his window again. "Efraim and I are going to put blindfolds on you for this next part. No vorries, though. I promise you von't vind up in a ditch, missing organs."

Jake made a show of touching his head and said, "I'm not sure I find that funny. Can you tell us why we need to do that?" He pointed to the acres of undeveloped land all around them. "There's nobody within several kilometers of us—no buildings, cars, people. It's no-man's-land out here."

Moshe responded, "My friend, I understand your concern, especially after vhat you've been through. But my hands are tied. I can't tell you vhy right now. Maybe soon." He shrugged his shoulders and added, "It's your choice. You can go back and see if there is another vay. Maybe the French can smuggle you out. Or you can come vith us. Besides, if ve had wanted to trade you to somebody else, ve'd have already done it."

Jake thought about it. Red looked at him, eyes begging him to proceed. Moshe was right. He had to leave. What choice did he have?

Moshe and Efraim tied the blindfolds on their "captives" and continued the journey, driving deeper into the country.

The Jeeps stopped a few minutes later. Moshe and Efraim led their passengers into a house. Jake, Red, and Robert heard a door open, and then they were led downstairs.

Moshe said, "Don't vorry! Ve're almost there." Another door opened, and they went further underground.

The air was now dank and cold, and it smelled like mold and dust. They could tell the lighting was dim. Moshe handed them flashlights.

Red said, "Can we take these things off? It's pretty obvious where we are."

"Yes, of course," Moshe said.

They looked around. The tunnel was about eight feet tall and three feet wide, its walls reinforced by concrete. The only light source was their flashlights. They heard rats in the distance.

Robert said, "Wow. This is incredible."

Efraim said, "We're surprised the Syrians haven't discovered it. We've been using it for years."

Jake asked, "How far do we have to go?"

"About five kilometers," Moshe responded.

"But that could take hours going at this pace," Red said.

Moshe explained, "Ve need to valk faster. Think about it. Ve couldn't have ended the tunnel too close to the purple line. The international press already hates us. Can you imagine vhat the UN vould say about it? And ve needed to pick a location that vouldn't be discovered by the Syrians. Ve also had to start it in an area far enough away from the fence."

They continued walking. Efraim had brought along water for everybody to share.

Moshe pointed to a mark in the concrete and said, "Velcome to Israeli-occupied Golan!" It reminded Jake of the sign in the Lincoln Tunnel that he had passed thousands of times, announcing the separation of New York from New Jersey—except the marking here was actually cleaner.

About an hour later, Efraim told them to be quiet. Moshe and Efraim put the blindfolds back on them, and they continued. A few minutes later, they ascended. They were in a house, this one much nicer than on the Syrian side. The Israelis led them through the structure and into a large SUV with tinted windows. There, they were finally able to relax and discard the blindfolds. They would remove the rest of the props later, when they had more time and space to maneuver.

Jake sat next to Efraim, leaving the seat next to Red vacant. Red grunted. Robert got in last and sat next to her.

"Ve have a lot to discuss," Moshe began. "Ve're heading to our headquarters in Tel Aviv. You guys should relax and take a...how do you say...snooze. Ve'll be there in about two hours."

Chapter 12
Israel

They arrived two hours later without a hitch. It had been a long time since Red had visited Tel Aviv. She thought it looked a lot like Miami with its tall, sleek buildings, glass facades, motorcycles, cars, and an eclectic collection of people walking around.

They drove into the parking garage of a building. The structure featured a bright sign.

Efraim noticed Jake staring up at the sign and, knowing that a lot of American Jews cannot read Hebrew, volunteered, "It translates to Complexity."

"Complexity?" Jake repeated.

Efraim laughed. "Sure, why not? We like to say it stands for two principles that sum up our business. The first is the truth. And that's what the word means. The second is the facade behind the truth. And that's where people like Red, Moshe, and I come into play."

They took the parking elevator up from the garage into the lobby. The lobby was first-class, with marble floors and a fountain. Passersby who peered inside would think that Complexity was a successful technology company.

Red was surprised to see very little security in the lobby.

Efraim whispered, "You'll get the search upstairs, don't worry. Remember, appearances from the outside are important."

The elevator had no buttons other than the number "2."

"Everybody goes to the second floor?" Jake asked.

Efraim nodded and added, "And there are no staircases you can take from the lobby."

Red pointed out the obvious. "Brilliant! That way you can perform a more intrusive search in the comfort of a private area."

Efraim added, "True, and the second floor is actually below the building in a bombproof vault. It should be labeled negative two. Remember, 'Complexity.'"

The doors opened and they arrived. Sentries armed with machine guns were posted on every wall. Different stations and rooms were set up for retinal scans and intrusive body searches, including the application of bomb and chemical sniffers. Even seasoned agents like Moshe and Efraim had to go through the testing. Red marveled at how much more secure the building was than the headquarters of MI6.

The group sailed through the search, thorough but efficient. Jake and Red were issued temporary identification badges, and everybody boarded a different set of elevators. Efraim said to Jake and Red, "We've proven we're clean. Now we have access to the floor we've been cleared to visit."

The elevators opened outside a large room where identification badges were checked and access granted. Red thought about how everybody worked at cubicles, probably part of the counterterrorism strategy, with less opportunity for rogue agents to sell secrets. Sure, there were briefing rooms, but not for individuals to use by themselves.

They walked into the large room and then to a smaller room off to the side of the cubicles. There, a young female soldier wearing green army fatigues handed each of them a set of clothes and, without saying a word, pointed them to an inner room to her right.

Efraim instructed them to join him, one at a time, in the inner room, where he removed the props he used in Syria and they changed into their "civilian" clothes. Jake yawned while Robert signaled for Red to proceed. Ten minutes later, the three of them felt partially restored, at least physically. Restoration of the mind would take longer.

Efraim and Moshe led them back towards the cubicles and into a tense collection of serious men and women working as if preventing Israel's annihilation hinged on the success of their efforts. Agents looked up to Moshe, some even getting up to shake his hand. He was revered, no doubt by successfully completing dangerous missions with great risk to his life. Agents saluted Efraim as well, but it was obvious to Red who the real hero was.

The five of them entered a briefing room located beyond the cubicles where they took their seats around a conference table. Two other agents joined. They had the look of "don't ask who I am." Red knew not to ask.

Moshe looked at Red. He sat back in his chair and bellowed, "Can you tell me vhy you and boy vonder dropped everything to run to Syria?"

Red blushed but then quickly replied, "You already know. Leatherneck's GPS activator went off, his boss called the *Times*, and the *Times* called my boss..."

Moshe interrupted, "Yes, ve vent through that already. And the *Times* knew to call your boss because of the case you vorked with Jake before on, blah, blah,

blah. I get it. But! Vhat I don't get is are you here in your official capacity or just because it is Jake?"

Red surveyed the room. Jake tried to look uninterested, even biting his lip to suppress a nervous smile. Robert looked down at his feet. Efraim leaned forward, ready to take notes. Moshe rocked back in his seat. He was having fun, ready with his next question, like a lawyer leading his prey down the wrong path.

"I don't have to justify anything to you. What's the difference anyway?" Red pouted.

Moshe took a sip of water from a glass in front of him and held up his index finger as if lecturing Red. "We have a saying in this country that I think applies here. 'Ask about your neighbors, *then* buy the house.' Understand?"

But Red wouldn't give in. "Not really, Moshe. I'm not selling real estate or anything else for that matter. This is just a debriefing, and I don't see how our personal lives matter. *Understand*?"

Moshe responded, "You may not be selling real estate. But for us to provide you vith information, ve need to make sure your interests are not tainted. It's not like Jake is CIA. He's a private citizen. My young friend, you vant information from me, I need to know more about who I'm talking to and vhy you are really here. Get it?"

Red paused for few seconds and then blurted, "Jake. I came because of Jake." She looked at Jake, who perked up and grinned.

Moshe didn't buy it though. "Bullshit! I know MI6, and they vouldn't let you go for that reason. You aren't even allowed to have any feelings! And vhat about him?" Moshe pointed at Robert.

Red looked away.

Moshe raised his voice. "You telling me MI6 let Robert come because of *your* concern about Jake?

Remember, you and Robert share, Jake shares, and then I share! Vant to try again?"

Red took a gulp of water. "It's true I was called because of my case with Jake. I wanted to come. I was crushed by the news." She looked over at Jake. "But it's also true that my boss, Monty, wanted me to go. Have you ever heard of Rift Valley or Lake Turkana?" Red proceeded to relay her story about the Mogobishi tribe being wiped out by the Mustavi tribe.

Efraim chimed in. "That kind of stuff happens all the time in Africa."

Red said, "True, but the one survivor told the Kenyan authorities he saw a white man leading the Mustavi tribesman as they wiped out his friends and family. His last words before he died were 'the white man cometh.' Well, through my investigation—excuse me, *our* investigation—we determined that the real killer was anthrax, not arrows shot by the tribe. We even traced the strain of anthrax to the same kind embedded in dead rodents buried in Anthrax Island. You know, by the Aral Sea."

"Interesting," Moshe said.

"And wanna know the most bizarre part?"

Everybody nodded their heads and leaned forward—even Moshe.

"I, *we*, went back to Lake Turkana. And we talked to the Mustavi. I drew a sketch based upon their description. Guess who they identified as the white man?"

Red looked at Jake and said, "None other than Saddam Hussein. They don't know Saddam, of course. They don't get any news down there. But they described him to a tee! I even confirmed it by showing them a picture of him I had downloaded on the satellite phone we were carrying."

The group ordered food while they contemplated what Red revealed. Jake was on the hot seat next.

Moshe looked at him and said, "Jake, now it's your turn. Red share. *You* share."

Red admired the way he was managing the meeting. *So different than Monty*. She also wanted to know what Jake knew.

"And if I share, you share, as you said to Red?" Jake said, looking at Moshe. "Is that how this works? One big, happy family, right? Except I'm the one who almost lost his head, and so far you're the one who's asking all the questions. Doesn't sound fair. I'll tell you my story, but I want you to look me in the eye and tell me you won't back down from telling us what you know after. Deal?"

Efraim and Moshe looked at Jake closely. Red smiled and looked first at Jake and then at Moshe.

Moshe said, "Agreed. I talk next. OK?"

Jake said, "You know about my story?"

Moshe replied, "I think so, but how did you get involved in it?"

"My paper, actually. At first I didn't like the assignment. I thought of it as a dead-end story. Former senior advisor to the president and chief of police of the NYPD now working for the *New York Times International Edition*. I figured they were either testing or turkey farming me."

Efraim said, "What do you mean, eh...turkey farming?"

"Sorry, that's my years in the government coming out. It is hard to fire somebody working for Uncle Sam. Too much paperwork, you know? Union's too strong. So a lot of people who *should* get the ax are instead relegated to some position where they can do no harm. The hope is that they'll quit out of boredom."

Moshe said, "Like somebody vorking for your FBI being sent to count cattle in Texas?"

"Exactly. I figured the paper was just testing me, hoping I'd quit. I'm sure some higher-up at the paper thinks I got the job because POTUS called in some favors after I—excuse me, Red and I—saved his life. Truth is, I decided to change careers. I couldn't work for the government anymore.

"In any case, the assignment grew on me. What happened to all of the doubles? Did they get executed? Are they working? Do they have jobs? The human element of it piqued my interest."

"How many doubles are there?"

"I'm not sure, but Jabal told me there were about four. He didn't seem too sure, though."

"He let you interview him?"

"Yes, but then something made him freak out. I mean, he didn't like me from the beginning, but then he...snapped."

"Vhat?" asked Moshe.

"Ah, I'm not sure."

"Come on, Jake. I can read you like a book."

Jake hesitated but then said, "I told him about meeting with his mom, Aisha, in their apartment. That surprised him. It must have hit too close to home for him."

Moshe pressed. "But he knew you vere investigating him. Is it that much of a stretch to have visited his home looking for him?"

"Yes, but Aisha gave me a note. I didn't say I had it, but I think he knew."

"Note?"

"Yes. Here it is." He showed the group the note. They took a few minutes to read it.

Efraim said, "Wow, I don't know why they let you keep it. You'd think they would've taken it from you."

"Believe me, I thought about that a lot. They never searched me other than for bulky weapons, though. Strange, but it's true. They weren't the brightest bunch of guys."

"How does the note tie to the massacre in Africa?" Efraim stated the obvious question. Moshe began to say something, but Efraim spoke over him and continued, "What if the double in Africa cut a deal with the Mustavi tribe?"

Red snorted. "Like, what, you mean they become his mercenaries in exchange for slaughtering the rival tribe?"

Efraim said weakly, "Sure, why not?"

Moshe addressed him directly. "That doesn't make any sense. The double, vhether Jabal or someone else, vouldn't have to go through all that effort to hire mercenaries. There is a whole network of disaffected Baathists alrcady champing at the bit to join the fight. No, this goes deeper."

A brief silence ensued until Moshe stood and began pacing. He said excitedly, "Ah! Vhat if vhat happened down there vas an experiment—to see if the anthrax vould vork. And the double used the Mustavi to finish them off vith arrows to throw off the authorities. Are you guys following me?"

Robert conceded, "Yes, that makes sense. That's what Red and I discussed before as a possible theory."

Moshe cut him off, talking faster. "But it goes deeper than that. Agree? The note speaks to something that vould be difficult to achieve vith anthrax. Note speaks to the resurrection of his people, the Baathists, and teaching a lesson to the infidels. Anthrax vouldn't achieve this, at least not easily. You'd need a lot of the stuff to achieve something significant. It's not contagious like a cold or other virus. One has to inhale or eat the spores. It's possible to infect a few, but you vould need too much of the stuff to kill a bunch of people. Something else might be employed, but anthrax isn't exactly the best veapon to use to achieve resurrection. See?"

Red chimed in, "That's been in the back of my mind. It is also difficult to reproduce in high quantities. And they used some of their stockpile on the tribe. I agree—something doesn't add up."

"A mystery," Jake said. "And one with catastrophic implications." The others nodded in agreement.

Jake looked at Moshe and said, "What do you have for us?"

Moshe leaned forward in his chair and replied, "Ve've been tracking the whereabouts of senior Baath party members for a while and picked up some chatter that could have been your man. Ve don't have a lot of solid evidence, but ve've learned from their communications about a planned shipment possibly going to America through a port. Not sure if this is related, but it's a rabbit hole you might vant to enter."

Jake said, "Any idea of what it is?"

Moshe said, "No, but I would start by looking into Jabal's background. Ve'll continue to monitor their communications, but you guys vill have to do the rest. It seems this is more of an American issue. I'm glad MI6 is involved. And I vill let you guys coordinate vith your counterparts at the CIA vhen you're ready. I know how it is—too many cooks can screw up the broth. You decide and run vith this one. Ve've got enough problems on our...how do you say...plate—yes?"

***

Jake, Red, and Robert met privately over dinner that night in the lobby of the historic King David Hotel. The hotel, with its pink quartz exterior, dates back to 1931. It was partially destroyed when bombed in 1946, but it was then rebuilt to its glory. Heads of state and other dignitaries frequent the premises. And tonight, mixed in with the dignitaries were two spies and their partner in crime, Jake.

The Mossad, which was paying for the accommodations, had stocked their rooms with clothes and toiletries, knowing none of them came prepared to visit the upscale hotel. Jake didn't have any provisions, his clothes being in Damascus at the Farzat Hotel, owned by Leatherneck's cousin, Ahmad Farzat. Red had only packed a simple change of clothes before meeting Moshe and his crew to rescue Jake.

Red used a pocket-sized meter, checking the three separate rooms for bugs. She located twelve, three on their clothes and nine in the rooms. "Par for the course," she told Jake.

Robert said, "Hard to blame 'em. Good fellas, they are. We'd do the same."

Jake rested in his room before meeting Robert and Red downstairs for dinner. He couldn't believe Red was staying next door. *True, she saved my life. But can I work with her again? She seems distant. But is that because she knows I haven't forgiven her?*

He poured the brandy he found stocked in the mini-fridge over ice and walked out onto his balcony. The old city beamed in the distance. He knew he would have to work with her, but that didn't mean he had forgotten what she had done.

He perused the clothing purchased for him. Funny, he thought, how his only dinner options consisted of clothing he would wear when dressing up, looking his best. Leather shoes, white collared shirt, paired with a brown sport jacket and beige dress pants. Moshe supplied him with a razor blade and aftershave, located prominently next to the sink. He would have to avoid the spots on his face that were still bruised, but he relished the idea of a close shave. *What are you trying to tell me, Moshe?*

Jake walked to the hotel's restaurant, which overlooked colorful sculpted gardens and pristine pools. Red was already at the table when Jake arrived.

She had on a red mini dress with shiny black high-heeled shoes. She said, "Can you believe this is what Moshe bought for me to wear? He even left me perfume. Don't worry, I didn't use it! The only other outfit isn't something I could wear to dinner at a hotel like this."

Jake grunted.

Red continued, "And look at you! Is that what he left for you? You look a lot better than the last time he dressed you up."

Jake tried not to laugh, practically biting his lip, but he couldn't help himself.

He said, "Where's Robert? He should be here."

"Oh...he's got a headache. He gets these migraines. Real bad. He ordered room service."

"Ha, sure," Jake said with a twinkle in his eye.

"Honest, Jake. Scout's honor."

"Scout's honor? Now I know you're not telling the truth. Do they even have Boy or Girl Scouts in Britain?"

"Jake, why is it that you Americans think you've monopolized everything? You *obviously* don't know, but scouting started in Britain, and it still runs strong today. But now that we're alone, we can talk more freely. Don't you think?"

"Sure, why not. You got something to say?" Jake fidgeted in his seat.

The waiter brought menus, and a busboy followed with bread and olive oil. Red reached for the bread while Jake buried his head in his menu.

Red dipped her bread into the oil and casually said, "I have a feeling this may get a whole lot worse. Why don't you stand down? Write your story. I'll fill you in. You've already gotten captured once, and I don't..."

Jake put down his menu hard, accidently bumping into the candle in the middle of the table, and stared at her. "Don't..."

Red interrupted, "Don't? Don't? You almost got decapitated. You're no longer in the game, Jake. When was the last time you even shot a gun?"

Jake responded by raising his voice. "Red, I'm not trying to arrest anybody! I'm a reporter, for God's sake. I'm just interviewing and writing a story. You really think I'm in danger? Fine, I'll be more cautious. I'll stay in the background."

Red spoke in a calm voice. "Jake, lower your voice and relax. I just don't want something to happen to you. That's all. I care. I..."

Jake wanted to make a snide remark in return but held back. She was right, after all. He couldn't protect himself. Leatherneck wasn't even able to do that, and now he was dead.

Red surveyed her menu and then put it down.

The waiter returned. Red ordered the sea bass, lightly spiced and served over couscous. Jake ordered the seared scallops.

Jake was quick to refuse any wine, a peace offering to the abstinence Red displayed last time the two were together. They settled on bottled water.

Neither were in the mood for small talk. Red broke the ice first. "I took something back where they were keeping you in Damascus. Moshe doesn't even know. I don't fully trust him. He seems like he's holding back."

"You took something? In the middle of all that fighting?"

"You realize I was guarding the perimeter, right? That was my role. And yes, I had the opportunity before I became entangled, and I slid a book..."

Jake didn't let her finish. "A book? You stole a book? What's wrong with you? Felt you needed something for the plane?"

Red laughed. "Let me explain, you dolt. Are you familiar with the Punic Wars?"

"The what?"

"Salting the earth. Ever hear of that expression?" Red asked.

"No, I can't say that I have. And besides, what does that have to do with the book you took?"

"It may be nothing, and I didn't think it was worth discussing until we learned more. I saw two copies of the same book just outside where they were holding you. You know, where you caught up to me? Anyway, the book is on the history of the Punic Wars."

Jake asked, "So what is this salting the earth?"

Red answered, "Interesting history at play here. You've heard of Hannibal, right?"

"Lecter?"

"Really? Hannibal Lecter the Punic War general? No, you silly man. The great Carthaginian general. Do you even know who the Carthaginians are? You bloody Americans need to think outside of your little pond. There's other people in the world, you know."

Jake said, "Why didn't you just say that? Of course, the Carthaginians. The guys who fought in the Punic Wars."

Red looked in Jake's eyes. "You're such a dolt. One minute you never heard of it, and the next minute you're an expert. Yes, *those* guys. They took on the Romans in three separate adventures, fighting over land and islands located not too far away from here, as a matter of fact—in and around Italy, Spain, and Tunisia. The Romans whooped them in the first war but suffered some defeats at the hands of Hannibal, who invaded Italy, in the second. By the third war, they had enough."

Jake leaned forward. "What happened?"

"They captured the city of Carthage, the center of the Carthaginian empire—a grave threat to the Punic culture. They were a tad pissed, you might say. Defeat wasn't enough. Legend has it that they cursed the land by salting the earth."

Jake said softly. "You mean with actual salt? How would they get enough to do this? It's absurd."

"You're probably right. Salt was a valuable commodity back then. It's a bit of an allegory. What they really did was to scorch the earth by razing the city. Kind of like what your General Sherman did in the Civil War by burning everything in his march through Georgia to the sea, chasing those pesky rebels.

"Well, the Romans did the same thing. They burned the city to the ground. Then they built it back up from scratch, this time under Roman control. The ultimate revenge and then resurrection, you might say."

"And you think that Jabal and his clan have something like that in mind?"

"It's possible."

"But isn't it also possible that one of the doubles or henchmen is a history buff?"

"Oh, I'm sure they like history. And yes, that could account for one of the books. But two of the same books? I think that is more than just a coincidence. And you yourself said you didn't think they were too bright."

Jake thought about it and then asked, "Is that what led you to encourage Moshe's thinking this isn't really about anthrax? That anthrax is a pretext for something larger?"

"Yes and no. I would've had my doubts even without discovering the book. The book just made the case stronger."

"Why didn't you mention this to Moshe?"

"What? You notice how he tries to control everything? He'd take it over. You know how this works, right? Moshe already suspects this goes deeper. He's willing to let MI6 take the lead...for now. Mention the book and we'll have the Mossad up our asses so deep that a plunger will not even work. Don't mention the book, and we just have to deal with them bastards bugging our rooms."

The food came, and they ate in relative silence. Neither of them dared to venture beyond a few polite requests to pass the bread, butter, salt, and pepper. Red caught Jake looking at her once, but when she reciprocated, he quickly looked away.

For dessert they ordered baklava, strudel, and European coffee. As they were eating, Jake asked, "So where do we go from here, Red?"

She said, "Well, that's a loaded question, don't you think?" She laughed, but Jake didn't. Red continued, "As I said before, I think you ought to leave this to the pros. This could get nasty."

"Pros? Really? You forget I was a detective for many years and then ran the NYPD, with a budget that was probably bigger than your ceremonial Queen's secret service. I also advised the president, a man much more powerful than your smug PM, on national security matters."

She laughed. "Touché, mister secret agent man. But you have to admit that you're on your own, whereas I have the backing of my smug PM and ceremonial Queen." She added in a more serious tone, "If you continue to insist on working on this, why don't we work together then?"

"Like the last time?" He glared.

"Professionally, of course. Robert and I will use our resources to look at the whole network. I have a feeling this goes deeper than Jabal. Remember, one of the dead guys also looked like a double. I'll get the tape we took of the dead guys from Moshe. You should concentrate on Jabal. Moshe suggested we look into his background. Deal?"

"What about my story and editor?"

"Tell them they'll get the exclusive if they don't print anything until we're ready. Deal?"

They shook on it and then headed upstairs after adding the bill and hefty tip onto Moshe's tab.

Chapter 13
Washington

J ake landed at Dulles, exhausted from the flight
back from Israel. He couldn't sleep on the plane.
His face and body still hurt. His thoughts were filled
with a mixture of rage, confusion, longing.

A taxi dropped Jake in front of his building, a ten-
story white brick building located near Adams
Morgan, a block down from Connecticut Avenue. Jake
moved to Adams Morgan as part of his rebirth after
resigning from his post as senior advisor to the
president.

Jake had become something of a celebrity after
helping to save President Tucker's life. Tucker was
smart enough to realize that Jake's actions, although
questionable because of the risks he took, had
ultimately saved Tucker's life. He sang Jake's praises
to all who would listen.

Tucker didn't know, however, that the event and
his praise had provided the catalyst Jake needed to
escape the Washington machinery. At first, joining the
Tucker administration was an interesting and
provocative challenge. And, he was part of the
winning team, after helping then-Senator Tucker
capture the presidency.

But it didn't take long after Tucker's first term began for the required horse trading, twisting promises, and truth spinning to slowly wear Jake down. Being a newspaper reporter had been a career Jake thought about pursuing since college. The opportunity to unravel mysteries, objectively report uncomfortable facts, and safeguard against naysayers was more noble than kowtowing to the power structure. It also brought Jake full circle from his first real job as a detective.

The door to Jake's condo squeaked as it opened. He heard a loud thump emanating from within and proceeded with caution.

Jake turned on the lights. Charming, his Javanese cat, spied him from the side of the couch. Jake could see Charming's piercing blue eyes, slender body, elegant beige coat.

He was usually playful but, like a petulant dog, didn't like being left alone. Charming's revenge—a tipped-over plant, scattered papers, and spilled cat food and water—didn't upset Jake. Jake missed his cat and could hear him purr. Charming settled down on the recliner next to the couch, Jake's invitation to sit and then for the cat to jump onto his lap. Jake hesitated and then assumed his rightful position.

**

Jake called Joseph Brommer, his editor, the next day. Joseph had read the recap of Jake's experience that he had emailed him while in Israel. Jake emphasized the arrangement he made with Red, and Joseph liked having a secret agent as the paper's new exclusive source. The editor agreed to not print anything about the case until Jake and Red were ready, but he gave them only two weeks.

Jake accepted, knowing that he would be able to push for an additional extension if needed. Editors, after all, were like athletic coaches: they knew not to push their star players out the door. And his story, now exclusive to the paper, was big, potentially very big.

Jake entered the search term "Jabal Shamoon" into his computer's web browser, seeking to create an outline of Jabal's life and service as a Saddam double. He hoped for anything that could shed light on his plans, friends, other doubles, and their whereabouts.

A few hits instantly appeared in light blue, green, and black lettering. Several of the hits were of people living in the United States and Europe. The remaining links were to people who didn't look anything like Jabal. For kicks, Jake Googled Aisha Shamoon. Nothing. He struck out on all accounts.

Next, Jake looked into Saddam. Millions of hits emerged. Not surprising. Then it dawned on him: *Some of these pictures might actually be Jabal.*

Charming approached, wisely deciding to watch instead of intervene. He knew his boundaries.

Jake compiled a chronological listing of all available photos, using software he had downloaded for the task. Jake blew up each in the highest resolution available and examined them closely. Each had the obvious characteristics: jet-black hair, large exposed ears, pudgy face, two cheek moles, elongated forehead.

It was painstaking work. Jake began measuring the angles and length of eyebrows, foreheads, noses, lips. He also recorded the width of eyes. The differences in image sizes made the work difficult but not impossible. Developing a scale helped. He had a headache after a few hours, but eventually he began to notice a pattern.

It helped when Jake realized photos of Saddam early in his presidency were more discernable. It took many years for his security detail to perfect the art of impersonation.

Saddam had a pronounced lisp. His doubles rarely spoke in public. Pictures taken at engagements, showcasing an important speech, were usually of the real Saddam.

Jake also noticed the real Saddam had a mole above his left eye, straight set of teeth, dimple in the middle of his small chin, elongated forehead. While some of the features were easy to duplicate, others were more difficult. A mole could be modeled but not a dimple, at least not without extensive plastic surgery. And plastic surgery carried the risk of discoloration and difference in aging, the same problem that painters have when patching a wall.

By the end of the first day, Jake developed a file of about fifty photos he knew were of the real Saddam. Jake stood up and stretched, proud of his accomplishment. His reward? A break and then Chinese food. Moo shu chicken could be enjoyed at any hour of the day or night. Charming joined him for some scraps and a quick volley of petting.

The next day, Jake began sorting the photos he thought were probably not of the real Saddam. About one hundred photos populated the "possible non-Saddam" file. He began sorting this pile into different categories, with more measuring of foreheads, angles, noses, lips.

A few hours later, he had developed six different buckets in his non-Saddam collection. Jabal had told Jake in Damascus he thought there were four doubles, but he didn't sound confident in his answer. Six was not out of the question.

Before proceeding further, Jake wanted to validate his work. Since doubles were most likely used in photo ops or other nonspeaking engagements, he hoped each of the six buckets in the non-Saddam portfolio were of photo ops or nonspeaking engagements.

By the end of the day, he had his answer. The process worked, confirming the accuracy of his work with a ninety percent correlation of the non-Saddam buckets to photo ops or other nonspeaking engagements. He was ready for the final step, which he would begin the next day.

On the third day, Jake tried to determine which of the six buckets represented Jabal. Charming offered him purrs of encouragement while he was contemplating how to do this. Identifying Jabal from the doppelgängers would not be easy.

Then he remembered Jabal's birthmark on his right shoulder, just below his neck. It was a long shot, but it might work.

Jake studied the neckline he could see in the photos from each bucket. In the last group of photos, the skin in the exposed neckline appeared darker in the area of the birthmark compared to the rest of the skin. The painter analogy again entered his head. Another clue was that, compared to the other five buckets, the last cluster contained fewer photos showing the neckline.

He now had a likely candidate for Jabal. As a final step, he looked at the photos Moshe sent of the dead double from Damascus. He confirmed his picture was different from what he now believed were photos in the last bucket of Jabal.

Jake was feeling confident but exhausted. He left the photos he had printed scattered on his kitchen table and flopped onto his bed next to Charming for a good night of sleep.

***

Jake awoke and put on a pair of shorts and a running shirt. The elevator took him to the lobby, where his doorman, a lanky Ethiopian named Dawit, greeted Jake with a broad smile and said, "Good mornin', Mr. Kessler." They talked about the upcoming Redskins season until Jake bid Dawit farewell. The temperature was already hovering around seventy degrees, and it was only 8:00 a.m. It would reach ninety by noon.

Jake put on his headphones, cranked up the volume to the classics, and headed for Rock Creek Park. Like Central Park, Rock Creek offered both refuge and recreation to the gamut of Washingtonians—from the homeless to guys like Jake. Its wooded areas offered shade. Its streams, forests, and rock bridges offered beauty, and its occupants reciprocated in demonstrating that life doesn't always have to be stressful.

After a few paces, he slowed down to reduce the pain in his sore body. A brisk walk would have to do; maybe he could jog in a few days. At least he was able to relax.

Jake thought about Red. *Was I being too hard on her? She didn't have to rescue me.* He also thought about his new career. *Am I willing to risk my life for this? Have I reached the point of no return?*

Jake reached the halfway point and turned back toward his building.

***

Charming looked at Jake upon his return. Jake tended to Charming's needs and then returned to the photos on his kitchen table. Today he wanted to focus on Jabal.

It took him a couple of hours to sort the images chronologically. Jake noticed Jabal was usually the most serious of the doubles. He never smiled. Although the real Saddam often didn't look happy, he at least showed some range of emotion.

The pictures Jake had of Jabal ranged from the year 1995 until early 2003 when Saddam went into hiding. The Americans discovered his spider hole in December 2003.

Most of the images of Jabal were at domestic events ranging from public works projects to visits to military installations or parades. Jake didn't notice many international events. Maybe a more senior double was assigned those trips.

Three of the images stood out among all the others. In one, he was inspecting what looked like chemical facilities at the Iraqi National Laboratories. In the second, Jabal was dressing in protective gear, ready to enter the Tuwaitha nuclear complex located approximately twelve miles south of Baghdad. The final picture was of Jabal in an unidentified underground bunker.

Jake finished classifying and studying the photos two hours later. The glory he felt the day before was replaced by a sinking feeling that he was wasting his time, spinning his wheels round and round. Sure, he had learned about Jabal's life as a double, but would the clues be of any use?

Chapter 14
London

The morning after Red dined with Jake in Jerusalem, the two MI6 agents left for the airport in Israel to take an early flight to London. While in the taxi, Red thought about how relieved she was that she had rescued him, while at the same time sickened by what could have happened had she not arrived with seconds to spare. If she had failed, she would have been driven deeper into her personal abyss.

She enjoyed talking to Jake and remembering happier times while they were together. Jake may be ready to forgive her, eventually. *But am I ready, and would forgiveness even matter? Would he follow through on his promise to stay in the background? Would I have to try to rescue him again?*

Robert was in a foul mood. He started in with Red as soon as their taxi dropped them off and they were alone in the airport café. "Why didn't you tell Moshe about the book you found?"

Nag, nag, nag, she thought.

She leaned over the dirty table and said softly, "Don't be such a pisser, Robert. I didn't lie. I just didn't tell him everything."

Robert whispered, "True, but that would confirm his theory about this not being about anthrax. The book explains what they're thinking, don't you think?"

"Don't be an arse. I have my reasons. Trust me when I say this: We don't want the Mossad interfering at this point. They did their job helping us in Syria, but this is our investigation."

***

The next day, Red entered the Central Line station on her way to meet Monty. It was crowded, but she immediately heard the unmistakable sound of Jasper's saxophone blasting a tune that even she recognized, the solo from *Jungle Land*. Jasper greeted her after his solo ended and then gently patted his stomach. She produced a bowl of his chicken fry and left him alone to enjoy his feast.

Twenty minutes later, she was sitting across from a scowling Monty seated uncomfortably behind his desk. Robert was sitting next to her. She wore a loose-fitting leopard print blouse with a bright orange miniskirt.

Monty, still in the closet with his sexuality, continued with his awkward mannerisms while working for the type A, macho-driven MI6. He could end the madness by coming clean and divorcing his wife, releasing her and everybody else from the sham.

Monty's wife was a real porker who kept a tight leash on her dog. Red imagined she didn't know his true preferences, and he tolerated her control to suit his cover. He used the office as his escape, arriving early with a pastry and coffee in tow. He dawdled at the end of the day, leaving late, even if it meant playing solitaire alone on his computer.

Today he didn't even say hello, a sign of trouble to come. Instead, he said, "Did you have fun on your little sideshow trip?"

Red wasn't in the mood. She leaned forward, making sure her blouse separated from her body. Her verbal response went too far. "Sideshow? I don't *need* to *travel* to give or participate in any sideshow."

Robert suppressed a laugh, although he couldn't have any idea she was serious.

Monty replied, "Let's get down to business, shall we? After you returned from Africa, GCHQ decoded a communication we believe occurred right after the massacre." GCHQ, which stands for Government Communications Headquarters, is responsible for providing signals intelligence for the British government, including MI6.

Government Communications Headquarters

"And?" she asked.

"The communication confirms what the Mustavi tribe told you—that the white man looked like Saddam."

"Jabal?" she asked.

"Yes and no, my lady. It was someone with an Arabic accent. It could've been Jabal, but it could've also been another double."

"By Arabic, can you be more specific?" Red chided.

Monty glared at Red. "Regardless of which double it was, we know who he took his orders from."

"You going to tell us, or keep us in suspense?" She detested Monty's flexing. *Get on with it already.*

"He talked to Sasha Krupin right after the massacre. You may have never heard of him by that name. You are probably familiar with his alias, the Wolf. Here, look at this." Monty tossed each of them a manila folder with the words *Top Secret* written in red boldface on the outside.

Red had always thought this naming process to be idiotic. If you're trying to protect the Queen's secrets, why label a document with a subject heading that strangers looking to identify material to steal can understand?

"You didn't find out much," Robert pointed out.

"Yes, our information is a bit sketchy. But here's what we do know. Study the file, and then let's discuss it tomorrow."

Chapter 15
London

The two agents returned to Monty's office the next day. They had studied the files, verified what they could on their own in the short period of time, and were ready to discuss.

Red commented first, "The Wolf's file is pretty sparse, especially the past fifteen years."

"We think he went under deep cover, even changed his appearance. Nobody has seen him. He never married and has no family. He's very difficult to track. Our first clue he was still operating happened when Putin annexed Crimea in 2014 and then fomented unrest in eastern Ukraine. Your dossier has a few pictures taken by Ukrainian intelligence of a person who would be about the Wolf's age, sixty-two, giving orders. They think he might be the Wolf, judging by some distinct facial features. We agree," Robert said.

Red leaned back for a little stretch and asked, "And you think the Wolf was the person talking to Jabal or another double in the discussion GCHQ intercepted? How would the Wolf have slipped up so badly?"

Monty shrugged his shoulders and leaned in, trying to impress the agents with his importance, as if he was revealing top secret information that only he possessed. "Our analysis of the vocals confirms the voice is likely that of the Wolf. They spoke in code, but it was easy to figure out. They kept the discussion short, and don't tell this to GCHQ, but it's amazing they found it. The Wolf probably thought he took enough precautions. We think it took place immediately after the massacre. Listen to what we have on tape."

Monty faced his computer, pressed some keys, and they listened to the discussion in Arabic, following along with their English translations.

> *Double: "The party went well. Our guests drank a little too much, though, and went to bed early. I just checked on them. They're in a deep sleep."*
>
> *Wolf: "Did everybody have fun? Was the wedding a success?"*
>
> *Double: "Yes, it went as planned. Everybody arrived on time, including the folk singer."*
>
> *Wolf: "Did people dance?"*
>
> *Double: "Of course! They were dancing by the time she arrived. People were chanting. They didn't even need the singer to get them going. They were in such a good mood."*
>
> *Wolf: "Terrific! I'm glad to hear that. You cleaned up or just left?"*
>
> *Double: "We cleaned as much as we could in the time we had and left."*
>
> *Wolf: "Great, good job. Why don't you return home? I'll call you soon."*

"It's brilliant they found this, a forty-second conversation," Robert said.

Monty beamed. "Yes, a good find, indeed."

Red jumped in, thinking about what was being overlooked. "Hold on, fellas. Hate to bring a womanly touch to this. But don't you think you're moving a little too fast here? We know the Wolf was high up in the KGB and in Russia's intelligence services. He also has deep financial ties to Russia's military contractors and was helping advance Russian interests in Ukraine. Wouldn't he have access to phones that can't be traced? I mean, we're not talking about the Russian Revolution ages ago or some terrorist organization you might watch on the telly news. We're talking about a high official with experience working for very sophisticated intelligence services."

Monty looked at Red like she was his mom breaking up a teen party. "Well, I thought about that, Red."

Oh, sure you did, Red thought.

He continued smugly, "GCHQ told me they didn't want to risk using the latest and best Russian equipment."

"Meaning?" she asked.

"They didn't want to take any chance on being traced back to Russia. There's not a lot about the Wolf out there. It's difficult to directly tie him to the Russian government, especially if he and his cronies don't use the more sophisticated Russian equipment. And there's lots of the older stuff out there."

Touché, Red thought. At least Monty asked the right question and the answer seemed plausible.

"But let's talk about the code, shall we?" She looked down at the English transcript in front of her. "For starters, how many tribesmen make international calls after a party in the bush?"

They laughed. Monty said, "That's a good way of putting it. It does sound strange hearing you say it that way. But remember, we don't know precisely where the call took place. It could've been made in a nearby town. GCHQ picks up conversations all the time with people in remote areas. And they used a wedding as a cover. Smart move on their part. People travel to weddings of important tribesmen, some even with cell phones. It's not that unusual."

"But do they use people from outside their own village? Jabal sounds like an outsider—like a party planner!"

Monty had enough. "Don't get your knickers in a twist, Red. You know this business. Not everything is easily explained. It's plausible they would communicate this way, and yes, I agree, strange and somewhat cavalier. But that's our business and that's why we need you to investigate this guy, the Wolf. If you want certainty, I'll transfer you to accounting."

Robert chimed in, trying to break up their little row. "And this also corresponds to what we discussed with Moshe and Jake."

"How so?" Monty asked.

"Well, think about it. The working theory is that anthrax is not the endgame. It may be part of the story but it might just be a diversion. At first I didn't believe in the theory." He looked at Red when he said this next part. "Red, I didn't say anything when we talked to Moshe about it, but I wasn't convinced. I mean, Jabal's small-time. Aisha even conceded he wasn't the smartest. Guys like that threaten catastrophe all the time and rarely achieve anything other than a few meaningless deaths."

Red said, "But now you agree because of the Wolf?"

"Yes," Robert said. "The Wolf's involvement is a game changer, you've got to admit. A guy like that has resources, experience, connections all the way to Putin. This is not a good development."

Red added, "Not to mention that Jabal is the perfect tool for the Wolf to manipulate. I mean, poor Jabal happily served as Saddam's double."

The three of them nodded their heads in agreement.

They took a break as Monty had to use the loo, and they reconvened a few minutes later.

Monty took the initiative. "I have an idea."

Red and Robert looked at him, expecting one of his usual lame schemes. Monty was a decent administrator, but that is where his talents ended.

IIe explained while Red looked at him with growing horror.

Even his male coconspirator was alarmed. "Don't you think that is a bit audacious?"

Monty looked down at his desk and then immediately up at them, recoiling from the sight of the crumbs from his morning biscuit. "Do you have a better idea? We need to cut the head off the snake. And then we go after the body."

Robert and Red looked at each other. "You've got to admit, Red. It could work," he said.

"No way."

Monty said, "Don't let your feelings for him..."

"Feelings?" Red interrupted. "Don't talk to me about that. We're over. Besides, having an attachment is bad for business."

Red realized her mistake immediately after she finished.

Monty seized the opportunity. "Well, then there shouldn't be any issue."

Red stormed out of the room.

PART TWO
THE WOLF

Chapter 16
Ten Years Earlier:
Flagstaff, Arizona

Sally Shimmerman yelled, "Abe, get down here now! This is your last warning. If you miss the bus, you're in *big* trouble, mister!"

His twin brother, Shmuel, counted his blessings. He was already downstairs and knew his mom was upset—fortunately, not at him this time. Her use of the word *mister* was the telltale sign she was done playing games. Don't cross Momma. They were in the first grade at Raker Elementary School, and their mom insisted on their taking the bus.

Abe raced downstairs. "Sorry, Mom. What's the problem? I got plenty of time."

He always reacted that way, Shmuel thought. His brother's laziness and failure to listen would be Abe's downfall.

"I've been calling you for the past ten minutes! And now you barely have any time to eat. The bus picks up at 7:10."

"Ah, come on, Mom. She's never there at 7:10, usually 7:15. I got five more minutes," Abe replied.

Shmuel cowered on his side of the table. He didn't want his mom taking out her anger on him just because they were identical twins. Abe was the one acting up, after all.

Sally replied, "No you don't, and *don't* talk back to me."

"Yes, Mom," Abe replied as he shoved cereal into his mouth. Half the food came right back out, landing on the floor, his shirt, or the white kitchen table. Abe picked up some of the pieces as they fell before his mom could see them, but after a while it became an exercise in futility.

Sally shouted at Abe, "I hear it now. Quick. You better run!" Shmuel already had his backpack on, ready to race out the door.

Abe was still dawdling, a trait that drove his mom crazy. "Why can't you be more like your..." Sally stopped herself before saying the next word, but they both knew what she wanted to say. Shmuel smiled while Abe shot him a nasty look. The brothers, best friends, still had the usual sibling rivalry.

Abe slung his backpack onto his back, and the twins ran out the door together before saying good-bye.

Sally ran after them. "I love you guys! Remember, Abe, I'll pick you up at five after play practice. Shmuel, don't wait for your brother. Take the bus home as usual..." Her voice trailed as the twins reached the end of the driveway. Sally watched from the door, still in her nightgown.

***

The bus driver, Kylie Rotterdam, looked forward to seeing the twins board her bus every day. They were just the cutest with their straight black hair, dimples, and freckles. And there were two of them! She had difficulty telling them apart, like most people.

She wondered where Sally was. She was usually at the stop dropping the kids off, kissing them on their cheeks as the bus approached. Shmuel usually accepted the attention while Abe cowered in embarrassment. Kylie finally spotted Sally by the door and waved.

***

"Hey, bro," Shmuel shouted to Abe. Abe was leaving math as Shmuel was entering. They could be together for lunchtime, homeroom, and gym, but their parents had asked the school to split them up for the remainder of the day. Fred had showed his decision-maker wife some articles highlighting twins who developed problems socializing with other people. Her boys were falling into the same dangerous pattern of becoming inseparable.

Their different personalities meshed perfectly together as if they were one. Alone, Shmuel was too hyper and outwardly focused, and Abe was too shy. Together, they had the perfect blend, like acid and alkaline neutralizing each other.

Abe punched Shmuel softly in the gut. Shmuel exhaled. "What'd you do that for, Abe?"

"It's not fair that I have to go to this stupid play practice while you get to go home and watch TV," Abe responded.

"Aw, shucks, you'll be fine. Just try it. I was Tin Man a few months ago. Remember? Now it's your turn. Isn't that what Mom said? Besides, I'd rather be Mr. Smee than the Tin Man any day of the week."

"Yeah, I guess you're right. Besides, *The Wizard of Oz* is for girls. I'm going to be in *Peter Pan*." Abe was feeling a little better. "I got to go," Abe said in a nasally drawl, beginning his slow walk to Ms. Harper's English class.

Shmuel returned home after school as expected. He took advantage of his thirty minutes of television, watching a cartoon, enjoying Oreo cookies and his mom's obligatory fruit, strawberries. Once his downtime was finished, he began playing soccer with his best friend and next-door neighbor, Jason. Jason's mom supervised the impromptu playdate, allowing Sally to fetch Abe from school.

Sally raced to the school. She was late as usual, busy running errands all day. The Fylermanns down the street knew to watch out for her, joking, "Here comes Momma Mafia!"

She pulled up to the curb at the school and waited. Five minutes went by. *That little troublemaker. I'm going to wring his neck*, she thought to herself.

Five additional minutes later, she screamed "Goddamn it!" and hoped the other moms hadn't heard her cuss. At least she didn't drop an F-bomb, and fortunately her windows were rolled up given the unusually hot weather.

She slammed her door and marched into the building. Other parents and kids were mingling in the theater room. She approached Mr. Thompson, a handsome man who Sally thought the children admired, but who also was the subject of her fantasies. She loved her husband, Fred, but his stomach was starting to bulge, and she knew a few years from now he would develop the same turkey-flap neck as his father. She was sure many of the other moms would admit to having the same thoughts. Women were women, despite social norms that suppressed their true feelings. *Why do men get to have all the fun?*

"Excuse me, Mr. Thompson, have you seen Abe?"

"Abe? He left a while ago. I was told you were picking him up. You haven't seen him?"

Briefly panicking, she blurted, "If I'd seen him...sorry. No. Hmm. Maybe my husband picked him up."

Sally dialed Fred's cell. *Come on, pick up!* He didn't answer. Sally dialed again. *Come on, you fuckin' lazy shit!* She alternated between being upset with

Abe for not being at his usual spot and *I'm going to kill my low-down husband who never answers his cell phone!*

She tried a third time. Still no answer. She and Mr. Thompson searched the rest of the school, but they couldn't locate Abe.

Sally hurried back to her car and raced home. No sign of Abe there.

Fred finally returned her calls. "Honey? You've been trying to reach me?"

She answered hysterically, "Yes, I have. Why don't you answer your phone? What good is it to have one if you don't answer? Huh? Huh? Do you have Abe?"

Fred, used to Sally's outbursts, replied calmly in monotone, "Honey, I'm at work. You're supposed to pick him up, remember?"

He obviously didn't understand the situation until Sally began screaming, crying, and panicking all at the same time.

Fred agreed to come home immediately. He arrived thirty minutes later, flying through the front door. "What is going on? You still haven't seen him?"

"No," Sally cried from her seat at the kitchen table.

"What about Shmuel?"

"No."

"Did you call all of his friends?"

Sally jumped up and began shouting, "Nobody, nobody has seen him, OK? If only I was there on time." She slumped back into the seat.

Fred walked over to her and gave her a big hug. Sally initially wanted to fend him off by punching him, but she accepted the empathy. "It's OK. It's not your fault. He'll show up. Maybe one of his friends' parents gave him a lift, you know?"

"We've got to call the police. It's already been an hour and a half."

The police arrived fifteen minutes later and asked the same questions of Sally that Fred asked her before.

Amber Alerts were broadcast, causing cell phones to buzz at precisely the same time all over Arizona: 7:30 p.m. But it didn't work. No one responded.

***

The Flagstaff police department assigned Detective Ken Chalmers, a veteran of the force, to search for Abe. Chalmers had a pretty good record for solving missing children cases. Other municipalities located in the same county as Flagstaff, Coconino County, often pined for his services.

His messy upkeep belied his success as a detective. Not only was he out of shape, needing to lose more than a few pounds, but he didn't even make an effort to dress appropriately. His partner, Steve Smitters, had to remind him that he missed a middle button on his brown uniform, exposing his white undershirt, and to tuck in the bottom before he met the Shimmermans. His hair, fortunately covered by his Stetson, had looked like a pile of randomly cut pieces found in the corner of a barbershop,

Chalmers knew the meeting wouldn't go well. He never had good news three weeks after a child had gone missing. He and Smitters knocked on the door. Smitters, promoted to detective three years ago, let his veteran colleague do the talking.

Sally answered the door. She looked dirty, and her hair was a mess. Chalmers had witnessed the same pattern many times.

"Good morning, ma'am," Chalmers said in his Southern drawl, cheeks bulging from the wad of chewing tobacco squirreled away in his mouth.

She nodded and let him in. Fred emerged from the basement. It was obvious to Chalmers that he had been sleeping there—also part of the pattern.

"Ma'am, sir, you may want to sit down for this," he said.

No pleasantries were needed; no coffee was offered. He knew to get right to the point—they were already crying and moving around on the couch.

"We found a body," Chalmers said.

Sally screamed before he finished the sentence, as short as it was, and making matters worse, he noticed Shmuel creeping down the stairs, probably after hearing his mom's hysterics.

Fred shouted to him, "Son, go to your room, now!" Fred reached to hug Sally, but she turned and pushed him away.

Chalmers sensed Fred was blaming Sally in private but covering it up by playing the supportive spouse in public. He had seen it happen before and was glad to see Sally sticking up for herself.

Chalmers continued. "Two boys were playing in the woods at a park near Plano, Texas. A ball went into the woods, and they saw a patch of disturbed earth. It was obvious to them and us when we got there. Maybe too obvious. We're following up on that. Anyways, the body was badly burned, not recognizable. We did match the teeth, though, to Abe's teeth through his dental records. And we found these near the body." Chalmers held up a bag of Abe's clothes. He added lamely, "I'm very sorry. I'll leave you two alone. We'll talk later."

With that, Chalmers and Smitters left, and Fred went to fetch Shmuel. They buried Abe a few days later.

Chapter 17

Flagstaff, Arizona to the
Land of Baklava

But Abe didn't die. He was alive thousands of miles away. The kids playing in the woods near Plano, Texas, discovered the body of another boy, planted there. And Abe's dental records were switched to match the teeth of the boy found in the woods. A simple break-in to the dentist's office was all it took.

Abe had no clue where he was—how could he? He was only seven years old. He eventually remembered parts of what happened and learned the rest later.

***

Mr. Thompson had stopped play practice and addressed Abe. "Abe, I forgot to tell you. Your mom called the school earlier today. I received a note from the office. You need to leave practice ten minutes early, something about an appointment. Your mom will meet you outside. See you tomorrow." Mr. Thompson had, of course, followed this up with his traditional signal that the short one-way discussion was over: two staccato bursts of "bye, bye," followed with a flimsy wave of his right hand.

Abe started to speak, but the always busy Mr. Thompson had already turned his back to him. His mom had forgotten to tell him about an appointment before. A few weeks ago, his mom had made a dentist appointment at the same time that Abe had play practice. She apologized and said that when she booked the appointment she didn't realize at the time he would have practice.

Abe didn't put up a fight the time it happened before or this time. He didn't like practice to begin with and would rather be home anyway.

While waiting, a car drove up driven by a man and woman. The woman, who was in the back seat, rolled down the window and said in a sweet voice, "Abe, here. Over here. Remember us? I'm Mrs. Stevens, and over there is Mr. Stevens. He's your dad's cousin. It's been a few years. My you've grown! Remember? We saw you and your brother and parents at your house?"

Abe stared blankly. The Stevens didn't look remotely familiar, and the woman, with a narrow face and mangled hair, spoke in a strange accent. She tried to cool herself from the hot air rushing in through the window by waving her hand as a fan.

The man looked too big for the steering wheel and front seat. His body looked thick, and his hair was jet black. He had a full but groomed mustache and beard.

He cocked his head towards Abe and smiled weakly.

The woman continued, "Well, you were probably too young to remember. It doesn't matter. Anyways, we're in town for a few days and just helping your mom out. She had to take Shmuel to the dentist, you know him, Dr. Palmer? Anyways, he has a toothache. She asked us to take *you* to your doctor, Dr. Adams. You've been there before, she said."

Abe didn't know what to do. He didn't remember them, and his parents told him not to get into a car with strangers. The woman also spoke kind of funny, not like people around his town.

But maybe the Stevens were not strangers after all. They seemed to know a lot about the family and their doctors. And Shmuel *did* complain of a toothache the day before. How would the Stevens know about that unless his mom told them? Mrs. Stevens explained they weren't from these parts, explaining her strange voice.

"Come on, Abe. Get in. We're going to be late," Mrs. Stevens said waving at him to get in the car. Mr. Stevens turned further around from the driver's seat, smiled deeper than he had before, and also waved.

Abe decided to go, ignoring the growing knot in his stomach, holding back his urge to take a sudden poop. He hopped into the car and they drove away. They seemed very nice, talking to him about sports and Shmuel. The car smelled like his dad's car when he used to smoke and then cover it up with a car deodorizer purchased from the local car wash. It was kind of gross, but he didn't complain.

The Stevens knew everything, including Abe's role as Mr. Smee in *Peter Pan*. He began to relax. They drove by the McDonald's that his mom took him to when they were running late on an errand or to an appointment, without dad in the car, of course. He didn't like going there.

The McDonald's whizzed by when a truck came out of nowhere, forcing their car to swerve. Mr. Stevens had to suddenly apply the brakes. Mrs. Stevens knocked into Abe as their car turned sharply before coming to a screeching halt. Abe felt a sudden pain in his head and left leg from when they collided -- and that was the last thing he remembered.

Mr. Stevens continued to drive the car, with Abe's head lying on his wife's bosom. Abe was stirring, sleepy and unaware, but still partially awake. She held his head firm, turning it away from the windows and putting an Arizona Diamondbacks baseball hat over his head. Abe mumbled something incomprehensible.

A few minutes later, they pulled into an industrial park in Flagstaff. Mr. Stevens signaled with his hand alerting two assistants to open the garage door. Mrs. Stevens took the boy's pulse and measured his blood pressure. Satisfied with the results, she inserted a small needle into Abe's forearm, starting a drip of Propofol and fluids.

The drip forced Abe into a deep coma-like sleep for the long journey. With Abe properly secured and ready for travel, they disconnected the drip and carried their patient into a different car in the garage.

They drove to a private airfield, where they boarded a Cessna that would take them across the border into Mexico.

"You filed the flight plan, correct?" Mr. Stevens barked at one of the assistants, a tall, slender, white man wearing baggy clothing. The assistant nodded, and Mr. Stevens began piloting the craft down the small runway.

Several hours later, and after applying another drip of anesthesia and fluids, they approached the border. A border control helicopter approached, trying to get a glimpse of what or who was inside.

"Don't worry. He's already run the numbers by the wing. They'd send the cavalry if there was an issue. I think he's just visually checking us out. Just make sure the boy appears to be merely sleeping, not in distress," Mr. Stevens said calmly.

The border control helicopter approached from a safe distance, spied on them, and left. After landing in Mexico, they traveled to the east coast, where they boarded a ship to Ukraine.

***

Abe heard a knock on the door, and then Mrs. Stevens walked into the room. She had a wide smile and carried a tray with his favorite breakfast cereal, Captain Crunch, and his favorite morning beverage, apple juice. She even had his favorite toast prepared just the way he liked – two pieces of white bread basted with a little butter and then sliced diagonally.

"Good morning, sunshine," she said as she approached the bed. "You slept a long time. Are you feeling better? Does your head still hurt?"

"Where's Mom and Dad and Shmuel?" Abe asked in a whiny voice.

Mrs. Stevens replied, "Honey, don't you remember what happened? We got into an accident on our way to see Dr. Adams. You're all right, don't worry about a thing. But you hit your head and need to rest. Your mom suggested we take you with us until you feel better. She even told me what you liked to eat."

"But..." Abe said in a confused voice.

She cut him off, "Now, I don't want you to worry about school or anything else for that matter. You'll be back home in no time, and Shmuel's been taking careful notes, so you won't miss anything." She felt his forehead and cheek. "Oh, my, you're burning up. Please drink some of the juice." She inserted the straw into his mouth and said, "I don't want you to worry about anything, okay? I just talked to your mom. That's how I knew what to feed you. Okay?"

Abe nodded after he was done drinking and then fell fast asleep. The same pattern continued for a few more days until he began to feel better. He remembered having several chats with the Stevens before going to sleep. They told Abe to call them "Auntie" and "Uncle." They were really nice.

One day after Abe began to feel better, he again asked, "When am I going to see my parents and Shmuel? I miss them."

Uncle replied, "Your parents want you to stay with us for a while. To experience a new and wonderful land. We live in the country of Baklava. We even have a dessert named after us!" He and Auntie laughed.

Abe didn't get the joke. He didn't understand geography, but he didn't feel safe, either. Other than at school, he had never been separated from his parents or Shmuel. He asked, "But they didn't tell me. Why didn't they tell me? And where is Shmuel?"

While Abe missed his parents, he yearned for Shmuel even more. His parents tended to his needs, but, they could be bossy at times, especially his mom. Shmuel, on the other hand, was usually willing and eager to play soccer with Abe or ride bikes and explore the woods together. Shmuel also cared for Abe, encouraging him to be more active, friendly, and sociable. Sometimes Shmuel even knew what Abe wanted to say before Abe talked. They were as close as twins could be, and he felt lost without him being around.

Auntie said, "Ah, that's simple. Even though you're now better, they told us you can stay here for a little bit longer. It'll be good to get to know each other—after all, we're family!" Abe began to interrupt wanting to call his parents and Shmuel, but Auntie talked over his voice, "And you know what the best part is? Big surprise."

Uncle began shouting for Spider to come in.

A pudgy boy with black curly hair and a dirty face walked into the room.

"Hey, Spider, come over here. Meet your cousin, Abe," Uncle called to a boy kicking a soccer ball in the distance. "Abe, Spider is our son, which also makes him your cousin! He's five. Two years younger than you!"

Spider offered his hand to Abe. "Nice to meet you." Abe took Spider's hand. Spider said "I didn't even know I had a cousin until my parents told me. Weird, huh? You want to play soccer?"

"Sure. I'm not very good at it. I play a little at home." Abe laughed nervously, forgetting all about calling his parents and Shmuel. Then he remembered that Shmuel told him to try and be more friendly, to stop being so shy, and he quickly added, "But I'll try!"

"You boys come back to eat in about thirty minutes, okay?"

***

Six months passed. Abe got tired of asking the same question about when he was going to rejoin his parents and Shmuel. He began to like the land of Baklava and missed Shmuel less. There seemed to be no rules, unlike back home in America. He didn't have to go to school or play some dumb role in a stupid play. He was free to do whatever he wanted. He and Spider became best friends.

Uncle approached Abe while he was playing soccer. His breath smelled like smoke, and his beard was no longer groomed. He took Abe back to his house where Auntie was waiting. Abe noticed her eyes were watery. She and Uncle were very serious. *Am I in trouble?*

Auntie hugged him tight and then released him. Abe was now facing Auntie and Uncle. *This must be real bad, he thought to himself.*

"Let's sit on the couch," Auntie suggested.

Abe sat across from them. Uncle looked at him and said, "Abe, I have some bad news. There's been a terrible disaster." Uncle told Abe that his parents and Shmuel had died in a tragic car accident.

They looked at him, waiting for Abe to respond, but he didn't. He didn't know what to say. He never heard of anybody dying before. *Will they wake up at some point?*

Abe thought about them. He missed Shmuel, his twin, more than his parents, but Spider had already sort of replaced Shmuel in Abe's life over the past six months.

Then he thought about how the news would affect his life. He knew he should feel sadder than he actually did, but he couldn't help how he felt. *Will Auntie and Uncle continue to take care of me? Can I stay here?*

Uncle seemed to read his mind. "We want to let you know that you are welcome to stay here. We have enjoyed having you. Do you want to stay?"

Abe nodded hesitantly at first.

***

A year later, Uncle called Abe and Spider into his study. He was sitting with his favorite ashtray on the table next to him, filled with ash and butts. The room was filled with smoke.

Uncle gestured for them to sit on the couch. "It's time we began teaching you about life. So you can learn. One day, the two of you will become adults like Auntie and me."

Abe said, "What are we going to learn? In America, I learned about nothing. Spelling. Math. Boring."

"We have something special in mind! You're going to love it."

Chapter 18

Four Years Later:
The Land of Baklava

Abe and Spider became best friends in addition to being cousins, as Uncle had first described their relationship. Spider was quick to pick up on the clever twist to Abe's name – Abram – that Uncle started using. What Uncle suggested, you did without question. Everybody living on the estate had learned that lesson.

Abram and Spider did everything together: eating, playing, listening to Uncle rant and rave when he was in town. They didn't understand everything he said, but they knew it was important, grownup stuff. They secretly referred to it as "The Talk."

They also learned together from Ms. Borash, their heavy-set teacher with a large mole implanted to the right of her nose. She held a fly swatter in her hand as she taught them math, English, Russian, and her favorite topic, world history. Not the same simple history Abe began learning in America about the pilgrims, Thanksgiving, and the Founding Fathers. Ms. Borash, when she wasn't swatting to keep them still, taught them a different type of history, about the world and how America liked to take advantage of other countries. He grew to hate America and its main allies, like Israel. At first, Abram was taken aback, but then he began to understand their rich history of meddling, exploiting, and conquering.

During their free time, Abram and Spider explored every inch of the walled compound. The armed guards ignored their silly games, pretending not to notice their frequent trips outside the gate to investigate their surroundings. They could even take their paintball guns and other toys.

The guards knew they would never get past the heavily fortified fence forming a large circumference around the compound about five kilometers down the mountain. Abram could make it that far, he had become stronger and more confident than his days in America. But he would never leave the slower, flat-footed Spider behind, and Spider had no chance of hiking that far, particularly without food, which the guards never permitted past the gate.

They were told it was against the rules because it could produce crumbs, attracting wild animals. But it really was a security precaution. Taking food would allow them to remain in the neutral zone for too long, potentially leading them to try and explore further. They would never get past the outer fence and the guards watching them, but it was best not to have any issues.

Abram, dressed in shorts and the soccer jersey of his favorite team, asked Spider, "What do you want to do today? We're out of school until Monday."

"Let's play Zions and Palions. I'll be the Palions and guard the pit." The pit was an area roughly half the size of a large soccer field.

Abram made up the game after becoming upset by a lesson taught by Ms. Borash. Spider liked to play the Palions. He didn't like to move that much, preferring to take a defensive position guarding his land, which was divided into different sections, each representing a settlement. Spider had to shoot the invading Abram with a paintball before his cousin entered the pit, attempting to capture territory.

If he succeeded, his prize would be to claim the portion of land within the pit he had captured. Abram had ten minutes to grab what he could before getting shot.

On days when Abram was particularly agile or Spider was a bad shot, the cousins changed the rules to favor Spider. Abram would have to capture more than one tract of land in the pit to win. And on days when Spider was accurate or Abram was slow, they revised the rules, requiring Spider to shoot his cousin more than once in order to win.

Abram found his hiding spot from which he would launch his attack once Spider blew his whistle for the game to begin. But today's game would never take place. A car approaching from a distance stopped them cold. The passenger waved, and the boys screamed hello.

Abram's uncle was returning from a long trip. Abram ran back toward the compound, hoping to catch him before somebody else got there first. Spider trailed behind him, struggling to keep up.

Chapter 19
December 25, 1991:
Saint Petersburg

Sasha Krupin prepared his two-bedroom apartment in Saint Petersburg for that month's Durak card game. He was a muscular man with dark hair that, unless combed right, looked like a toupee. His bulky nose bent to the left, the result of a right hook he received in a boxing match. Like many Russians, his thick mustache and beard provided him with protection against the cold winter winds.

Sasha's longtime girlfriend, Maya Romanoski, cleaned the dishes in the sink, scrubbing off the dried grease and sauce. Maya had a petite figure that seemed proportionate to her small nose and shoulder-length hair that was dark and straight. Her complexion was attractively clear with a light-brownish hue.

They spoke in Russian.

"You pig, Sasha. Why don't you clean up after yourself? You leave these for me?"

Sasha grunted. He knew Maya would take care of it, so why should he?

Maya shouted to Sasha from the kitchen, "You left a half-used cigarette with ash on the counter! I'm sick and tired of cleaning up after you!"

He gave it right back. "Maya, you talk too much, you know. Now shut up! I'm readying the den for Vlady and Dmitry. Did you pick up an extra bottle, like I said to? We can't run short like the last time."

"Yes, yes, who else is going to pick it up? And you know there is less and less of this stuff because of all the fuss. People are stockpiling. They don't know what's going to happen."

The doorbell rang. Maya fetched their guests.

"You guys came together? You a couple?" Sasha chided Vladimir Putin, Vlady as he liked to call him, and Dmitry Moosecravic as they entered. He poked Dmitry's plump belly for emphasis.

Sasha, Vlady, and Dmitry grew up together in the same Saint Petersburg neighborhood. They were good friends, although not as close as they used to be. Each had enjoyed different levels of success or failure at the KGB, driving a wedge between the once-impenetrable bond they previously enjoyed.

Sasha enjoyed stellar reviews with relatively minor stumbles. His star began to rise after his bold killing of the U.S. ambassador to Afghanistan, Adolf Dubs, in 1979 as part of an operation to cover-up the failings of another KGB officer, Sergei Batrukihn.

Sergei had orchestrated the kidnapping of Dubs by the National Oppression in order to force the release of its communist leader, Badruddin Bahes. The Afghan government was holding Bahes, and the KGB hoped the U.S. would pressure its ally into releasing him.

However, when it became apparent that Bahes wouldn't be released by the recalcitrant Afghans, the KGB had a major problem on its hands. Enter Sasha, who reportedly stoked an exchange of gunfire, which he used as cover to assassinate Dubs and the kidnappers, eliminating the key witnesses to the botched affair.

Dirty work was his specialty, and people learned not to cross him. His associates called him by his given name. His enemies knew him as the Wolf, a nickname Sasha gladly perpetuated.

Vlady, on the other hand, lost standing after leaks revealed him as the key actor in burning mounds of KGB material in Dresden following the collapse of the Berlin Wall. He adopted an "I don't give a fuck attitude" after being blamed. He also worked for Sasha until retiring from the KGB to pursue politics.

Dmitry was known as an out-of-shape drunk, resembling more of a philandering clown than super-agent. His deep friendship with Sasha was the only reason he hadn't already been fired or sent to some godforsaken place.

***

Maya served bread and vodka, and the four took their seats at the table in the den.

"We playing teams or individual?" Sasha asked.

Dmitry responded first. "Teams—I call your girlfriend!"

"Good choice," Sasha responded. He blew Maya a kiss. She looked away from the gesture, and Sasha added dryly, "She's a *real* winner."

Sasha looked at Vlady. "That leaves you and me, Vlady."

Sasha dealt each player six cards out of the deck of thirty-six cards. Four suits of nine cards each, ranging from ace down to six. The goal of the game was to get rid of all cards that the team held before the other team rid itself of its cards.

"Anyone have a six?" Sasha asked.

Maya smiled and showed her six of hearts, entitling her to start.

"Appropriate, darling," Sasha said. "You begin."

Maya looked at her hand and eyed her opponents—Vlady and her boyfriend. She attacked Sasha with a king. He was now forced to defend himself with a higher card. Only an ace would work. He didn't have one, so he picked up the king and added it to his pile.

They continued for the next hour and then took a break.

Maya filled their glasses. "You miss the organs? You worked there for a long time. How you making out?" she asked, referring to the nickname used by insiders to describe the KGB.

Vlady took a swig of his drink and replied, "I miss it. But I can't be a part of the security services anymore." He looked at Sasha. "As you know, elements of your agency supported the coup against Gorbachev. Communism is dead. We need to move forward, not back."

Sasha sat back in his chair, puffing heavily on his cigarette. He was surprised that Vlady would poison the game with politics this early in the evening. He didn't have to answer Maya's question so directly.

Sasha could reprimand him, but he reconsidered. He wanted to remain friends at all costs. *Vlady may be useful later.* Sasha did enjoy a friendly banter though, and said, "Communism may be outdated, but our union was strong at one point and is now collapsing. We'll be a joke if we continue down this path. We've lost too much of our power to the republics as it is. We can't live without a strong nation to stand up to imperial America."

Vlady pressed. "We can transition away from communism without losing our union, that much I agree. But I can't support any attempt at a coup. That would weaken us further, make us look like a joke."

Sasha smiled. He had considered joining the hard-liners in the August 1991 putsch against Gorbachev. He couldn't stand the thought of his beloved county being reduced to a peppercorn overnight. However, he preferred to stay in the background, able to hedge his bets.

His pager went off suddenly. He excused himself to call his boss.

He rejoined the group a few minutes later and announced, "It's official. Gorbachev's going to resign. The union is done. Turn on the television. It's happening now."

Dmitry turned on the tube, and they watched the dramatic events unfold from Sasha's den. Vlady looked at his friend, Sasha. "You don't seem too upset. I suspect you wanted this all along."

Sasha shrugged his shoulders. "It's time. We all know that."

Vlady didn't know Sasha had received assurances from Boris Yeltsin. Sasha would receive a plum appointment in Russia's intelligence service agency. He would also control a key supplier of armaments to the Russian army, opportunities far beyond the paltry salary he would continue to make as a cog in Gorbachev's Russia. Someday he might even accumulate enough wealth to help restore the Soviet Union back to its glory days.

Vlady, on the other hand, had already resigned, hitching his fortunes with the liberal, Mayor Anatoly Sobchak. A political career was in his cards.

***

March 2003:
Near Donetsk

The Wolf stepped out of the building and onto the landing atop the steps. It was cold outside but with little wind. He spat out bits of tobacco that accumulated in his mouth from the cigar he was enjoying. He also watched the sky through his binoculars. Nothing. No sign. Just clouds.

He returned to his table beside the bar and to his consolation prize, his Stolichnaya, which he now had more time to enjoy. He drank alone. His security detail watched him and the surroundings carefully, knowing they would be harshly reprimanded if any uninvited person came within a kilometer of him. The Wolf previously shot a guard in front of his remaining security detail after he caught the unfortunate soul drinking while he was on duty—an example to all.

His phone rang a few minutes later. He cursed and then went back to the landing spot, squawking for his guards to give him space to speak without being heard. "Yes," he said.

"Did the package arrive yet?"

The Wolf calmly replied, "No, Vlady, not yet. I'll call you as soon as I hear anything."

The Wolf sat down and refilled his vodka. He began drumming his fingers on the table. His leg bounced in tiny movements up and down under the table until he couldn't take it anymore. Neither could his security detail, watching from their nearby perches.

He was in a waiting room outside the runway of a small local airport outside of Donetsk. The airport was used by the Wolf and his cronies, Russian and sympathetic Ukrainian tycoons, to ferry goods and people to and from their large nearby estates. Today the Wolf was waiting for a package that could one day help to restore Russia's status. The Soviet Union may have dissolved, but that didn't prevent Russia from collecting the union's former fruits.

He finished his drink and then jumped up, racing onto the tarmac, readying his binoculars. He waited. He was not a patient man by nature, except when he had no choice. Five minutes. Ten minutes. Nothing.

Finally, he had enough, whipped out his secure satellite phone, and called Major Hassan of the Iraqi National Intelligence. He was disorganized and sloppy, not the type of person the Wolf had expected Saddam to appoint to such an important position. He guessed it proved how Saddam's resources were stretched, preparing for the pending American invasion.

The Wolf couldn't speak Arabic, and Hassan couldn't speak Russian. They settled on English, which they both spoke well enough.

The Wolf demanded, "Where is my plane?"

"Relax, it's on the way."

The Wolf barked into the phone, "Relax? I'll rest when it arrives. And if it doesn't, then you'll be the one who will have trouble relaxing. Did it take off on time?"

Hassan responded calmly, "Yes, and with the package."

"Good," the Wolf said as he clicked off the phone.

He heard a distant buzz coming from the sky a few minutes later, white streaks tailing the source of the noise.

***

The Wolf greeted Jabal with a bear hug after he walked off the plane. "Good flight?" Jabal looked a little less like Saddam than he had before, his face and mustache were thinner while his hair was bushier.

Jabal seesawed his hand. "A little bumpy."

The Wolf didn't care. He wasn't even listening. "Show me the barrel."

They walked to the cargo bay. The light-beige barrel stood alone, strapped in tight to the metal racks. The Wolf gingerly touched the top, afraid it would come off but needing to make sure it was secure. One could never be too careful with Jabal. He sometimes didn't pay attention to the details, the little things that sometimes festered into headaches. The Wolf tolerated him because, well, he had other qualities.

"What does this say? Give me the English translation," the Wolf asked, pointing to a sticker in the middle of the barrel.

Jabal replied, "'Place of Storage: Tuwaitha Nuclear Research Center. Date Sealed: December 5, 1990. Date of Next Check: December 5, 2020. Serial Number: XX45198523RX.'"

The Wolf shook his head and chuckled. He was amazed at how thorough Saddam required his people to be. He wasn't surprised; even Hitler recorded the names of people destroyed and itemized property stolen. And the Baath Party was influenced by and learned a lot of its early tactics from the Nazis.

The Wolf gave orders on his cell phone. "Bring the truck to the plane."

While waiting, the Wolf wanted to discuss an important detail and addressed Jabal. "Any movement out of the Americans?"

"How should I know? I don't have access to those reports."

The Wolf shook his head in disgust at having to coax this moron. "What do you hear? Certainly people are worried, no? Or do they all think they're bluffing, like your bumbling leader?"

Jabal ignored the insult to Saddam and said, "A lot of the higher-ups don't believe it will happen. The grunts and their immediate overseers are more worried. Some have even committed treason, daring to whisper they believe Saddam is ignoring the tea leaves."

The Wolf replied, "I'm not sure that is completely true. How do you think I managed to get Saddam to give me the barrel? He's not completely hiding his head in the sand."

Jabal looked surprised that the Wolf would talk to him in this way. But he was curious.

"Money?" he guessed.

"Money? No. He already has enough of that. Try insurance."

Jabal thought about what the Wolf meant. It made sense. Saddam was always thinking ahead.

As the truck arrived, the Wolf hoped Jabal knew enough not to ask any important questions in the presence of the driver.

It took about thirty minutes for Jabal and one of the Wolf's trusted employees to load the barrel onto the truck. The Wolf then paid the pilot and crew in cash. IIe needed to kccp thcm happy. They worked exclusively for him, and while loyalty was a virtue he sought when hiring workers, money always helped seal the deal.

The Wolf instructed Jabal to sit in the back next to the barrel on the way to the estate. They both knew the road was filled with potholes, and the Wolf was not taking any chances that his prized material could get damaged along the way.

The compound was located roughly ten kilometers from the airport. The wind and cold in the unprotected back made Jabal's olive skin redder and puffed up his clothes. His head whipped up and down and side to side as the truck's worn-out shocks failed to smooth out the ride. Life as a gopher, but the Wolf had no sympathy for him. Everybody pays their dues. Simpletons pay forever.

They approached a fork in the road. The Wolf looked back at Jabal before they turned off the main road to begin their steep ascent up a mountain via another street. Jabal looked pale.

They reached a black iron fence fifteen minutes later. A guard emerged from his stone gatehouse, nodded at the Wolf, and opened the gate. They continued climbing.

As they inched closer, the landscape changed. Before and after the fence lay a ring of thick trees and shrubs that obscured the compound from anybody foolish enough to traverse the private road. A kilometer past the fence, the land was rough and completely barren of any trees. The Wolf had his people raze any obstacles that could be used as cover by any interlopers foolish enough to bypass the outer fence without permission.

A few minutes later they arrived at an inner decorative fence made out of stacked shale stone that surrounded the compound consisting of four colonial-styled structures, a courtyard, and a loose gravel road connecting them all. The largest building was a large symmetrical three-story estate house with twelve rooms and a chimney on each side. The façade was made out of different shades of grey and brown stone that the Wolf had imported for construction. The roof was made out of light red Spanish tile. A winding shale stone path, which matched the inner fence, led from the gravel road to the estate house's large white porch and red front door. Smoke from burning firewood filled the air with a light smoky aroma.

Two other buildings were located off the gravel road flanking the back of the main estate house. They looked like model homes compared to the main house with all the details except for only one chimney and only a simple elegant door.

The fourth structure was different. It was known as "the brick house," having a red brick exterior and a black tile roof. It also had a metal door and no windows. Everybody understood that it was off limits, except for a few special invitees. Nobody dared to find out what would happen if they violated the Wolf's strict instructions. The two men protecting it had Kalashnikovs draped over their bodies.

Two men emerged from the brick house and directed the Wolf's truck toward the back, where they unloaded the barrel, placing it in a secure location inside. The Wolf walked inside, made a final inspection, and walked out, locking the door behind him.

***

March 2015:
Near Donetsk

The Wolf returned to the compound after a lengthy trip. The residents of the estate were used to his coming and going frequently, but this time they hadn't seen him for over three months.

He spotted the two boys playing in the field between the outer and inner fences, amused they had become close. He didn't really care, except that it made his job easier. They were weak and content, and that was all that mattered.

The Wolf had arranged for the extraction of one of the boys, Abe, from America several years ago, claiming to be a distant relative. Abe called him "Uncle" as a convenient reference. He was pleased at how easy it had been for Abe to forget his life in America. Abe had even accepted his nickname of Abram, which the Wolf began using after the initial assimilation period.

The Wolf grudgingly waved at the boys, and they screamed with excitement, waving back. The gate opened, allowing his car to enter. The boys returned from the field.

The Wolf hesitated but then opened his arms, continuing to play his role. The faster boy, Abram, collided with him. The slower boy, Spider, caught up and also received a hug. Others approached, greeting the Wolf warmly but more cautiously.

A small Asian man wearing thick, black-framed glasses emerged from the second row of the car.

The Wolf told the crowd, "Everybody, meet Kim Jae Rok. He's going to be staying here for a while." An impromptu receiving line formed as the guests introduced themselves to Kim one by one.

As the crowd dispersed, the Wolf and Kim ventured toward the brick house. They walked inside and guards began carrying in boxes from the trunk. The Wolf and Kim walked toward the barrel that had arrived twelve years earlier.

"What do you think?" the Wolf asked in an excited voice.

"Ah. So good. I test," Kim said in a high-pitched voice. "One moment."

He scampered away. Like a rat looking for food, he searched the boxes that had been delivered by the guards. He moved items out of the boxes in a frantic effort to find what he needed. The Wolf watched him, worried the eager scientist would accidently break something.

A few minutes later, Kim found what he needed: a square yellow box made out of hard plastic. The upper portion of the box contained a smaller area in the shape of a rectangle with a clear plastic covering, a needle, and a clicking meter. A wand, held by a wire and encased in thick black rubber, hung below the box as Kim bounced up to the Wolf with his toy.

Kim waved the wand over the barrel. The meter made a noise, but the needle moved only a little.

"No good?" asked the Wolf.

"This to be expected. How long stored here?"

"Twelve years," the Wolf answered.

"Such long time, long time."

The Wolf responded, "We took advantage of an opportunity that presented itself. The barrels would've been destroyed had we not acted when we did. I knew it would come in handy one day, and that day will be upon us soon."

Kim didn't know it, but Putin had recently called the Wolf. It was time to activate the dormant.

"And the equipment, it's all here?" Kim asked.

The Wolf smiled. "Of course. I had it purchased and delivered over the past several years. I could only get a few pieces at a time without raising serious questions. But we did it. Let me take you there. Right this way."

The Wolf escorted his prized scientist into the next room, through the glass doors. He thought about his accomplishment and his unfolding plan. He had already spent millions on this project, money transferred from his armament company.

"See?" The Wolf moved his arm and pointed to the far side of the room. He let the moment sink in and then asked, "How long until you are ready to begin the process?"

Kim looked at his boss and shrugged. He didn't want to say what he truly thought. He had learned before escaping his country about the need to try answering a superior in a manner that didn't risk jail, beheading, or banishment. His own brother had been sent to a camp when he stepped out of line and didn't properly salute the Dear Leader at a parade.

The Wolf repeated his question. "How long?"

Kim deflected. "Let me see." Surely the Wolf knew it wasn't as simple as he was making it out to be. He walked around the room.

The Wolf said louder, "It's all there, I can assure you. I bought all of it, all of the pieces you told me to get."

Kim walked up to his boss. "Yes, I see. I assemble, test, and then start. This take time, Mr. Krupin."

The Wolf frowned. "I know, blah, blah, blah, but how long?"

"Depends. Process go faster with assistance. Any help available?" Kim hoped that the Wolf wouldn't offer his own services.

"Yes, I've the perfect person in mind. I'll introduce you to Abram."

Kim asked, "Is he a scientist? Background?"

The Wolf grinned. "Well, not exactly. Let's just say he's been training for something like this for a long time."

Kim looked at him funny. *He know risk? What at stake?* Kim knew he should respond carefully, but he couldn't resist. "I no work well with rookie. This very difficult."

The Wolf replied in a stern voice, "Don't patronize me, or I'll ship you back home in a box. I'm paying you a small fortune. You'll get it done."

Kim sighed. "Yes, Mr. Krupin."

"So, let me ask you for a final time. How long?"

"I no know for sure. Several years, yes? Five? Process take time. We no careful, and kaboom!"

The Wolf took his time replying while a nervous Kim waited. "Yes, yes. No kaboom. Kaboom would be bad for business and very bad for you."

Chapter 20
Present Day:
Near Donetsk

The Wolf fidgeted on the trip from the airport to his compound. The main road had recently been paved, making his journey smooth. But his careful plans were coming to fruition, and he was too anxious to relax and enjoy the ride.

He had been gone for a long time and was not planning on returning yet, until he received a call from an excited Kim. Kim was finally ready to show the Wolf what he had accomplished.

The Wolf generally believed in disciplining his subordinates. Treat them like garbage but pay them well, and they'll be careful not to make any mistakes. Make examples out of those who screw up. Kindness leads to complacency.

But the Wolf also had to be smart. Throwing the baby out with the bathwater made sense only when you have another baby. He also didn't, and probably would never, understand the complexity of what Kim was trying to accomplish.

He had received low grades in any chemistry or science class he took in school, having no interest in molecules and atoms. Any object that needed a microscope wasn't worth his time. He had bigger fish to fry, even as a youngster.

So he treated Kim differently—not in front of the others, of course. Sure, he made Kim aware he was being carefully watched, monitoring his progress. But he had to rely on reading Kim's reports and interpreting his broken English to learn what he could absorb.

The Wolf reached the compound, and his driver rolled down the window. It was raining, and the gravel road had turned from its normal light whitish color to a dark grey. The air smelled like a mixture of smoke from burning firewood and wet earth. The guard nodded at the Wolf, opening the gate.

They drove to the brick house, where the Wolf hesitated before walking up to the door. *A lot of time, effort, and money went into this place. It's finally happening.* The rain was dripping off the house's black tile, and the red brick took on a burgundy color. A drop of rain landed on the Wolf's nose.

The Wolf knocked. Kim carefully opened the door just enough to let his boss enter.

The Wolf pushed himself past Kim down the main corridor and began to open the glass doors leading into the chamber, stopping only when Kim screamed, "Stop! Clothing, clothing!"

The Wolf looked back at him, annoyed. He had not seen the operation since Kim finished assembling the equipment and building the containment chambers.

Kim pointed to a protective white laboratory coat, dark cover pants, and blue surgical slippers. He put them on and gestured for the Wolf to follow. Kim explained, "Dirt cause contamination."

The Wolf grunted and moved toward the gear.

They donned the protective clothing and entered the chamber.

"What's in those tubes?"

Kim was astonished at how little his boss knew. He could have said anything, but then again, maybe the Wolf was testing him.

"Uranium contain both isotope U-238 and U-235. Need to get rid of U-238. First we use hydrofluoric acid, make cake into gas. This happen over here." Kim pointed to a series of cylinders made out of metal with lines protruding out and into the contraption.

He continued, pointing to a series of metallic objects, "Gas then go here into spinners."

"Spinners?" the Wolf asked.

"You know them as centrifuges. Spin gas in tube to separate the heavier U-238 from the lighter U-235."

"Sounds simple the way you explain it," the Wolf said, feeling giddy.

But Kim was not to be underestimated. "In theory, yes. But no in reality. Start, U-235 only point-seven percent. Must increase to three percent to five percent for commercial reactor. The rest U-238. Your cake begin at twenty percent. Must increase to seventy percent to ninety percent U-235 to work. Take time. Lots of time. Lots of time."

The Wolf felt his stomach tighten. "But you said on the phone..."

Kim understood his mistake. He spoke fast. "Over there. That cylinder contain enough for one."

"Gas?"

"Yes, but over there, apply chemicals, and voilà! You have end product."

"When will you be finished with the whole process ready to ship?"

"Six months."

The Wolf looked at him. He was pleased, but he couldn't let Kim know. He said stridently, "You have four months. Make it happen."

"Yes, Mr. Krupin."

Chapter 21
Moscow

Dmitry Moosecravic sat at his designated center seat, reserved at his permanent table at Moscow's trendy new bar, Rasputin's Dagger. An ironic name given that Rasputin, known for his dark influence over the repressive Imperial Romanov dynasty, didn't wield a dagger, as his reputation might have suggested. Rather, he was stabbed by one in an assassination attempt against his own life.

Dmitry didn't even bother to secure the top three buttons of his dirty white Oxford shirt. His dark matted chest hair was visible from a distance, as was the plume of cigar smoke surrounding his table. Dmitry's guests—two blondes, one on each side of him—laughed at his racy humor. He loved blondes, although he realized they were attracted to his money and powerful friends, not his plump, unkept frame.

They were already into their second bottle of top-shelf vodka when Dmitry noticed a lanky man slap a woman with purple hair and a black leather club dress on the dance floor. The woman pushed back at the man, who then stormed off. She continued to dance, now by herself, provocatively swinging her hips even more than before.

The blonde sitting on Dmitry's right pined for his attention. "What you lookin' at, baby?" she breathed in his ear.

Dmitry replied tersely, "Nothin', babe. Pour me another."

A few minutes later, the lanky man returned to the dance floor for round two of their skirmish. He grabbed the woman, trying to drag her off. She resisted and broke away, swiping at him in the process. They shoved each other until the man decided to end the dustup. But she must have said something to him, causing a violent reaction. Dmitry heard the vicious slap from across the bar and witnessed her crumple to the floor.

Other patrons passively watched, not wanting to get involved. But Dmitry was not a passive person. He considered chasing the man who ran out of the bar, but he knew better. The out-of-shape man probably would have a heart attack before he made it to the next table.

The blonde on Dmitry's right again tried to get his attention, but he put up his hand. She knew to remain silent. Dmitry was known to have a sharp temper and no patience, but his money brought him eternal forgiveness. Women knew to speak when he wanted to hear them, not before.

Dmitry got up from the table, walked to the dance floor, and offered the woman his hand. She shook him off, preferring to get up on her own.

"Are you OK?" Dmitry said in Russian.

She ignored him, instead touching the sore spot on her cheek.

"Can I get you anything?" Dmitry asked, raising his voice to her back as she walked away. She didn't respond, much to his dismay. Dmitry wasn't used to watching a woman walk away from him, much less one thwarting his rare attempt at being a white knight. *So much for that*, he thought.

He continued to stare, eyes unable to refocus on the girls at his table, instead watching the purple-haired woman as she walked into the restroom. She emerged a few minutes later, looking as if nothing had happened, and sat down at the bar.

Dmitry returned to his table but couldn't take his eyes off her. Through his peripheral vision, he watched her order a shot. She downed it quickly and ordered another. Dmitry couldn't resist. He could have his blondes any day of the week, but to rescue a princess? That was a rare opportunity.

He stood up as the blonde on his right gently grabbed at his arm. She knew what was happening and didn't want to lose her sugar daddy. He poked her arm away, gave the blonde a nasty look, and approached the bar.

"May I?" he said in Russian, placing his hand on the seat next to her.

She looked at him and slurred in Russian, "Let's get the fuck out of here."

"As you wish, my princess," Dmitry said as she walked out the door. He nodded to the bartender, a cue to add the shots to his monthly tab.

Dmitry walked outside while the blondes at his table took stock of their backup plan, the free bottle of vodka they had just inherited. At least they could share it with the other fish in the bar.

***

The purple-haired woman watched with amusement as Dmitry jogged past her, desperately looking around the parking lot. She was smoking a cigarette immediately adjacent to the door, letting him suffer for a few minutes until he looked back at the entrance like a lost puppy. Dmitry spotted her and laughed.

She leaned back against the wall. He bent down to kiss her, but she stopped his approach, touching his lips with her index finger, saying, "Not here."

Dmitry eagerly led her to his car and they drove off.

"You have a name, my princess?"

She laughed and bit down on a strand of her purple hair long enough to exit the other side of her mouth. She looked at Dmitry seductively, staring into his eyes and pouted. "Princess will do, for now. Be a good boy, and I'll tell you my real name."

Dmitry drove as fast as he could to his luxurious Moscow condominium. They pulled up to the front entrance of the building. The doorman greeted her warmly as he opened the car door, leading her out by her hand.

Thank God they were alone in the elevator, Dmitry thought to himself as the elevator climbed towards the 20th floor. He lunged at her until the elevator unexpectedly stopped on the sixth floor, where, to his dismay, Mrs. Panavory entered with her idiotic white hat and wrinkled skin. She looked like a prune, and Dmitry wanted to kill her right then and there. Making matters worse, Dmitry knew she didn't even realize the elevator was going up. And in his pique, he stupidly didn't point this out until it was too late. Fortunately, she realized her error, and after a civilized womanly cuss, hit the button and exited on the eighth floor.

They were alone again, at least until the twelfth floor. There, Mr. Amorov entered. Dmitry huffed so loud that Mr. Amorov looked at him as if Dmitry was having a problem. Thirty seconds later, Dmitry and Princess reached the twentieth floor. Princess whispered to him her real name, Irena, as he opened the door.

Irena took in her new surroundings: the shiny wooden floors, off-white walls, open floor plan, twelve-foot ceilings. The furniture, floor, and kitchen were in pristine condition.

Dmitry directed her to sit at one of the six stools at the bar. He proceeded to pour both of them a drink.

He walked to his lavish stereo equipment and, thinking himself as suave, put on some Stravinsky.

Irena laughed and said in Russian, "No. Not going to work. I have something better." They would continue in Russian for the remainder of the evening—a language in which she was comfortable, albeit a bit choppy at speaking. She covered up her deficiency by making herself sound uneducated but in a provocative way.

Dmitry watched her carefully open her handbag and fish inside for her phone. She scrolled to her playlist, synced her phone to Dmitry's equipment, and pumped up the volume, letting her music fill the two-level condominium. It was not the soft classical music of Dmitry's tastes but Russia's own infamous dolls, Pussy Riot.

Dmitry grudgingly conceded, "Music for my purple-haired friend." He learned his lesson. She would be in control this evening.

Irena encouraged Dmitry to finish his drink and poured another for both to enjoy. She then began dancing in the living room, a few feet away from the bar. She pulled both straps on the top of her dress toward her shoulder blades, drew him in with her finger, and after he came within striking distance, she pushed him away. He returned to his chair and finished his shot.

She repeated the drill when the next song began playing. But this time she pulled her straps too far down her arms, exposing the tops of her breasts. Irena again pushed Dmitry away, but this time he resisted.

He had had enough. She had to push again, this time a little harder, wagging her finger from side to side, saying "sit down" with her lips.

He got the message, returning to the bar. Toward the end of the song, she pulled her straps even further, motioning again for him to join her. This time she accepted the embrace and then pointed upstairs.

He enthusiastically led her to his bedroom where they both jumped on the bed. She maneuvered to be on top of him.

He pawed after her. But she had other plans. While blowing in his ear, she retrieved blindfolds from her handbag and dexterously maneuvered them onto his face. He laughed.

Next, she cuffed him to the poles holding up the backboard. He started to protest, but Irena knew how to handle him. He was no match.

She lay down on his body while he thrashed under her, unable to handle the situation. But she wasn't done. She used leg cuffs and secured his legs, spread wide, to the end of the bed.

He was becoming agitated. She knew the great Dmitry was not used to being controlled, certainly not in this way. More of her body made him more agreeable, until she tied a sock around his mouth. Now she controlled all of his movement and any noise emanating from his mouth. She had reduced him from kingpin status to that of a mere peasant.

She went to the bathroom and emerged a few minutes later, noticing Dmitry had started to sweat in her absence.

"Don't worry, honey, I'm just trying to excite you, make you crazy." Dmitry moaned.

She climbed on top of him, nestled her lips into his neck, and began to gently nibble on his ear. At the same time, she used both hands to pin down his arm. She located his track marks and inserted a needle into his forearm. Dmitry began squirming but couldn't shake free as she emptied the contents of the needle.

"Aw, relax, honey. I saw your track marks and decided to amp it up a bit. You know?"

Dmitry raised his voice, but it came out gargled as she inserted more heroin. She let it sink in for a bit. "You feel the rush?"

She faked her own use and then comforted him with her body while waiting for the adrenaline to curtail. After a while, he calmed down and she said, "So, tell me about your friend, Sasha Krupin—the Wolf. How do you know him?"

He began thrashing, this time violently. She continued, "Here's how it's gonna work. You answer my questions right, and I stop and, let's say...I release your tension. You answer wrong, and I use more. How much can you tolerate? I'm going to remove the sock to let you speak. Nod your head if you understand."

He nodded, and she said, "Good."

She removed the sock, and he yelled, "You're dead, bitch!"

She secured it again and said, "Nobody's gonna hear you over the music blasting downstairs. I knew you'd fail the test. You testing me?"

She pinned down his arm again and jammed the needle back in, nearly emptying the contents. His heart began to slow down—unusually slow. She feared she had gone too far.

"I'm going to ask you again. Do you know the Wolf? Nod your head if you do." He nodded his head as his heart continued to beat slower. He began gagging.

She took his head and, as much as the arm cuffs would allow, leaned the upper half of his body to the side. He vomited, forcing the sock, now covered with vomit, out of his mouth and onto the bed.

"There. Now you feel better?"

He didn't respond.

"Trust me, you'll die if I use more of this stuff, so I suggest you cooperate. OK?"

He nodded.

"How can I get in touch with this Wolf?"

Dmitry cried out, "I don't know! I don't know. I swear!"

"That's not a good answer." She began moving items around in her handbag.

Dmitry screamed, "No. No more! OK, OK, he's got a place. I don't know it very well. I was only there once. We landed at a small airport in Donetsk."

"Anything else?"

"No, I swear!"

"I need more. Give me an address, a phone number, a name. Something."

"I don't know. The man blindfolded me. He's paranoid. It's in the middle of nowhere. A private road leads to it. That's all I got. Please! We good? We good?"

Irena said, "We're good. But remember, if you tell anybody and it gets back to the Wolf, then he'll probably kill you for ratting on him. That's just the way he is. Paranoid, as you said."

She secured the sock, kissed his cheek, and said in her seductive voice on her way out, "Sweetie, if you get sick, turn your head."

Chapter 22

Moscow

Red removed her faux fingertips—designed by MI6 to feel and look exactly like skin—purple wig, fake mole, and nose implant in the bathroom of a popular hotel, cleaned herself up, and exited through a rear door. Then she hopped in a taxi to a hotel on the other side of Moscow, where she and Robert had rooms. She was exhausted and needed to sleep.

They met at the lobby restaurant for a late lunch. Red watched him approach from her table in the back corner, away from any prying ears. He sat down and looked at Red closely.

"Well?" she said. "You look...ah, like you want to say something, get something off your chest. Bad night alone?"

He grunted. "Let's order first."

Their waiter, a middle-aged man with a mustache, delivered dark-brown rye bread and butter to their table while they pondered the selections. The bread looked hard and felt tough but tasted surprisingly sweet.

The waiter returned a few minutes later with water. Red ordered the olivye, a mixture of potatoes, hard-boiled eggs, carrots, pickles, and ham. A colleague introduced the dish to her on her last visit to Russia. It sounded gross but actually tasted quite good. Robert ordered safer, a plate of chicken cutlets.

The waiter left. Red sat back in her chair, arms across her chest. "You got a problem?"

Robert ignored her question. "Why didn't you call?"

"Call? Who are you, my freakin' mum?"

He leaned in and said in his dramatic but low tone, "Red, we're partners. Remember? The plan was for you to call once you got him under wraps."

Red said quietly, "I don't remember it that way. I was to call *only if* needed. I had the situation under control. Didn't need you. No need to have a row over this."

He looked at Red, pondering his next shot. He wanted to talk about how he was concerned for her safety, but he was afraid, so he settled on, "That depends on what you learned. And could you have done better. So, what did Miss Wonder Woman learn?"

"Not much...except for one of the biggest secrets about the Wolf," Red said, voice rising triumphantly as she talked.

"Yeah, like what?"

"The location of his den."

"You learned that?"

"That's right. Any other questions?"

Robert looked confused. "You're telling me you learned where he lives? You did this by yourself? By going into his friend's secure condo, and he just...blurted it out to you. By yourself. Without a gun or any significant weapon. Just—what—your Swiss Army knife?"

"You look surprised. Why? Why is that so hard to believe? And..." She realized her mistake as soon as she said it.

"And what?"

Red could lie, but that wouldn't be smart. He might find out, and it would be worse if she didn't tell the truth. "You remember the photos Monty showed of Dmitry?"

"Yes."

"Well, do you remember the one that showed his left forearm?"

Robert stared at her but didn't answer, not at first.

"Are you saying what I think you're saying?" he shouted.

Red responded tersely, "Lower your fucking voice."

He leaned in. "Well...?"

Red nodded.

"I can't believe this!" he shouted again. "Monty's plan was to gain his trust, not dope him up with heroin."

"I said lower your goddamn voice or this discussion is over! I knew I shouldn't have told you. You're so high and mighty. You act like you've never been on a case...out in the field before. Sometimes you have to make tough choices. Get it?"

The waiter came and served their food, providing them with a cooling off period. When he left, Robert asked, "Where'd you get it?"

Red teased, "Why, you want some?"

"Very funny."

"In every city there's always a place, usually under a bridge or in a sleazy park in a shitty section of town. You dig enough online and you can find out anything. Now that you know my dark secret—which I would appreciate your not repeating, by the way—did you learn anything interesting?"

"As a matter of fact, I did. Monty called when you were on your date."

"And?" she asked impatiently.

"And he provided me with the address for Maya Romanoski."

"Who's Maya?"

"She's an old girlfriend of the Wolf. MI6 thinks they broke up a long time ago, but Monty suggested I pay her a visit, which I did while you were sleeping this morning after your...rough night."

"Ha-ha. Well, did you learn anything important?"

"For starters, she's clearly still pissed at the way the Wolf handled her. She's got blood in her veins, ranting and raving against him. He apparently treated her like crap at the end. Abusive in some way."

"I hope you learned more than that, hotshot."

He glared. "She told me something interesting, but I don't know how it fits. She heard that about ten years ago, a boy from America mysteriously appeared at the Wolf's den—the den that you learned about by poisoning Dmitry. The boy was six or seven."

"How did she find that out? Was she ever there?"

"I pressed her on that, but she claims she received the tip from somebody at the estate. She wouldn't tell me who."

"Description of the kid?"

"Just that the boy was white and had a dimple on his cheek and straight black hair."

"That's a start. But what would the Wolf do with a little kid from America?"

"That's what we need to find out. It may be tied into this, whatever this is."

Chapter 23
London

The agents decided to return to London. Red exhaled once the plane left. Dmitry would've been too embarrassed and scared to report the incident to the Wolf. What would he have said? That he had been duped by a purple-haired junkie woman who forced him to shoot up? That he had invited a fan of Pussy Riot into his luxurious two-level condo?

But still, he had many friends. And Red knew he and his band of subordinates would be looking for her.

The agents prepared and submitted their reports to Monty soon after returning. Monty knew the plan was for Red to get to Dmitry—indeed it was his idea in the first place. But he wouldn't have approved of her methods. Robert didn't approve either. It was too risky. It worked, but MI6 was a process-oriented organization, and Red would be fired if the agency discovered her trick.

Robert promised to not mention her use of the smack. And in exchange, Red agreed to give Robert a greater role in planning future endeavors. They both knew he would have to take her pledge with a grain of salt. Red was, by far, the more experienced field agent.

The agents debriefed Monty. He must have been concerned more about next steps than their methods since he didn't ask many questions. Better for them.

After the conference, they logged onto two adjacent computers. Red swiveled her chair toward Robert, ignoring the creaky noise. Government quality. He looked toward Red, and she said, "I think we're looking for a boy born around seventeen years ago, who disappeared ten years ago." Throwing him a bone she added, "Do you agree, partner?"

A faint smile formed on his lips.

He is too much of a patsy. It's too easy, Red thought. *Cute with his yellowish hair and reddish hue in his cheeks, but in a little boy sort of way.* "Tell me," she said in a bid to make nice, "do you have any brothers or sisters?"

He responded, "Of course. Can't you tell? I'm the youngest of three boys. Surprised?"

Red wasn't. It explained a lot. "What did your dad do?"

"Pa? He was an accountant—until he lost his job. My mum got a job as a baker. She was good—the best in the town. We had to live on her income, and she did well."

"Did he ever work again?"

"No. You see, he had worked for a city agency until he got blamed for some missing money, which was a joke, of course. My pa is one of the most honest persons around. Years later, they caught the dolt who stole the money, but by that time it was too late. He was an old man close to retirement age, already crushed."

"And did that make you want to join the agency?"

"Sort of. I mean, maybe. I never thought about that as a reason until later, until right before I graduated from SLIP. But it makes sense. How about you? What led you to join?"

"Well, I grew up on a farm in a wee bitty town a few hours' drive from Gloucester. Dad was a pisser—always loaded. Never hurt my mum or me, but he was a real arse, plain and simple. He wanted me to stay home. I suppose he looked at me as insurance in case my mum died—stay, take care of him. That crap. 'Girls can't be spies,' he said when I told him. I haven't spoken to him since."

"So you did it to rebel?"

"Absolutely. And also to get out of that shit town. I'm glad I did. I've never looked back."

"How about siblings?"

Red looked at him blankly and simply shook her head.

Robert said, "I'm sorry about that. Interesting—two different backgrounds, but both of us are doing the same thing. Look, I know you have more experience in the field. I think my strength is in the analysis—my pa's skill set that he passed down to me. I'll take a crack at coming up with a list. Deal?"

"Deal. I need to see someone. I'll be back, and then can help narrow down what you find. Try not to include any child that was either found or confirmed dead. Otherwise, you'll have thousands. Also, you're looking for white kids, not Asians, Hispanics, or blacks."

He rolled his eyes at Red as she left.

***

Red thought about checking up on Jasper, but she didn't want to leave Robert alone for that long, and she had something else to accomplish. She walked half a kilometer to her destination and looked up at a modern glass building standing tall in front of her. People were going in and out at a fast clip. Ambulances turned into the emergency room lane, dropped off patients in stretchers, and then quickly left.

She gathered her thoughts and approached the glass doors, which opened automatically, beckoning her inside. There was no turning back. Red put her head down and blew past the volunteer manning the information kiosk. She didn't feel like talking.

Surprisingly, the hospital had a confession booth in the lobby. Red figured that a lot of upset people used the hospital, some needing spiritual relief. She noticed a person waiting. But not her. If she wasn't going to talk to the strangers working at the check-in station, she certainly wasn't going to discuss any personal issues with a priest.

Red took the elevator up to the third floor, where the sign pointed her to the hallway on her right. This time, Red greeted the nurse staffing the desk before she looked up from the book she was reading.

The long-term critical care wing smelled like a toxic combination of urine, fecal matter, bleach, and air freshener. Machines barked brief signals, some half-notes and some whole-notes, but all in a distinctive pattern. If you weren't sick upon arrival, you would be after about ten minutes. This partially explained why patients rarely left the floor, except in a body bag to the morgue.

It had been about eight years since her last visit. She wasn't even planning on going today, but her discussion with Robert had gnawed at her, drawing her.

She ventured into room 305 only to find one empty bed and an elderly woman lying still in the other bed with her mouth open. Tubes drained water accumulating in her mouth and fed her nostrils with oxygen. A bouquet of red and pink tulips in a crystal-like vase and six or seven greeting cards and pictures rested on a table to her right.

By contrast, the empty bed was stripped down to its mattress. No flowers, toiletries, or equipment were housed on the nearby shelves. It looked like the occupant had left a long time ago.

She raced into the hallway, frantically looking for the nurse, the pit in her stomach growing bigger and heavier. "Where's Jimmy?" No response. "Where's Jimmy?" she shouted louder.

"Jimmy?" a skinny black women in a white coat said, looking up from behind her desk. Her carefully braided hair had colorful beads mixed in the cornrows.

"Yes, James McDandy. I'm, uh, his..."

"Sister? Girlfriend? Honey, I've been working here for five years and ain't nobody seen Jimmy since I've been here. You got the right Jimmy?"

"Look, ma'am, here's my identification." Red flashed it quickly. "And here's a picture of him and me before he got sent to this place."

"Sent? What do you mean sent? Where else would a comatose person go? They changed his room is all—he's in 308 now."

Red thanked the woman and walked toward Jimmy's room, hesitating before walking through the door. She approached his bed gingerly. His eyes still had that same amber hue as Jasper, but his body looked frail. She ran out crying hysterically.

Red didn't make it far, the nurse stopping her in the hallway. "Honey? Where you going, girl? You ain't been here in a long time, right? You need to face him."

"What's the difference?" she stammered.

She took Red's hand and said, "For you, sweetie, for you. He's gone, and he's never coming back. His father should let him go, but he ain't easy to deal with. Know what I'm saying? Go to him."

Red thanked her, paused, and began walking back.

The nurse shouted after Red, "You his sister? His file says he has a sister. That you?"

Red wheeled around, tears spilling from her eyes, and said, "Yes."

Jimmy's room was neat. There were no flowers and only one picture.

The picture showed the family during its happier times at the farm. She remembered it clearly. Pa was posing from the front seat of his tractor. Jimmy stood directly below him on the dirt ground wearing a button-down shirt and the quarter vest he liked to wear on the more chilly days. He held a young pig, and smudge marks were visible on his face.

Mum had her arms draped around Red, standing on the other side of Jimmy. Everybody smiled. It was taken when she was seven and Jimmy ten, before Jimmy's accident and the troubles on the farm began.

Pa tried to turn Red into his helper to replace Jimmy after he died. But she wasn't interested in farming, being too self-absorbed as a young girl to try very hard. Pa couldn't keep up with all the work. Crop yields plummeted, and he started to drink.

Red focused on Jimmy's lifeless body. He bore little resemblance to the brother she remembered. His frame had shriveled to half its former size. His face was pale, his body lifeless. The facial scars he had received when the barn loft collapsed onto him were still visible. She took his hand and began to cry hysterically, for the second time in the past fifteen minutes.

Ten minutes later, she walked out. The nurse greeted her warmly.

"What's going to happen to him?" Red asked.

"Ain't nothin' going to happen until your father dies. Don't you know that? He is insisting he be kept alive, still hoping."

"He probably hopes his life will go back to normal. Our family was happy before Jimmy's accident."

"I've seen that before. He's gotta let go, though."

"Yes, he does," Red said before walking back to the elevator.

Red bounced down the stairs to the lobby level, not wanting to run into anybody by taking the elevator. Once in the lobby, she headed outside. But then, just as she had been drawn to see Jimmy, something drew her back inside. She walked into the confession booth and sat on the hard, wooden seat.

Red paused. "Forgive me, father, but I'm not sure where to begin. It has been a long time." No response. *Great, just my luck.* She started to leave.

"Wait. Don't leave. I'm here for you, my child. Start with signing the cross. Relax."

She kneeled and said in synchronicity with the movement of her hand, "In the name of the Father, and of the Son, and of the Holy Spirit." That was the easy part. There were so many things she could have discussed next. She didn't even know which topic to raise. This was a mistake. She was now trapped.

"Yes, my child?"

"Ah...there's a patient upstairs. His name is..."

"No need for last names, my child."

"Right. I'll just refer to him as Jimmy. He's my brother, and he has been in a coma since a farming accident a long time ago."

"Is he going to improve?"

"No."

"This must be hard on you. Do you visit him often?"

"No, never. I'm not good at this sort of stuff."

The priest chuckled. "Not many people are. Don't be so hard on yourself. Do you have anything you want to confess?"

"I just need to talk to somebody. Is that OK?" She wasn't ready to bare her soul and ask for forgiveness.

"Of course. That's why I'm here. I was just helping you along."

"Sorry. As I said before, it's been a long time."

"And you feel bad because you don't visit him enough?"

"Yes, it's too painful. He's never going to recover."

"That's a common reaction, and I understand where you're coming from. But you should understand there's nothing you can do for him at this point. I think you understand that. You feel guilty, but the truth is visiting him is more important for the visitors, not to him. That's the reality you need to face."

Red shook her head glumly, tears collecting again in her eyes. She knew he was right. She needed to visit more often. And maybe one day she could sense a subconscious reaction coming from Jimmy, something in his body still recognizing her, responding to her voice and touch. Doubtful, as the priest implied, but hope can be soothing anyway.

The priest said, "Is there anything else you want to talk about? I sense you're holding back."

"Actually...maybe another time. My boss is trying to make me see a therapist."

"It might help. You seem like you have a few more dragons to slay."

Red nodded and left.

***

An hour later, Red joined Robert, feeling like she had cleansed her soul, at least for a while.

"How's the list coming?" she asked, sitting back down.

Robert didn't even look up. But he did speak. "I tapped in to an FBI database that made it a lot easier. I compiled a list of 206 kids who went missing and were not found during our time frame. I whittled the list down to twenty-nine white kids between four and eight years old who have black hair."

"Wow, that was fast. You're good."

"Ha! You mean the FBI is good. The database allowed me to plug in the parameters, and voilà! It was easy—right down to the black hair. I could have sorted by blond hair, red hair..."

"Great. Your turn for a break. Let me look at the list."

"Break? Thanks, but I'm good. Why don't you take the first half, and I'll take the second half. Here," Robert said, eagerly handing her the first page.

Red looked at him and smiled. He grinned, happy at his progress and her attention. He quickly looked back at his list, afraid she would disapprove of him staring into her eyes — the time not right for something more.

She began pulling up news stories on the disappearance of the first boy on the list. The American media did its usual job of overanalyzing the story—interviewing neighbors, relatives, friends, coaches, even school teachers. Tim was last seen walking to the bathroom at an amusement park. He was never found. A similar incident—a kid named Clovis—occurred nearby in the same county as Tim's amusement park (Sequoyah, Oklahoma) three years later. Again, no knowledgeable witnesses. The police never found Clovis either.

She didn't discover anything else about them. The boys were possibilities to investigate further, although Maya only talked about one child coming from America. She made a note to call the local police for more information. It was a lead, albeit a slim one.

A few hours later, she had eliminated everybody else on her list as not fitting the profile provided by Maya. Discouraged and tired, she needed some coffee.

Red stood and walked over to Robert, who had switched to a computer on the other side of the room.

"Hey, hey," she said, tapping Robert on his shoulder. He looked up at Red from his chair and squinted. He had that look like, *You're disturbing me. Get lost.*

"You want some coffee or something to drink or eat?"

He reached into his pocket, withdrew a protein bar, and pointed to a water fountain. Red left Robert for the second time that day, this time for a stronger drink.

She returned forty-five minutes later. "You making any progress?"

He shook his head in disgust. "All of the kids on my list were buried. And it's standard procedure for the deceased child to be identified through verifiable means, visible confirmation, dental records, et cetera."

"Frustrating, I know. I also didn't learn much. Slim lead about two kids disappearing under similar circumstances three years apart in Sequoyah County, Oklahoma. Both never found. I'm going to follow up, but I'm not sure if it's going to trace back to the Wolf based upon what Maya said about there being only one boy kidnapped from America. What makes you so sure that Maya was telling you the truth in the first place?"

"I dug into her background. I confirmed she had lived with the Wolf for a long time, and then something happened. Next thing you know, she relocates to an apartment building in Moscow. She's lived alone ever since."

"When did this happen?"

"About twelve years ago. *Before* the kid supposedly arrived."

"You got more than that?" she hated how he liked to drag his out explanations, like he was pacing a novel.

Robert gave Red that look. "Of course! I discovered a hospital admission record. He beat her so bad, she wound up in the hospital."

"I see. You're guessing this confirms her story about having an ax to grind."

"A big ax, indeed, don't you think?" Robert asked, mocking Red.

"But you said she also appeared to still...what was the word you used...yearn? Yes, I think you said that. How would that be the case?"

"That's not uncommon. Haven't you heard of traumatic bonding? An emotional tie develops between the abused woman and her partner. The more she gets beaten, the more her self-esteem plummets and she becomes dependent on him."

Red thought about what he said. Her mum became somewhat dependent upon her abusive husband, Red's brilliant pa. It explains why she stayed with him until her death.

She looked at Robert and said, "That makes sense. Nice work. But why wouldn't the Wolf—the terrible, horrible Wolf—have killed her if she knew about his new guest at his hidden lair?"

Robert considered this. "It's a good question, and I thought of two possible explanations. The first is that he still loves her. They were not just long-standing partners, but they loved each other very much. This is not uncommon in abuse situations. Husband beats wife but knows he needs her. He can't help himself. Maybe the guy has a heart after all?"

Red laughed uncomfortably, again thinking about her parents. "I doubt that. What's the second theory?"

"He may not even know she knows about the boy. Remember, they had been close for a long time. And she would've gotten to know some of his associates. Maybe one of them told her at some point."

"Any ideas who?"

"No, not a clue."

Chapter 24
London

Ben Sequoyah was chatty on the telephone. He volunteered that his lineage dated back to George Gist Sequoyah. George, according to Ben's story, invented the Cherokee alphabet in 1821. Red didn't even realize the Cherokee had their own alphabet until Ben informed her.

Ben next asked about Britain, the typical stuff. Is the food in London really that bad? Is there still a king?

He finally answered her real question. He was 99.99 percent certain Tim and Clovis—the two Oklahoman kids that Robert had discovered— didn't wind up in the Wolf's den. Several years ago, a prisoner in the Sequoyah County jail, Marcus Whitmore, was overheard talking about what he had done to the boys.

Marcus refused to reveal where the bodies were. Ben couldn't generate enough evidence to convict, despite Marcus providing him with details that were known only to the police. Marcus died the previous year, shanked in the jailhouse shower.

The agents now had no leads into the identity of the boy who the Wolf had supposedly kidnapped.

Their only real lead was the Wolf and the mysterious body doubles for Saddam. Monty was starting to raise holy hell.

***

They flew into Donetsk International Airport. MI6 had very few assets in that part of the world, and Monty didn't want to involve any, as he put it, foreigners. Operational security. Red had learned not to question such decisions, although in this case it didn't make a lot of sense. The CIA or France's Directorate General for External Security could have resources they could bring in. Without them, they'd be flying blind.

The airport was active, with people bustling all around them. Police patrolled the crowd, some with bomb-sniffing dogs. Other officers armed with machine guns watched warily from their posts.

They hurried through the formalities of landing in a foreign country as best they could, rented a car, and drove to their hotel.

The hotel, a product of the Soviet era, was a six-story structure made out of concrete and little else. Sure, there were windows, but the barren gray concrete overwhelmed the building's facade. It could have been worse; other buildings in Donetsk showed signs of damage from sporadic fighting over the past several years.

The lobby looked just as drab. The floors were covered with cheap linoleum and the walls and ceiling with painted drywall. The owners didn't even bother with flowers. The paint was off-white, and the furnishings were sparse.

Their separate rooms each had one double bed that lay bare on iron springs. Red found stained, threadbare sheets stacked in the closet. A table, dresser, and bathroom with a sink, shower, and pit-squat toilet completed the room. There was no television.

They searched each room for bugs, more for curiosity than any other reason. Removing a bug would be out of the question, as that would only arouse suspicion. Living with an intact bug would preserve their cover story, assuming they didn't say anything stupid.

***

Red and Robert walked into the offices of the Donetsk version of a chamber of commerce. They had an appointment with its chairman, Mr. Alexi Amelin, an elderly man wearing a wrinkled, overused navy suit, white shirt, and red tie. He looked like he had spruced up for the meeting. Red hoped they would not disappoint him. They spoke in English.

Alexi showed them to the chamber's freshly cleaned and potpourri-scented conference room and gestured for the agents to sit down. He leaned forward and began like an excited child, "How pleased I am to make your acquaintance. Your assistant said you are interested in doing business here?"

Robert explained, "We're with a survey team."

"Survey? Ah, yes, you have decided to buy?"

Robert continued, "Our employer is a tire company. We are investigating the area as a possible location for a new plant."

Alexi began his pitch, excitement in his voice growing as he talked. "We have lots of business activity. This is an excellent area to consider. As you probably know, it will be easy to transport the tires you make here to the port in Mariupol. From there, you can ship to anywhere in the world. There also is an ample supply of labor, and most people speak English fluently, like myself, as you can hear."

The agents had prepared for Alexi overstating the case. International businesses generally were not interested in Donetsk. The constant threat of fighting between pro-Russian and Ukrainian government forces made the area too risky.

They hoped to exploit the tenuous situation. The chamber would be eager to answer any question, hoping to land a new business to highlight and begin to rejuvenate Donetsk's tattered economy and image.

Red looked into Alexi's eyes. He looked tired but anxious. She said, "We are looking at five other locations in other countries in Europe and Asia. And I must tell you, our survey is secret. One of the factors used by our superiors is industrial secrecy. If word gets out to our bosses, well, they'll want to go somewhere clse. Do you understand?"

"Of course! I'm used to these types of visits. Happens all the time," Alexi answered with a slight facial tic.

She asked him, "What can you tell me about the area?"

"Well, I already mentioned Mariupol. Then there's the airport. It is busy with lots of activity going on and located only about ten kilometers outside the city. People also get around..."

Robert asked, "What about the other airports?"

Red looked at him again with a scowl, thinking it too soon for that type of question. She quickly added, "Robert, I think the international airport and port are sufficient to bring in people and material. And we'd be shipping out by truck to the port."

Robert sulked. *Too bad*, Red thought. She tried to get Alexi back on track. "Sorry, you were saying..."

"Yes. Eh...people get around by car, bus, and train in these parts. You may have passed by the central train station on your way to the hotel. The workers are educated, and there is plenty of good housing, some of which you may have already noticed."

Robert recovered, asking, "How is the economy?"

Alexi took his time answering. "The area is stable now, and as I said before, we have lots of business activity. People are looking for jobs, and lots are already working."

Red thought to herself: *Stable? And looking for work? Monty told them the unemployment rate was in excess of twenty percent. There's also still intermittent fighting that sometimes encroaches on or close to the area.*

"Are there large tracts of land available?" she asked, already knowing the answer.

"How big?"

"About one hundred acres."

Red noticed Alexi trying to suppress a smile. "We have lots of available land." He barked in Russian into the intercom at his assistant to bring the land reports. A heavyset middle-aged woman walked in carrying a thick document. She seemed like she wanted to throw it at Alexi, probably for disturbing her game of solitaire.

Alexi thumbed through the report and identified numerous available tracts.

Red asked, "Do any of these tracts have more developed infrastructure than others?"

"What do you mean?"

"Like a nearby power plant, telephone lines, reliable Internet connectivity, local airport..."

"Airport?" he asked.

Red answered in a measured tone, "Yes. I said before, the international airport and port are sufficient for our needs. But a local airport can come in handy—you know, small charter flights for company executives, that sort of thing. So, we still need to ask the question. I doubt it will matter much, but you never know, and if we don't ask, they will think we didn't do our job."

Alexi responded by flipping through the report his assistant had handed him earlier. "There are a few local airports. Here is a listing." He tabbed the page and told his assistant to copy it for them.

Robert moved on. "Can you address the rest of my colleague's question? You know, about the power plant, telephone lines, and connectivity?"

Alexi considered how to answer. "Some areas have more access and infrastructure than others. But we're actively seeking business and can work with you."

"How? What do you mean by that?" she challenged.

He leaned back in his chair. "If your company commits, we can help widen roads and anything you need—within reason, of course. Tell us what you want, and I'll let you know. I have connections in the government."

Robert asked, "What about taxes?"

"Same answer, really. We can help, depending upon your level of commitment."

Red smiled. "That's what I hoped to hear. Sounds like there's some flexibility to suit our needs. Why don't we get back to you after talking to our bosses?"

She stood and extended her hand. Robert did the same.

Alexi stood. They shook as he made his last pitch. "Great. I look forward to hearing from you. Let me know what you need, and we'll make it happen."

***

The agents sat in the car after leaving Alexi and scanned the list of airports. They agreed to start their search in the northwest suburbs of Donetsk—an area the MI6 analysts thought was a likely location for the Wolf's lair.

They drove to the first airport on the list. It had started to rain, and the ground became slick. A curvy road led to a small parking lot, and a boxlike building sat a few yards beyond the lot. They opened the door to the building. An eerie feeling pervaded the emptiness. The bare walls looked like cheap scenery, made of thin pressboard.

Red said loudly, "Anybody here? Anybody speak English?"

No response.

Robert spoke even louder than Red, "Anybody here? Anybody speak English?"

No response.

They walked further into the building until a chunky woman with jet-black hair greeted them in dry Russian. "Oh, I wasn't expecting anybody. What do you want?"

Robert replied in Russian, "We are looking to rent a private plane. Do you have any available?"

"No."

"Not even a charter flight?"

"No. This is strictly for private planes to land and take off," she said in a monotone voice before starting to walk away. "Have a nice day," she added as an afterthought.

Red called after her. "Excuse me, but I was wondering if you could help me with something else."

She turned back toward them, unable to hide her displeasure. "Yes?"

"Do you recognize this man?" Red asked, pointing to an old photo of the Wolf. She knew it was a long shot, but they didn't have much else to go on.

The woman looked at it while they studied her reaction. Nothing.

"No," she said woodenly before walking off.

They walked back to the car and drove to the next airport. Having had no luck there, the agents decided to return to the hotel for a quick meal before retiring for the day.

***

The restaurant was located in a plain, square room with threadbare green carpet and white walls. Pictures of scenery that looked to be cut out from a calendar and then framed decorated the walls. The tables, positioned close together, were only about a third filled.

They looked at the menu. Red inquired, "I can understand the borscht and pork, but what is that?" She pointed to the third entry.

Robert looked up and smiled, "That is a Ukrainian fish delicacy. It doesn't say the type of fish, but in these parts, there's a good chance it's pike. Whatever they use is baked in a sour cream sauce and then flavored with carrot, celery, and butter-sautéed onion. It happens to be delicious."

Ugh, thought Red, *that sounds gross.*

"I think I'll pass and stick to the borscht with a side of gefilte fish. I have to use the loo. Can you order for me?"

Red left, and Robert ordered, dutifully obeying Red's command—with one exception.

Red returned just as the waiter was delivering two shots of vodka and water for the table. She didn't want to hurt Robert's feelings by explaining she was a very light drinker. Instead, after the waiter left, she asked, "Vodka? Are we celebrating something?"

Robert looked down and then into Red's eyes, ignoring the direct question but stating, "You know, I never thanked you, Red."

"Thank me? For what?"

"For your help that day at SLIP."

"It was nothing. Any one of us would've done the same thing." Red looked down at her feet; she was not good at accepting congratulations, praise, or thanks.

Robert held up his shot glass to Red, who met his with a loud clink. Robert chugged while Red took a small sip.

"What, you don't like vodka?"

"I'm not a big drinker. But you can finish mine if you like," she said, shifting the glass to Robert.

Robert said, "Thanks. You know that's not true about our group at SLIP. Are you kidding? They would have left me in the pool for a trainer to fish me out. But you came back for me, helping me to the edge of the water to our next station."

"But it wasn't your fault, really. It could've happened to any one of us."

"No, Red. I let the chute collapse on me after landing in the pool. I should've dived down to get around it, but I lost my sense of direction, disoriented after the jump. I had no business passing that test, advancing to the next."

Red took hold of Robert's hand. "We're a team, Robert. Isn't that a big part of what we're supposed to learn at SLIP?"

Robert blushed at Red taking his hand. *Is she trying to say more?*

She slowly let go, her pinking lacking behind, and Robert said, "There's something else about that day I don't understand. What did you tell the instructor about what happened?"

"What do you mean?" Red asked.

"You remember. You think I don't know? You didn't tell him I made a mistake, right?"

She looked at him. "Yes, I lied. That much is true. I told him there was a problem with the pull cord, that it was ripped and it didn't separate properly."

"But they would've inspected the pull cord, to make sure it was broken."

"That's right," Red said, waiting for him to figure it out.

"So...ah...you ripped it yourself?"

"Yes, yours truly. I didn't even think about it, to tell you the truth. I just did it."

"Wow, and you did that knowing you could get caught. The trainer was nearby. He could've seen you, and then you would've been thrown out of SLIP yourself."

Red looked at him and smiled. She had always liked Robert and looked back upon what she had done with pride.

Robert took Red's kindness too far, though. He didn't want to let the moment slip and could no longer suppress his feelings. He reached out, taking hold of both of her hands, and in an awkward gesture, he stood up slightly and pulled her towards him. He bent over the table, kissing her on the lips.

She recoiled. "Wow, that was unexpected. I didn't mean to give you the wrong impression. I'm sorry."

Robert quickly let go of Red's hands and sat back. He felt bad, knowing he had made a mistake. "I'm...sorry, Red. I was just thanking you. Nobody has ever done anything like you did for me before. That's all."

Red paused to gather her thoughts and said, "Apology accepted. I told you, isn't that part of the training? For the trainees to stick together?"

"Well, thanks again, Red."

"How did you figure it out, by the way?"

"Isn't it obvious? They didn't even talk to me about it. Remember what happened to James? He got kicked out for his mistake. Perhaps I should have as well. Maybe I'm not cut out for the field. You've said that yourself."

"No, Robert. I didn't. I said you were a great analyst. That's your strength, but that doesn't mean you can't also be a great field agent. And I've come to trust you even though we haven't been working together for a long time. I wouldn't lie about that. Not with our lives on the line."

"Well, let's drink to that!" Robert said.

They clinked, Red with her water and Robert with the remnants of Red's shot.

The waiter brought the food. They began eating, Robert gingerly pecking at his fish and Red slurping her soup.

"You don't look like you're enjoying your meal, Robert."

"It's ok. It's not like what I've had before."

Red took the opportunity to restore Robert's self-esteem. "Here, let's switch. Your dish actually looks better to me. Would you like to try mine?"

Robert smiled and they switched. Red added pepper to the fish and began eating. It tasted surprisingly good.

They finished their meals and then dessert. The waiter added the bill to their rooms.

Red looked at Robert and chose her next words carefully. "I've enjoyed our talk about something other than the case." Robert perked up until she added, "But I think I'm going to head in for the evening. Busy day tomorrow, you know. Let's meet for breakfast at eight."

"Sure, Red. That sounds great. I'm going to head to the bar for a few drinks first. You want to join me before you leave?"

She considered it but knew better. "I think I'll decline. See you tomorrow."

She stood, kissed him on the cheek, and walked to the elevator.

Chapter 25

Robert watched Red walk away from their dinner table. He had misread her signals over dinner and had taken a chance, something he had wanted to do for a long time, dating back to their days at SLIP.

He should have been disappointed. But strangely, he wasn't. He could finally move on while Red seemed stuck in mud.

When they were first reunited on this case, she seemed manipulative, controlling, demanding. She treated him like a rookie, even though they had graduated from SLIP at the same time. Sure, she had more experience in the field, but her condescending attitude initially irritated him.

However, lately, and especially after their recent time in London, she seemed to be more in control and likeable. She reminded him of how she was at SLIP: stunning, confident, warm—even sticking her neck out for him after his training accident.

Now, he felt sorry for her. She was an emotional wreck, having a lot of deep issues: her dominant, abusive father, tragic history with Jake, and the cat-and-mouse relationship with Monty.

He wanted to protect her. But her problems evidently ran deeper, and dating her would have been a disaster.

Robert walked to the bar, a small room next to the restaurant. He sat in front of the bartender and ordered a shot of Maker's Mark on the rocks. He looked around.

Only a few tables were occupied. A petite woman with dirty-brown hair sitting at one of the tables caught his eye. She was nicely dressed and looked familiar, but her head was down. He couldn't see all of her face even when she had looked up, periodically scanning the room, as if waiting for somebody.

He returned to his drink, positioning his body in a way so he could periodically glance over at the woman. He was drawn to her. She looked up in his direction, and he quickly looked away, not wanting to get caught.

He looked over at her again. She was now in a hurry to finish, pay her tab, and leave. And suddenly he figured out why. Not many women had that same dark hair kept at shoulder length, smallish nose, and clear, light-brown face.

"Maya Romanoski, what a coincidence," Robert said in Russian as he approached her table.

"Hi...I've got to go."

Robert couldn't pass up on this opportunity, though. "Let's chat for a few minutes before you leave. Please, just a few minutes." He sat down without waiting for a response and said softly, "I'd like to continue the discussion we had in Moscow."

He studied her expression. Her face went blank, as if she had been caught cheating. She seemed scared and waited a long time before speaking.

Finally, she said, "I can't talk to you. I'm sorry." She started to stand up.

Robert quickly said, "Maya, sit. I don't want to make a scene. I just have a few questions. Nobody knows me, and nobody knows you, right? So what's the harm? We can talk here or somewhere else. Either way, you're going to answer my questions."

Robert wasn't comfortable putting her in this position, but he had no choice. He imagined Red's reaction if he let her just walk out. Besides, Maya had more to lose. She wouldn't scream for help—that could implicate her for having talked to Robert back in Moscow. If they were quiet, nobody close to the Wolf should notice their discussion, despite his reach.

She seemed to arrive at the same conclusion, saying, "What do you want to know?"

Robert asked, "You told me a boy arrived at the Wolf's den about ten years ago. Correct?"

"Yes."

"OK, how did you know about that?"

"I told you, I heard rumors."

"Yet you described him as having a dimple and straight black hair, even though you never saw him?"

"So? What's the problem? My contact described the boy. Isn't that obvious?"

"Maybe, but I checked, and nobody like that got kidnapped in America ten years ago."

"How do you know? You know everybody that got kidnapped?" Maya asked.

Robert responded confidently, staring into her eyes. "It was actually easy to determine. My partner and I checked the FBI database, looking at all boys that fit the description you gave. We checked on all possibilities and struck out. So, let me ask you, why did you lie to me?"

Maya looked at the ground.

"You're really working for him, aren't you?" Robert asked.

She looked up at Robert, unsure of what to do next. She rose from her seat, but Robert grabbed her arm and held her down. The bartender began to approach, but she waved him off.

She drew a breath and pleaded, "You know the Wolf and I were once madly in love. We were going to get married. But he changed after the Soviet Union broke up in 1991. He became obsessed with America, blaming it for all of our troubles. He turned his anger against me, trying to control and demean me. He even began sleeping around. I couldn't take it anymore and eventually walked out. The asshole didn't even care.

"We broke up, and that's the truth. I've never been to his estate. I heard it's somewhere in this area of the country, but I have no idea. You must believe me. I don't know why you didn't find the kid in some stupid American database kept by the incompetent FBI!"

Robert considered her answers, realizing she was telling the truth. Information provided by MI6 confirmed she was not only abused but beaten. He switched topics.

"Is there anything else you can tell me about the kid?"

She hesitated. Robert knew she was hiding something.

"Maya, you want this conversation to end, right? I promise I'll leave you alone. Or, if you want, I can call for my friend upstairs, and we'll both question you. Tell me what you know!"

"I'm not sure it even matters that much, but my friend also said he spoke to the boy soon after he first arrived."

"He spoke to him? What was the boy's name?"

"Abe."

"What else did the boy say?" Robert pressed.

"Just that he missed his brother, Shmuel. I think they are twins."

"Can I talk to your friend?"

"I'm afraid that's impossible," Maya said, looking dejected.

"Why?"

Maya said softly, "He died of an overdose several days ago."

Robert's stomach churned, and he instantly felt sick. He finally said, "Really? That's a little convenient, don't you think?"

"It's the truth, I swear."

"His name?" he asked, even though he knew she was referring to Dmitry.

"I can't tell you. If I told you, the Wolf could trace it back to me. He knows that I know him. He used to come to our apartment back in St. Petersburg."

Robert appreciated Maya's position and didn't want to press further. Instead, he asked, "What are you doing here?"

Maya looked at him and stared. "I actually live in Moscow and am here on business."

"Business?"

"Yeah, I'm a sales representative for a truck parts company. I like this place and stay here when in town. Great bar to pick up guys! That a crime? I don't work for the Wolf. That's all you need to know."

Robert thanked Maya, pleased with what he had accomplished. He and Red had their first solid lead.

Chapter 26
Donetsk

After a good night's sleep, Red met Robert at the scheduled time of 8:00 a.m. for breakfast, at the same restaurant as the previous night. They ordered light and were served black bread, watery juice, and hard-boiled eggs. The restaurant was more crowded, and the tables were again crammed close together.

Robert said, "Red, something interesting happened after you left. At the hotel in the bar over there I met..."

Red immediately leaned her head in and interrupted in a soft voice, "Is this about the case?"

"Yes."

"Let's chat in the car then. We'll have more privacy, and we've got to get going anyways."

They paid and began walking to their car, parked on the side of the street opposite from and diagonal to their hotel. Robert suggested he drive. He was tired of her zigzag turns, abrupt stops, and rapid accelerations.

"Robert, I forgot my notepad in my room. I'll be right back," Red said, turning around before opening the passenger door. She picked up her pace, knowing her blunder was holding up the morning's adventures.

As she reached the hotel's driveway, a large explosion suddenly ripped through the street, knocking her down. People screamed, and smoke engulfed the air.

She looked back at the car. Robert burned inside, his face in agony. He was struggling, trying to get out.

Red rose and ran towards the car, but the fire was too much. He looked towards her as she approached and dropped to the ground. The fuel line ignited, causing a secondary explosion. Shards of glass, metal, small fireballs, and plastic fell around Red. She heard and felt nothing.

***

Red dreamed...

Pa is in a drunken stupor, ridiculing Mum and herself, treating them as his personal slaves. Fetch him some Scotch. Clean up his mess. Fetch him a beer. Fuck him!

Jake barges into the house through the front door, tackling Pa, pinning him down on the living room floor. Jake smashes Pa's head against the floor. Blood gushes from Pa's nose while Mum looks on, a rare smile forming on her lips.

Robert enters his car immediately before it explodes, killing him instantly. Red watches nearby as if she knows what would happen and set him up to die.

Pa reemerges: drunk, hitting Mum while Jimmy looks on. She doesn't even recognize the lad she is sleeping with. Empty beer cans are on the floor, and a painting of Mum, frowning in her favorite blue holiday dress, hangs crooked on the wall. Jake is looking in through one of the windows, tears running down his face.

Red feels empty, light as a feather.

***

Red's eyes opened for a second. She saw a little girl staring back at her. She closed her eyes, they opened again, and the girl ran out. Red thought to herself, *Where am I? What is this place?*

Red heard a knock, and then a woman entered without waiting for her response, as if used to receiving none.

"All of us speak English. My husband picked you up from the driveway. You would have died. They would've killed you. We're part of a group fighting for Ukrainian nationalism. You are now safe. How do you feel?"

Red stared back, not knowing what to say. The room looked empty, except for Red's small twin bed on a metal frame and an old wooden chair used by the girl. A framed picture of Jesus wearing a golden sash around his chest adorned the otherwise beige bare walls.

"Do you remember what happened? Your car exploded, your friend died. I'm sorry for your loss."

Red whispered, "Who?"

"This is the work of a man—you have a picture of him in your pocket. It's his trademark, his...handiwork. Our people get bombed the same way. But you, we don't know. You're obviously not from here."

"But...police?"

"Dogs." The woman spat on the floor for effect. "They would have taken you to him! Get some rest. We'll talk about this later. Wait for my husband to come home. He may know more."

Red awoke later that day, stinging pain coming from her shoulder and head. She sat up and again saw the little girl watching her.

"How old are you?" Red asked the curious child.

"Seven."

"What is your name?"

"Dasha."

"That is a pretty name. Do you know how long I've been here?"

"My papa brought you here three days ago. Papa! Mama!" Dasha shouted.

A lean, muscular man with a scruffy face entered. "I'm Petro. I believe you've already met my wife, Katerina."

Katerina carried a tray with a bowl of borscht, hot tea, and a roll. Red started to get up, but the woman held up the palm of her hand and said, "Stay! Save your strength."

"I'm OK. I've...got to...go to the bathroom."

"Here, let me help you," Katerina said, helping Red to her feet and escorting her to the bathroom. Red did her business, and Katerina walked her back to the bed.

Petro said, "We helped you to the bathroom before, but you were still delirious. This is the first time you regained your senses. You must have had a pretty bad concussion. You were knocked to the ground, unconscious. You also had a piece of metal sticking out of your shoulder."

Katerina interrupted, "He's a doctor. He works at the hospital." She smiled and looked up at her husband.

"Well, not a doctor, not really. She likes telling people that. I help out. I have some medical training, but not much. I've seen men, women, and even children with injuries like yours. It happens too much in our country, I'm afraid." His voice trailed off softly.

"I...need to get out of here." Red tried to get up, but a wave of nausea sent her back onto the bed. She sat up against the backboard and began eating from the tray of food Katerina brought.

"English?" Petro asked.

"Yes."

He asked, "How long have you been in town?"

"Few days."

"Have you been here before?"

Red looked at him, not used to being interrogated, at least by civilians. But Petro may have saved her life. And what if Katerina was telling the truth about the police? She couldn't know for sure, but she knew she could learn as much information, if not more, than she would give.

"No. Look, I understand why you're questioning me. You want to know about the picture? Let's just say I'm...looking for him. What about you? Katerina said you are a Ukrainian nationalist?"

"Yes, that much is true. The man in your picture—you might know him as the Wolf—is a rat from the Soviet era. He's living in the past and is fighting to turn the clock back to the 1960s or even earlier."

"How can I trust you?"

Petro and Katerina looked at each other. Katerina looked like she was about to cry. "Dasha, please come here." Dasha entered the room. "Tell our guest what happened in your class."

Red could see Dasha's eyes begin to tear.

"Mr. Stavocheck was teaching us about Ukrainian history when the bad guys came in." She pulled her shirt to the side and showed a scar running across her right shoulder.

Katerina said, "Thank you, sweetie. That's enough. You can go back to what you were doing."

Red didn't know what to say, settling on an inadequate, "I'm sorry."

Petro explained in a low tone, after making sure Dasha was not nearby, "The Wolf and his band of rebels came to her class. They must have had the teacher on some sort of list. They wanted to make an example of him and started to drag him out of the room until Dasha went to intervene. Poor child. The Wolf slashed her with his knife."

"What happened to the teacher?"

He looked to the ground. "We don't know but can assume the worst. Nobody has seen him since. We fear he may be in one of the burial grounds. We already discovered two where civilians have been buried after being tortured and shot. He wasn't there, but there are other places."

She thought about what to say next. Taking a chance, she said, "I'm actually looking for his compound. Do you know where it is?"

"Of course. Everybody knows where it is. You just need to know who to ask. But I'm afraid you're too late."

"Too late?"

"Yes. We have a source who said the Wolf left two days ago, maybe even for good. I just came from there. I can take you when you are ready."

***

Petro and Red ventured to the compound two days later, the first day she could walk far without getting nauseated. They pulled off the main road into a wooded area and parked the car.

Petro looked at her for reassurance. She said, "Don't worry about me. I'm probably in better shape than you are, even at half strength."

He laughed.

A car approached. Red gave Petro a worried look and scampered into the nearby bushes for cover. He looked at her with amusement.

The car stopped, and two burly men toting semiautomatics jumped out. Petro gave each a bear hug, motioned for her to appear out of the bushes, and introduced Red to his associates.

She asked, "What's with the muscle? I thought you said this place was abandoned?"

Petro stated the obvious. "You want to take a chance? After what happened to you? We've also lost a lot of men. This guy is smart, unpredictable, tough."

They hiked to a point high above the compound where they scanned the compound and surrounding guard posts for the next twenty minutes. Nobody came into view—not a child, woman, man, or even a dog. It looked quite abandoned.

They hiked down, preserving the element of surprise. A quick scan of the guard towers from their different vantage point verified the posts were indeed empty.

Petro opened the gate, and they ventured inside. The buildings were empty. Red spotted an odd-shaped brick building with no windows. It had a high ceiling. She motioned for Petro to join her, and they walked up the steps together, Petro in front, gun at the ready.

It took about twenty minutes for them to break the lock. They walked in and noticed debris covering the floor: a pair of rubber gloves, a soiled laboratory coat, broken glass, twisted metal, rubber hoses. A barrier separated them from an inner chamber, which contained even more debris.

Petro looked at Red in horror, but she didn't think he truly understood the magnitude of their discovery. Red looked at him, her gut aching more than the pain in the rest of her body.

PART THREE
THE LOCKKEEPER'S HOUSE

Chapter 27
Washington:
Thursday, September 14

Adams Morgan is a trendy part of Washington, rich in diversity, restaurants, and bars. The blues are played at Madam's Organ, whisky and other spirits are nonchalantly sipped at the Jack Rose Dining Saloon, and tourists and residents gawk at the colorful row houses, murals, and other street art.

Jake enjoyed the street vibes on his terms, knowing he could escape the busyness at any time to the solace of his nearby 10th floor penthouse condominium located on a side street one block from Connecticut Avenue. His building had plain white brick on the outside but was immaculately maintained on the inside with an elegant lobby guarded by Dawit, the building's helpful, lanky Ethiopian doorman.

Dawit held the door open and greeted Jake with a wide smile. They bantered their usual small talk about the Redskins. How many games are they going to lose this year? Do they have a shot at making the playoffs? Should the coach be fired if they don't?

The elevator took Jake to his floor. He opened the door, stepped inside, and called for Charming. No response. "Charming?" he said again louder. Still no response. *Was he sleeping at 3:00 in the afternoon?*

The front door had been locked as Jake had left it, but he could see a light in the kitchen from the open living room. His plush, white carpet was mushed with the shapes of a trail of footprints. He tiptoed through the room and approached the kitchen, bracing to meet his intruder. A tub of ice cream sat atop the counter.

No robber would stop to have ice cream. Still, he couldn't be sure. He grabbed a steak knife from the counter near the door—not much protection against a gun, but it was better than nothing.

He called out, thinking his brother had entered, "Samuel? Samuel, you here?"

Nobody responded to Jake's call. He peered around the kitchen wall to his right into his bedroom. Nobody. He looked through the living room to the left on the other side.

The door to his study was cracked, and the light was on. He tiptoed, knife in hand, and pushed the door open. Red was sitting on a chair by the window watching his blood parrot fish swim in his sixty-gallon tank. Charming was on her lap. A bowl with traces of ice cream and a dirty spoon rested on a table in front of her.

She chuckled softly and leaned back against the chair.

"A knife? Really? That's the best you got? My, my, my, you really are a Boy Scout, aren't you?"

Jake towered over her. "You scared me. What the hell are you doing here? And why didn't you call in advance?"

The look on her face answered his question. They moved to the living room. He sat on his leather reclining chair, and she sat on the coach.

His voice softened. "You're in trouble. What happened?"

Red's hair looked dirty, she smelled foul, and her face was greasy. Her eyes glistened as she told Jake about Donetsk, she but steered far from her trip to Moscow. She started to sniffle as she described the bombing. She pointed to the tissue box when she reached the part about her failed attempt at rescuing her partner.

Jake handed her the container, which she promptly invaded, taking a wad to her nose.

Jake choked up, listening to her talk, and lamely added, "Wow, oh my God, I don't know what to say. That sounds awful. He sounds like he was a great person. Red, why do you think the two of you were targeted?"

She knew better than to tell Jake what she feared the most: that her adventures with Dmitry may have gotten back to the Wolf, putting him on alert. Maybe he had his cronies waiting for her in Donetsk. Somebody had tipped them off, scaring him. Why else would he have abandoned his estate within days after the bombing? But she didn't feel comfortable telling Jake any of this, instead choosing to suggest a leak in MI6 as the culprit.

"Don't you think it strange that two days after we landed we got bombed? We didn't even find out anything, and I'm not sure we had made any progress."

"So, you think someone at MI6 gave the Wolf a warning that you were coming, that you were looking for him?" Jake asked.

"It's the only thing that makes any sense. They were probably trailing us since we landed. It turns out the Wolf's compound was near one of the airports we investigated. We were getting closer, a little too close."

"You said you met with the economic development official. Couldn't it have been him?"

"I'm not sure. It's possible, I suppose. But does it make sense to you that the Wolf is going to place a valuable source at a chamber of commerce–like position? There are so many other better uses for informants. Wouldn't you place folks at other agencies within the government, like police, military, intelligence?"

Jake shrugged. "He has tentacles everywhere. His payroll is huge."

They talked some more until Jake couldn't resist. "Red, you've been through hell. I'm sorry you had to deal with that. What are you going to do about Monty though? Don't you need to let him know? I'm sure he's looking for you. He may not even know what happened. He's going to want you to return to London, which probably makes sense, don't you think? Has he tried to contact you?"

"Oh, I'm sure they have, but my satellite phone batteries died. I got rid of the damn thing and haven't tried to contact them. By now they surely think I'm off the grid. Maybe I died in the explosion, with my body taken by the Wolf or his people. That's what any witnesses would say, that I dropped to the ground and somebody picked me up. Yes, definitely, could've been the Wolf."

"Hmm," Jake murmured, rubbing his chin. "Leave anything important in your hotel room?"

Red leaned back again. "Not really, nothing important that can be traced to anything meaningful."

"How about the passport you used to get here?"

"Fakes. I got them outside of conventional sources. People I know and trust."

"Anything else?" asked Jake.

"Well...yes, I left my notepad. That was what I was going to get when I turned away from the car. I left it in the room."

"Anything important in the notepad?"

"No, no concern there. We pretty much struck out, and I didn't have any old notes. Standard protocol. What do we do now?" She straightened up and looked at Jake, a twinkle in her eye. Charming purred.

Jake tried to suppress a smile. He coyly said, "Well, how about you take a nice, hot shower. You look like crap."

***

They ordered delivery, General Tsao's chicken for Jake and, like a good Londoner, curry chicken for Red. They agreed to split an order of pan-fried dumplings, moving to the kitchen table after their feast arrived.

"Let's start by reviewing a few key facts, shall we?" Jake said as his chopsticks crossed too far, causing him to fumble a dumpling onto the floor. Jake pretended it didn't happen, quickly scooping it back up onto his plate before Charming could attack it. "What, never heard of the five-second rule?"

"We're a tad more civilized in Britain, Jake. That's an American habit. Why don't you start with the review?"

"You said you found glass, rubber, and even a lab coat. Are you thinking this connects to the anthrax?"

"Not sure," she said, although the doubt in her voice told Jake the real answer.

"I also don't think so. Remember what Moshe thought, that Jabal's note spoke to a larger plot than anthrax?" Jake rose and retrieved a file from the living room. "Let me show you what I found while you were deep inside the former Iron Curtain."

Jake stood at the table, searching the file for some pictures and handing them to Red.

"I came across these while researching Jabal. See these?" He pulled out the three images he had separated from the others. "Look what he's doing in this one." He pointed to the one where Jabal donned protective gear, ready to enter the Tuwaitha nuclear complex.

"Remember what you found in Damascus about the Punic Wars?" Jake asked.

"I remember you had no clue what I was talking about," Red laughed. "But continue."

"Moshe and you both felt this is not *really* about anthrax. It is something bigger."

"Like salting the earth," Red said.

"Yes, like salting the earth. Well, I think I may have discovered something that ties into that. First, some background."

Red sighed, telling Jake to get to the point. But Jake was enjoying himself.

"Did Bush find any weapons of mass destruction in Iraq?" Jake asked rhetorically.

Red hesitated and shook her head indecisively.

"You're right to hesitate, because he did. Any guess where?" Jake looked at Red.

"At Tuwaitha?" Red said, voice wavering.

Jake answered. "Correct. Score one for her majesty's secret service. In 2003, the Americans discovered about five hundred tons of yellowcake at the Tuwaitha Nuclear Research Center, not too far away from Baghdad. The stuff was low-grade, sitting in old barrels. The US sat on the discovery for years, fearing it would lead to others trying to capture it. They didn't know what to do, other than guard the material."

"What finally happened to the stuff?"

"The Americans shipped it off to Canada!" Jake exclaimed as if delivering a punch line.

"Canada?"

"Yes, can you believe it?"

"Makes sense, I guess. They get all of America's crap: draft dodgers, pollution, criminals escaping to the north," Red said.

"Funny, real funny. It was actually a great idea. Operation McCall. They moved about thirty-five hundred barrels by road to an airport in Iraq. Then they flew it, using thirty-seven different military flights to an atoll."

"An atoll?"

"Atoll is an island reef, in this case Diego Garcia, located in the Indian Ocean. From there they put it on one of our largest planes—a Globemaster—bound for Canada."

"What did your northern friends do with the bloody stuff?" Red leaned forward.

"A Canadian uranium company used it to fuel its reactors in Ontario." Jake shrugged his shoulders.

"Brilliant. Your country recycled the stuff. Very green, I must say," Red said. She next asked the obvious question, "Well, if it was disposed of, then how does that fit into your...little story?"

"Right. Good point. Well, Jabal would've been there well before the Americans. Who's to say there wasn't a barrel or two missing from what they found?"

"And you think Jabal had at least one of these *missing* barrels?"

"Could be. Think about it. We know the Wolf was high up in the KGB. The KGB had ties to the Baath Party. Jabal was in the Baath Party—even respected for his work as a double. The Wolf could've been working with him during the buildup of US forces *before* the invasion. Heck, he could've manipulated members of the Iraqi military, including Jabal, into shipping him the missing barrels on the *pretense* that it made sense to spread the resources around in case the Americans discovered Tuwaitha. In fact, at one point, people in the US thought Saddam himself ordered the material be split up and buried in people's backyards."

Red looked at Jake and said, "I must admit, it makes sense. Using your theory, the glass and debris we found wouldn't have been lab equipment to make anthrax. There was too much for that anyway. The debris could have been centrifuges used to enrich the yellowcake."

"And the fact you found the building destroyed, presumably by the Wolf?" Jake asked.

"I suppose the Wolf was spooked by my visit. And remember, I still believe it is plausible somebody at MI6 tipped him off," Red said, feeling guilty for not telling Jake what she really thought. Jake would never understand the manner in which she elicited information from Dmitry about the Wolf's compound.

"But wouldn't he double down and fight to protect the valuable equipment? After all, this is his turf. Who's going to barge in on him, your Ukrainian nationalist friends? There are enough separatists in that area to help the Wolf."

"Unless…" Red paused.

"Unless what?"

"Unless he had finished whatever he was doing. Then it might have just been easier to destroy everything and move on to the next phase," Red said, her voice trailing.

Chapter 28

Washington: Friday, September 15 to Saturday, September 16

Jake awoke on the couch to Charming's purrs for food as the sun began to rise. He had forgotten to fill his bowl. The cat had just jumped on top of him, after having slept in his bed with Red. She had insisted on taking the couch, but Jake wouldn't agree—she needed sleep more than Jake. Tired and a tad jealous, he pushed Charming, but that just increased the cat's resolve. *Did you enjoy your night on the bed sleeping with Red?* he thought.

Jake tried to go back to sleep but couldn't. He had tossed and turned all night, unable to fall into a deep sleep. His back was hurting, his mind racing.

He decided to go for a morning run. Nobody was around on the jogging trails. He could enjoy Rock Creek Park, his personal backyard. The only humans around whizzed by in cars: a lobbyist bound for K Street, a diplomat headed for Embassy Row, a staffer off to Capitol Hill.

But Jake had more mundane issues to consider on his run. *Could I trust and work with Red again? Is she being paranoid about not involving MI6? How long can she remain "off the grid," and what happens when MI6 finds out she is alive and...working with me?* No easy answers.

***

Jake walked back into his condo, sweat dripping out of every pore. Red had taken over the kitchen, rustling up some bacon and eggs.

"Hey, running man, food's getting cold. Work out your dark thoughts?"

Jake looked at her approvingly. It had been a long time since anybody had cooked for him. His mood changed when he saw Charming standing by her side. "I see you have a new friend. What'd you bribe him with? I'll be back in a few."

The refreshing water allowed Jake to think more about his new roommate. His feelings alternated between confused, upset, and excited.

He emerged twenty minutes later, taking his place at the table, allowing Red to serve him. She sat and they enjoyed their second meal together. Red broke an awkward silence at the beginning with a profound womanly burp. They laughed like children.

After the meal, while drinking coffee at the table, Jake declared, "Let's play out the yellowcake scenario."

"OK, shoot."

"The Wolf enriches the uranium and shuts down the operation. Presumably he's now onto the next phase. He has enough for a dirty bomb or other concoction, and the target is the good old USA. Jabal and the Wolf *both* have a beef against America."

Red sat up straight and continued the story. "Next question is how does he move the stuff. Moshe mentioned traffic about a possible shipment. Makes sense—I can't imagine flying it, especially through his chummy private airport. Can't go that far on a Cessna, with the delicate, enriched yellowcake. What's the closest port to Donetsk?"

"I'm not sure, hold on." Jake left to retrieve his laptop from his office, feeding his blood parrots their dried pellets while there. He emerged a few minutes later, turning it on midstride as he walked back to his chair in the kitchen. "There appears to be several ports: Mariupol in the Azov Sea and others in Crimea—Kerch, Sevastopol, Yalta, Evpatoria, and Theodosia, to name a few."

"Distances?" Red stood and began pacing.

"Looks like all within an eight-hour drive of Donetsk."

"And you can drive the stuff by truck?"

"Don't see why not. And the Wolf would've had resources for protection on the trip," he said.

Red returned to her seat. "OK. So now what? You've moved the yellowcake to a port."

Jake stood and began washing the dishes. He looked back at Red. "Wait a minute. It would have to be a large ship, right? You're not getting far with a small vessel—just like your Cessna example."

"OK, I'll bite."

"Ships have preplanned routes. They make several stops, like a bus route. Cargo companies, freight forwarders, workers—they all need the schedules planned like clockwork. Otherwise the system would break down. Say you're an iron company shipping goods to America. And you need to get it there by July first. You'll need accurate information well in advance so you can plan which ship to get your product on."

"And?" Red asked, not quite getting the point.

"And? Don't you see? I'll bet there are schedules you can find online. The information's got to be out there."

"Brilliant! You start checking. I've got to use the loo," Red said.

By the time Red returned, Jake had figured out how to get the schedules. He told her, "I called a friend of mine. He's with the FBI, works with the customs bureau. We go way back. I told him I was working on a story and what we needed. He pointed me to a database that shippers use. It'll take me some time, but I think I'll be able to get what we need."

Red replied, "Resourceful. Good. But what's bothering me is how would they get the stuff through customs? Aren't there detectors?"

"I've been thinking about that too. Look, don't discount their abilities. It would be difficult but not impossible. People smuggle drugs in all the time."

Red interrupted, "This isn't drugs, though. It's yellowcake."

Jake said, "True, but the system for checking is complicated. They can't check all the containers, and I bet there are ways to dampen the signature of yellowcake. It's a good question, though."

"I'm going to get a refill on my coffee—bit of jet lag to get over. How can I help you pull the information together?" she asked.

"Not sure yet. Let me begin, and I'll let you know. You can use the computer in the study to do a deeper dive into what I pull."

Jake called her an hour later. "Red, let me show you something."

She returned, standing over him, her breath reaching his neck.

He continued, "Look here. These are screen prints of the routes for fifteen ships that docked at one of our ports around Donetsk within the past two weeks and that are also headed to the US. The list is not complete. I just want to show you the information out there."

"Why two weeks?" asked Red.

"I thought you said your friend, Petro, said the Wolf disappeared shortly after the explosion. I expanded it to two weeks so we don't miss anything. Make sense?"

"Right, I'm tracking. What about the future? I mean, he could've stored the stuff in another place temporarily."

"I'm going to look at the next four weeks after I finish with the past two weeks, so six weeks total.

Red leaned on the back of Jake's chair, slumping forward even closer to Jake. Troubled, she said, "I'm not sure four weeks into the past is enough. If he moved up his timetable because Robert and I were on his trail, he'd store it until the ship he was going to take originally docked."

"That's a risk. I agree. He must've been close enough to finishing though. Otherwise, he wouldn't have destroyed his lab. His bomb killed Robert and wounded you. He could've stayed to finish. Let's start with four and see where that gets us. Agreed?"

Red nodded, "You want me to start looking at the first fifteen? What am I looking for?"

"Well, I actually think that part of it is easy—just a lot of grunt work. Right up your alley," Jake teased.

"Funny man you are not." Red chuckled, suddenly aware she was standing a little too close to Jake.

"I would create a spreadsheet with all the ships. Maybe classify them by name and record the arrival date in the US, name of US port, size of ship, type of cargo, et cetera. See here? This link is to a website that lists the entire routes." Jake pointed to a web page and continued. "We know the starting point, and we're looking to eliminate any that don't go to the US for, say, a year. This could still be a long-term plan, but the Wolf's not going to have this stuff out at sea for more than a year."

Red jumped in. "So you continue with the master list of all ships going to the US over the six-week period, and I build the spreadsheet with the particulars for the possible culprits?"

"That works for me. You can start with the first fifteen—I'll send the list and links to your private email account."

"Brilliant."

***

They worked in tandem for the rest of the day and the next, until they finished.

Jake looked at the list. Eighty were listed, but most weren't serious candidates.

"Phew, only twenty. Let's sort it by ports in the US. I mean, do we both agree they would be targeting the east coast, most likely DC?" Jake asked.

"Probably, especially since the Wolf is calling the shots, not Jabal. The Wolf would want to go after the organs of your government, not symbolic places like Hollywood or Vegas," Red said.

A few clicks later and Jake reduced the twenty to five: two in New York, one in Philadelphia, one in Baltimore, and one in Norfolk. They studied each of the ships.

Jake said, "These all look like good candidates. How do we narrow this down further? We can't handle this by ourselves."

Red replied, pleading, "We can handle it. Besides, what choice do we have at this point? Who else is going to get involved when all we have is some broken glass from a lab near Donetsk and an interesting story?"

"My credibility. I've still got a lot of friends I can call at some point."

Red ignored him. "Wait. Wait a minute. Check this out. See the ship name? *St. Pete.*"

"So?"

Red beamed, "So, isn't it obvious? St. Pete for Saint Petersburg? I bet you didn't know the Wolf actually grew up there, with Putin as a matter of fact. They also worked together before the breakup of the Soviet Union. What better way to bring back the Soviet Union."

"When does it arrive?"

"It says here it arrives in Baltimore exactly three weeks from today. No need to make your call," Red said and then added, "We don't have enough at this point, just a few hunches. If you call too soon and we're wrong, you'll be like the boy crying wolf when we finally have something."

Chapter 29
Baltimore:
Saturday, October 7

They travelled to Baltimore in time to watch for the *St. Pete*. Jake ignored Red's caution about calling for help, contacting the person he talked to three weeks prior, FBI customs bureau agent Bud Dupree. The stakes were too big, and Jake was sure they were onto something. *Can't Red see that?*

Jake knew Bud from when he supervised the man as chief of the NYPD. Bud was a big guy with a scruffy face who walked with a slight limp, the result of getting shot while working as a detective. He got a job in FBI customs thinking he wouldn't have to be as active. This time, Jake explained more about the situation, without mentioning Red.

Jake and Red watched for the *St. Pete* from a hotel room they rented across the Baltimore harbor. Jake borrowed a pair of high-power binoculars, telling Red he hawked them off a "friend." They were hoping to spot the Wolf or Jabal leaving the ship.

They knew the ship would be in port for three full days for scheduled maintenance, the perfect amount of time for the Wolf and Jabal to put their plan in motion. The cramped crew would be eager to leave the ship. It was just a matter of waiting for them—and the marks—to leave.

But the ship didn't arrive at 11:00 a.m. as expected. Jake looked at his watch with growing concern. Red looked calm. Jake watched her with envy, her shiny red hair blowing in the light breeze on the balcony. He suddenly wished there was no case, that he and Red had normal jobs and were here stealing a few hours together, a midday romp, playing hooky from their jobs. He grew hard thinking about it.

He wished for another chance with her. She was there for him. She had said as much through her actions of traveling across the pond, as she liked to say, to see him. Even going "off the grid."

They ordered room service at noon. Lunch arrived a half hour later. They ate in silence, taking turns watching for the ship. A few hours after lunch, they began discussing the worst-case scenarios: What could have happened? How could an entire ship have disappeared?

After a few more moments of panic, Red suddenly shouted to a sullen Jake, "It's here! It just pulled in. Just a tad tardy. Better late than never. Isn't that what you Yanks like to say?"

They continued to watch the port from the balcony, sharing the high-power binoculars. It was crowded. Mobile cranes were busy unloading and loading other ships. Trucks and equipment raced around, some going to meet the *St. Pete*, unaware of its dangerous cargo.

As if on cue, four unmarked black cars raced into the port, surrounding the dock where the *St. Pete* had arrived. Men jumped out and cordoned off the area. Bud barked orders. Sharpshooters provided security.

Jake felt a knot in his stomach. He looked at Red and smiled.

Red frowned. "You're such a donkey. Do I need to leave? I'm not ready for questioning."

Jake replied before running out of the room, "No, I'll go down. They don't know about you, I swear. I trust Bud, my contact. He's the guy I called before about the shipping database. I'll come back here soon. Watch me through the binoculars. If I think you should cut bait, I'll raise my right arm before scratching my head."

Red put her hands on her waist and puffed up her chest, glaring at Jake. Jake looked back at her, winking before letting the door close.

***

Jake drove his car from the hotel to the Port of Baltimore. Security had brought life to a standstill. Forklifts were in suspended animation, some with pallets raised above the machine, others empty. The tall white and blue cranes looked like King Kong just before the colossal ape fell to the ground after being shot, stabbed, and netted. Jake felt back in the game, proud and important, having caused the chaotic freeze.

Bud waived him through the security cordon. They shook hands.

"Thanks for coming," Jake said, "you tell the crew to come out in groups? Standard procedure?"

"Of course. Groups of five. We'll know soon enough if your guys are on it. You know what they look like, right?"

"I've seen pictures of the Wolf, and Jabal and I are like...old friends." Jake grunted.

The crew disembarked over the next hour. "You see your men?" Bud asked.

"No."

Bud motioned to his subordinates to search the ship, which by this time looked empty except for the customs agents who looked tiny in the distance. The ship was blue on bottom with a flat, brown open cargo bay. Containers were lined up, stacked four high. A white, sterile control tower, exuding authority, towered over the containers in the middle of the hold.

The agents emerged about a half hour later, shaking their heads. The team lead squawked to Bud over his walkie-talkie, "Nobody except for a skeleton crew of engineers. We took pictures of them."

He brought the pictures to Bud, and he and Jake surveyed them. Jake shook his head a few minutes later in disgust.

Bud said in an irritated voice, "Well, it looks like they're not on it. This was a complete waste, Jake."

Jake sighed, dropping his shoulders. "I'm sure this is the right ship, though. Do you mind if I search the cargo with your men? I'd like to look at some of the containers."

Bud shook his head. "Jake, you and me, we go way back, and I know you know your shit. But I got different bosses now. I can't keep spending *my* resources on *your* hunch."

Jake raised his voice. "Hunch? I literally almost lost my head on this case. You *seemed* to understand how all of this fits together on the phone. So don't give me that hunch crap."

"What evidence do you have this is even connected? Unless you're holding back on me," Bud snapped back. He then softened his voice. "Develop something, and then we'll talk, but for now, we're out of here."

Bud released the ship's crew, telling them, "Sorry—spot checks, you know. Normal. Have a nice day." He then gave his boys the all-clear sign, and they left to return to the local office while Jake walked to his car.

***

The Wolf watched it all unfold from a hill overlooking the Port of Baltimore. He enjoyed watching the stupid Americans run around with their walkie-talkies, no doubt using their weak curse words like "shit," "crap," and "damn."

He had looked at the couple watching from the hotel balcony on the other side of the port. He thought they were tourists until he saw them passing what looked to be binoculars back and forth, although he couldn't quite see from the long distance. It didn't matter, they would die with the rest of them as DC was scorched, dealt a mortal blow, allowing Russia to once again rule the world.

The Wolf fit his tall, muscular frame into his car and scratched an itch on his bent nose. He drove about thirty minutes and waited at a table at a rest area near Columbia, Maryland. America's weakness was on display even in the rest area, apparently infesting every facet of American life. Children running around in a field adjacent to the parking lot, unclogged toilets, machines that blew hot air to dry wet hands, and two workable vending machines, one with drinks and one with a wide variety of snacks.

He drummed his fingers on the wooden outdoor table, watching the cars and trucks arrive. *So many blacks, Asians, and Hispanics. And Jews. Lots of them.* People running around like they didn't have enough time, as if their world was about to end. Well, maybe they were actually right for once.

The red Chevrolet rented by Jabal and Abram approached cautiously, bringing a sense of normalcy back to the Wolf. He greeted them in English for appearance's sake but with a bearhug, uncharacteristic for him. The Wolf's cell phone interrupted the exchange.

The Wolf did more listening than talking during the brief exchange in Russian through his voice scrambler. "Yes, Vlady, they've arrived. We're on schedule." The Wolf said into the phone.

The Wolf clicked off and turned to face Jabal. Abram had gone to use the bathroom.

"You got it? Our boys give you, eh, the material? I just told the boss you had it. Yes?" The Wolf asked Jabal.

Jabal nodded, pointing to the truck.

"Good," the Wolf said as Abram approached. "My boy," he said playfully slapping his sparse beard, "You look handsome. No?"

The Wolf turned to Jabal and beamed, "Great. Now, next part. Good luck. I won't see you for a while."

He said this knowing he would never see them again, at least in this life. Even if they escaped the mayhem, he had plans to dispose of them later. Loose ends.

***

Jake returned to the hotel and opened the door. Red stood with her arms crossed, at first frowning and then smiling.

She asked, "Plan B?"

Jake grumbled, "Whose side are you on? What's plan B, now that we won't have any backup support?"

"You'll see."

Chapter 30
Baltimore:
Sunday, October 8

Captain Romonov wasn't in a good mood. The damn FBI had raided his ship the day before. *These stupid Americans profiling. Not every Russian is thief.*

He was in the local offices of Trans-Asian Holdings, the Russian conglomerate that owned the *St. Pete*. The offices were located in the seedy part of Baltimore on the second floor of a strip mall featuring an adult book store, strip bar, liquor store, and funeral parlor.

The captain was sitting at the company's put-together, faux-wood desk that central command back in the mother country had provisioned for use by visiting captains. The third shelf of the bookshelf had collapsed into the second shelf after somebody lost the pin holding it in place. The right front corner of the office had collected crumpled up balls of paper, mushed into the corner by the door compacting the refuse when being opened.

He was completing paperwork when his phone buzzed.

"Front desk, Captain. There are two agents to see you." *Po'shyol 'na hui!* he cursed to himself. He was hoping he could finish today, allowing him to take in Baltimore's finest sites tomorrow. Not the touristy ones, the ones downstairs.

"Agents? I no see agents. They leave."

"They're with the FBI, Captain. You really want me to say that?" his secretary, a husky black woman manning the front desk said.

The captain charged up to the front desk and shouted, "You guys searched..."

He looked around. Other tenants and guests in the office space his company shared with other unrelated companies were staring at him.

"My office," he barked.

They walked to his office, where he shut his door and said, "Show me IDs."

The agents flashed their badges and sat down, motioning for the captain to sit behind his desk, the one he was borrowing for today.

***

Jake and Red didn't give Captain Romonov a good look at the badges Red had picked up earlier in the day. She had purchased them from a covert contact who lived outside of Baltimore after assuring him she wasn't rogue. She knew her contact well enough to know he wouldn't report her. She didn't want to get called back home to face Monty, not yet.

Red began speaking in a confident voice. "Captain, I wasn't at the ship earlier today. I want to apologize for my agents' behavior."

The captain smiled. Red knew the trap was set.

She asked, "You mind if I ask you some questions?"

The captain glanced at his watch and said in his stilted English, "Fifteen minutes."

"Anybody on your ship you didn't know?"

"*Nyet*."

"How about these two?" Jake showed him pictures of the Wolf and Jabal.

"*Nyet*, no seen them."

"Anything unusual happen?"

"*Nyet*."

Jake said, "Really? Are you usually late on arriving? We checked the logs—your ships are never late. What happened?"

"Mechanical problem is all. We anchor away from port. Operators want fix before arrive. Standard procedure in Baltimore. Harbor too busy for broken ships. Parts brought to ship offshore instead."

"What happened?"

"Boiler broke." The captain shrugged his shoulders. "Sometimes happens, you know? With this shit company, no money. Look around here, this place, you see?"

"And you ordered some parts?"

"Yes, boiler smoky." He waved his right hand back and forth. "We no have part we need."

"Who did you call?" Red asked.

"These guys..." He looked around, gesturing showing them an invoice. "Ace Engine. I call from ship, and somebody here call Ace."

Jake followed up. "Here?"

"Yes, sir. Where else? That room over there, the local agent." The captain pointed to the room to their right.

"And after it was called in, how did they get to your ship?"

"Supply boat, of course," the captain said, as if it was an idiotic question.

"Did you recognize the guys from Ace?"

"*Nyet*, but that no mean anything, eh." The captain shrugged again and continued. "Never met anybody from Ace. Never had a problem here before, you know. Not here often."

Red said, "OK. Thanks, Captain. I think that's all we have. We'll get out of your hair."

Jake and Red stood to walk out while the captain watched.

Jake turned around as he reached the door. "Captain, I have one more question." The captain nodded. "Anything unusual happen when you were docked in Crimea?"

"*Nyet.*"

"Any unusual activity in the port, in the water?" Jake asked.

The captain looked at Jake and paused. "Well, not really...uh...nothing."

Jake raised his voice. "Well, what?"

"I no know, it probably nothing, you know," he said. "But when we, how do you say...stationed, idling, I noticed the boobles, lots of boobles."

Red laughed. "Boobles? Bubbles, you mean?"

"Yes, boobles—coming from water near hull. 'Out of place,' I say to myself. I've never seen so many boobles. And it no my ship—not from where coming."

Jake raised his eyebrows and said, "How so? I mean, certainly you've seen bubbles before, right?"

The captain considered the question. "Yes, of course, but usually just few. Not so many, many boobles. And no divers there, not with us there."

Jake shot Red a glance. Interesting information, but it didn't seem to fit.

"Can you introduce us to your local agent?" Red asked, politely switching gears.

"Yes, yes, come with me," the captain replied in an annoyed tone, not even trying to hide his irritation.

The captain knocked on the door. No answer. He said softly to them, "She's in there. Hiding. Stupid game with that woman. I no here often, and she's hiding. Coward." He pounded his fist. "Open up! We got guests. Want speak to you! Answer them!"

Roberta answered, and the captain left them alone. She spoke fluent English, which was understandable despite her distinct Russian accent.

"Please come in. Sit." She pointed to the two seats in front of her desk.

As Jake and Red were sitting, she put out her cigarette and waved at the plume of smoke in front of her in a desperate attempt to clear the air. The air purifier next to her desk looked clogged.

"I can't stop. I grew up where everybody smoked—in offices, restaurants, homes. It didn't matter. But this country? Too many patsies. I'm not supposed to smoke here, but I'm addicted. I've been the local agent here for twenty years. What are they going to do—fire me and get someone else to run this shithole?" She chuckled to herself.

Red spoke next. "Thank you for seeing us on such short notice. The captain tells us he called you from the ship. What did you do after getting the call?"

"You came to ask me that? I called Ace, of course."

"And you spoke to...?" Red asked, taking out a pen and small notepad she carried in her purse.

"Tommy. He's the owner over there. He would have called some of his fellows to fix the problem."

"You know who he used?"

"No, and I don't care. As long as they get the job done."

Red said, "I see. Well, do you have Tommy's number?"

Roberta fished around her desk, located a yellow sticky note, and read the number out loud, which Red jotted down in her notepad. Jake and Red then left the building.

***

They drove back to Washington and entered Jake's condo. Charming looked at Red and then at Jake. He made his choice, rubbing up against Red's leg and purring as he strutted to his litter box, tail upright and curved at the end.

Jake shook his head in disgust and went to the kitchen to boil water. "Pasta?"

"Sure, Jake. You cooking? My, oh my, another talent. Where does it stop?"

"Probably here, boiling water. It's getting late. Should we call Tommy from Ace now?"

"Yes, sir. I'll call while you prepare dinner. Deal?"

"Deal."

Jake watched Red dial. She had changed into a brown halter top, exposing her shoulders, which were partially covered by her hair. She had lost her traveling wardrobe in her room in Donetsk. Still, she had been able to buy enough from the local stores in a limited amount of time. If it were him, he wouldn't have been able to buy everything he needed so easily.

She caught him looking and smiled back.

She's getting a little too comfortable in my apartment, he thought.

He sliced and spread fresh garlic on bread he had already buttered and placed on a cookie sheet. Jake pointed to a bottle of Cabernet. Red shook her head, and Jake felt foolish, remembering she didn't like to drink. But Red surprised him by pointing to the Chianti. *Good choice*, he thought to himself.

He listened to Red speak. Her questions were clear, but her face became serious. There were lots of "ohs," and then the discussion ended with her saying, "That's OK."

Jake looked at her as she said goodbye.

"The water's bubbling over!" she said.

"That's what he said?" They laughed.

"No, silly. I got Tommy, and you know what he said?"

"Of course not. What?"

Red waited a moment, deepening the suspense. "He said he called the two-person team he usually uses in an emergency, and they agreed to take care of it."

"That's what you have to tell me?"

She ignored his reply. "But guess what? *Both* men have been AWOL since."

"AWOL?"

"Tommy can't reach them. They always check in after a job, but they haven't returned any calls. He even called their homes. One of them is married, and his wife hasn't seen him since he left for the job."

Chapter 31
Washington:
Monday, October 9

Tommy's revelation about the two missing Ace mechanics provided the first positive validation that they were making progress. One missing mechanic could be chalked up to the bloke being out of town. But two missing mechanics? And a wife who didn't know where her husband was? They now could start making noises, and Jake knew how to start a symphony. He called Bud.

Jake felt bad about the *St. Pete*, knowing Bud had taken some heat for believing in him. He wanted to redeem himself and Bud at the same time. And Bud had told him to call when he had more of a lead.

Bud didn't let him down. Red even agreed to join in on the fun after Bud promised to not rat on her whereabouts. She still refused to call Monty. She wanted to see this through and didn't want to rest until Robert's killer was captured or killed.

The three of them met for breakfast at a quiet coffee shop ten blocks from Bud's L'Enfant Plaza office. Jake stared at Bud's hair as they sat down.

"You looking at my hair? You don't like my new look?" Bud asked.

Jake laughed. "I didn't want to say anything at the dock in front of your men. Very distinguished. You're now silver and have grown it out a bit too. You look like Richard Gere in that movie...*Runaway Bride*, I think it was. The one with Julia Roberts. Ever see that movie?"

"*Runaway Bride?* Are you serious? It is a new look, though. As soon as I started a little bit of salt and pepper, I went all in, dyeing it silver, growing it out."

The men ordered coffee and eggs with bacon. Red ordered tea and pancakes.

"Tell me about the case. I don't have a lot of time, and it didn't end well at the dock," Bud said impatiently.

Jake talked quickly and moved his hands wildly, walking Bud through everything he knew, including the anthrax, the dirty bomb theory, and the Wolf's lab. Red watched, nodding for emphasis and adding to the story when needed.

Bud yawned from the opposite side of the table as the waitress served their drinks. He fished a few ice cubes out of his water glass with a spoon, placed them in the coffee, and took a few satisfying long sips. The more Bud heard, and with the caffeine starting to work, the more he too became excited.

Bud let Jake finish, knowing not to interrupt. At the end he asked, "Did the captain notice anything out of place? I mean, the boat from Ace arrives with two people, right?"

"As far as he knows, yes," Jake responded.

"And they fixed the boiler?"

"If it was broken in the first place."

"OK, I'll bite," Bud said, sipping more coffee.

"I'm sure you're familiar with the use of a torpedo for smuggling drugs?" Jake asked. Red looked at him funny.

"Remember that case we had at NYPD where the Colombians used a ship for smuggling cocaine?" Bud looked confused. Red perked up.

"You don't remember? Well, I do. They welded..."

Bud finished his thought: "A torpedo on the hull."

"A torpedo?" Red asked.

Jake answered, "Yes, only it wasn't a real one, of course. It was a hollow pipe with cocaine in protective packaging stuffed inside and a metal plate welded to the end, sealing it shut. It was submerged, but no water could reach the drugs."

Red said, "That's it! You remember what the captain said about bubbles?"

Jake replied stoically, "How could I have missed the connection?" He faced Bud. "The captain said he noticed bubbles coming from the hull while in port in Crimea."

Bud's face looked blank.

"Don't you see? The bubbles would have been caused by workers hired by the Wolf, welding the torpedo onto the hull," Jake said excitedly.

Bud took a sip of coffee, contemplating their theory. "Seems obvious—like with the Colombians—it would've been welded on at the home port."

Red added, "Only this time it was done in secrecy without the captain knowing."

"Didn't you say there were only two mechanics on Ace's boat?" Bud asked.

"I said as far as the captain knew. The divers could've gotten off before the supply boat reached the *St. Pete*," Jake said.

"Yes, I see," Bud responded.

They were silent for a few moments, contemplating what they learned while eating their food. Bud chewed with his mouth open, as if in a trance. He took another drag of coffee, this time with some dribbling off his lip.

"You have pictures of Jabal and the Wolf I can have? I'm going to put out an APB—we need to find them," Bud said.

"What about footage from the docks?" Jake asked.

"Forget about Crimea, of course, but I'll get the tape from Baltimore. Meet me at my office around one for a full debriefing. I'm gonna get going. There's a lot to do." Bud stood, wiped the crumbs off his lap, and threw a couple of crinkled dollars on the table. "You pick up the rest?" He walked out, not waiting for a response.

***

Jake moved to the other side of the table. He was now across from Red. He looked into her eyes but couldn't hold the stare. "Are you good with this? I mean, it looks like you're being dragged in. This is now an American problem. We can hand it over to Bud and walk away."

Red ignored the question, taking a sip of tea. Jake waited patiently while she weighed her response.

She stiffened her spine and said, "I need to see this one through. I feel responsible for Robert's death. That was on me."

"What do you mean? He was killed by a bomb in the car. Right?"

"True, but he shouldn't have been there in the first place," insisted Red.

"I don't understand what you mean. It was his job. That's what he signed up for. He knew the risks."

"Oh, Jake. You're so kind. But you don't understand. You see, truth be told, he was a lousy agent. Always had been. Great analyst, but lousy in the field. You ever hear of SLIP?"

"Of course. I can't tell you what it stands for, but I know it, that's your training ground. CIA has the Farm, and you have SLIP. What about it?"

"Well, Robert and I were enrolled together. He was failing. He had a training mishap, and I intervened when I shouldn't have stopped Darwinism from happening." Red choked up and said loudly, "It's all my fault, don't you see?"

"I'm lost. I need some more coffee. You're not making sense," Jake called the waitress for a refill, which she brought a minute later. "Please slow down." He took her hand from across the table and began stroking it gently.

"He would've been kicked out of SLIP, but I intervened. I stopped the process from weeding him out. He even conceded he preferred being an analyst," she said sadly.

Jake stared into her eyes. "You know your eyes are starting to match your hair?"

Red laughed at the comic relief. Jake took a sip of coffee and continued.

"Look, I know you've been through a lot, Red. But you can't blame yourself for the Wolf's bomb. Robert wanted to be an agent. He knew the risks. Let's talk about something else, Red. Isn't your boss looking for you?"

"He probably still thinks I'm dead," Red replied.

"At some point you'll report, though. You'll have to."

Red looked at Jake. "Maybe. But Monty, he's not such a bad person. He may understand how I handled this. And if he doesn't, then, well, I'll get a job where nobody shoots at me. So even in the worst-case scenario, I come out OK."

Jake considered this then added, "I think you should call him."

***

For the 1:00 p.m. meeting, Bud assembled a team of experts from different facets of the government: CIA, NSA, DHS, DIA, and, of course, the FBI. They met at the FBI headquarters office in Washington. Bud set the tone, establishing himself as the point person—at least for now.

The conference table was dark and homogenous with the men, including Jake, wearing dark suits and white shirts. Nobody dared to wear a striped or colored shirt. Ties were red or blue. The two women, not including Red, wore navy business attire with white shirts. They were part of the club, except for the Brit, who had to rush into a local store before the meeting to purchase her attire: a beige pair of pants, pink shirt, and button-down red sweater.

Jake thought he was walking into a funeral and was immediately reminded of one of the drawbacks of public service. He shared a bemused look with Red.

Bud began the substantive portion of the meeting after introductions were made. Large-scale pictures of Jabal, the Wolf, and some of their known associates were displayed on a screen. There was even a picture of Saddam's ace of spades card next to Jabal's profile. Jake and Red briefed everybody on what they learned and how they had learned it.

The participants were fascinated by Jake's description of his near beheading and by Red's description of the bombing. Questions were asked, some for knowledge and some to boost the ego of the questioner. And when the dust settled, the expected happened—no surprise to Jake as he had been the decider of such fates in another life. They were dismissed, relegated to the role of spectators and asked to wait outside the room—in the office's lobby, of all places.

Jake fought the urge to tell the receptionist to wipe the smirk off her face as he and Red took their seats. She had seen this happen before.

They were summoned to return to the conference room about an hour later. Bud addressed them.

Scott A. Dondershine

"We thank you for helping in this, but we're going to take this over from here. You understand, I'm sure. We'll be in touch. Please stay close to your cell phones. That is all."

Chapter 32
London:
Tuesday, October 10

With nothing to do, Jake went to his office to catch up on paperwork and brief his editor.

Red called Monty, who was furious, at least until Red screamed "What, you rather that I was dead?" Monty calmed down long enough to order that Red return, and she took the red-eye, arriving early in the morning. They had a lot to discuss.

During the plane ride, she had an epiphany. She nearly told the pilot to land immediately, even though they were over the Atlantic at the time. She called her old friend Moshe soon after landing, and she took a taxi to the office to meet Monty after a brief stop home. She didn't have time for the Tube. She would see Jasper another time.

Monty and his merry band of uppity suits were miffed, and rightfully so. Robert's death put a blemish on MI6's otherwise stellar safety records. It was bad for morale and worse for recruiting. And after it happened, Red, the only reliable witness, disappeared. They initially thought she also was dead, but they couldn't be sure because her body couldn't be found.

Monty's Star Chamber entourage asked: How did Red and Robert become such a threat to the Wolf in the short period of time they were in Donetsk? They seemed to understand Red's answer that it was not possible for her to know. The Wolf was like an octopus. How was Red to know where and how she or Robert tripped a wire?

They next asked: Why did Red "flee" to America instead of coming home to England, paying her respects to Robert's family, and immediately facing her superiors? The Star Chamber wouldn't accept Red's response that there was an imminent danger to America. They pointed out that she could have debriefed them, and they could have called to make arrangements with the CIA through official channels. Blah, blah, blah.

The Chamber also dismissed any implication that somebody at MI6 could have tipped off the Wolf to their presence in Donetsk. It was preposterous, and any further casting of dispersions on this fine organization without even a shred of evidence was simply not acceptable.

One person had the gall to ask how Red managed to escape the car. He seemed to insinuate she knew a bomb was planted and at the last minute conveniently remembered she had forgotten something in the hotel. Monty rescued her from having to answer that insulting question, but not the others.

Besides, Red thought to herself, *if I was in on it, does that jerk think I'd confess in answering his question?*

The drill continued for several hours, although at one point it morphed into individual meetings with psychologists and other specialists. Red was sent to various rooms, bouncing back and forth like a ping-pong ball—dismissed from one room, summoned to the next.

The madness ended as abruptly as it had begun. Two agents escorted Red into a back room and told her to wait. A subordinate brought her coffee, telling her not to leave.

Monty's secretary fetched her an hour later, bringing her to his office, where he said, "I'm sorry, Red, but you're going to have to recuse yourself from this case. We're not blaming you for Robert's death, but we still have too many questions." Red began to reply but Monty held up his hand. "We're done talking for now. Take a few weeks off."

Red considered how to respond and then asked, "Am I on suspension?"

Monty looked at her sternly. "Let's not go there at this point. Just take a few weeks off is all I'm saying right now."

At first, she didn't know how to respond, but then she realized that Monty had handed her a gift. "Am I allowed to travel?"

Monty looked up to meet her gaze, tried unsuccessfully to not smile, and said weakly, "Not in an official capacity."

***

Washington:
Tuesday, October 10

Jabal walked towards the Washington Monument. The gneiss stone—a mixture of marble, granite, and bluestone—was cleaner than Jabal had expected and lacked the worn-down look that had taken over many of the public statues and monuments in the Middle East. He had been told that it looked like a pencil, and pictures of it justified the description. But not up close since he couldn't see the top.

The sun was shining brightly, but the air had a slight chill, enough to justify his wearing jeans, a baseball cap, and a long-sleeve shirt. He was careful to change his clothing and appearances given the two rotating cameras he spotted trained on the monument and its grounds.

Jabal looked around quickly like his head was on a swivel, avoiding eye contact, becoming paranoid when others looked at him. He knew that despite his attempt to blend in, he looked out of place, especially since most of the tourists were in groups. Watching the children with their fathers made him even more bitter. He never had the opportunity to have a real relationship with his father, who died fighting the Iranians, and the Americans working with the Shia scum had brutally hanged his surrogate father, Saddam, ruining his beloved country in the process. Now the Shia were in power, and the Baath party was in disarray.

At first, he was impressed by the buildings on the National Mall, the prosperity of the people he saw, the fresh air and cleanliness. But then he realized the superficiality. People ran around without any care for others, in a rush, tripping over strangers, spitting on the ground, cutting lines. Women, and even some girls, seemed to proudly show off their decorated faces and bare skin, not caring that it caused men and boys to ogle, gawk, lust.

***

Abram was drawn to the Smithsonian Museum of Natural History. He didn't understand why, but he had to enter. Jabal had told him to find a location somewhere close to the Washington Monument. He saw the monument but kept walking. One long block later, he saw people filing in and out of the imposing museum building. Kids were running to the entrance, smiling, waving. People took pictures. Abram felt oddly comfortable.

He bounced up the steps and then froze. Security. He stopped himself, turned around, and walked back to towards the monument.

With the monument now on his left, he froze again. This time he didn't feel relaxed, not at all. His forehead became damp. His muscles tensed. His head ached. Images flashed in his head. A house, near the busy intersection of 17th and Constitution Avenue, shined in the distance. He had seen it before, many times, in his dreams, and he had a strange feeling he had been inside before.

The exterior of the house was made of a medley of very old gray, white, charcoal, and yellowish stones mortarcd in place. A triangular roof featured chimneys on both ends of the house. Two dormers with dark-brown peeling paint protruded out of the roof. The house had two wooden doors, one at the front and one at the back.

A National Park Service plaque outside the house said, "LOCKKEEPER'S HOUSE." He walked around the structure, yearning to enter. Other people were around, so he decided to try later. The door to the house was towards a set of trees along the National Mall, making it possible to enter at night undetected. He would come back with Jabal.

***

Late Tuesday, October 10, to Wednesday, October 11

Abram and Jabal were staying with an acquaintance of the Wolf who lived in an apartment building on Maryland Avenue, away from the downtown bustle, but not too far from the action. The building, three stories of painted dark-brown brick with narrow but tall windows, had a black wooden door.

Abram approached the door and paused, noticing the food truck parked outside that the Wolf made

Scott A. Dondershine

arrangements for Jabal to use. Jabal must have returned the red Chevrolet they had rented for their trip from Baltimore to Washington, Abram thought to himself. The Wolf had told both of them about the need to switch vehicles, and the food truck offered them cover for putting their plan into action.

They talked in Arabic. "Abram, let's take a walk," Jabal said, looking for privacy. They left the building and walked down the street.

When they were alone, Abram said softly, "I found the perfect place. I can't believe it. I know the place. I feel like I've been there before, and I've seen it in my dreams." He proceeded to tell Jabal all about the Lockkeeper's House, and at the end he asked, "What do you think?"

Jabal couldn't believe it. *The Wolf has really brainwashed this kid, stolen his mind. He sounds like a child. But if this is where Abram wants to die, then so be it.* And it did have its advantages, being located near the monument and masses of people.

Jabal looked Abram in the eyes, clasped his hand on his shoulder, and said, "I think it's perfect. Let's get some rest. We're going to leave at 3:00 in the morning."

They left on time, driving the food truck offering hotdogs, pretzels, drinks, and candy to outside of the Lockkeeper's House. The streets were empty, except for a few taxicabs and other vehicles. Another food truck was setting up for the morning rush a few blocks away. Jabal checked to make sure the door to the house was not in view of the vendor. No security cameras were pointed on the neglected house either, Jabal confirmed.

The National Park Service reluctantly agreed to keep the historic building standing. The main attractions—the Washington Monument, Vietnam Wall, World War II memorial, Roosevelt memorial—

were all within walking distance. Even Albert Einstein's bust across and down the street garnered more attention. Nobody cared about the little out-of-place house standing by itself with nothing but a plaque.

They began unloading the equipment and provisions Abram would need inside the house onto a cart. Buns, candy, and beverages were stacked on top as cover.

Jimmying the lock free was easier than expected. It was spooky inside, and they heard a few rats scramble when they opened the door. No lights were on; it was pitch black inside.

It took a few minutes to unload. Abram was nervous, as he would be in the house alone for a few days. But he knew what to do and felt a strange familiarity. They tested to make sure nobody from outside the house would see Abram's flashlight. Jabal issued his final instructions and then left, knowing he would probably never see Abram again.

***

Jabal gave a sigh of relief after leaving Abram. His work was done. The Wolf had already left the area, and he would also soon. Jabal had other aspirations and refused to risk his life by staying in DC. He would be able to capitalize on the publicity, bringing money, people, and other resources to his group attempting to resurrect the Baath party. And, just as important, he would have his revenge against the infidel Americans.

Jabal packed up the provisions not taken by Abram and drove away back towards the apartment. He was within a few blocks of Maryland Avenue when he saw the flashing lights on top of the police car. Jabal pulled his truck over, trying to remain calm. He rolled down his window.

"Sir, your tail lights are not working," the officer told Jabal.

"Lights?" Jabal repeated, silently cursing the food truck owner.

"I'll be right back," the officer said sharply.

He returned five minutes later, instructing Jabal to "exit the vehicle." Jabal opened the door, at first thinking he should run but then realizing he had no choice. Maybe it was routine. Should he offer the officer money?

The officer quickly dashed Jabal's hopes as he forced Jabal to stand with his body against the truck, legs spread. Backup arrived. The officers arrested Jabal, responding to the all-points bulletin with Jabal's picture and name released by the FBI two days prior.

Chapter 33

Washington:
Wednesday, October 11

Dawit, the usually friendly doorman working at Jake's building, scoffed at the scene. Two black SUVs arrived, blocking the entrance.

The front-seat passenger of the first car jumped out, immediately giving orders.

"Get these cars out of here!" he commanded the doorman, pointing to two cars currently occupying spots where the SUVs would park. He flashed his badge for emphasis.

Bud called Jake, enlisting his services, as soon as Bud learned about Jabal's capture. He was needed at the Bayou. Jake knew of the place, but he had never been there before. Only people with the right credentials knew about and had access to the Bayou. The nickname came from its location, just off Louisiana Avenue in southeast DC.

A park near the intersection of Louisiana Avenue and C Street offered tourists refuge from the sweltering heat in the summer or the converging mess of couriers, staffers, lobbyists, big shots, and no shots, pimping the American political system the remainder of the year. It was circular, divided into four quadrants of green grass.

Each section was separated by a gravel path that lead to a statue of the French general who had helped the Americans win their civil war, Marquis de Lafayette. Lafayette has a horse whose head faces upward. Water drips from the horse's mouth into a catch basin, *tat, tat, tat*. The catch basin contains a hidden microphone that, when activated, collects the sound of the dripping water. Visitors to the park consistently question why it is a drip as opposed to a normal spray. They would never know the truth.

The FBI built the Bayou underneath the park to provide a place where agents could quickly interrogate a person picked up in downtown DC. It has only a few rooms, the most important of which is a holding cell used to contain the prisoners. When activated, the noise picked up by the microphone is piped into the holding cell. The noise can break the will of those held down under, before interrogations even begin. No need for torture. *Tat, tat, tat*.

Bud escorted Jake down a set of steps, obscured by landscape, leading to an iron door. Bud pointed his scruffy face at the camera located above the door and flashed a forced smile. The camera scanned his retina, and the door opened five seconds later. An elevator took them into a secured area, and after passing that test, Bud brought Jake into a narrow room. He raised the blinds on the far wall, revealing to Jake why Bud needed him.

Jake looked through the one-way mirror. Jabal was sitting motionless at a metal table in an interrogation room. Two rows of fluorescent lights punctuated the white ceiling tiles, lighting the otherwise dark room.

Bud said to Jake, "You've done this before. Once you've done it, you never lose it. It's like riding a bike. I'll play good cop, and you play bad cop. OK?"

Jake agreed, and they walked in. The room reeked of mildew. Jake didn't know whether that was an intentional effect to disquiet the suspect or government neglect. Bud suppressed a grin.

Jake could see Jabal's face twitch as he looked at his former captive, now turned interrogator. Jabal didn't look as much like Saddam as the first time they met. This time his mustache was trimmed and thinner, looking more like Hitler's than Saddam's. His face was lighter and skinnier. He looked stoic.

"Some reporter, you...a spy now?" Jabal spit on the ground.

Jake slapped him across the face hard, causing Jabal's lip to bleed slightly.

"You should've used your machete sooner back in Damascus, *before* my friends stopped your sick plan!" Jake boomed. He took a step forward, but Bud held him back.

Jabal said, "Hit me more, I no care. My mission over. I got nothing to say to you two or anybody else you parade in here."

True to his word, Jabal stopped talking. Jake and Bud alternated roles, trying everything in the book. Two hours later, they gave up.

***

London: Late Tuesday, October 10, to Wednesday, October 11

Red ventured back to her flat after leaving the uppity Star Chamber on Tuesday. She greeted Jasper with a polite nod from afar as she marched past him at the Central Line station near her Holland Park flat. Red couldn't see his amber eyes that reminded her of Jimmy, but she admired Jasper's casual yet hard-working attitude as he worked the crowd, playing his sax. Jasper was smart enough not to slow her down. A simple wave would have to do.

Red noticed the red blinking message light on her answering machine as soon as she entered the flat. "This is the Royal Flower Store. We have your violets," Moshe's voice on the machine said. *Boy, he works fast*, Red thought.

She dialed the number Moshe had given her. He answered on the third ring. Red hung up the phone two minutes later, smiling for the first time all day. She called Jake and made arrangements to meet him at Dulles airport the next day, needing sleep and time to log onto her computer at work.

***

Wednesday, October 11

Jake waited outside of customs holding a sign made out of cardboard that said, "Red." She wanted to run to him as soon as she noticed his goofy smile, fedora with a red feather sticking out, and dark suit.

She had gone through hell over the past couple of weeks, between Robert's death, her injury, and then the discovery at the lab, arriving at Jake's apartment in her down-trodden emotional state, and then being called back to London for interrogation. She relished the idea of Jake pampering her.

But she decided to play it cool, ignoring Jake while strutting near and then past him. After walking past the distraught Jake, she quickly whirled around and embraced him with a romantic kiss.

Red initially had intended to discuss the lead she had developed in London with Moshe's help. But after seeing Jake at the airport, she decided it could wait. She would "ruin" the reunion later.

"We have the night off while Bud and his crew figure out the next steps after Jabal stonewalled us,"

Jake said as they were climbing into his 911 Porsche Carrera.

"Nice," she said as she looked around at the interior. "You're full of surprises, Jake."

"Thanks. This car's been in my family for years. I don't drive it often but figured, for this occasion, I'd give it a spin."

Jake began weaving through traffic, not reckless but quick.

A few turns later, she asked, "With the night off, what do you have in mind?"

"You hungry? I made reservations at one of my favorite restaurants. The type of food you can't get back home."

Red hid her disappointment, saying, "You bet. But I need to change first, if that's OK."

Jake laughed. "And I need to get out of this silly suit."

***

A half hour later they were still stuck in traffic. Jake was taking Red to eat at DC's waterfront, an overlooked area a few blocks south of Georgetown's bustle. Residents from all classes and cliques roamed the area: working poor hustling from one job to the next, students on dates, congressional staffers and government workers splurging on their big night out, corporate types looking for some working-class charm.

They took their seats at a posh restaurant located in a sleek glass office building sitting tall on top of a promenade on a Potomac River bank. The restaurant was on two floors, the first offering tables on the same level as the promenade. Jake preferred the second floor, with its richer view of the river. Dinner cruises were visible as their lights reflected in the waters of the surprisingly crowded river for the unusually warm October evening.

"Do you mind if I order a glass of wine?" Jake asked.

Red touched Jake's hand and replied, "No. I enjoyed the wine we had the other night. I'm not an alcoholic, you know. I'm just careful."

"You want one too?"

She thought about it and said, "Pick out a bottle. I'll have a little."

The waiter came and Jake ordered a bottle while watching Red struggle with the menu. When he left, Jake asked, "Don't like seafood?"

"No, I like it. But crab cakes? I mean, we have fish and chips, but crab cakes?"

"Of course. Nothing but the finest. You can have your fried cod wrapped in old, dirty newspapers back home. I'll take my select lightly fried crabmeat painstakingly picked from the best Chesapeake crabs any day of the week. Just try it."

Red looked at Jake from across the table. She hadn't felt this content in a long time. The waiter arrived and placed in the middle of the table a basket full of crisp, warm rolls. A thick candle in the middle of the table illuminated the white linen tablecloth, crystal, and china. Even the silverware sparkled.

Neither wanted to discuss their previous love affair or the past. Bringing up memories, even great ones, could lead to another discussion about Red's car accident while chasing Saajid Badat, an accomplice to the Shoebomber, Richard Reid.

Politics was safer. Red knew Jake worked closely with the Democratic president, Tucker, and she wasn't surprised when Jake implied the government needed to prevent corporations from taking advantage of the unprotected masses. "We need more taxes, not less."

Red pressed her viewpoint. "The government is inefficient, though. I've witnessed firsthand the damage caused by high tax rates and socialist policies.

The government doesn't know how to spend money, leading to waste. Like a cocaine addict that can't stop snorting, the fat cats keep spending yours and mine. The result? Huge budget deficits. The pressure builds and builds like steam trapped in a clogged teakettle.

"Bills accumulate, only to be paid by the next generation. Some of the steam escapes. At some point, though, the next generation can't keep up, and the steam is too much, until finally—boom! It explodes. Indeed, the bubble doesn't just burst—it goes out in an inferno, ravaging society! Remember what happened to Greece, Spain, and Italy?"

"We've had our problems too, Red. And a lot of the time it's because of lax regulation, leading to the creation of an artificial bubble of economic activity, caused by a small group manipulating the masses. Nobody notices it until one day, when nobody's looking, the bubble bursts. Millions of Americans lost their homes and retirement savings in 2008 because of under-regulated banks. Then suddenly there's outrage. Hearings and investigations. People are jailed. But the damage has already been done."

They continued to talk throughout their meal, dessert, and coffee. Red liked discussing politics with Jake. They didn't agree on much, but they respected each other's opinions, encouraging the banter.

***

Jake opened the door to his condo, and they walked in. Charming gave his approval and, understanding he wouldn't be the center of attention, meowed and scampered away.

Red threw herself into Jake, wrapping her arms around his waist, pulling him close, thrusting her tongue into his mouth. Her shiny, red hair flew towards Jake as she collided with him.

Jake had been waiting for this moment, but he didn't plan on it happening so quickly. He had planned to break out a bottle of wine, play some Beethoven, and set the mood. Then he would play passive-aggressive until the moment arrived.

But Red had other plans. She took Jake by the hand and led him into his own bedroom, where she pushed him onto the bed and began a slow striptease. Her movements briefly exposed to Jake her birdcage tattoo, located on the small of her back.

She's changed since before, Jake thought to himself. Jake was turned on, but he wasn't exactly sure how to reciprocate, and he sure didn't want to send the wrong signal. He watched her large, firm breasts emerge from her top and longed for the rest. Her naked body looked leaner than he had remembered.

Jake squirmed as Red seductively slinked her way onto the bed, slithering up Jake's body, starting at the feet and stopping at his crotch. Although he had developed a bulge in his stomach since the Project MKUltra case, he was still in good shape.

She unbuckled his pants using her teeth. Jake tried to touch her, but she slapped his hands away. His pants now unbuckled, she used her teeth to move one pant leg down his body while her left hand did the same with the other pant leg.

With the pants removed, she looked up, winked, and went down on him. At first, she teased, nibbling at the edges. Then she got more intense, taking him deep inside her mouth. Jake tried to gently pull her hair up as a primitive signal she was being too rough— her teeth were beginning to bite—but she wasn't paying attention. She continued with greater intensity, overwhelmed with passion and increasing the thrust of her mouth.

But it was too much, starting to hurt. At first, Jake tried to ignore it, not wanting to destroy the moment. He continued to use her hair as a lever. Red didn't get the message until it was too late. Her teeth got too far in the way, causing Jake to yelp.

Red jumped up and ran to the bathroom, where she locked the door and cried. Jake sat there, startled. What had happened to her?

He put his pants back on and knocked on the door. He could hear her sobbing hysterically.

"It's OK, Red. We'll try another time."

"No, no, it's not OK. You don't understand. I've been…I'm so embarrassed, confused."

Jake knew that already. He was also confused. But how did confusion turn into this? He heard the toilet flush and the tap turn on.

"You want me to get your clothes?"

She whimpered, "Yes, please."

She opened the door a crack and stuck out her hand. Jake handed her the clothes and a few minutes later she emerged, fully dressed.

They didn't speak for the remainder of the night. Jake tried to talk to her but she didn't respond. Jake gave her the bed, and he took the couch. Charming slept with him that night. Jake would've laughed at the irony had he been in a better mood.

***

The next morning they ate in awkward silence in Jake's kitchen. Jake reached for her hand over the table, and Red recoiled. Attempts at small talk generated only one-word answers. They finished the meal quickly, each wanting to end the awkwardness. They settled in different rooms.

Red approached Jake about an hour later in the living room, where he was sitting on a couch. She sat down next to him.

"Oh, Jake. I'm sorry about what happened last night. I was…I don't…"

"It's OK, Red. I understand. It happens. Let's get past that." He moved closer to her, and she moved closer to him. They met in the middle and kissed passionately.

When they separated, she said, "Jake, I hate to do this now, but there's been a development we need to discuss. I worked on this before leaving London, but I didn't want to spoil last night."

He chuckled. "Of course! Perfect timing as usual."

Red sighed. "I know, but I've called a taxicab." Jake looked deflated until Red quickly added, "We're taking a little trip to Austin of all places. Let me explain. As I was flying to London, I remembered what Robert said to me at breakfast before the bombing. Maybe the trauma had repressed the memory, but it started to come back on the plane."

Jake cuddled up to Red and began stroking her hair. "What did he say?"

"Well, we were eating breakfast, and he began to talk about how he met somebody at the hotel bar the night before." She looked down at her feet.

"And?"

"I interrupted him. You see, the restaurant was crowded, the tables close together. I didn't want to continue the discussion there. We were going to be alone in the car in a few minutes."

"And you never got the chance to follow up on it." Jake finished her thought, his voice trailing at the end.

"Unfortunately not."

"Who do you think it was that he met?"

"Maya Romanoski."

"The Wolf's ex-girlfriend?" Jake asked in an excited voice. He separated from Red on the couch, facing her instead.

"Why do you think it was her?"

"That's the easy part. Robert met with her when we were...eh, investigating. He knows what she looks like. I have a hunch they ran into each other at the bar.

It fits with the way he described it to me. Probably just a bizarre coincidence."

"Really? Coincidence? They just happened to meet there? I'm not sure there are coincidences in your line of work," Jake said. He added, "How do you know she's not actually working for the Wolf? She could've been at the hotel to plant the bomb."

"I considered that, but it doesn't fit. Monty had told Robert that MI6 learned they'd broken up a while ago. An abusive relationship is what he said. And Robert confirmed this with Maya. She hates him.

"Anyways, I called Moshe right after I landed in London, before my meeting with Monty and his clowns. He agreed with my assessment that she probably detests the Wolf. There's no evidence she's working for him. He offered to call in a few favors and send one of his local agents to meet with her where she lives in Moscow."

"And what happened? I assume he got back to you?" Jake asked.

"Yes, he worked quickly, and before I left London I had a response. Turns out the bombing shook her up. She was still at the hotel when it went off. She didn't have any problem telling the agent what she had told Robert."

"Which was?" Jake prompted.

"The boy at the Wolf's estate had a twin, they lived together in America. She didn't have any other information, but knowing about the twin made it much easier to discover their identity."

"So, how does this figure into going to Austin?"

"Patience, I'll get to that," she chided before continuing. "I logged onto my computer at work from my flat and uploaded the printouts Robert and I prepared of the missing kids in America. At first, my search struck out, just like last time. And then it hit me. Maybe Abe wasn't kidnapped?"

"Huh?" Jake asked.

Red chuckled, "I meant to say, he wasn't listed as being kidnapped on the FBI database. What if, and bear with me for a second, the Wolf faked Abe's death. I've seen cases where dental records are switched. In other words, the Wolf kidnaps Abe but makes it more difficult for it to be discovered by making it *look like* he died instead. The police, or cops as you blokes like to say, would tell his parents they found his body. He could've been badly burned, so they don't recognize his face. The police would convince the parents that the body is Abe's since the dental records they receive from Abe's dentist are really of the dead boy. The Wolf could've easily broken into the dentist's office to switch the records."

"I don't know Red, it sounds like a stretch. You have any proof of this?"

"Actually, I do. But I'll get to that in a second." Red beamed. Jake perked up as Red continued, "I reran the query with an 'Abe' dying and having a twin brother, Shmuel. And you want to know the best part? I found this."

Red handed Jake a copy of a newspaper article she had printed out. The article, from the *Arizona Daily Sun*, discussed the discovery of Abe's badly burned face and body discovered in a park. Dental records were used to identify him.

Jake paused, still skeptical. "Hold on for a second. I'm still not convinced Maya running into Robert is a coincidence. I still think it's odd she was there."

"Maybe, but you have to admit it makes even less sense she would plant a bomb to kill Robert and me and then hang out at the hotel bar. Why would she do that? I don't know why they met at the hotel, but I don't think it was because she planted the bomb."

"Didn't Moshe's agent ask her why she was there?"

"Yes, she apparently was there on business."

"Business? What kind of business would the ex-girlfriend of a ruthless villain have? Is she a mortician?"

"No, she's actually a sales representative for a truck parts company based in Moscow. She had an appointment with a company in the area. The agent called and verified her story."

Jake considered what she had said. "So what's your plan?"

Red looked at him. "My plan? We're going to get creative, think outside the box. I've been thinking about what Jabal said when you were questioning him."

"Said? He didn't say anything—that's the problem."

"True, but don't you think that in itself is revealing? You described him as being almost smug. No?"

"OK, I'll bite. You're on a roll. Continue." Jake gestured with his hands.

"Here's what I have in mind." She noticed Jake's eyebrows rise as she talked.

Jake didn't respond for a few minutes. Then in an animated voice he said, "I like it! It's brilliant. Don't ever let them talk you down, Red. Between your pop and Monty...you're not getting a lot of support. I say fuck them. You're one heck of an agent. I'd have hired you in a heartbeat at NYPD, and...not just for your looks, you know. We have policies against that!"

***

Jake's landline rang, and Red looked at her watch. He hung up the phone and announced, "Taxi is here. We've got to go."

Two hours later, they boarded the plane. Red was surprised to see it half-empty; people were spread out, enjoying the room. Jake and Red disregarded the extra space, instead cuddling next to each other and catching up on long-neglected sleep.

Red jerked her head up as the plane landed and the wheels touched the ground. She wiped her drool off Jake's shoulder as he looked at her. And at that moment she felt worse than she had the night before. *How do I deserve somebody like him? Why does it have to be so complicated?*

***

Austin:
Thursday, October 12

The temperature outside the airport was hot, but the air was dry. They rented a car and headed to the University of Texas campus near Austin.

"You sure about this, Red?" Jake asked, looking at Red in the driver's seat. "If you're wrong, we're screwed."

Red looked at the floor of the car and said quietly to Jake, "I know I'm right. You didn't object when we talked about it earlier." She looked up at him. "Having second thoughts now?"

"No. Of course not. After everything we've been through together?" He looked at her even though her gaze was elsewhere, as if in a trance. "Are you sure Shmuel is visiting his friend this week?"

Red replied, "The crap you can learn on social media these days. The hours of teenage bullshit I had to wade through. Yes, I'm sure. I even hacked into his account to arrange this meeting."

They walked down Sixth Street and headed to a tapas restaurant a couple of blocks from campus. Red watched the lucky college students talking and laughing as she passed them in the busy hub. She had never experienced a college town.

They were early and took a seat at the bar. Students looked at them, and they defended themselves with awkward smiles. Onlookers turned red and found new objects at which to stare.

Red poked Jake a few minutes later and said, "See that guy in the red shirt who just entered? The one with the long black hair? That's our guy."

Jake said nothing.

Red continued, "Poor guy. He's got no idea."

They watched the young man talk to the host, who then led him to a four-top table. A waiter took away two place settings. They watched as the teenager ordered a drink and produced an ID. The waiter nodded and brought him a beer a few minutes later.

Red looked at Jake. "Must be a fake," he said.

They watched him type something into his phone, and then Red's phone buzzed. She showed Jake the text: "I'm here." Red typed back, "So am I." She and Jake headed towards the table.

Startled, the teen looked up and said, "What? Who are you? I'm meeting somebody. You must have the wrong table." He looked around the room. When Red and Jake didn't get up from the table, he turned to them. His greasy face didn't mask his wrinkled brow. He looked around again and said in weak voice, "But I'm supposed to be meeting my friend Jackson."

Red responded, "Don't worry about that. He thinks you canceled. Social media is a two-way street, young man."

His face became pale.

Red continued, "Look, I know you're scared. But we just want to talk. We're with...the government. You're not in trouble. We think you might be interested in what we have to say. May I continue?"

He looked at them for a long time. Red and Jake didn't know if he would scream or hear them out. In the end, he just nodded.

Chapter 34
Washington:
Friday, October 13

Jake sat on a wooden chair on one side of the same metal table as he had sat at when at the Bayou two days before, same room with the same mildew smell. Bud and Red watched through the one-way mirror. A guard escorted a hooded Jabal into the room and then pushed him into a chair on the opposite side of the table. Jabal had been forced to listen to that *tat, tat, tat* dripping sound for the past two days.

His hands were cuffed together, and his feet were chained by metal restraints loose enough to allow him to shuffle. The guard pulled off the hood, unleashing static electricity that caused his hair to dance. Jabal looked tired, and his face was dirty.

Jabal grunted, "I know nothing. I told you...I got nothing to say."

Jake ignored him. "I visited your mother a while ago. Do you remember we talked about that? I was in *your* house with *your* mother. You don't care what happens to her? She served me tea. Nice lady. Shame she's going to get caught up in all of this."

Jabal looked up. "Go fuck yourself. I wish I had offed you when I had the chance back in Damascus."

"Ah, Damascus. The place *you* failed to secure, that *I* escaped from? You think you can get away with what you're planning here? You're going to wind up in jail or dead...like your poor mother. Have you thought about..."

Jabal's ears perked up. Jake heard a blast, then gunfire, followed immediately by intense screaming in the background. The noise got louder as it continued, getting closer to where he was sitting. A bullet smashed through the one-way mirror, cracking it wide open. A man in black with olive skin shot Red. Another attacker shot Bud, the big man making a thud as he fell to the ground.

Jake stood and looked at Jabal, who started to move toward the door, his foot restraints slowing his movement but not immobilizing him. Jake had no weapon. He lunged at Jabal, tackling him. Suddenly, two bullets tore through his clothing and into his flesh, one hitting him in his right thigh, the other in his back. He screamed in agony and went limp, releasing Jabal.

Jabal turned to Jake and tried to kick him, but his restraints held him back. The door opened, and a figure wearing a black hood appeared, motioning for Jabal to join him.

Jabal, his rescuer, and the rest of the attackers moved into the hallway beyond the room, looking for the exit from the Bayou. Blood and bodies littered the floor.

The rescuer took off his hood, his black hair clinging to the hat as it was removed. Jabal brightened, embracing his hero.

"Abram, my savior. Who are the other men? The Wolf?"

The rescuer nodded his head and ran ahead, clearing the path, putting his hood back on his head as he moved.

"Abram, you have keys for these?" Jabal shouted.

Abram didn't respond. *Too far away*, Jabal reasoned. He slowed to allow Jabal to catch up.

"Coast is clear," Abram grunted, the hood muddying his voice. "And no, I don't have a key. We'll deal with that later."

They entered a staircase, a safer escape route than taking the elevator up to the ground level.

"You plant the stuff?" Jabal asked.

The rescuer responded, "By the Lincoln Monument?"

Jabal raised his voice. "Lincoln? No! I told you by the Washington! You didn't follow..."

Multiple agents suddenly streamed down the staircase. Other agents blocked the door leading to the staircase. They were trapped.

An agent shouted, "Freeze!"

Jabal started to hop up the steps, but the rescuer tripped him.

The startled Jabal bounced on the steps and looked up at the rescuer, who removed his hood and stared down at Jabal before kicking him in the ribs.

"What, you don't recognize me? You never knew that Abe, Abram as you call him, had a twin brother, huh?"

***

Jake, Red, and the others who had been splayed out on the floor as part of the ruse to trick Jabal were in the kitchen, which had now turned into a makeshift recovery room. An assistant pushed the microwave, kitchen utensils, coffee cups, and drying rack to the side, making room for hydrogen peroxide, bandages, ice packs, and body wraps. They all sat on white kitchen chairs as the assistant helped the injured apply first aid wherever needed.

"Those plastic bullets pack a lot of punch, Bud," Jake shouted as soon as he saw the silver-haired Bud arrive.

Bud suppressed a smile and ignored the reprimand, instead asking the entire group, "Nothing stuck in, right? All superficial?"

Everybody shook their heads "yes" or said "yes, sir."

Bud said, "Then suck it up. We've got work to do."

He took Jake and Red to a separate room. "I sent Moshe's men home. Their Middle Eastern looks came in handy as people the Wolf might hire to retrieve Jabal. Now it's time for them to leave."

"Is the Washington Monument blocked off by now?" Red asked, hands resting on her hips.

"Yes, and we've activated the Red Team to begin searching the area. We're not taking any chances."

***

The Navy has the SEALS, the Army has the Green Berets, and the Marines have the Raiders. A more elite and exclusive subset of warriors exists within each special operations department, the most famous one being SEAL Team 6, credited for killing Bin Laden.

The FBI employs a similar structure. Bud called for the Red Team to quarantine and search the Washington Monument for anthrax after they had tricked Jabal into revealing the location.

Abram heard the voices from inside his position in the Lockkeeper's House. Fortunately for him, his house wasn't located in the search zone and quarantined area.

He had planted the anthrax and its delivery mechanism in a concrete flower pot even though Jabal had told him to place it on the underside of a large trash container after garbage pickup. The flower pot seemed a better idea, and he would likely never see Jabal again anyway. He did this late the previous night, making sure the security cameras were pointing elsewhere at the time.

Abram wasn't sure what the authoritative voices he heard were saying. A knot in his stomach grew tighter, and he knew he would have to fight until his death if the cops suddenly broke in the door.

The voices grew louder and more prominent. Panic set in, until he heard somebody shouting in the distance that they had found it. The agents near his house shuffled away.

Abram smiled, knowing he would be left alone with the main plan still intact.

***

Bud, Red, and Jake rejoined the group recovering in the kitchen at the Bayou. An assistant had picked up pizza that the group was enjoying while they waited for news.

An hour later, Agent Newcomb, a rookie errand boy, knocked on the kitchen door twice and then opened it enough to stick his head through.

"Bud, we have an update. The Red Team found anthrax at the monument. Congratulations."

"Thanks," Bud said, cuing the errand boy to close the door.

Red and Jake looked dispassionate. Bud didn't even look convinced knowing about their dirty bomb theory, nodding to them to move back into their private room.

After the three of them relocated, Bud looked at Red and Jake and said, "You think this is over?"

Jake spoke first, "Bud, you know what we think. We're talking about the Wolf. Think he's satisfied infecting a few dozen tourists hanging out at the Washington Monument? No, he's interested in salting the earth of DC with a dirty bomb. Remember, we talked about that? We even briefed your colleagues at the meeting we had on Monday at your headquarters."

Red piped in, "I agree with Jake, Bud."

Bud shifted the discussion. "What have you learned about Abe and his brother...Shmuel?"

"Show him the article, Red. The one you showed me," Jake said to Red. He turned to Bud and pointed at a computer, "Can she use that to retrieve a newspaper article?"

Bud nodded, entering a password in the login screen.

Red retrieved the *Arizona Daily Sun* article that she had shown Jake in her apartment.

Bud took his time reading it and even reread portions that caught his attention.

"Wow, this is incredible. Abe's face and body reportedly burned in a fire. Matched his identity through dental records they must have doctored? They even buried Abe. That grave will have to be exhumed and the body reidentified. Did you contact the parents yet?"

Jake answered carefully, "No. Can you imagine what they would have done? They would've swooped in, and we would've never been able to convince Shmuel to work with us, putting a seventeen-year-old kid in harm's way after losing Abe. It was too risky."

"Won't they miss Shmuel, though?"

Red explained, her expression blank, "Nobody even knows he's missing. We hacked into his social media feeds, setting up a fake meeting with his friend, who was away at school. He's not even missing yet!"

"Brilliant," Bud said. "Here's what I don't get, though. Why would the Wolf have picked a twin for this? I mean, ten years ago he kidnaps a twin from America after doctoring his death? Isn't that more risky?"

Jake responded, "I've given that a lot of thought. He could've kidnapped a kid with a younger brother or sister instead of a twin or just an only child. It sounds odd. But think about it. Using a twin provided the Wolf with options. He could've instructed Abe to recruit Shmuel at some point, if needed. And if the twin is not needed, then he's just like any other sibling, except that now he's an only child living in America."

Bud said, "True. But somebody like the Wolf doesn't like loose ends. How well do you know Shmuel? You've known him for what, a day?"

Chapter 35
Friday, October 13

Every federal agency has an operations manual, thousands of loose-leaf pages stored in multiple three-ring binders, making it easy to swap out new for outdated procedures. All matters were covered, even how to buy a hammer.

Except for this situation. Nobody knew what to do with the tall and pimple-faced teenage Shmuel. The dimples he had as a child had flattened, and his freckles had disappeared. How to house and feed a seemingly innocent high school student whose twin brother was about to kill thousands of people. There wasn't enough time to figure it out. The FBI chose the easiest option, the Marriott Hotel in downtown DC, a moderately priced twenty-one-story, thirty-year-old hotel.

Bud placed an FBI agent outside of Shmuel's hotel room. Shmuel didn't know what to make of the large man with a protruding beer belly. He didn't look tough, not that Shmuel wanted to test his resolve. Shmuel periodically peered at him through the fish-eye lens of his door's peephole. The man just paced until he was replaced by another large man wearing the same navy suit with a white shirt and black tie.

They were definitely not part of the A team. These two must have done something wrong to be banished to this duty, Shmuel mused.

Bud told Shmuel to wait for further instructions, as if he was part of the official team. He told Shmuel it was better to not call his parents. Their meddling would just make it more difficult to recover Abe. *Recover*, as if Abe was a lost dog.

Shmuel had a lot of time to think. When the agents met him in Austin, he initially didn't really remember a lot about Abe. Sure, he remembered the funeral and everybody being nice to him for a while, but then life went on. His mom stopped crying as much and saying, "You look so much like your brother." She encouraged him to grow his hair long and part it down the middle.

He initially agreed to help the agents out of a sense of obligation to his family and to Abe. It would be great to get to know his twin brother again. The grand reunion would be insane, as would the media coverage. He would be hailed as a hero.

Since meeting the agents in Austin, Shmuel began to feel different. The sense of obligation turned into the realization that he and Abe were forever linked. Synapses grew back, reinstating memories of their relationship.

Indeed, if it weren't for Shmuel, Abe might not have even disappeared in the first place. He had encouraged his introverted brother to participate as Mr. Smee in *Peter Pan*. Shmuel had recently been the Tin Man in the *Wizard of Oz* and he told Abe it was his turn. The Wolf had snatched Abe after play practice.

Shmuel also recalled an incident that he had suppressed for a long time. It occurred when they were both in the first grade, a few weeks before the Wolf kidnapped Abe.

***

Abe walked into the cafeteria at Raker Hill Elementary School. He had the same straight black hair, dimples, and freckles as his identical twin brother.

Kids were either sitting, walking, or—much to the dismay of Ms. May—running around the large room stomping on the white and black checkerboard linoleum flooring. The seated kids were talking, punching, motioning, and eating.

The lucky eaters enjoyed whole sandwiches purchased by their on-the-go moms, more interested in getting to yoga class than preparing a nutritional lunch. Others suffered through the house specialties *du jour*: cardboard pizza, flat hamburger patties, or syrupy chucks of fruit. And a few, including the Shimmerman twins, ate homemade sandwiches prepared by their caring mothers.

Abe couldn't hold in his gassy bowels, forcing him to miss the first few minutes of lunch period. Fortunately, Shmuel had saved him a seat.

Abe greeted Shmuel with a smile and a light friendly punch to his arm, saying, as he sat, "Where'd you get the chocolate milk? Mom didn't pack one for me." Shmuel ignored the question and continued eating his peanut butter and jelly sandwich while Abe retrieved his own food from his knapsack.

Abe left the table ten minutes later to get a napkin from a stand in an empty part of the room. Jelly had dripped onto his shirt.

Sam, a large child in second grade with even darker freckles than the twins, tapped Abe on the shoulder while he reached for a napkin. As Abe turned around, Sam hit him hard in the gut.

"That's for what your brother did, stealing my milk."

Abe, holding back tears, looked at the mortified Shmuel as he stood. He accepted Shmuel's apology and agreed to keep the incident to themselves. Twin secrets, they called it, each knowing that one day the roles could be reversed.

***

Shmuel began to imagine that he himself had been kidnapped, raised by the Wolf, and mentored by Jabal. The hell Abe had to endure became Shmuel's hell.

Once a twin, always a twin.

He would help Abe, even if it meant putting himself in danger.

***

Shmuel's reminiscing was interrupted by a knock on the door. Shmuel opened it, letting Bud, Jake, and Red enter. Jake reached for Bud's arm, trying to slow him down.

Bud addressed Shmuel as he lay on the bed against a pile of clothes. "They didn't find anything at the Washington Monument!"

The visitors stared at Shmuel, waiting for his response. He jumped off the bed and stood to meet them at eye level.

"Why are you asking me about it? How the hell am I supposed to know where it is? Maybe you didn't look hard enough."

Bud replied, "I don't think so, smarty. We searched every inch of the entire monument and the grounds, with agents and dogs."

Shmuel cocked his head at Bud like a perplexed dog. He addressed Jake and Red. "Are you with this clown? He's blaming me, as if it's my fault. I think I'm done with this, done cooperating. I need to speak to my parents. We'll figure out some other way to save Abe."

Bud boomed, "Abe? You think this is just about Abe? What about the thousands of people who could die?"

"What else do you want me to do?" whined Shmuel.

"How about telling me everything you know? You can start by telling the truth. When was the last time you saw Abe?"

Shmuel replied loudly, "I told you, I DON'T KNOW ANYTHING! I haven't seen him in ten years!"

They stared at each other until Jake interrupted, "Bud, that's enough! Tell him. Tell him, or I will. He's just a kid."

Bud glared at Jake, composing his thoughts. "OK, OK. We believe you, Shmuel. And you were right—it was at the Washington Monument. I'm sorry I had to put you through that. I needed to make sure you don't know anything." He looked at Jake and Red and added, "This wasn't their idea."

"What? But you said you didn't find anything. You were testing me? Seriously?"

"Look at it from my perspective. I need to be able to trust you to do the right thing."

"The right thing?"

Bud explained, "Abe's your identical twin. You guys have been bonded since birth. We needed to find out if he contacted you. And the other question you should ask yourself is how are you going to react if he's ready to blow up downtown DC?"

Shmuel considered the dilemma and eventually said, "What did they find?"

"Anthrax, enough to kill scores of innocent people," Jake offered.

Shmuel exhaled and ventured, "So is this over? You guys have a bead on Abe?"

"Not exactly," Bud said on his way out the door. "Wait here. We'll be back."

"But..." Shmuel said as the door closed.

***

Bud, Jake, and Red climbed into Bud's car. Bud answered a call on his cell. The call started to come through his car speakers, but he quickly turned off the system.

Jake and Red were on a need-to-know basis. They could hear a lot of "ohs" and "ahs" but little else. The call ended a few minutes later.

Bud volunteered, "That was the lab. They confirmed the anthrax came from the Aral Sea—the same island Red infiltrated months ago."

"And in Kenya, used as a sick lab experiment, wiping out a tribe, creating a ghost town in the process," Jake reminded them.

"What did they discover about the delivery method?" Red asked.

"That's the most interesting part. Apparently, our friends set it to go off, releasing the anthrax at noon this coming Saturday."

"And it would get detected?" Jake asked.

"Yes, the Park Service installed an anthrax detector just last year," Bud responded.

Red looked at Jake. "That supports our theory that the anthrax is a pretext—a diversion, if you will."

"For a dirty bomb," Bud chimed in. "They'd probably time it to go off for maximum effect when the first responders arrive."

"Which means..." Jake started.

"That we know when the dirty bomb will be released unless we stop it from going off," Red said finishing Jake's thought.

"And the location?" Bud asked the obvious question.

***

Shmuel couldn't stay in the hotel room any longer. Bud had tested him, demonstrating he didn't fully trust his loyalty. He had seen movies where people like him were blamed as the fall guy when the police failed to stop a threat.

What right does he have to doubt me? Heck, if I was working for the bad guys, I wouldn't have helped trick Jabal! Haven't I already proven myself?

He knew he had to act fast, having overheard agents talking about the dirty bomb. Time was running short, with noon on Saturday the most likely time of detonation.

The link he had recently rediscovered with his twin was growing stronger. Even ten years after Abe's kidnapping, Shmuel had a bond with his brother nobody else could understand. He *felt* Abe. What's more, he knew where Abe would be.

Those clown FBI agents couldn't possibly understand any of this. They would kill Abe at the slightest provocation—and maybe without one. He couldn't allow his brother to be slaughtered, even if he hadn't seen him in over ten years. Eliminating Abe would be akin to killing a piece of himself.

He decided to take a chance. He wasn't under arrest, and they never said he couldn't leave. Unfortunately, the guard outside his door had that look—the kind that tells you not to do something, like walk out.

Shmuel got used to the food delivered by room service. He had previously tested the limits of what he could order with the FBI's money. Nobody cared. And so for Friday night's dinner he ordered two entrées, dessert, and a milkshake.

The food cart arrived thirty minutes later. The attendant needed a large cart to carry the feast.

The agent let the attendant through the door.

"Right on time, Alfonso," Shmuel said. "Ready to get off of work? You've been here for what, eight hours already?"

Shmuel could see Alfonso was a hard worker. He learned he had graduated from washing dishes to room service a month ago.

Alfonso replied, "Yeah, man, life's tough. But not for you, huh? Crammed up in this penthouse suite, guarded by Mr. Friendly and served whatever you want."

Shmuel laughed. "That's right. Treated like a pampered criminal—you conveniently left that part out. Put it over there, please. And can you do me a favor when you're done?"

"Sure, my friend. What is it?"

Shmuel told him what he had in mind.

***

Early Saturday morning at 7:00 a.m., a nervous Agent McAdoo approached Bud in front of Jake and Red.

"Agent Dupree, I have some bad news."

"Don't tell me you lost a high schooler!" Bud screamed.

McAdoo, a ten-year veteran of the force, knew how to handle bad news, an all-too-common occurrence these days. It was better to be up front. Supervisors hated it when you danced around.

McAdoo said, "Yes, we did. I'm not sure of all the details, but here's what we think happened."

"Happened? Isn't it obvious? You got tricked by a pimple-faced teenager!"

"Yeah, well, he had help. It turns out he befriended the room service attendant, a guy named Alfonso."

"And?"

"The kid is pretty smart. He ordered a lot of food. Alfonso had to bring a bigger cart. Then the kid pays Alfonso a couple of hundred out of the spending money we left him to allow Shmuel to hide in the lower cabinet of the food cart. They emptied out the space, and he hid in there. Alfonso simply wheeled him onto the elevator."

"You arrested Alfonso, right?"

"On what grounds? The kid's not a prisoner, right? He could have walked out on his own. Alfonso didn't harbor or allow a fugitive to escape."

"So now we have identical twins running around DC—one with a dirty bomb and one we allowed to escape. You telling me we can't do anything about it?"

"Unfortunately, no."

"Should I put out an APB on Shmuel?"

Bud thought about it. His answer surprised McAdoo.

"No, not necessary. We already have one out on his twin. And we're searching the entire town anyway."

Chapter 36
Washington:
Saturday, October 14

Experts claim children can remember events starting as early as the age of three. But when they turn seven, they start forgetting what previously happened. The phenomenon does not apply to traumatic events that stick in a child's mind, similar to the way a person with dementia can remember long-term memories while forgetting what happened earlier in the week. It also doesn't apply if there is a triggering event, like Abe's rediscovery of his twin.

Shmuel's and Abe's fifth birthday party was a traumatic event stored deep inside the hippocampus part of Shmuel's brain—that is until he became involved with the FBI combatting Abe's radical conversion. Sally and Fred, the twins' parents, took them to Washington to see dinosaurs at the Smithsonian Museum of Natural History. The parents had purchased for the boys one-foot-tall plastic replicas of the animals—T. rex for Abe and triceratops for Shmuel—and they were to visit life-size artifacts of the animals. Abe loved to sneak up on Shmuel and attack his triceratops. They played well together and often.

The family stayed in downtown DC, not far from the boardinghouse where Abraham Lincoln died after getting shot at the Ford's Theatre. Shmuel vaguely remembered the museum, but he recalled other happenings of that weekend in greater detail.

Chapter 37
Twelve Years Earlier

Abe, the more demonstrative of the twins, whined to his father in his singsong voice, "I'm hungry."

Shmuel followed, also complaining of dire hunger, as if he hadn't eaten since arriving in DC, even though they had recently split a giant hot pretzel.

Their mom, Sally, treasured her twins, but she was sick of the complaining. She told Fred they should go. Fred was glad for the opportunity to leave the museum floor. He touched his gut, inhaled, and said, "Yeah, food sounds good right about now."

They entered the museum cafeteria. The twins marveled at the diverse selection of sustenance: pizza, burgers, pasta, and strange international food. They stuck to their familiar favorite: pizza with salted pork toppings.

Sally, being unusually mischievous, took a chance on the chicken kebabs. Everybody loaded up on French fries and drinks. They tossed half their food in the garbage twenty minutes later. It was time to go.

It was Abe who made the next suggestion. Shmuel wanted to go back to the hotel to swim in the pool. Abe, though, wanted to go to the top of the Washington Monument, and as usual, he got his way.

They were walking down Constitution Avenue when Abe spotted an old stone house several blocks away. It stuck out, unusual for an area of town filled with large fields, monuments, and museums. He screamed, "Look!" before sprinting away. His parents shouted for him to stop, but it was too late.

They ran after Abe, glancing at the White House on their right in the distance. Shmuel stayed behind with his parents.

"What's he looking at, Dad?"

Fred panted. "That's the...Lockkeeper's House. You see...there used to be...a canal that was...used to transport supplies and people. The dirt roads were too muddy. I read about the house on the plane. It goes back to about 1833. It's a run-down building today...but it used to be where the lockkeeper stayed."

"Lockkeeper?" Shmuel asked.

Fred looked back as he was running. "Yes...the...keeper would...collect tolls, and he kept records of people using the canal."

Shmuel didn't understand the explanation. He didn't know about tolls and records, and he couldn't imagine a world without cars. But he quickly forgot his confusion. He was getting worried about his brother. Then something horrible happened. A door to the house opened, and a man pulled Abe inside.

"Abe!" the three of them shouted. But it was too late. The door locked just as they got there. Fred began pounding on the door while a hysterical Sally called the police using her cell phone.

The police arrived a few long minutes later. A man opened the door after begging the police not to shoot.

One of the cops said, "Whew! Don't worry about him—it's just Crazy Al. He's not altogether there. He usually lives on the streets, but he sometimes ventures into this place. He's never hurt anybody. He probably just thought your son was going to trespass into his space."

Abe ran outside into the waiting arms of his mother, crying hysterically but otherwise intact.

"Did he hurt you, son?" one of the cops asked.

Abe shook his head.

The cops arrested Al, who kept repeating, "This is my house. This is my house. This is my house."

The cops handcuffed him and locked Al in the car. Then they interviewed Abe and the rest of the family. Abe got to show everybody the inside. Other than being musty, dirty, smelly, and grungy, Al's house looked intact.

Chapter 38

Washington:
Saturday, October 14 at 9:00 a.m.

Shmuel walked a few blocks towards what looked like a main street, away from where he slept Friday night after his daring escape, under a bridge filled with garbage, feces, and even a few abandoned shopping carts. It had been cold during the night, but he was lucky enough to find a blanket strewn amongst the trash. He imagined it had been used by other homeless people who had moved onto better places to sleep, leaving him with an area not even fit for them.

He didn't want to stay in a hotel using the rest of the money the FBI had given to him. He had seen television shows where the bad guy checks into a hotel and then immediately gets caught. And he was now the bad guy.

Shmuel hailed a taxi driver who reluctantly stopped to pick him up. He didn't know Washington that well and told the driver the first thing that came into his head: "Take me to Georgetown."

He slithered down in the backseat as the cab drove away. The driver dropped him off in front of a store, which Shmuel entered to purchase a pair of dark baggy jeans and a light-blue sweatshirt with the words

Get Tough written in large letters across his chest. It was the only sweatshirt he could find that seemed to work. Besides, he could use it as inspiration. He also bought a baseball hat.

He took his purchases to a nearby coffeehouse, where he conned the barista into lending him a pair of scissors, watching her frown as he took them into the bathroom. There he cut his hair short, flushing the cut locks of hair down the toilet, and dressed in his new clothes. He tightened and pushed down on his hat, hiding his remaining hair and much of his face, the same way movie stars did when being photographed by the paparazzi. It would do for now.

But what would the barista think of his metamorphosis? Would she call the police? *She's probably seen worse*, he concluded, handing back the scissors.

Shmuel threw his dirty, smelly, preppy outfit in a dumpster behind the store. He looked at his watch: Saturday 9:00 a.m. He had only a few hours to locate his brother and somehow diffuse the bomb.

He ate a pretzel from a street vendor and walked into a bookstore. Shmuel found a book about DC and began flipping through pictures of old houses. He didn't find anything remotely close to what he was looking for.

Then he remembered: It was close to the White House. He had seen the iconic white structure twelve years ago while running after Abe, looking over his shoulder. But was it on his right or his left? And what was the museum with the dinosaurs that they had visited before going to the house?

He looked around the store. Patrons were browsing in the aisles, and kids looked studious in the children's section. *These are not normal kids*, he mused to himself. Kids back home didn't waste time reading in a bookstore. Nobody seemed anxious except for Shmuel.

An employee approached, addressing him in a confident voice. "May I help you? You look like you need some help." Her name tag read: Chelle. She was old enough to be Shmuel's mom, but she was very attractive.

"I'm looking for information about the local museums."

Chelle put her hands on her hips and shrugged, as if to say, *Is this kid for real?*

"Around the mall, Virginia, Maryland? Where, honey?"

"Mall?"

"You're not from around here, are you? You know, the mall, the National Mall?"

Shmuel nodded, suddenly afraid to speak.

Chelle went away and then came back with a map. "Look here. This area is where the Smithsonian museums are located. All kinds. What are you interested in?"

Shmuel mumbled, "Dinosaurs."

"OK, now we're getting somewhere. Aren't you a little old for them, though? Never mind. It's not my business." She laughed to herself and then continued, "You must mean this one, the Museum of Natural History."

Shmuel read aloud, "Constitution Avenue. Hmm. Is the White House off of that?"

"Honey, you can see the White House from lots of streets in that area. But you got a great view a few blocks away from the museum down that same street."

"Any other houses in that area?"

"I thought you wanted a museum?"

"Ah...I do. Just curious. How do I get there—to the museum?"

"From this part of town...probably bus or taxi. Short ride."

Shmuel thanked Chelle and left. Ten minutes later, his second taxi ride of the day dropped him in front of the museum. He looked at his watch: 10:15 a.m.

He walked west on Constitution Avenue. It was Saturday in October, a popular tourist season. The street was crowded with people hustling to nearby museums and monuments—people sure to die from radiation poisoning, if not killed instantly by the explosion, and land that would be forever contaminated.

He saw the White House over his right shoulder and the Washington Monument up on the left. The images from his dreams and memories became clearer. He was getting closer. He had a vision of running with his parents and looking over at the White House. He glanced at the hundreds of people congregating around the back of the White House. It looked like a dollhouse from where he was standing.

He walked further down the street, and then saw it—a different and much older house near the vibrant Constitution Avenue, with its taxis, bicyclists, and tourists racing up and down the street. Chills ran through his body. He had found it. A plaque next to the building read: LOCKKEEPER'S HOUSE.

He remembered the antiquated exterior, the old gray, white, charcoal, and yellowish stones mortared in place. The triangular roof with chimneys on both ends looked really old. Although he didn't know anything about archeology or architecture, he knew the house dated back a few centuries. The two dormers protruding out of the roof stood tall, despite the peeling paint.

The house had two wooden doors, one at the front and one at the back. He carefully inspected the side facing the street and then walked toward the front door while reading his watch—10:15 a.m. The door wouldn't open. No response.

He walked around the house to the back. Unlike the front, which faced the street, the back faced an empty part of the mall and seemed quiet. He tried to look through the windows, but heavy curtains blocked his view. He tried to turn the handle to the back door in case it was open. It wasn't.

He circled the house, arriving again at the back door. He tried the door handle one more time, out of frustration. He turned his back against the house and contemplated his next move.

Then, without any notice, his world suddenly went blank.

***

Saturday, 10:45 a.m.

Shmuel stirred and mumbled. His head hurt. Where was he? Then he remembered. He must be inside the house.

He opened his eyes but couldn't see much. Nothing more than a sliver of light shone through the edges of the thick curtains. The National Park Service, owner of the house, had made it difficult for tourists to look inside.

He tried to get up and immediately tumbled, making a loud clatter.

From the dark, a voice familiar to Shmuel's said, "Don't. You tied up. You go nowhere."

"Abe? Is that you?"

"Name is Abram."

"You know who I am?"

"Trespasser."

"Ah! That's a good one. You own this place, right?"

"Done with you! Don't test me."

Shmuel tried to talk to Abe, but he wouldn't listen. Shmuel focused instead on loosening the ropes binding his hands behind his back and feet. But Abe had been trained well, tightly binding his limbs.

He heard Abe walk into the next room. He felt his cell phone in his right front pocket, but his hands were tied too tight. Shmuel tried to contort his right shoulder to allow room for his hand to pressure the phone through the opening of his pocket. He made progress until his hand slipped back down. Gravity pushed the phone back to its original place. Shmuel's shoulder ached.

He tried again, ignoring the pain. It took a few minutes to make progress as the phone fell to the ground, its screen illuminating the room. He was able to cover it up with his body, but he didn't know if Abe noticed the light.

The phone rang. The mute button had clicked off as he pushed it up through his pocket.

A voice boomed over him, and he cowered, anticipating the blow.

"Now you learn!"

His world went black again.

***

Shmuel came to and looked at his watch: 11:30 a.m. He smelled the fresh blood on his face and tasted it in his mouth. His head screamed as if it were on fire, as if his scalp were burning away.

Shmuel looked at his brother, sitting in a chair ten feet away. The small amount of light peeking from the edge of the thick curtains supplied enough to see. The floor contained debris and mouse droppings, except in the areas Abe had cleaned.

Abe looked a lot older than Shmuel, with a bushy beard that looked like an afro and a thick mustache growing into his lips. Shmuel could smell his sweat. A mechanical device with wires lay by Shmuel's feet.

"You remembered this place. I know you've dreamed about it. I have too. Who did you see in your dream?" Shmuel asked.

Abe jumped up and threatened to hit him again. But he didn't. He stared at Shmuel instead.

"How much time do we have?" Shmuel asked.

Abe replied sternly, "Thirty minutes...less if anybody else knocks. Button right here." He showed it to Shmuel.

Shmuel continued to work on his binds. "What do you remember? The T. rex you used to love, my triceratops, huh?" Shmuel just remembered the play. "Or the play? I think you played Mr. Smee in *Peter Pan*, right?"

"Lies! Information available everywhere."

Shmuel's heart sunk. He didn't anticipate Abe would deny their relationship. *Was this the way it was going to end? In and out of the world with his twin?* The ties on his hands were loosening, but what was he going to do even if they were freed, with his brother looming over him next to a button he could press, triggering the bomb? Abe was prepared to die for the Wolf.

He began to sing: "Hush, little baby, don't say a word. Mama's gonna buy you a mockingbird. And if that mockingbird won't sing, Mama's gonna buy you a diamond ring. And if that diamond ring turns brass, Mama's gonna buy you a looking glass."

Abe snorted, "Enough!"

His voice was strong, but Shmuel detected a slight hesitation. Abe approached Shmuel again, this time with an old piece of lumber. He raised his arm, preparing to strike. Just then, Shmuel broke free from his hand restraints and lunged at him. They both fell to the ground. The sudden burst of sunlight from the opened door revealed the twins wrestling on the bare floor, the plank of lumber laying nearby.

Bud, Jake, and Red rushed into the room. Other agents followed, some with portable lights. Jake launched himself onto Abe, ensuring he remained pinned down until another agent could apply handcuffs.

"Don't hurt him!" Shmuel screamed. "You have to work on the bomb over there. There's also a button somewhere on the floor. Watch out! Don't step on the damn thing!"

Bud shouted at Abe, "How long do we have? How do we disable this?"

Abe stared at the wall, his face blank except for an occasional blink. Shmuel also tried to break Abe's trancelike state, but he was not successful.

Red and Bud frantically searched the ground. Red looked at her watch, synchronized with everyone else's before entering.

"Two minutes before noon. We don't know how much time after twelve o'clock we'll have. Heck, it also could've been set to go off at the same time as the anthrax. We need to find that bloody thing now!"

Bud directed two other agents to disable the bomb.

Agent Charlie, an expert in triggers, cautiously approached the bomb. Cutting the wrong wire might set it off. Bud called for a sealed truck designed to contain an explosion of nuclear material as a backup plan, but they couldn't be sure they would have enough time to make the transfer.

"Found it!" Red screamed, securing the button and eliminating one of the possible triggers.

Charlie began to sweat. His heart was racing. He stammered, "I...haven't seen this one before. I...I...don't know what to do."

Shmuel began crying. He screamed at Abe, "I don't want to die this way! We're brothers, for God's sake. Remember, what we used to say, 'twin secrets' and 'once a twin, always a twin'? Wake up!"

Shmuel slapped Abe. Abe looked at him, tears forming.

Abe finally spoke: "Cut the red wire, the red wire."

One minute to go before noon.

Bud said, "Listen to him, Charlie. Do it."

Charlie cut it. "Damn, there's another red wire. This thing is still ticking."

"Cut it!" Abe screamed.

"God help us!" Charlie said as he cut the second red one.

The bomb stopped ticking as soon as Charlie cut the second red wire.

Shmuel hugged his brother. "It's going to be all right."

Abe ignored him, refusing to speak.

Shmuel asked Bud, "How did you find me? I'm sorry for leaving the hotel."

Bud laughed. "Don't worry about it, son. Alfonso—you know, the food server? Well, he works for us. We tracked you the whole time, hoping you'd lead us to him. The device was in the food you ordered. It will pass through you in a few days."

Bud looked at Jake and Red. "I didn't tell you that last part, but we staged the whole escape, including when Agent McAdoo told me about it in front of you. We have our reasons for handling it this way."

Bud said in a softer tone to Shmuel, "It was the only way we could think of to save Abe and stop the plot at the same time. We would have rushed in sooner, but we heard your exchange about him having the button, and we had to wait for the right moment."

"And our parents?"

Red said, "Let's call them right now."

Chapter 39
Washington

In the end, the group decided Red would make the call. Dead children cannot call their parents to pick them up, as if they had run away and become homesick a few days later. And Shmuel couldn't find the words to say. Red, with Robert's help, had discovered the connection between Shmuel and Abe. She gladly accepted the task as a small way to honor the death of her friend and colleague, Robert.

Fred Shimmerman didn't believe it when Red reached him on his cell phone, hanging up on her after calling her a bitch profiteer. Red was incredulous, in part because she didn't understand what he meant. They tried Sally's phone next, but calls to her were not answered until Shmuel relented and left a message.

Sally and Fred both returned the call, which Red answered with Shmuel by her side. "Oh, my god! Oh, my god!" they said. Arrangements were then made for the grand reunion.

The Shimmermans flew to Washington on the first available flight from Arizona the next day. Bud picked them up at Dulles Airport, holding a sign to attract their attention at the gate. He explained the situation as best he could in the car, but they still were in shock until they saw Abe in the flesh.

While Sally, Fred, and Shmuel were excited, showering Abe and each other with tears, hugs, and kisses, Abe was much more reserved. He needed time and extensive therapy, paid for by the United States government, which also decided to forgo any charges after testing confirmed his being brainwashed by the Wolf.

***

Like the Shimmermans, Jake and Red were facing a pivotal moment – with a major difference, of course. They could have easily departed, ending the reunion. And while they decided to take a test drive, they did so in classic passive-aggressive style.

Red asked for leave of absence from her service, a request that could easily be ended, although if Monty had his way, it would be permanent. He accepted Red's request with the silver lining being the potential that she would fall madly in love with Jake and would eventually quit - termination of the pesky, insubordinate girl without having to plead his case to the dreaded personnel office.

Jake reciprocated with a leave of absence, although in his case, the *New York Times International Edition* sent him off with a well-earned applause. The newspaper initially planned for one human interest article on the body doubles, placed in the societal pages to be read by people whose attention span lasted to Section C. Editor Joseph Brommer had secretly hoped Jake would tire of his new career as a reporter after seeing months of work boil down to one article read and then disposed of without much fanfare.

That didn't happen. Jake had stumbled onto and then exposed a fiasco that could have salted the earth of Washington, converting the boisterous capital of the free world into a barren wasteland. He could even have had Joseph's job, if he wanted.

Temporarily freed from their employers, the couple spent their time at Jake's condo when they were not enjoying the unseasonably warm November weather in DC. At night, they cuddled in bed after enjoying Jake's favorite take-out Chinese food or Red's new fondness for crab cakes and seafood at Washington's Georgetown waterfront or Alexandria's Old Town. Sex began tentatively after the last fiasco where Red hid in the bathroom, but it then graduated into passionate displays of warmth, unselfishness, and kindness. Days were spent in the Smithsonian museums, where Red learned to appreciate that America had defeated the Brits not once but twice in two wars within a period of less than fifty years.

Three months later, when winter finally arrived late—in January of the next year—Jake decided to up the ante. He surprised Red with two plane tickets for a vacation in St. Martin. Red happily accepted, but she added one condition.

Chapter 40
London

Jake and Red's venture away from the safety offered by Jake's condo began in London. Red wanted to bring closure to Jimmy's vegetative state. Jimmy's doctors made sure Red understood he was never going to get better and pulling the plug was long overdue.

Red used her resources at MI6 to discover the whereabouts of her father. He had wasted his years after Red moved out of the house and eventually lost the farm to creditors by spending too much time getting smashed at the local pub, drinking his new favorite drink, room temperature Guinness.

"You're just making it difficult on yourself, Jimmy, and me. He's never coming back, and you know it," Red told him during a tense phone call.

He would not relent until Red used her A-bomb. "Pa, how many times have you visited him since he's been there?" Crickets.

Red, Jake, Pa, and Jimmy's nurse and doctor gathered around Jimmy's bed. The priest Red spoke with during her last visit to the hospital gave the last rites. The doctor disconnected the machinery and feeding tubes.

It took eight hours. Red and Jake alternated time at Jimmy's bedside, while Pa watched television in the lobby. Red noticed the twitching first. The doctor and Jake rushed into the room. Pa lagged behind. Red wanted to choke Pa as he entered the room, but she focused on Jimmy instead.

Jimmy expired a moment later, his amber eyes centered on Red at the last moment. She thought briefly about her subway performer friend, Jasper, before bending over to kiss Jimmy's cheek. She forced herself to stay strong in front of her father; it helped that Jake held her moist hand. She walked out with Jake, avoiding any eye contact with Pa.

***

St. Martin

Red awoke and removed Jake's arm that he had wrapped around her during the night. An ocean breeze permeated through the open balcony doors and slit in the drapes. She could see the bright sun from her position on the bed. They were in a private villa, located in an elevated area above the beach.

Red walked to the bathroom and looked back at Jake. His eyes were closed, but she sensed he was just pretending. She glanced at the turquoise water, which seemed to smile back at her. Jet Skis and kayaks moved in the distance.

Jake turned on the television once Red entered the bathroom. She couldn't hear the words clearly. When she finished and walked out, Jake was sitting against the headboard, concentrating on the news, motioning for Red to be silent.

Red climbed into the bed and listened to the exchange in French. She knew Jake was relying on the English subtitles.

Anchor: "Fred, I hear you have some information for us from the Eastern District Court of Virginia?"

Reporter: "Yes, I do, Sheila. Jabal Shamoon entered a plea of not guilty at his arraignment. The case will proceed with the government hoping to bring the case to a trial within the next twelve months."

Anchor: "What did you learn about why yesterday's hearing was delayed until today?"

Reporter: "A reliable source in the Department of Justice told me that Judge Thomas made the decision, but she wouldn't tell me why. A second source, this one an attorney working for the law firm representing Shamoon, shed some light on the situation. He said that Judge Thomas used a technical flaw in the complaint filed by the Justice Department as an excuse to give the American government additional time."

Anchor: "Do you know why the government would want a delay?"

Reporter: "They were apparently negotiating with Shamoon for a deal. The government wanted to drop the charge that carried the possibility of a death sentence in exchange for Shamoon's testimony against Sasha Krupin, better known as the Wolf."

Anchor: "And Shamoon refused to accept the deal?"

Reporter: "Yes, he did, despite the urging of his defense counsel. He hasn't cooperated with his counsel since the beginning of the proceedings. My source working at the law firm told me he refused to testify against the Wolf."

Anchor: "And so the death penalty is still on the table for Shamoon?"

Reporter: "That's correct, Sheila."

Anchor: "Is the case against Krupin weak without Shamoon's testimony?"

Reporter: "The prosecutor said the government is still confident it has a strong case against the Wolf. But multiple sources tell me that without Shamoon's testimony, the prosecution will have to rely more on circumstantial evidence."

Anchor: "Has the American government been able to locate the Wolf?"

Reporter: "No, they haven't, Sheila. People within the United States government believe he's being protected by insiders in the Russian government. They may try him in absentia."

Anchor: "And what about Putin's role? We reported yesterday they had grown up together, were friends, worked together in the KGB, and he may have been directing the Wolf all along."

Reporter: "That's right, but prosecutors were hoping to have Shamoon testify about a call he allegedly overheard between Putin and the Wolf, and now that won't happen."

Anchor: "What are you hearing about the twins?"

Reporter: "Abe is home with his parents. He fully cooperated with the government and received immunity, but he remains in extensive therapy. His brother, Shmuel—credited with locating the dirty bomb—has enrolled at the University of Texas."

Anchor: "Thanks for the report, Fred. And on to other news..."

Jake looked at Red and smiled. "Jabal will get what he deserved," he said.

As for the Wolf, Red knew he probably would never face justice in the United States. Red glanced at the balcony. A heavy rain had replaced the sun.

They decided to sleep in.

Author Bio

Scott A. Dondershine is an attorney who practices law in Northern Virginia. His numerous articles have been published in national journals. His newest work is **Double Conundrum**—his second full-length novel. **The Project MKUltra Legacy** was published in October 2014. Scott lives in Vienna, Virginia with his wife and fully grown, yet still rambunctious, boys.

www.ingramcontent.com/pod-product-compliance
Lightning Source LLC
Chambersburg PA
CBHW072117250626
47159CB00007B/2480